Walled off from a world it no longer remembers, the city of Thryn decays in arrogant isolation. Its ancient scriptures tell of the god, Gomath, who will one day return to perfect his city. But his return has been long awaited.

In a bizarre coincidence of events, Lupio, a cynical and decadent young aristocrat, is unwillingly entangled in the prophecy. Appalled, he decides to break ancient law and flee the city. He joins up with Dubilier, a failed poet and dreamer, who is trying to escape from the death of inspiration and love. Together they travel through uncharted lands in search of the lost god. One of them wants to find him. The other certainly does not.

Daybreak on a Different Mountain

Daybreak on a Different Mountain

Colin Greenland

London
UNWIN PAPERBACKS
Boston Sydney

First published in Great Britain by George Allen & Unwin 1984
First published by Unwin Paperbacks 1986

UNWIN® PAPERBACKS
40 Museum Street, London WC1A 1LU, UK

Unwin Paperbacks
Park Lane, Hemel Hempstead, Herts HP2 4TE, UK

Allen & Unwin Inc.,
Fifty Cross Street, Winchester, Mass 01890, USA

Allen & Unwin Australia Pty Ltd,
8 Napier Street, North Sydney, NSW 2060, Australia

Unwin Paperbacks with the Port Nicholson Press
PO Box 11–838 Wellington, New Zealand

British Library Cataloguing in Publication Data

Greenland, Colin
Daybreak on a different mountain: a fantasy novel.——(Unicorn)
I. Title
825′.914[F]   PR6057.R3/
ISBN 0–04–823346–3

Printed in Great Britain by Cox & Wyman Ltd
Reading

for Melanie
all too many candles later

As Moses was admonished of God
as he was making the Tabernacle,
See that ye do all things according to the pattern
shown you on the high mountain.

Robin Williamson (after Heb. VIII, 5)

The time has come for poets to proclaim their right and duty to maintain that they are deeply involved in the life of other men, in communal life.

On the high peaks! – yes, I know there have always been a few to try and delude us with that sort of nonsense; but, as they were not there, they have not been able to tell us that it was raining there, that it was dark and bitterly cold.

Paul Eluard

Flaming mountains in the dead of night
Can't stand these nightmares, please turn on the light.

Peet Coombes

1

'There must be some way out of here,' said the joker to the thief.

Bob Dylan

Something had woken him. He slipped out of bed and reached towards the pile of clothes, but it was only roisterers straggling down the street. What was it they were singing? Something about forsaken love and broken promises, but alcohol mangled tune and words. They had a lantern bobbing on a pole; in the shadows and alleyways shapes ducked and twisted from the touch of its light.

Dubilier turned from the window, confused, half-asleep; unsure where he was. But that was Ali, that white glow on the pillow; she didn't wake. He thought he could see her smiling in her sleep.

All evening she had been trying to tell him something, leading him through a maze of cryptic phrases and meaningful looks. It seemed she kept the secret intact in her dreams.

At dinner: 'What do you think's the worst thing about the city?'

'The poor, the freaks . . . '

'No . . . '

'Disease. The rubbish everywhere.'

'Do you really think so?' She contrived to look amused, as though she never gave such things a thought and was entertained that he let them worry him. 'Don't you think boredom?'

'Ali, darling, you're not bored.'

'I am. Thank you, Ibet, that'll be all.'

'You've got this place, and the villa; the antiques; the birds . . . '

'I'm bored. It's always the same. Nothing ever happens. Nobody goes anywhere or does anything. People are so predictable.' She referred to them as to an inferior species, renowned for unsociable behaviour.

'People?'

He was not good at concealing a disadvantage, was hopeless in card games. Alita pounced.

'Oh, well, *you*, darling, you're different. You've got your poetry . . . '

Which had been ambiguous enough. Ibet was standing in the background smiling, head bowed: it looked like the conventional posture of servitude, but he sensed collusion, conspiracy, elaborate traps closing.

He started to dress. The only thing he could match his mistress at was elusiveness; he'd shut himself up at home and try to concentrate on the poem. Whatever her plan, Ali couldn't manipulate him if he wasn't around.

He found her book. She'd been reading it all evening; she'd picked it up when Ibet had cleared the bowls and brought the amel jug, and had ignored him for an hour or more until he'd practically had to assault her. For a while he thought that might be it, that she wanted a little more challenge and a little less facility in their love, but she had stayed distant even when they were coupled, and when he thought he could safely complain to her about her book and the way she was neglecting him, he found he had only cued a ready and over-meticulous apology which turned into a rapturous description of the story. There was a Thrynian hero and his love, a simple wasteland maid, who managed to be surpassingly fair and graceful despite coming of commonplace parents, marsh-trolls, deshingen-aw-Jeswed. For her he undertook feats and journeys without end (this was when Gomath was still a youth, before the Walling), and as they grew more tedious and repetitive, Alita grew more eloquent and Dubilier more annoyed.

At last he'd succeeded in interrupting. 'And does he win her in the end?'

'Oh, I don't know – I haven't finished it yet.' She sighed. 'But I think he must do, don't you, after he's worked so hard?' Even lying beside her in complete darkness he'd felt that cool look.

Dubilier was not a decisive man. He usually found himself hesitating until forced to act. He sat at her feet and wondered about waiting for dawn, having a confrontation; but he knew he couldn't face her eyes when they opened again and focused on him, mildly surprised to find him perched on the end of the bed. He finished dressing and crept out onto the landing. The house was dim and fragrant. Automatically he took a handful of petals from the bowl and scattered them into the basin, nodded his head and then looked up. Gomath was smiling benignly down on him. Slightly guilty at his lack of attention, Dubilier summoned his thoughts and addressed the god with proper reverence. Guide me, Gomath, guide me today. As usual, the petals crumbled in the water, dissolved and left it clear. Yesterdays, thought Dubilier, sweet and gone. He was a child again, as so often when negotiating the eternal. His religious upbringing had been orthodox and exact. Now that old unconditional faith welled up: Gomath would come back and perfect his people, and he would have Alita again, like that day in the orchard. He found he was still holding her book. Resting on the sill of the shrine, he turned to a blank page at the end and wrote her a message. It started off very cryptic and cutting, but dwindled into lachrymose self-remonstration by the fourth sentence. He hated it. He tiptoed back to drop it by the bed again, his heart hammering in case she woke and caught him; but she didn't. He felt quite brave and determined by the time he got down to the hallway: like a phantom in the night, he'd –

'Aigu?'

It was the housekeeper, Ibet, coming from her cubicle by the front door.

'Is there something?'

She stood like a shadow in her grey gown of service – did they wear them to bed too?

'Oh. No, nothing, Ibet, I'm sorry I woke you. No, don't bother, I'll get my own cape. Please go back to bed.'

'Yes, Aigu.' She let him go by and open the front door. Mist sneaked in.

'Ibet? Ibet, is that you? Who's down there?'

An upstairs door opening.

'Ibet, where's Aigu Dubilier?' Alita's voice was drowsy.

Caught for a moment in the doorway. Ibet looked from him to the landing where her mistress would appear any second.

'He – '

Panic and resolution united in him. The door shut quickly.

'He was here a moment ago, Aigui. He said he had to leave at once.'

Alita was hurrying downstairs, pulling a robe about her. Dubilier, hugging his cape closed, headed into the labyrinth of crooked streets, raging. Like an adolescent boy surprised in the maidservants' quarters; you graceless fool.

A dark shape grew limbs and scuttled out of his path, tripped and fell down a flight of steps, shrieking feebly. It bumped into something else, another clot of darkness that sat in the doorway gnawing. The little shape stopped, made no sound. The larger one snapped and spat.

Not far away in the gloom was another noise, a whine that continued without faltering. It was like a whimper of pain or misery, except that as it proceeded it rose and fell with measured regularity, as if it did for music to the creature making it.

The eater shook itself and growled. It had dropped the eaten and was grubbing unsuccessfully for it. 'Worm,' it said.

'I – I'm sorry,' said the little shape.

'Ghuric. Little Ghuric. Yes, well,' said the large one.

'Who is it? I can't see as well as – '

'Ghuric. Tell you by your smell.'

'Abri, oh, Abri, I should have known, you're so clever in the dark – '

'Worm,' he repeated with satisfaction, and belched.

Ghuric was trembling, not daring to move away.

'Tell me something.'

'What, Abredos?'

He didn't answer at once. In the hiatus the voice keened on through its lonely cadences.

'That,' he said at last. 'I've heard it before, nights, down at the river. What is it? It's got a rotten pain in the gut, whatever it is,'

'Oh, Abri, can't you smell her out too?'

Unerring, the fist crashed out of the blackness. Ghuric screamed and skittered up the steps again. As she ran she was flashed in silhouette against the low windows of a tavern: the body of a six year old, though the legs were short even for that, and she had to scamper like a maimed spider, putting her huge muscular right arm to the ground for support.

Abredos waited. Ghuric wasn't very clever. When she was

tired out, she'd run back and fawn on him rather than wait in the darkness for him to pounce on her.

'Ghuric.'

'I went to find out for you, Abri, come on, I'll take you, she's only just over here, this way.'

He grinned and hauled himself up.

'It's Kavi.'

Kavi was dreaming she was lighting the candles. Kavi was dancing. Each time she turned, there were fewer citizens there. A candle in the corner wouldn't light. Something was stirring in that corner, in the shadows, but when she looked it wasn't there. Lead us, Gomath, lead us, she sang, and the citizens followed her. Lead us from the marsh of the Outwall. Lead us from the lairs of Jeswed. Lead us to the citadel of perfection. In the pool someone was jumping up and down. Lead us to the mountain of our inheritance. There was rumbling in the vaults. If only she could dance better, she could save the citizens; but there were no citizens left. Husband, she prayed. The statue pushed its face into hers, its expression twisting, strangely regretful. They had grabbed hold of her to pull her off the dais – as if they knew how to save anything! But there was a horrible shadow on the statue's face, the shadow of something behind her. She tried to sing, but no sound came. In the lurching pool the blossoms became brown frogs which swam away at once. Kavi was out on the hillside, looking down on a desert whose sands seemed to writhe and swirl. Someone was trying to make her accept a flower. She felt regretful, relieved. Kavi tossed in her blanket, crooning ceaselessly. There were cobwebs in canopies around her, and everywhere the green mist. Framed in the opening of the cellar two figures sat hunched.

The sun rose and wearily began to clear the mist below. A few figures appeared in the streets, moving lethargically or with furious haste. In an Aigudan district a cleaner came out to pick half-heartedly at the litter and poke a drain. A scrawny teenage girl led a line of smaller children up the hill to play in the deserted temple. Queues grew at the food dispensaries. At last the boy could be seen coming back with a basket on his arm. He dawdled through the streets, jostling other boys, glancing upwards from time to time apprehensively.

Lupio smiled grimly. Come on, lad, he thought, you know I can see you.

The boy stopped to rest several times on the way up. The basket was growing heavier and he changed arms repeatedly. He was plumper than most boyservants because Lupio was more prodigal than most masters. He pushed open the massive door and squeezed into the Iigril. At length Lupio heard him faltering breathlessly upstairs. The footsteps paused at the door while Hifran tried to compose himself. Lupio waited until he knew the boy was just about to knock and then called, 'Come.' He leaned back on the balustrade and watched him stagger to the table, lifting his burden with both hands.

'Jumox said I should bring it to you first, Aigu.'

'Bring?'

'The food, Aigu.'

'Ah.' He came and stirred the basket's contents with a languid hand. 'So this is what you've left me, is it?'

'Aigu?'

'Pinched all my breakfast and went back for another lot.'

'No, Aigu!'

'You took your time, Hifran.'

'I haven't taken anything, Aigu!'

'Well, I hope not. You're far too fat anyway.'

'You said you liked me to be fat!'

Lupio looked into the injured, uncomprehending eyes. 'Hifran, for Gomath's sake unpack that basket and let's eat.'

Hifran beamed. This he understood.

When his Aigu had been eating for a while, he felt things might be a bit less delicate. 'Aigu?'

'Mm?'

'Shall I go home afterwards?'

'Yes.'

A pause.

'Aigu?'

'Yes?'

'Why do we come here?'

Lupio reached for a slab of grey bread and broke off a corner.

He sniffed it circumspectly, grimaced, and ate some before replying.

'Do you know what this place is, Hifran?'

'It's the Iigril. All the Aiguda used to come here and discuss important things.'

'That's right.'

'They don't come here any more, do they, Aigu?'

'No.'

'Why not?'

'Why do you think?'

Hifran paused mid-mouthful to consider. 'I suppose because there aren't any important things left to discuss.'

Lupio laughed. 'That's right. You're absolutely right.'

'Then why do you still come?'

'I like the paintings,' said Lupio. 'I like the books and the tapestries and the scrolls and the carvings and the mouldy old instruments and the rusty old weapons.' But there was no joy in his eyes as he said it.

Hifran thought about it. He twisted round in his chair to look at a wall-hanging behind him. It was heavy and very, very old. He recognised the pictures: that was Gomath, and the Cirnex, going to the mountain.

'That's a tapestry, isn't it, Aigu?'

'That's right.'

'Do you like that one?'

'Yes.'

'Then all those ones in the dancing room, the ones you cut up with your sword – were those ones you didn't like?'

Lupio stood up without answering. He went back to the balcony and gazed down for a while. Then he returned and stood at the head of the council table. 'Hifran,' he said, 'come here. Come to me.'

The boy looked worried as he approached. The Aigu Lupio took him in his arms and hugged him. The boy struggled. 'No, Aigu, please, not in here – '

'Why not?'

The boy's eyes hung fearfully on the dark tapestry. 'Gomath,' he said.

Lupio didn't even glance over his shoulder. He bent and kissed his mouth. 'No such person,' he said.

Dubilier crossed out the fourth word of the five hundred and sixty-second line and wrote another word above it. Then he crossed that out and rewrote the original word. Then he crossed out the whole line. The light from the window crept gradually over the desk. He stared at it unseeing, chin on hands.

Alita woke late, turned over, and reached across to the other side of the bed. She found only an empty pillow. She opened her eyes in surprise; then amusement; and then something like pity. She wriggled deeper under the covers and lay diagonally across the bed, flexing her toes against the cool sheets.

There was a clepsydra on Dubilier's desk. All the water had run through. He'd forgotten to refill it, and Jumox, the housekeeper, was not allowed into the study. Now the water was evaporating: time, stagnant, running backwards even. He shouldn't have been so impulsive. It wasn't as if she'd said anything, after all. Now she'd be upset and frosty with him. If he went back straightaway – No, he let himself be pushed around far too much. She'd always said so. He was resolved: the poem. He counted what he'd achieved that morning. Minus eleven words. Just what you'd expect, with time running backwards.

She put the other pillow behind her and shook a handbell. Ibet came in with a steaming mug and fruit on a tray. Alita sipped and set it aside. 'Sing to me.'

They'd spent most of that summer in her neglected orchard, persimmons ripening in the branches overhead like promises. Dubilier frowned. He wanted to get all that into the poem, for the symbolism, but the season had escaped him again. He wondered who had eaten the fruit.

Now it was nearly spring. Outside his window the lawn sloped away, dull and colourless. Even the buds looked tight and mean. The gardener went by with a bag of poison.

> *'Take these eyes so swollen and red,*
> *Swollen and red from weeping,*
> *For my heart is yours, but my heart is dead,*
> *And they wept it out of your keeping.*

Take these lips so pale and wan,
So pale and wan from crying,
For my heart is yours, but my heart is done,
And they mourned it a long time dying.

Take these hands so withered and worn,
Withered and worn from pleading,
For my heart is yours, but my heart is gone,
And they nursed it as it lay bleeding.

Take all of me, mistress, or leave me alone;
You have worked all your will to defeat me – '

'Ibet, Ibet, what a dirge!' said Alita, and laughed.

'Yes, Aigui, it goes on:

And while I am yours, I am dead as a stone,

but it ends:

But a new love is waiting to greet me.'

The Aigui Alita studied the placid woman in grey. She learned nothing.

Casting about the room for something else to entertain her, she found the book lying by the bed and read his note again.

'Why did he have to write it on the last page?' she demanded pettishly. 'I haven't even finished the story!'

Kavi came up with her blanket under her arm and nearly fell over the huddled form. It squeaked.

'What is it? Who's that?'

'Hnnn . . . '

'Don't you know better than to sleep where citizens can fall over you? Who are you?'

'Forgive me, Previs Kavi. Ghuric. I'm Ghuric. I was one – '

'Speak up!'

'My name is Ghuric. I was one of your temple-girls, Previs, when I was little – when I was young.'

'Before you stopped growing, eh? Well, yes, I can see now. Ghuric. Yes, you still look like a little girl, but I can see now you're old, aren't you? Old enough to have been at the temple. Ghuric.'

'Yes, Previs Kavi.'

'Faithless, the temple-girls. All of them. What are you doing here?'

'Forgive me, Previs Kavi, I'm sorry for being in your way, but we were so disturbed last night, I must have just dropped – '

'What do you mean, disturbed? Who disturbed you?'

'You did, Previs. Your singing, I mean. I mean, I mean – it was very beautiful – '

'Was I singing?'

'Oh, in your sleep, Previs, I mean, please.'

'What was I singing?'

'I – I don't know, Previs Kavi.'

'You were a temple-girl, what was I singing?'

'I – it was – what you used to sing, Previs, in the temple. Spells, and – '

'Spells?' That seemed to enrage the old crone. Ghuric felt dizzy. What could she say to appease her? Frantically she tried to remember, anything. She looked around. Abredos had gone to work.

'I don't know, I – Gomath-songs, it was. You used to dance, and sing – '

'Cretin!' That had made it worse. Hopelessly she looked round again.

'I was so young. He's older than me.'

'Who?'

'Abredos.'

'Who?'

'The rivergateman.'

'He was here? He'd know what I was singing?'

'Abredos. He's clever, he's not little and silly like Ghuric, he's got a good brain, he's got sharp ears, he'll remember for you, anything you want, Previs.'

'Take me to him. Wait. Carry my blanket.'

She bent and laid it across the little creature's back. The two women hurried off down the fetid street to look for the remnants of a dream.

Jumox came into the kitchen. Cheredep looked up from the table where he was marshalling the crumbs into a pattern with the tip of the breadknife.

'Where's that boy?'

'Is he not back yet?' he asked idly.

'No he's not.' Jumox was irritated, though this was evidently not a new annoyance. 'Next time I shall tell him to come home first and Aigu Lupio'll have to wait for his breakfast.'

'You sent him there first, did you?'

'I did.' She sat down, shifting uncomfortably. 'He's got to eat or he'll drink himself to death.'

'We should just pretend we don't know where he is,' said the cook. 'Then he'd have to come home.'

Jumox pursed her lips and gave a disapproving frown. She knew the suggestion hadn't been made seriously, but that kind of talk wasn't right.

They sat in silence for a long while. Cheredep stroked the crumbs into a long snaky line. 'There's no food in the house,' he said needlessly. A door creaked and Jumox looked up, but no one was there.

'Where *is* that boy?' she said again. 'What's the Aigu doing up there – giving the boy history lessons?'

'Physical education, more like,' grinned Cheredep. 'Physical jerks!' Seeing that he was being ignored, he rewarded the joke by laughing loudly. He picked up the knife again.

The yard door opened suddenly and Hifran hurried down the steps with his basket. 'I've brought the food,' he said. 'I'm sorry I'm late.' He was red and out of breath, his grey tunic crumpled.

The cook put down the knife. 'Why,' he said slowly, '*are* you late?'

Hifran looked at the floor. 'Aigu Lupio needed me.'

The cook leered at the housekeeper, but she wouldn't notice. 'Physical jerks,' he said softly.

'Here's the food,' Hifran said to her, 'and here's the drink, though the Aigu kept most of it – '

'What's your hurry now?'

'He said I could have the rest of the day off once I'd brought it.'

'Well, tidy yourself up before you go,' Jumox told him as she bustled back and forth to the pantry. Cheredep sat and watched both of them. 'You're a proper mess. Just look at your tunic.'

Hifran didn't, but he brushed at it with his hands as he ran back up the steps.

'Afternoon off,' said Cheredep with casual scorn. 'There's work to do here, you know,' he called after the hurrying boy.

'He's a disgrace to us all,' muttered Jumox; but she didn't define who she had in mind. Bottles clinked on stone flags. Cheredep stretched. He began to fill a pipe.

The great door boomed behind them, shutting out the weak light and air. Ghuric hesitated at the top of the steps, eyes and lungs adjusting to the smoky gloom. 'Can you see him?'

'Idiot! I can't see anything in this – ' She waved her stick impotently, beginning to cough. Ghuric reached for her with her lesser hand. Like some old and crippled crustacean, they stumbled down together into the Hall of Beggars.

On the floor the air was slightly clearer but no less rank. Piles of battered and discarded objects lay everywhere, and lying among them were animals and people in rags scarcely distinguishable from the refuse. At the far end a large fire burned an ill-tempered and uneven red. This was where most of the inhabitants were gathered; a flame occasionally revealed more of them clustered on ledges and balconies, in niches of disintegrating sculpture. Ghuric and Kavi trod between bodies to the fire. Several recognised Kavi, the Previs-aw-Gomath. The younger ones roused themselves to jeer but others, closer to her own age, looked aside uneasily as though catching sight of a mirror. The greatest fraction, and the oldest there, gaped vacantly, so that there was nothing to distinguish them from those who gaped and did not see her, or did not see anything at all – or from the antics and gargoyles whose faces blistered the architecture. Children believe that a grimace made when the wind changes will be fixed, frozen, forever. It had been centuries since the wind had changed in Thryn.

A man stood up, arms akimbo, to block their path. 'This isn't the place for you, Kavi.' He was a burly old man, grey-skinned and completely hairless. He seemed to hold some authority among the freaks and derelicts. 'Why did you bring her? Take her away.'

'She wants to see Abredos,' said Ghuric.

He gazed around. Finally he said, 'He's not here. You'll have to go down and find him.' Ghuric made to scuttle off. 'Don't leave her here. Take her with you.' He gave her a flaming stick out of the fire.

There was a recess, more steps, and a low door. Once through it the women found they could breathe more easily. The predominant stench changed from stale flesh and smoke to damp and decay. The dancing light showed that they stood at the top of a stone staircase curving down to cellerage. They descended, haltingly, into dank arcades of stone. Ghuric swung the torch. On all sides pillars marched motionlessly away into the dark.

'You've blinded and choked me with smoke; do I have to rot in the damp now?'

'Shh, shh,' hissed the midget, agitated. 'Listen.'

'What?'

There was a faint trickling of water. Ghuric strained her ears. 'This way, Previs.'

For a long time they walked without speaking. Their flame carved columns out of the blackness ahead and the blackness behind dissolved them again. The new columns started to be dimmer.

'Can the Previs-aw-Gomath walk faster? The fire's almost out.'

'The Previs-aw-Gomath does not scurry like a thief or an animal.'

They limped on. The torch went out. Ghuric moaned, but fear of Kavi was stronger than fear of darkness, and she reached for the withered hand again. They found that the columns were solid even though they were invisible.

As her eyes grew to the dark Ghuric began to see the faintest of glimmers a long way off, like the glow of diseased water. 'The river, Previs,' she said eagerly, 'can you see it?'

At that moment there was a scuffling, scampering sound ahead. Ghuric gave a little cry and stopped, petrified. Towards them hurtled a shadow, fast and low.

'Who?' it cried, its voice oily and threatening.

'Abri!' yelped Ghuric, terrified.

A face made itself in the dark, black on black: the grimy face and vacant black eyes of Abredos. 'Ghuric,' he said. 'Well.'

'Abri, the Previs-aw-Gomath, Previs Kavi. Here she is. She wants to ask you something.'

'Well.' He grinned, malevolently. 'Honoured.'

Ghuric explained. He sniffed at the Previs and then roared with laughter. 'She!' he wheezed. 'Mother of Perfection! Sings the same song all night; can't remember it in the morning!'

Kavi struck out with her stick. There was a crack and a cry of pain. Disembodied, her voice was even more imperious. 'What was the song?'

He sniffed. 'You were dreaming. What's the matter?'

'Gomath, you faithless, ignorant hog – '

He snorted and laughed.

'Gomath is coming.'

'Pthegh!'

'He sends his night-messenger the Cirnex, who speaks in dreams, the language of night, that men don't understand. What was I singing?'

Abredos thought about it. He scratched himself, growing bored with this. 'You sang "Lead us, lead us" for a good while.'

'I remember that,' said Ghuric.

'Shut up. Then you sang something else.'

'What?'

'Some rubbish, I don't – '

'Tell me or I'll beat you.'

'Like you were welcoming somebody. Somebody come a long way.'

'The Cirnex.' It was a whisper. 'The Cirnex-aw-Gomath.'

'Ay. Right.' Abredos cleared his throat and spat. There was a pause.

'Is he here?' The Previs seemed to be having difficulty speaking.

'What, here?'

'He comes in dreams and in the dark places of the city.'

'That's why you sleep in cellars?'

'Is he here?'

'Don't know, I'm sure. Dark enough for him, is it?'

'There's no one here,' Ghuric said in fright, 'no one but us, Previs.'

'I need my books,' said Kavi faintly. 'Take me out. Take me to the Iigril.' Nobody moved.

Abredos laughed. 'Come on. I'll show you. This way, ladies.'

Dubilier sat mesmerised. Time ebbed. He picked up his pen, looked at what he'd written, and put it down again. The paper was scarred with deletions. Too much revision's not good, he told himself helplessly: he'd done too much already. But as darkness fell he walked back over the hill. Below, the first tendrils of mist fingered the desolate waterfront.

'Aigui, the Aigu Dubilier is here,' Ibet announced.

A languid hand twisted a flower stem.

'Some amel, Ibet.'

'Yes, Aigui.'

'Ibet?'

'Aigui?'

'One cup, Ibet.'

'Yes, Aigui.' She bowed and retreated.

'Oh, and Ibet – lock the door when he's gone.'

'Yes, Aigui.'

He watched her come downstairs, silent and self-possessed as a temple-maid.

'The Aigui Alita is not disposed to see you, Aigu.'

'Does the Aigui Alita always turn away beggars?'

'Not always. You get out of bed and greet them all personally, do you, Aigu Dubilier?'

She's not so docile, he thought, correcting the image. A grey stone that gives back sparks. 'No, but I give my servants instructions – '

'*My* instructions are to lock the door when you've gone.'

'Do they say how soon that has to be?'

Ibet paused. 'No,' she said, 'but they do say I have to go and make a cup of amel for my mistress.'

'So?'

'No housekeeper worth her position would let a beggar stay in the hall while she went into the kitchen; so you'll just have to – '

'I'll have to come with you,' he said quickly. Was that a trace of a smile? 'The kitchen's the place for a beggar, after all.'

Ibet shrugged. 'There's nothing in my kitchen that'd satisfy a hunger like yours, Aigu.'

He reached out as if he wanted to shake her. 'I only want what Alita wants. You know, don't you? She tells you everything. Tell me what it is and I'll do it!'

'A cup of amel, that's all,' she said, turning towards the kitchen, 'and I can manage, thanks all the same.'

Dubilier followed her and installed himself miserably at the table. He watched her take the amel pods from a jar, and he was certain there was amusement in those carefully lowered eyes. She was friendly. He coaxed her.

'Ibet, I know you like me. Last night, you let me escape.'

'I didn't know what was happening. You took advantage of me.'

'And you haven't called a manservant to throw me out tonight.'

Ibet looked up. 'You reckon I'd need help?'

'It's what she'd tell you to do if she came in now.' Ibet shredded amel and didn't reply. He took confidence from that. 'Ibet, she's rejected me. Even before I ran away.' Ibet set water to boil, took a mug and spoon and put them on a tray. 'If I knew what I'd done, I could do something about it. But I don't understand, it's – she does things I just can't understand. I never know what she really wants.' Ibet put the shredded pods in a jug and steeped them in boiling water. 'You understand, Ibet. You interpret her wants every hour of the day. You anticipate them. You live by them. Please, Ibet.'

'Yes, Aigu, I know what my mistress wants,' she said, 'of a servant. She wants a cup of amel.' Ibet picked up the tray and went out.

Hifran had played uneasily all afternoon, wondering if his master could see him from the Iigril, high above the city. He knew that once Aigu Lupio started drinking he often finished in tears, raving over ancient and incomprehensible disasters and bellowing for his boy to come and comfort him. Hifran was afraid that if he weren't close at hand when that happened he would be punished, whatever the Aigu had said that morning. So as the day passed, his wanderings tended gradually not towards home, but back up the hill to the Iigril's lonely tower.

Nevertheless, when he came to push the door ajar and squeeze through, his independence revived. There was no point, after all, in presenting himself to the Aigu before he was summoned; that would be pouring away the last of a rare and precious liquor called freedom. He tiptoed upstairs and held his breath outside the council chamber, expecting any moment to hear his name called, but there was no sound. Hifran had no intention of knocking. He opened the door as softly as he could. The room was deserted.

He began the long climb down, wondering which other areas to investigate. A quick search of galleries, conservatories, studios and the vast museum did not find him. The library, thought the boy, and then I'll go home.

As he turned a corner of the basement stairs, a noise below made him duck back. He glimpsed a figure in green rush unsteadily past, its footsteps accompanied by a muffled tapping. Who else came to the dead old Iigril? Curiosity and silence beckoned him out, and he went stealthily along the corridor to the head of another stair which wound down into the main hall of books.

The room seemed empty when he got there, and he was just about to leave and look for another way the stranger or his master might have gone when he saw movement behind one of the central bookcases. He crept sideways into the room, close to the wall, keeping the bookcase between them. He found a recess on his right – a shrine. The pool was dry, but the statue of Gomath was especially large, near lifesize. It would hide him well. He sidled into the gap. This hall, he remembered, was the place for books about Gomath and Jeswed, magic stories about the past, the days before the Walling even. Aigu Lupio hated this room; that couldn't be him over there. Perhaps the green thing was a ghost, or a demon, deshingen-aw-Jeswed. Hifran hugged himself. His heart had jumped up inside his head. Save me, Gomath, save me, save me, save me, save me.

Ibet came back. 'You'll have to go now,' she said.

'Please, tell me!'

'Go away. Please.'

Defeated, Dubilier gazed into her eyes. They were grey too. 'Isn't there anything you could tell me?'

'No.'

'If you think of something, anything at all, will you tell me?'

'I can't help you, Aigu,' she said brusquely.

'But tomorrow, or the next day – if she says something, something happens, will you let me know?'

'I can't – promise anything.'

She hesitated while she spoke. Dubilier seized the lacuna: a crack in the adamant. And her refusal was at least not an unconditional one. Anxious not to spoil things by any more violence, he left in silence, thanking her with his eyes.

The streets were empty. His echoing footsteps beat a retreat. A breeze plucked his cape and he turned, almost expecting to find someone at his side. He prayed: Wind, no one can see you, no one knows where you come from, where you go. Are you the unknown spirit that moves the Aigui Alita? How can I understand you? But the wind seemed to be whispering to itself.

He was the Cirnex; any other name he had ever borne had been forgotten, as he had requested, wishing no higher place than to walk before the Aigu Gomath and sweep his road for him. At the time of the Tivori he had escorted his master to Hisper Einou, bid him farewell, and watched until he was out of sight. The Cirnex had built himself a pavilion there, to watch over the Outwall wastelands, to meditate the way of perfection, and, at every hour, to look for Gomath's return. On the great day he would herald him back to Thryn. The perpetual duty of the Previs, the bride of the god, was to be correspondingly vigilant, like a good housewife for the messenger who will announce her husband's arrival.

Kavi knew it by heart. '*He comes in dreams; he comes at twilight and in the dark places of the city; in his eye will be fire, and fire in his hand; he will laugh with joy, and speak strange things, that none may understand him, and men shall say one to another, Surely this is not he.*' The young beggars had laughed. Abredos had laughed. '*But in this may you find him, and know him who he is, that the Aigu shall speak to him and he shall obey.*'

There had been generations of high theological dispute on that phrase. Would Gomath have to return and speak before his messenger could be recognised? Would there be a public annunciation, a supernatural voice, or would that come in a dream too? The scholars had sat in the Iigril unpicking scriptural knots while, below, the citizens had strayed out of the temple and into despair. Kavi was the last Previs. She had watched the rot creep from the city, up the hill. The last. Her husband would come now, to find no one waiting for him, his servants asleep and the lamps out. Bereft of other responsibilities and of the comfort of training a successor, she turned the vigil into a search, intensifying it as the years fled her. She had haunted dark places, combed the twilight, and, though she could never remember her dreams, the former temple-girl and the rivergateman had both witnessed her singing the ritual welcome song. He was at hand. The long story was drawing to an end. She looked at the illumination that filled the page beneath the last line of text: an Aigu giving a bunch of flowers to his Aigui who leans out of a window to welcome him. He was coming. Despite age, despite fading sight and tortured limbs, despite doubt and grinning beggars, she would live that long: she was the Previs-aw-Gomath; she was ready.

He came at her from behind, stumbling. His ragged forearm locked about her throat. She dropped the sacred book and clawed at his arm, trying to scream but, as if she were dreaming, unable to make a sound. She twisted in his grip, struggling to see his face – who would dare? – and glimpsed a haggard, ravaged profile before he jerked her head round again. She fought so that he snarled with the exertion of holding her, and then she knew why if not who, for his breath reeked. The drunkard was the slave of impulse. He growled like a dog and grabbed her free arm, twisting it up behind her. The effort cost him some of his hold on her neck and she began to yell.

'Deshingen-aw-Jeswed! Let me go!'

'What? What?' His voice was strained, but he spoke with an ironic politeness in keeping with that decadent aristocracy she had seen in his face. 'You confess your Aigu? Did he send you to defile the holy library? Did he?'

'Blasphemer! I cursed *you* – let me go!' And, as the arm released her, 'Don't you recognise me?' She confronted him in rage, thinking to awe him however drunk he was. Instead he gave her an enormous grin and a bow, kneeling at her feet and then sitting back on his heels.

'Of course! Kavi, Previs-aw-Gomath!' He studied her,

shaking his head with exaggerated chagrin. 'So long, I'd quite forgotten.' And he was on his feet, inspecting her face, tilting her head back and stroking her cheek: 'And you've changed, oh yes . . . ' His voice was soft and sad, oiled with the juice's melancholy. She struck him.

'Deshingen!'

He rubbed his cheek slowly. 'No,' he said, 'I am Aigu – '

'You? You're no citizen. You're no better than an Outwall creature, licking the slaver of Jeswed – '

'It's true,' he said thoughtfully, 'I have been drinking . . . '

' – attacking your Aigu's bride in a holy chamber, under his very gaze!'

He followed the indignant finger to the statue where it pointed, and began to laugh. It was quiet, but frightening: not the laugh of a malevolent demon, but a laugh of despair, as if he saw through the statue, through the Wall, out across the wasteland to the mountains and beyond, to the edge of the world, and found nothing but wind and rain.

He was young; not tall, but strong, of an Aigudan family whose breeding habitual indolence and vice had failed to erase from him altogether. The desperate laughter, the dilated, watery eyes were the marks of alcohol, but what possessed him was not liquor, nor Jeswed the fiend of the marshes, but a personal demon. Here was a great spirit born to frustration and bafflement; a prince whom powerlessness delivers at last to frenzy. Unkempt, unshaven, dishevelled, barefoot, he was not pitiable or absurd; his stance, the tilt of his head made him almost majestic in the half-light of the underground galleries, and, dim-sighted, it was Kavi who was awed. He stood with his back to her, dwarfed by the mass and age of holy doctrine, and said quietly, 'There is no Aigu,' – and why did that frighten her? Who was she to lack confidence when correcting the faithless?

'He is not dead,' she said loudly.

'He was never alive,' said the young nobleman. 'He's a man-shaped madness we catch, like a fever. When we lose heart, when we want someone to tell us what to do, he comes on strong – Lead us, Gomath, lead us. And then later, because things get worse and we want someone to blame, he's deserted us, and then last of all, when things can't get any worse, we want someone to make it better. Save us, save us.' His voice was calm and, with his face turned away, Kavi had to remind herself that this was not reason though it took reason's shape: it was the worst of unreasons, the blackest heresy to come from the brown bottle. She expected it and recognised it, so why did she need to remind herself?

'Who are you?'

He came and caught her up as easily as if she'd been a large doll. He sat her atop a bookcase and smiled at her with his crazy eyes.

'Tell me a story, Previs.'

She was the Previs injured, not a frightened old woman. 'I do not understand you.' Her stick lay on the floor. 'Set me down.'

'Tell me a story of the end of the first age.'

She was praying.

'No? Shall I tell you how it goes? *The citizens, seeing that they were to the marshdwellers as the man is to the pig* – '

'Stop it! Stop!' She kicked out.

He skipped out of reach. ' – *came to agree that they should build about themselves a Wall, such that none should pass in or out. They perceived in themselves* – '

'Gomath! Gomath!'

' – *the seeds and blossoms of perfection in all things that men should be and do, and they said, Let us also come to fruit in this perfection* – '

'Aigu, my Aigu, deliver me from your demon . . . '

' – *free from the taint and corruption of the Outwall. And the most perfect among them* – '

'Aaaa!'

' – *was one called Gomath* – ' He broke off and held her by the ankles, looking up into her eyes with a kind of sympathy. 'Kavi, the Previs-aw-Gomath. How are you these days? You don't look well. Are you sick?' He turned away again. 'We're all sick now, you know. Some of us are sick of the city. Some of us are sick of Gomath.'

'Who are you?'

'I'm sick of being sick.' He grinned. He bent and picked up the book, saw that she had been reading about the Tivori, the departure of Gomath and the Cirnex. 'It wasn't Gomath that quit,' he told her, more savagely, 'it was us. Ourselves. The people went away and just left the dead bodies. We're the bodies.'

Kavi was in shock, not understanding a word. She watched him manipulate a spark-box, heard the metal rasp on the stone. It flashed under his fingers. He set the flame to the corner of the page.

'Nooo . . . '

It caught.

'Oh, Gomath, nooo!'

The book was burning. The demon's eyes were twin flames. She reached out; he growled and made as if to hurl it at her, brandishing it like a torch. Agitated shadows scrambled up the shelves. She grabbed again; but the voice transfixed them both.

'No, no! Don't hurt her! She's the Previs!'

Kavi stared. The man with the blazing book looked over his shoulder. The statue gazed towards them across the empty pool. Arms outstretched, Kavi overbalanced and fell to the floor.

He dropped the book and walked away, ignoring her. Helplessly she saw his feet go by. The book lay within the uncertain radius of her sight, sprawling open, its spine buckled. Flames trembled at the edge of the page, beginning to die. It was the page she had been reading. The words mesmerised her.

He comes in dreams; he comes at twilight and in the dark places of the city; in his eye will be fire, and fire in his hand; he will laugh with joy, and speak strange things, that none may understand him, and men shall say one to another, Surely this is not he. But in this may you find him, and know him who he is, that the Aigu shall speak to him, and he shall obey.

Every day Dubilier threw another love poem into the pool. Unlike the flowers, they did not dissolve but remained to corroborate his fear that time had ceased to flow. The past lay all around him like silt in a stream, blocking the fountain of present joy. Memory poisoned everything: nothing escaped him, nothing would let him escape. Nothing dissolved except the ink that clouded the pool. He knew the facts of the parting as clearly as though he'd committed a murder, but every time the thousand implications burgeoned and diffused, obscuring him. On the thirteenth day he smashed the clepsydra, whipped a serving-man, took a crossbow and strode out along the ridge, away from the city.

When he came home Ibet was waiting for him. She looked at the dead cushats in his fist, at the blood on their feathers and his fingers. There was contempt in her smile. 'I see you've found a way to satisfy your own hunger, Aigu Dubilier.'

'Ibet, don't. You don't know what I've been suffering.'

'So you decided to share it around.'

He flung the birds down. Their broken wings described gestures of resignation at her feet. 'What is it? What have I got to do?'

'Go and wash your hands, by the look of it.'

The blood spread around the basin, reminding him of the ink. He grew angry with poets who were so glib about broken hearts, and ashamed of his butchery.

She had sat down, uninvited, and didn't get up when he came back in.

'You've got some news for me?'

'No.'

'Then – what – '

She didn't answer, looking around as if deciding whether to move in or not. Then she went past him into the hall again. Watching every gesture for a sign, Dubilier didn't dare speak. He followed her.

'This is a fine house.' She stroked a curtain. 'What have you been putting in the pool?'

He felt ridiculous but made himself tell her the truth: it might be vital. 'Old poems; old letters.'

'Love letters?'

'Yes.'

The smile. 'What d'you want to do that for? They've clogged it all up. Now you'll be getting someone to clean it out for you.'

'No. I don't want it – clean.'

'You can't have much respect for him, then.' She indicated the statue.

'I . . . I don't know. It's up to him, now, really. I suppose I've given up. I don't know what to do.' She didn't speak. 'You can't think of anything.'

'She won't talk. Won't even have your name mentioned.'

So why had she come? As she stirred the soggy mess in the god's pool Dubilier noticed she was murmuring to herself.

'What did you say?'

'Oh, nothing, Aigu.'

'What was it? Please tell me.'

'Just some nonsense you put me in mind of with what you said just now. A rhyme we used to say when we were kids. It just popped back into my head.' Smiling: 'Nothing to interest a poet like your – '

'Please!'

She smiled at him archly; then adopted the pose of a schoolgirl about to recite.

'Up along the mountains
Covered in snow
Lives a wise old man
Knows all there is to know.
If you've got a question – '

She broke off. 'You see? Nothing at all, Aigu Dubilier. What must you think, me standing here reciting poetry as if we've both of us nothing better to do.'

'Ibet, please go on.'

'I don't know that I can remember it, Aigu, it's that long ago . . . '

'Ibet, I – I order you to continue.'

'Oo, well, Aigu, if it's that important . . . Let me see, where'd I get to?

If you've got a question
Or don't know what to do,
Ask the old wise man
And he'll tell you!' she finished triumphantly.

Dubilier's mind went cold and blank. Up along the mountains?

'Are you suggesting that I should – an Aigu of Thryn should go – Outwall?

She smiled wider than ever. 'Me, Aigu? I'm sure I never suggested anything of the kind.' She was on her way out of the door. 'Just an old rhyme I used to say. You mustn't pay any attention to me.'And she was gone, undismissed, and without telling him why she had come.

The rugged old man was almost alone now in the Hall of Beggars. His name was Nelgion. He was not happy. He paused to light his pipe. Blue smoke flourished and spread, vanishing slowly. 'No,' he said. 'Dreams: lot of rubbish. My dreams, your dreams.'

'I do not agree,' Previs Kavi said curtly, drawing a line in the dust with the tip of her stick as if to demarcate defences for her argument.

'Well, I know that. I know that.' He sucked noisily at the pipe, anxious to hold the initiative but having nothing to say. 'You think – '

'I know.'

'*They* think . . . ' He waved vaguely at the door. 'They're leaving me. All except the young ones. Some of them, too. Well, the old ones, they're . . . headful of dreams anyway. Their dreams, your dreams, what's it matter.' Kavi tapped her foot impatiently. 'It's all they've got; they've abandoned sanity, years ago.' It seemed he had finished, but he burst out: 'But to abandon me!'

'They wouldn't need to abandon their Aigu – ' The beggar-chief looked up sharply at her sarcastic misapplication of rank. 'They wouldn't need to abandon their Aigu to follow their god if their Aigu were doing his duty. He'd have led them all back to the temple.'

He was staring at her without listening. He got up. The bulk of him dwarfed the Previs. Unconsciously, she held her head high as her crabbed old spine would let her. He jerked open the door and motioned her onto the balcony.

'Look at it.'

Kavi's eyes could discern little at such distance, through such gloom, but she knew what he was demonstrating.

'The Hall of Beggars is nearly empty.'

She said nothing, letting him fret if he wanted to.

'You took them away. Nearly empty. The Hall hasn't been empty since it was the Hall of Glory.'

'Isn't it time we all left off huddling round our miserable

hearths and found out what we're supposed to be doing?' She took a few steps towards the stairs. 'Come up to the temple – you'll find them all there.'

Nelgion grunted, scratching his bald head with chipped fingernails. 'Why have they abandoned me? Because of a dream!'

'Because the Cirnex visited me at the Iigril in the holy library, and the Aigu spoke to him and he obeyed.' She answered with more patience than was her custom, having repeated this explanation so many times that all the trembling had gone out of her, leaving the plain fact, with no emotional colouring.

'Ptha!'

Nelgion was not happy.

There was chanting.

'Oh my God.' Lupio opened his eyes and then squeezed them tight shut. 'Let me sleep.' He shook the boy. 'Hifran. Hifran? Hifran, go and see what they're making all the noise about.'

The boy rose awkwardly from the couch and pushed the shutters open. A stiff wind sprang into the room. Discomforted, Lupio began to dress.

'They're going to the temple, Aigu.' It stood below, to the south-east. Up the path from the city came the procession. They were having difficulty with the tune, which none of them had sung for twenty years.

'Sheep,' said Lupio, leaning next to Hifran.

They had already reburnished the metal on the gates, but had not yet succeeded in dispelling the general shabbiness which had set in when their parents had given the custody of their building over to the forces of exposure and neglect. There were still disgruntled wildfowl couched on the less accessible ledges; their droppings speckled the cracked flagstones. As they watched, somebody was hustling a goat out.

'Goats out, sheep in,' said Lupio. He was still drunk. 'Where did you put the stuff?' The flagon he found proved empty. With a giggle he brought it to the window.

'Aigu! No!'

This time he didn't listen. It spun gracefully in the early sunlight and burst satisfyingly on the ground. Two or three of the last supplicants turned to see what the noise was. One of them noticed the young man gesturing wildly from the tower, but didn't recognise him. They passed into the strange, disorientating glow mixed by candles with sunlight from high, sheltered windows. The pool, refilled, reflected the god Gomath, propped up again for a long cosmetic treatment of chiselling, plastering, and painting to redress his thousand blasphemous and casual stigmata. The temple, built for a larger, lustier populace, dwarfed its congregation which stood in awed, uncomfortable groups among the dust and debris.

Kavi looked down from the dais, acknowledging obeisance. She was pleased at the citizens' embarrassment – had had the floor left unswept not only through haste but also to remind them of their state of disgrace.

It was time to begin. She had no music yet, but that would come later. In the meantime her ragged croaking would doubtless frighten them to deeper humility. Suddenly and strongly she began to invoke. Uneasy voices fumbled the responses. Kavi forced more scorn into her stare, into the hard, clipped syllables of the chant. Now they were replying with more warmth, a stir of urgency. They were desperate to believe. The call droned on, dissonant and spiralling, reaching for the moment when the dance of reception would begin.

And stopped. 'I cannot dance,' said Kavi. She glared at them. They gaped back, not daring a murmur.

'My body is unworthy of the Aigu's embrace. It cannot dance. It can scarcely walk. It is crippled with disease, sick with error and doubt. It has skulked in the darkness so long it is unable to come out into the light. It has bent and withered to the breath of Jeswed.' She banged her stick. 'It needs a stick, this carcase, to stop it falling over and rolling in the dirt!' She swung the stick backwards to point to the battered idol. 'Yes, look at him. Look at your Aigu. Have we treated him any better?' Forwards to accuse the citizens themselves. 'Now look at your own bodies. What? Misshapen from birth, half of you – and the rest eaten up with depravity.' Pause.

'And you dare to come here – to worship and seek perfection? Perfection. Jeswed's guts!' She laughed.

If they had come in trepidation, they were terrified now.

Insults, oaths and laughter in the temple of Gomath, from his own Previs! If she were so contemptuous, how would her husband treat them? If she were so wretched, what colour must their own souls be? A white-faced epileptic moaned and stumbled backwards into the row behind. His fear caught and everyone began to wail together. Kavi waited with grim joy. There was the music. Let them scare themselves; let them fear vengeance; the Aigu is coming.

The tremor waned. She held the tension, poising for a second attack.

He flung open the door. She stared; dropped to her knees. That face, at any distance, in any light, even to her failing eyes – but the congregation shuffled, not knowing him.

'Pray, citizens, fall on your faces and pray – '

Someone was shrieking hysterically.

' – this is the Cirnex. This is your master's servant.'

Dark against the doorlight, he yelled incoherent rage. He leapt amongst the cowering worshippers, hauling upright one who prostrated herself at his feet.

'Stand up, damn you! Stand up!'

He was making for the dais. He thrust aside a cripple who stood gibbering in his way, shouting over their heads. 'Kavi! Kavi, you rot-brained, superstitious old crow!' He ploughed through bodies. They struggled to touch his feet, his clothes. He kicked them, scrambling up onto the dais and jerking her head by a handful of hair. 'Tell them! Tell them!' Her lips fluttered, mouthing ancient prayers. 'Listen!' he yelled. The congregation fell back, seeking shadows. 'Listen to old Kavi, your Previs. She has something to tell you. She made a mistake just now. Her eyesight's not so good. She thought I was somebody else. Didn't you?'

'Welcome the Cirnex Servant of the Aigu he who walks always before – '

'Tell them!'

She gabbled on. The citizens shifted and murmured.

'Well, don't you know me?' He appealed to them. 'Me! You know me. You know Lupio, the wild one, the drunkard, the pansy; the one you love to gossip about. Me! Lupio! The one you tell the kids to keep away from.'

They were uncertain.

'She made a mistake, that's all.' Inappropriately, he felt tears coming. 'I don't want anything to do with gods . . . ' He sniffed and shook his head to clear his eyes. There was somebody else at the door. 'Hifran! Hifran, come here. I need you.' The citizens turned to stare again. A small grey figure slipped between them. Lupio reached down and hugged him, drawing him up onto the platform. 'Say something. Listen to this, Kavi.'

The boy stammered helplessly.

'Say something!'

'What do you want me to say?'

'Tell them what happened the other day. Tell them that you hid behind the statue to watch me when I was drunk. It was you calling out to me, wasn't it? Tell them!'

Hifran opened his mouth. Terror paralysed his tongue, and he whimpered. Lupio laughed and cuffed him. 'Citizens of Thryn, the voice of your god. Kavi? Recognise it?' He flailed his arms and jumped clumsily into the pool, splashing the holy figure. 'Smiling idiot – ' He tugged at the supports. 'You've propped him up. You shouldn't have propped him up, he's dead.' He tugged again, lost his footing and sat down. Hifran ran into the water sobbing and clutched his arm, trying to drag him up. 'Go home. Everybody go home. Leave me alone.' Lupio lurched back to the dais, reached up and grabbed Kavi, pulling her over onto her side. 'Tell them to go away. Please, please, please . . . '

'The Aigu is just. He punishes us. He tests our faith. Abuse me, Aigu Cirnex, I deserve – '

'I am not the Cirnex! There isn't a Cirnex! Somebody died, alone, Outwall, on top of a mountain, ages ago. That's all there was. Nothing to do with me, nothing to do with anyone. Please let's all go home now.'

Kavi knelt, her eyes closed submissively; she began to pray again rapidly with her lips. Lupio watched them twitch and then turned away in disgust. Hifran lay huddled by the pool, still sobbing. Lupio picked him up and carried him. The citizens shrank from him as he passed. Now many eyes held anger and hostility. But from outside he heard Kavi's voice charming them back to herself, allaying their confusion with familiar lies.

'. . . *will laugh with joy, and speak strange things, that none may understand him, and men shall say one to another, Surely this is not he.'*

No one followed him from the temple.

Restless, Dubilier rose early and walked out to a spot where he could sit and look down at the city. The mist lay over it thick and green like pondwater, but this new wind made the mist eddy and curl. Again he was hesitating, not understanding, not knowing what to do. Ali's ambiguous dismissal had left him lost and brooding in the mist, but Ibet had called on him to gather all his drifting thoughts in a new direction. Outwall, the unknown. He was afraid of Ibet, to whom nothing was unknown, who was wise and sly; and Ali – they laughed at him behind his back.

He tried to force clear thought, knowing how his mind preferred to avoid a problem by pretending to examine it; the analysis smeared and spread it into something so vast and vague that it could not be comprehended, much less answered. Then he would wait, wretchedly, until the opportunity passed, until it was too late to answer; and then he would indulge in recrimination and regret. Mist, more mist. He tried to wipe it away. What did he actually know?

Well – that he was disturbed. Unsettled. His old, safe dependence on Ali had been overturned. Without that, time seemed empty and vile. The only thing he had seen that might replace it was Ibet's idea. Whatever *that* was. If anything.

Another wave of misery. But he clung to the wreckage, refusing to have it swept from him. All right, *if* anything, Ibet's song had been about a pilgrimage, to Taleg Tivoriun in the mountains. Whether it had been literal, or a riddle, or even the nonsense she claimed it was, that was what it had said. She might have been advising him to leave Thryn and become a recluse. She might have been mocking him for his importunacy. But intentionally or no, she had suggested a journey. As he sat here now, aloof from the convoluted city, the sun lingering on the horizon and a new day, unspoilt yet, lying in his lap, the suggestion returned to him. It almost seemed possible.

The base facts were that nobody ever went Outwall. That was what the Wall was for. In an ordinary citizen or servant the idea would be despicable, even suspect of madness. In an Aigu it would be cowardice, sacrilege, dereliction of duty. The facts stopped there, at the Wall, leaving the Outwall marshes wide and free for the exercise of fantasy. They had certainly been well used. Everything a Thrynian hated or feared had been spawned, was rampant, or would eventually find its way to perdition out there. The trolls and werebeasts and blind sucking worms, not to mention the degenerate tribes of cannibals and warlocks and snake-lovers, came and went through the marsh according to the generations of popular credulity – though always under the malign and baleful tutelage of Jeswed. Legends varied: Jeswed was immortal, or Gomath (or the Cirnex his servant) had killed him, or would do one day. Seen in the early morning from the hillside, the marshes were only their usual featureless grey; and Dubilier could not summon up much holy dread of Jeswed and his minions.

Gomath, guided by the Cirnex, had gone out across the marshes at the time of the departure, the Tivori. Since then no one else had been allowed to follow. At the summit of Hisper Einou they had parted: Gomath to go on into some legendless and unspecified Unknown, while the anonymous Cirnex sat watching for his return in the fastness of Taleg Tivoriun, citadel of the departure. The whole story was really rather unclear. Dubilier wasn't at all sure he felt inspired to pursue it. While in a feeble, unfocused way he still believed in Gomath, his social and educational level of sophistication made him unable to localise that belief as the ordinary citizen did. Gomath was a god, a supreme metaphysical being. The mythology translated him down into something banal and physical for the benefit of the unrefined intelligence. Dubilier's intelligence was refined. Going off to look for the old man on the mountain was an embarrassing idea, put like that. But a quest, for the secret behind myth: that was a temptation he could appreciate.

Whatever is out there, he thought, it can't be worse than some of what we have in here. He looked down at the dingy city. As the mist dispersed, what it revealed more and more was a broken, claustrophobic warren. It depressed him. He was sleeping badly. He felt ill-prepared for leaving, but reluctant to stay only to fence nightly with phantoms of desire. He remembered a masked ball, with midnight partnerings by torchlight.

Those men whose companions had eluded them, and those who had none, had had to run back and forth through the gardens at the behest of faceless sirens who beckoned or spurned them from behind every bush and tree. Brambles had torn at Dubilier as he pursued his blue-gowned spectre far from the others, and when at last he'd caught her by the waist a great exhilaration had possessed him; but laughing she plucked off her mask and kissed him deep and hard, and was not Alita at all. It had been a night of horror for him.

Masks obtruded from all sides now: citizens were beginning to glance and comment when they thought he wasn't looking and to effect unconcern if he glanced back. Did Alita's treasured face mask an unidentified enemy? Did Ibet's cowl shadow an unexpected friend? Masks at night are terrible enough; masks in daylight –

Alarmed, he got to his feet. He had actually begun to contemplate leaving Thryn. It would be madness.

But if all he could find in Thryn would be masks and mazes, then that would send him mad, perhaps more swiftly. Perhaps he had begun to be mad already. He turned round as if flinching from the sight of the city, but the cold wind slapped his face and provoked something cold inside him to take control and turn him again. Clarity, he insisted. If I can contemplate it, contemplate it properly, can I effect it? How can I get out? Over the Wall? Or under it?

He blinked as the climbing sun flashed on something bright. The river. He could see it only in fragments between buildings, but he knew it threw a broad loop through an open space in the cluttered city, where a tiny wharf and a dilapidated warehouse indicated that that unimpressive streak of grey had once been used by barges, for cargo – an age ago, before Thrynian self-satisfaction became absolute. It had to be still navigable, though it passed underground when entering the city. Where and how it flowed out, away behind him to the right, he didn't know; it might be that he'd have to find out and go that way to have the current with him, but at the moment he preferred the upper conduit and a direct route upstream to the mountains.

He was mad. The fact that he could be planning such an absurdity proved it. He had no experience, no assets, hardly any motivation. It would be impossible for him, probably for anyone. When the Thrynian patriarchs had built the Wall, they had not left gaps. Nobody had ever got out. Except that boy. Who was that? Where had he heard that? Someone had been telling him the story of a boy who'd swum out, for a dare. More mythology. Or perhaps it had been a joke, or an idea for a book. Improbable, anyway. And he'd been drugged or drunk, the man who'd told it.

How did he remember that? Crazy laughing face in the hot room, shouting about the boy – Shouting? Why? A smell . . . Smoke. The pipe and the bowl going round. Shouting above the music, and all the people singing and talking. A party. At a party. Somebody told him – but who was that? And, almost as an afterthought, slowly floating to the surface, that the crazy face was a mask, wasn't it? At the same masked party.

Dubilier shut his eyes to concentrate on what was coming up. But if it was at a party and he was wearing a mask, you'll never find him. Somebody else must know the story. What happened to the boy. But the laughing harlequin had bewitched him. He was running again round and round the black garden, hunting now not for his changeling lady but for a man with a laughing mask. The darkness was oblivion, the darting torches flares of recall too dazzling and brief to be intelligible. It was no good.

'Are you all right, Aigu?'

The tremulous voice summoned him back. A worried girl was looking up at him. Behind her a gaggle of pallid children waited fearfully to see what the strange man would do. Dubilier realised how formidable he must look stumbling about on the hillside with his eyes closed. 'I'm not sure,' he said ruefully. He sat down on the grass, to counteract the awe a grown-up creates in a child merely by being taller.

'Can I do something, Aigu?'

'No.'

Though frightened, she wanted to help him. 'What's the matter?'

He smiled at her. 'I'm looking for a man I can never find.'

'What's his name? Perhaps we know him.'

Dubilier shook his head.

'What does he look like?'

'That's the problem. He was wearing a mask with a silly face on.' He grimaced to demonstrate and make her smile. 'It doesn't matter,' he said. She gave him a look more of pity than fear and marshalled her charges. They began to play a few yards off, hide-and-seek among the stones. Suddenly Dubilier got up and touched her on the shoulder. 'I've remembered his name. Lupio.'

The shrieks and laughter stopped. The children stood staring. Then they bolted, without a word. The girl looked at him in shock for a second and then made to chase after them. He held her.

'What's wrong? *Do* you know him?'

The wind tugged her hair as if urging her to pull free.

'Oh, Aigu, pray to Gomath, say a prayer quick.'

'Because of Lupio?'

She nodded, dumb.

'Who is he?'

'Not – not that name any more, Aigu. He came to the temple. The Previs, she says he's the Cirnex. She says he's come back now and Gomath's coming back and they're going to punish everybody!'

He stood gazing at her, uncomprehending.

'Please, Aigu, let me go now. The children – I must – '

He dropped his hand. Round the curve of the hill she fled. He was trembling. Just reach out and snatch the mask away and you'll see: an unexpected god.

Lupio was drunk because the publicans were too scared to refuse him – and some too scared to take his money – but he was alone because all his old associates were too scared to come near him. Even the whores. Especially the whores. He laughed, splashing along the alley, mimicking them. 'Don't tempt me, Aigu Cirnex! Don't make me do it, holy master! I'm a poor girl, a wicked girl, but I've got to live. I couldn't go with you, it wouldn't be right.'

'What wouldn't be right?' asked a voice from the darkness.

Another one. 'Do you have a light?' he asked wearily.

A spark-box scratched. The shaky flame showed him her painted eyes, her sombre scarlet mouth: they didn't convulse with shock. She inspected him.

'You're the one they're calling the Cirnex.'

He bowed.

She studied him without speaking.

'Well?' he said. 'Aren't you going to ask me to bless you too?'

'Do you want to come in?'

He followed her dim shape up the alley, across a yard and into a cellar. There was a smell of damp. She struck sparks again and lit a fat-lamp, then scrutinised him again. 'You don't look like someone who gives many blessings.'

'No,' he said, 'but that doesn't stop them asking.'

'So what is the Cirnex doing drinking in the slums and talking with prostitutes like an ordinary man?'

Lupio swore. 'I am an ordinary man!'

She laughed. 'All right,' she said sardonically, 'I believe you.'

'You do?'

She shrugged. 'Seems to me a man should be able to tell whether he's a god or not. If he says he isn't, who am I to turn custom away?' She peered into a fragment of mirror to unpin her hair. 'What makes them think you are?'

'Kavi. Some ... prophecy.' He slumped on the bed, very tired, no longer defensive. He let the drink and this woman dissolve the bitterness.

She was undressing. 'He must have died ages ago. Centuries. Either that or he's hundreds of years old.' She started to unfasten his trousers. 'You look rough all right, but not that rough.'

'You're not so bad yourself.' He reached for her. She smiled and went to blow out the lamp. 'No, leave it,' he said. 'I want to be able to see the one woman in Thryn who's not afraid to go to bed with a god.'

'I'll have to charge you for the fat. It's not cheap, you know.'

'Come here.'

Even after midnight, the city did not sleep. Its dark silences held no rest, seeming to wait always for the next interruption. An old man came scavenging, sorting the day's litter and leavings with a practised toe and stooping only for the best. A woman holding torn clothes to her was yelling at the man who was about to hit her again. A drunken Aigu wandered homewards, stopping in a square to relieve himself in the dried fountain. A thief crossed the square from the other direction and they greeted each other. Past the house of the Aigui Alita came a legless man, thrusting his trolley along with rhythmical strokes. The jagged tune he whistled harmonised strangely with the squeak of wooden wheels. In a blue gown, the Aigui Alita watched from a taperlit window. The city could not sleep. It tossed as if in fever.

They lay listening. When the lamp failed at last, the woman rose, silhouetted against the dim green window high in the wall. Lupio got up to go. 'Lie down,' she said, bringing a blanket to the bed. 'I'll get no more trade tonight, you might as well stay.'

They squeezed together on the narrow mattress, the blanket over them. After a while, she said, 'Does it bother you, everybody saying you're the Cirnex?'

'Bother me?'

'Oh. Obviously it does.'

'It's not nice to see everybody jump as you walk down the street.'

'That doesn't amuse you.'

'Not often.'

'Can't you do something about it?'

He sighed noisily. 'I've tried. I've tried doing all the ungodly things I can think of – all the ungodly things I'm in the habit of doing anyway – and Kavi tells them I'm under commission to tempt them and test their faith.'

'The Previs?'

'Mn.'

'She came here once.'

'Here?'

'Yes. Came stumping in through the door when we'd just got going and dragged him off me.' She laughed. 'You should have heard him go for her! Jeswed . . . '

'Why? Was she trying to clean up Thryn single-handed or something?'

'Oh, no,' she said, 'nothing like that. She's got a thing about cellars – she thinks she's going to find her husband in one, so she barges in at random and if she finds a man, she hauls him out to make sure it's not him!'

Lupio thought of the text. 'It wasn't Gomath she was looking for, it was me.'

'What?'

'That's how it started. I got in the way of a prophecy.'

'Kavi decided you were the one she was groping round cellars after?'

'Mm-hm.'

Lupio stared up into the dark. He was comfortable. Kavi was a mere absurdity from this perspective.

'Why do people have to put their faith in a rot-brained old hag?'

'She's the Previs.'

'If only I could convince her I'm not her man, they'd soon lose interest.'

'It's taken them a good few years to lose interest in their last god.'

Lupio saw the prospect. Everywhere, at every moment to be shunned or importuned. Mistrust from one side and from the other only trust misplaced, deference he didn't want and demands he couldn't satisfy. And when faith faded, suspicion and resentment. So much attention, and none of it for him. The Cirnex, not him. To be lonely in the middle of all that. He'd never been lonely. He saw faces watching from the shadows of the long colonnades, heard children jeering. He could go mad.

'I'm going to have to leave the city.'

'You might as well, mightn't you?'

'You think so?'

She sensed his diffidence. 'Well, who's going to try and stop you? Who's going to care?'

'Kavi,' he said, 'I hope.' They laughed.

'Where are you going?'

'Somewhere – clean.'

'The mountains.'

'Are they clean?'

'When I was a girl I used to think so. I used to think that the tops of the mountains must be the cleanest place in the world. I suppose it was because they sometimes look all white, when there's snow on them. And they're right up above all the mist.' A thought struck her and she chuckled drowsily. 'While you're up there, you can call in at Taleg Tivoriun.'

He squeezed her reproachfully. 'What would I do in Taleg Tivoriun?'

'See if there's anyone at home.'

'Just a little pile of bones.'

'There you are, then. Bring them back. You can prove he's dead.'

Suggestible with sleep, he thought that made sense. But walking home through the cold morning, he recalled it with scorn and renewed his despair. The bones of the Cirnex: the bones of a man who had never existed . . . or his own bones, perhaps. Gruesome. No, this would all blow over as quickly as it had blown up; he just had to weather it. He could do that. But he knew how to get out of the city too, if he needed to.

It wasn't until he was five minutes from home that he laughed uproariously to find she'd rifled his pockets, his money-pouch, everything.

The house was deserted. Lupio ran through the empty rooms calling. Out in the courtyard he found a small figure struggling unhappily with a large broom.

'Hifran!'

He came forward. 'Aigu?'

'Where's Jumox? Where the marsh is everybody?'

'They – went, Aigu.'

'Idiot! Where? Why?'

The boy stammered. 'I hid and came back, Aigu, I didn't want to go away. I tried to clean up for you but the – '

'Jeswed's eyes!' Lupio grabbed his arms, almost tugging him off the ground. 'Where has everybody gone? Tell me!'

'The Previs made them go. She came, she – she said nobody was to live here any more, she – she – '

'She sent them away? My servants?'

'She said it's a holy place now, Aigu . . . '

Lupio dropped to his knees and clutched Hifran to him. 'You stayed.'

'She frightened me, Aigu, I don't want to go.'

His master hugged him in silence. Comforted, Hifran began to speak again. 'There was a man, Aigu; he was looking for you. I told him you were at the Iigril. Did you see him?'

Lupio stood, his arm on Hifran's shoulders. He looked at the dusty yard and at the identical cold grey shadows waiting at each window for him to leave so that they could take up full occupancy. Sitting out Kavi's siege would be a grim while. 'No,' he said. 'I'll go and see if he's still there.'

'Shall I stay here, Aigu?' He swung the broom unwillingly.

'No. Let Kavi have the house if she wants it. Go and play, Hifran, don't come back here. I'll come and find you when I get back and then we'll see what's to be done.'

The boy still looked frightened.

'What's wrong, Hifran?'

'Aigu – you will come back, won't you?'

'Yes, Hifran, of course I will. You know I will.'

He nodded, convincing himself. 'Yes. You'll have to come back, because you're the Cirnex now, aren't you?'

Blind with anger and love, Lupio hugged and kissed him. 'Run away. Don't look back. Go on, run!'

Lupio went inside. He found a haversack and filled it with food and a few clothes. He took a sword and a knife and a couple of bottles. He slung a stout cloak about his shoulders, left the door open, and went to the Iigril.

The man was in the council chamber. He was an Aigu, dark haired, dark featured, and darkly dressed. Lupio could not recall having seen him before. He seemed worried; and Lupio guessed that this was his general state rather than his dread of supposing he was meeting a demi-god. 'I'm Lupio. Are you waiting for me?'

The stranger rose, bowed and made the orthodox gesture of supplication. 'Aigu Cirnex,' he began, 'forgive me if what I say is confused and full of error – '

Lupio banged the bottles down on the table. 'My name is Lupio. Kavi is a crazy old witch. The Cirnex is dead, the prophets were all liars. Gomath – ' His eyes flicked involuntarily to the great tapestry. 'Gomath is a guilty dream, the after-effect of arrogance and indigestion.' He paused. 'If you've nothing more to say to me, I suggest you go and tell your Previs what I said.'

'Aigu – Cirnex – '

Lupio lost patience. 'My name is *Lupio* – is it me you're looking for, or a dream?'

The man surprised him by smiling at that. 'Both, I suspect,' he said. 'I'm sorry, I was told – You're not the Cirnex?'

'No. Sorry to disappoint you. Drink?'

He took the profferred bottle. 'On the contrary . . . it makes all this much easier if you're not.' He smiled, eager to propitiate the young man. 'My name's Dubilier. You won't remember, but we have met, at a party once. You told me a story, about a boy who swam up the river out of Thryn. Do you remember that?'

Lupio tried not to show that he was startled. That was exactly what had been on his mind since leaving the prostitute. 'I remember the incident, yes, but I must have told that story a hundred times; I'm afraid I don't remember you.'

Dubilier laughed deprecatingly. 'Oh, I'm immaterial,' he said, 'but tell me: is the story true?'

Even more bewildered, Lupio took a pull on the bottle before replying. 'Well, without remembering what fanciful embroidery I embellished it with on that particular night, the story's true, yes.'

'That's good. That's very good. Thank you.'

'Look, I hope you don't mind my asking, but what is all this?'

Dubilier looked at him. The young man's unkempt appearance, his exaggerated bluntness and insouciance, his condemnation of religion marked him as a dissident even if he was the only Aigu still to be found at the Iigril. 'I want to leave the city,' said Dubilier, making his decision in the same instant that he announced it.

'Why?'

There was a strange intermission. They regarded each other, each buffeted by the tempest of his own thoughts. This was the unforeseen. Across a table dulled by neglect, in an empty tower whose triumphal hangings were stained and shadowed with the deceits of time, two of the last Aiguda gazed at one another without understanding. Through them, Dubilier thought, a game was being played out, an irrevocable game for concealed, momentous stakes. Each of them had been dealt an unexpected hand, each was unfamiliar with the rules, but the sequence had been initiated and they could do nothing but follow suit. Dubilier had the feeling that whatever either of them did, the cards would make their own patterns.

He cleared his throat. How much more could he tell this irritable young degenerate? Should he admit that he was a failure with women and lacked the courage to do anything but run away? That was how it would sound, surely, to anyone else; that was perhaps how it actually was.

Lupio told himself: Coincidence. He turned away, bewildered.

Dubilier stood nervously looking around the chamber. A tapestry caught his eye, a huge picture of gods: Gomath and his servant the Cirnex, in the background a simple triangle standing for the mountain of the departure, Hisper Einou. They signalled to him out of history with angular gestures and imperious stares. All that embroidery had once been white and silver, turquoise and crimson. Now it was faded and grimy.

Dubilier said, 'Because I'm sick of the way everything gets spoilt here. Thryn doesn't give anything a chance. Everything's deformed or stillborn, if it's not aborted first. I'm sick of sickness being normal, sick of corruption and complacency, and I want to go and find something better.'

With his cynicism Lupio recovered some of his poise.

'That's an old song, Aigu Dubilier,' he said. 'I remember singing it myself, once upon a time.' And he sang a few bars of something about true love, before breaking off and saying, 'It's no good, you know. There isn't any true love – any true anything – wherever you look. Like those morons down there.' He pointed to the temple humming below them. 'Stare into the mist long enough and you start seeing all sorts of things. A man, maybe, standing a long way off. You call him: *Hey! Come and give us a hand!* But he doesn't move. And then you get angry.' He pointed at Dubilier. 'You get really desperate; all because you won't admit – he was never there in the first place. There's nothing there, nothing anywhere.' He tugged on the bottle again. '*That's* what's wrong.'

Dubilier didn't know what he was talking about. Lupio gave him a searching glance, thinking he'd underestimated him. He wasn't just a traditional reactionary – not if he intended to leave the city. Lupio felt an alcoholic surge of frustration and longing. He thought of Hifran trembling in the courtyard of his own home. This man Dubilier seemed to know what he wanted. Lupio beckoned him to the window. Dubilier approached, thinking he heard the last card fall.

'Look at it,' Lupio was saying. 'Blinded by the exhalations of its own decay.' He waved the bottle clumsily. The last of the green mist clung to the black back of the river. 'You know it. I know it. We don't need to climb this tower to observe that the citizens of Thryn are an insensate rabble of beggars and freaks. They've got nothing to look forward to, no more than we have. But you're right, Dubilier, that doesn't oblige us to lie down and fester with them.'

Dubilier looked and he panicked. In the derelict council chamber a tapestry flapped. It seemed that a corner of the mantle of their inheritance had brushed them there, Aiguda of Thryn, with the eyes of Gomath upon them and their city like a helpless child sprawling at their feet. They were throwing off the mantle; they were ignoring the crying of the child. What was he going to the wilderness to find? He didn't even know. And Lupio –

'We shouldn't waste any more time,' Lupio said.

'We – ?'

'I'm coming with you.'

'You don't know what I'm looking for!'

'Do you?' Lupio folded his arms and leaned back on the parapet. 'Let me tell you a remarkable thing. Last night I was with a prostitute. She told me, quite out of the blue, that she thought I should go to the mountains. Then she robbed me of everything I was carrying. The Previs-aw-Gomath, which is a ridiculous name for another sort of prostitute, assured me that, in some mystical way, I've actually *come* from the mountains. Then she robbed me of my home and all my servants. Today you turn up, equally out of the blue, and start talking about leaving the city, just as I'm beginning to wonder if the city isn't conspiring to expel me. Now I'm not – as you've probably deduced – a religious man. I don't believe in destiny and coincidence manifesting the will of Gomath and all that. But I am beginning to think that perhaps it's time I went and had a look at these mountains that everybody so cheerfully identifies me with. I can't imagine they'll be anything but great lumps of perfectly ordinary rock, but at least I'll be able to breathe there, and I won't have Kavi on my back. And I can come back, if I want to come back, laughing.'

The game was done. Dubilier felt relief and excitement.

'The mountains,' Lupio said. 'Does that appeal? Hisper Einou – that's where Teleg Tivoriun is, isn't it? That's where you'll find something better, don't you think?' He grinned fiercely. 'If it really exists.'

For a moment Dubilier thought of telling him a remarkable thing too; but he simply nodded. 'Hisper Einou and the Citadel of the Departure,' he repeated. 'That sounds fine.' And so, he thought, I myself at last adopt my mask too. All motives are questionable. Ali and Ibet are right to keep theirs hidden away where they can't be questioned. He felt suddenly light-headed. Lupio was smiling sardonically.

'So if you succeed, I fail,' he observed. 'You still think we have something to look forward to. I think we have nothing to look forward to, and that's why I'm going to look. Can you leave tomorrow morning?'

'I think so. Do you know this way out by the river?'

'Oh, yes.'

'You were the boy in the story, weren't you?'

'I was.'

With a histrionic flourish of his cape Lupio strode back into the room and snatched the second bottle from the table. Dubilier followed him downstairs. The eyes of the portraits reproach us, he thought.

'How do we get through the Wall?'

Lupio had begun to run, his boots clattering insolently in the corridors of immemorial silence. His bitter melancholy lifted for the first time in days; he felt wilful and lawless again.

'By the rivergate,' he shouted back, 'with a little help from the rivergateman.'

2

One learns to love reality better sometimes after a long detour by way of dreams.

Pierre Reverdy

Being absurd as well as beautiful,
Magic – like art – is hoax redeemed by awe.

Peter Viereck

Hifran waited until the sun set, then he stole some food and climbed up to the Iigril. There was no one there. He sat on a window-sill and ate Lupio's share too. The lapwings cried, going home in the twilight. Hifran yawned and went too, the night mist creeping up around him. The Aigu wasn't there either, and the empty rooms were suddenly strange, as if they'd forgotten him now they were holy. He curled up at the bottom of the steps outside the kitchen door and cried a little before he fell asleep. Something stung his nose and throat. He coughed and woke up. The house was all lit, orange and golden, though the sun was still down. That was what the holiness did. It was hot, and Hifran ran away. He saw a man in a cloak running away in the opposite direction, so he was afraid and ran faster. He hid in a thicket until it started to grow light, and then he came out and went along the path towards the Iigril.

Kavi was fussing at the gate of the temple. Hifran paused, dazzled by the glare on the white stone and metal. Kavi's robe shone green. She waved her stick at him. 'Hey! Where are you running?'

He approached her shivering, but only inside. He didn't bow, though you were supposed to. 'To the Iigril, Previs.'

'Servant of my master's servant.' She seemed to be talking to herself. 'Is he there?'

'Who?'

'Your master.'

He shook his head and tried to shade his eyes. 'I don't know. He's coming back soon.'

'Come inside.' Hifran didn't move. He felt half asleep still. It would be lonely in the Iigril. 'Well? Come in, boy. Do your duty to your master's master.' Kavi was frightening. She was the Previs, but Aigu Lupio said she was just a batty old woman. She was the first person to speak to him since Aigu Lupio Cirnex had kissed him goodbye. He went nearer. 'Can you dance?' she asked. 'Can you sing?' But he went past her, into the cool dimness of the temple, and stood at the edge of the pool. The youngest of the new girls looked at him and giggled together. They were throwing in the dawn flowers. The door boomed shut.

Even Nelgion the beggar-chief had gone. Lupio and Dubilier carried their packs through the Hall. There were some of the oldest ones left, crouched on litters of soiled rags around the dwindling fire, too feeble to be moved, but all the children, the cripples and the sick had been carried up to the temple for the morning ceremony. A hairless dog nosed a body: its eyes were open, but it hardly moved.

Dubilier was aghast. He looked around the walls with a sort of numb misery. The rotting sculptures looked like rotting flesh.

Lupio pushed the dog off with his foot and knelt to speak to the victim. It didn't reply, but the eyes followed him as he went to the fire and stirred it up, throwing on some of the refuse. Then he stood up. 'This way.'

Yellow lantern light danced down long avenues of mouldy stone. 'We can get to the river through here?'

'Yes.'

Dubilier was trying to reason it out. 'Where's the gate?'

'In the Wall. Mind – the floor's uneven just ahead.'

'You certainly know your way around. Have you been here before? – since you were a boy, I mean.'

'I know Thryn pretty well – the nastier bits of it, at least.' He held the lantern up and looked at Dubilier critically. 'The taverns and the whorehouses and the rat-holes – and most of the rats, too.'

Dubilier laughed sociably, trying to feel at ease. 'The ones with four legs or two legs?'

Lupio grinned. 'Four legs, two legs . . . one leg . . . three legs . . . All the places and people an Aigu should avoid.'

'But you were in the Iigril.'

'Well, there's some good things there still.'

'It looked as if a lot of it's been vandalised.'

'That's right,' Lupio said, and laughed, for no reason Dubilier could see. He wasn't boasting, he wasn't relishing his disreputable career, but it seemed to amuse him, distantly, as he might be taken with the adventures of some rogue in a book. Dubilier remembered nights in his adolescence when he'd crammed his head under the pillow, frantic with the drunks outside whose brawling stopped him from sleeping. This sure-footed, intelligent young layabout might have been one of them.

'I vandalised it,' Lupio added. 'Some of it.'

'What? Why?'

'Oh – something to do.'

There was a pause while Dubilier searched for a friendly, non-committal reply, annoyed at himself for being shocked.

'We are the leisure class, after all,' Lupio said lightly. 'How did you spend yours?'

'Oh, I – ' He rushed back to childhood. Somewhere there must have been something that wouldn't sound pathetic. The images flickered, brightened by the gloom around him. In his father's library, staring at a book or an ancient, half-legendary map, filling in the spaces between the words and the designs with creatures and castles and somebody singing to a harp. A warm fire. Years when he seemed to have been endlessly walking on the hills, and it was always autumn; or in the streets below, hooded, keeping to the wall when anyone passed, courting a mystery. Then the pain of transposing her music down to the callous, guttural tones of the city, conducting himself awkwardly by ideals high and unhelpful as the stars. Gatherings of the young nobles where ease and laughter made up the dominant, and he was pitched too fine or too deep. He seldom spoke and was never understood, but he couldn't go back and talk to the trees and statues any more. Frustration – depression – and compromise, the daily tragedy. And resignation: gingerly attempting parties, trying on the protective coloration.

At one or other of these, high on something, he'd lost sight of the gulf between himself and other men and discovered the more treacherous chasm that divided him from women. There was an old song about a sweetheart who lived on the other side of a deep torrent, and Dubilier had helplessly concluded that the only way he was ever going to cross that was by waiting for her to row across and pick him up. At last, Alita: she seemed to beckon, which was something, and he'd taken it for everything. Once again he lived in shuttered rooms, private orchards, and fulfilment was being on the right side of a fastened door. Only now it was barred against him, and in a few more minutes they'd come to the rivergate and go outside the Wall, where nothing was safe . . . He couldn't tell Lupio any of that.

He made himself smile. 'Avoiding the rats,' he confessed; and Lupio laughed, but appreciatively, not unkindly, so he felt relieved.

They stopped and looked from a broad stone ledge down into obscure water. A gleam ran along and showed the tunnels to right and left, the ledge continuing each way into shadow. There was a notional fence, wooden posts four feet apart, between them and the water. It reeked. Lupio held the light out. 'You'll soon make up for that,' he said. White and black and grey, they scrabbled in the scum.

At the rivergate Abredos was cursing the damp in his spark-box. He tugged its flint free and scraped it on the wet stone floor. Then he hit it on the rusty winch. Nothing happened.

'Jeswed's guts. All the water. Gets in everything. Rots.'

He pushed the flint back and hunched over it, cupping his hands. He jabbed the lever again, thrusting the tiny bowl right up close. There was a spark; gone.

'Plagues.'

Abredos's remaining teeth clenched the stem. He flicked again and again. Then he sighed and sniffed noisily, and spat. There was a splash. He stuffed the pipe into his pouch and crawled back to his cell in the Wall. A brick platform halfway up the hollow held a spread of mildewed straw and dead moss. With aged ease the cripple dragged himself aloft by his fingers and collapsed muttering into his nest. There was a long rustling; then silence, as Abredos started the dream.

It was his only continuous occupation, the dream. He made his patrols infrequently, without any attempt at regularity; he tested the gate perhaps twice a year; occasionally he monitored the level of the river by lying down beside it, holding onto one of the posts with his unco-operative legs, and hanging as far as he could over the edge. Normally that would not be quite far enough to reach the water; a few times, once or twice a year, he had hauled himself back with wet fingers, which indicated a rise of perhaps four inches. These perfunctory tasks he performed more as diversions than duties, though he had been trained for them half his life ago; for they were quite pointless. If he ever met anyone on his rounds, it would only be one of the idiots from the Hall of Glory, thrown downstairs for a laugh, or some urchin more inquisitive than his mates, or one of Nelgion's grisly concubines come to offer him food or drink. A few times Ghuric or someone would come down aimlessly and leave soon. Kavi's visit had been the only incident for over a month. The gate still worked: so what? No one was about to use it. And the predictability of the river's height was no more interesting than if it had fluctuated constantly and at random, for there was no one to interest – though it was lucky the river was so tame: a flood could cause a lot of damage among creaking vaults and decrepit masonry. Would he have time to give the alarm in an emergency? Who would he give it to? He scarcely thought about it. But Abredos remained the rivergateman. Sometimes he would scuttle about the waterfront; sometimes he would keep his bed and go into the dream.

In the dream it was the day when the last Aigu had died, and all the citizens gathered to choose a new leader. The Previs had meditated in the temple and announced a sign from Gomath: Abredos was the one. A cadre of twelve beautiful maidens was sent to escort him from the rivergate to glory. He often excited himself further by imagining that they would arrive when he was in the middle of dreaming them one day, and that all the Aiguda might really have died since he'd last emerged into the light. He persuaded himself that any day might be *the* day; any rehearsal of the dream might be interrupted forever and evaporate into actuality. The maidens (who were very often naked) brought him fine robes and carried him up into the Hall of Glory, which had been restored beyond its original magnificence for the occasion. It was filled with citizens of all ranks, his companions, his enemies, and sometimes any Aiguda to whom he felt especially hostile at the time, reprieved from the general demise for the sake of this humiliation. They would sing his praises and acknowledge him Aigu Supreme with ritual observations of fealty, religious and secular. He could sense the warmth and smell the incense of the ceremonial candles, and hear himself exalted by the Previs in rich, sonorous phrases which he glorified in without understanding. No longer would he have to feel his way around the dank, lightless cavern on the brink of a sewer; his fingers would be occupied with treasures brought him by great men (from where? He never gave it a thought). He would smile as they vied for his attention, despising them all, secure in a reward no less lavish than he deserved. The dream almost invariably dissolved into an undifferentiated ecstasy as one or all of the maidens came and made love to him in a warm and perfumed bath.

Approaching finale, Abredos sighed and sniffed with pleasure. Nothing would disturb the dream once begun, and now it was on the point of climax. Here they came, the maidens: he could hear their footsteps in the tunnel from the underhall, treading carefully on the uncertain floor. They were murmuring expectantly, playing torchlight around the sombre tons of stone. Abredos felt strangely relaxed. Soon they would locate the doorway of his cell, and then he would never need to dream again. The city had recognised the true prince dormant in his shrunken frame (there they were at the threshold) and had sent its fairest to lift him from darkness to the glad light. (Now they were gathering, looking up at him in awe.) It would be bright –

'Wake up.'

That was a man's voice. The hand on his arm was firm and strong.

'Is he dead?'

Another, more tentative.

'Smells like it. Come on.' Tugging him.

'Gomath, what a pit – ' broken off in a retching cough. Who were they? Where were the girls? Abredos jerked upright on the shelf. Soldiers: of course, they'd send soldiers to guard him. They should have more respect.

'I'm awake. Don't handle me. Don't you know I'm your Aigu? Whose orders? Dogs!'

'Mad – oh, Gomath. . .' The quieter one, edgy.

'Dreaming.' The bolder one, purposeful. 'Come on.'

'Idiots! Mad? Dreaming? Not any more. Take me to them. You'll see. Where are they? Where are the girls?'

A pause.

'Do you think we can make him understand?'

'Hey! Rivergateman!' The lieutenant.

'No. Not any more.'

They were going outside again – without asking leave! Abredos glowed with righteous indignation. Insulting him at his great time, because they wouldn't accept that a humble door-keeper had been put above them. When he was declared Aigu Supreme he'd show them how to treat him.

He sat in the dark and listened.

'Is he the same one?'

'Must be; he looks as ancient as the Wall.'

'What are you going to say to him? What happened last time?'

'I hid for a long while, watching: I thought he might open the gate, but he smelt me out. He must know every inch of the place. Then I ran up the tunnel and when I came back I made a lot of noise and told him I was a messenger from the Aiguda and I had to check the gate was working.'

The voice stopped, interrupted by the other one coughing again, and blaming the smell. Abredos snorted. What smell?

'He grumbled a lot, but he had to believe me, and when he opened up I slipped into the water.'

'You swam? In that?'

The lieutenant laughed. 'Like a fish – like a rat, and I thought I was being quiet, but he heard me. He must have good ears too.'

'So he can hear us now.' Abredos heard the fright in the voice and smiled.

'Probably gone back to sleep. The damp's got to his brain.'

The corporal he would beat; the lieutenant he would hang.

'Did he catch you?'

'Well, he tried lowering the gate first, which was a waste of time, and then he opened it again and came through in his boat, by which time I'd had a good look round. While he was fumbling about in the tunnel I swam back in.'

'What do we do now?'

'I don't know. I thought we might be able to get the key off him.' Abredos stiffened. What was this? 'We'll have to confuse him again. You go in and humour him while I get the boat. Then if one of us can fetch him out of his sty, the other can find the gate key.'

Abredos rummaged urgently for the key and hooked it to his belt. Treachery – he'd hang both. But if would be safe there.

The corporal was saying, 'You'd better take the lantern.' He came back into the cell.

'I heard you! I heard you! I know what you're doing, think I don't? Baughh! Rats. Now they're all dead you think you can run away, join your master in the badlands.'

'Give us the boat, rivergateman. You don't need it. You're not going anywhere.'

'Going? I could have gone. Any time. Any time! Out in the marsh, out in the – in – I didn't go! What would I want to go for? Women? You think it's women? Oh, no, soldier, they might look like women, d'ye see, but they're demons. I didn't go to them! I didn't desert my duty.'

'Women?'

'Yerrghh! Where are they? Hiding in the underhall, are they? Scared to come through?' The corporal was alone; his lieutenant had the lantern. That gave Abredos the advantage. 'They don't need you, they don't need a bogworm like you, soldier. Call yourself a soldier?' He was shifting to the edge of the shelf.

Dubilier stirred. Women hiding – demons disguised as women – Ibet, and Ali masked behind stone trees. The stinking old troll, what did he know? Humour him. 'Yes,' he said. 'It's you they're waiting for.' Outside something splashed. As if at a signal, Abredos flopped forward. Dubilier was thrown to the floor in an avalanche of darkness. Hands at his throat.

'Dubilier!' Running.

Kneeling on him the hunchback hissed in his ear. 'You have to take me. Take me, I'll burn you alive. I'll get – '

Then Lupio was onto him, pulling him away. Lantern light leapt crazily into the cell, caught monstrous fungi dripping from the ceiling. Dubilier gasped for breath, thrusting his knees up to heave the wriggling weight from him. Lupio was struggling to pin the cripple's arms but he struck out backwards. The lantern hit the floor and went out. A hand groped for Dubilier. He seized and twisted it, scraping it hard against the floor. There was a cry; the shadow slid to one side and he could see the dim oblong of the doorway. He ran into the cavern. Someone wheezed behind him. Had Lupio got the key? He couldn't see anything but coloured flares. His spark-box refused to ignite. Where was the boat? Stumbling, he sensed he was at the edge. A misshapen bulk lurched out of the dark. How could he see he was there? He flung himself into space and landed in cold water, shrieking. The filth seemed to clutch him. He forgot how to swim. He flailed his arms in panic and hit wet wood that bounced and reverberated hollowly.

Abredos came screaming to the edge. Lupio met him with a vicious blow from his forearm: seeing nothing, he felt a face give under it. Abredos clawed for his eyes. Lupio dodged and grabbed the arm, levering him off balance. There was a crack. Abredos lay still, his head against a post.

'Dubilier!'

'What happened?'

'Have you got the boat?'

'Yes. What about the key?'

'Hold on, I'll – no, wait.' Scuffling. 'I've got it. Have you got the oars?'

Dubilier found them. He could hear metal on metal, the screech of unoiled works.

'It's – lifting – '

The rivergate went up hesitantly, ripping a fat curtain of weed from the bottom. Lupio threw a rope and jumped down. They wobbled from the Wall, staggering helplessly into mid-stream and under the dim teeth of the gate overhead. Lupio took both oars and they were into the tunnel. A wail of angry bewilderment reached them. A blind man lay robbed and bleeding in the dark. Outside, the sun was shining.

Thryn was a low shoulder of rock bulging from soft terrain. A small, sharp hill jutted at one end of the bone like a broken neck, while grass and farmlands covered the shoulder-blade like the gathering of a cloak. There a topsoil could be persuaded to stay, and drainage was good down the ridge into the marsh below. The Wall outlined the whole anatomy precisely – an irregular ellipse around the long miles of rural land throwing out a loop to take in the hill where the citadel stood: the Iigril, Taleg Aigudun. At the foot of the hill the buildings of the city clustered in a crescent like stones from a shattered necklace. The river entered from the south-east, between the horns of the crescent and under the austere regard of the temple of Gomath, having dipped beneath the Wall in enforced submission to him. It browsed calmly through his territory, edging between the Wall and the rock, bobbed gracefully out at the other end, shook itself over half a dozen bends and wandered off through the silent wastes. Legend – or history – located its source in the mountain range that crumpled the horizon from east almost round to south-west; on an exceptionally clear day the river could be seen to flow directly out of the south-east for several miles, but there was no further evidence, and none at all for deriving its flow from the holy mountain, Hisper Einou itself, highest of the chain. Thryn was the largest and most solitary of a number of low islands in a vast tract of bog; doubtless the river had visited many others on its way, passing (perhaps) a few surviving Outwall primitives who preferred their own, more ignorant accounts of its murky origin.

The sun was near its zenith. Under it harriers and swifts flew without effort, uninterested that the river below was being disturbed by a dull brown wedge pushing laboriously upstream.

'Give me your oar.' Dubilier rowed while Lupio dipped his scarf and bathed the blood from the claw-marks on his forehead and arm.

'How far do we keep this up?' Dubilier asked, glancing briefly at the desolate landscape before returning his concentration to the new and backbreaking art.

'I don't know. Not far.'

'Do you know where to go?'

'No.' Lupio smiled rather wearily. 'I'm afraid my geography's not so good beyond the Wall.'

'Why do you think we'll be leaving the river? I mean, doesn't it lead all the way to Hisper Einou?'

'Instinct for the devious. They'll be following us upriver, so we go overland. . . More possibilities of escape, even in marsh.'

Dubilier considered. 'Following?'

'When Kavi finds her pet demi-god's slipped his leash and run away, she won't stop searching at the Wall. Can't you just see her, mobilising a crusade?' He was amused.

'I suppose you're right. But you're so calm. I'd be gibbering mad by now.'

Lupio shrugged. 'Isn't this madness? I nearly killed that old fool, just to steal his boat and get out of safety into danger!'

Dubilier handed him the oar back. 'Your madness fits in nicely with my own,' he said gratefully.

'I'd rather share yours than Kavi's, that's all.'

'You don't even know me.'

'I know one thing – you're not confident enough to stake everything on your delusions. Kavi is. She's confident. She's *certain*. It's her certainty that makes her so dangerous.'

'I don't know... Sometimes I'd willingly exchange all my doubt for an ounce of conviction like Kavi's – or the river-gateman's.'

They kept going until light failed, then dragged the boat aground and slept in it, under cover of thick reeds. Lupio proposed keeping watch in turn, but they were both too exhausted. Next day they came at mid-afternoon to a place where the river grew shallow and rocky. They moored, lifted their gear out and stood looking round on the bank.

'So we walk.'

An ancient, broken road followed the course of the river. Where it was sound they kept to it, but soon they were filthy from trudging through mud. Once Lupio slipped in up to his chest.

'We must find horses, something.'

Ahead, pale lagoons reflected a pale sky. They turned to look back at Thryn, a distant bulge half familiar, half indecipherable: the debris of an old dream.

Evening put a cold edge on the air; there was a lack of sympathy in the breeze that raised the mist. Fifteen minutes ago it had been a delicate lace on the pools; now it was thick and spreading.

'Where are we going to sleep?'

'Anywhere.'

'On the road?'

'You can try the marsh, if you'd prefer.'
'Isn't the road a bit hard?'
'Yes. The marsh is very much softer.'
'Ohh – '
'Come on, it's not so bad. We might be sleeping rough for a while, we'll have to get used to it. Eventually we'll find some shelter.'
Jeswed's lair, Dubilier thought involuntarily, and then reproached himself. Nonsense. Well, yes, but what would the Outwallers be like?
Lupio was pointing. 'Horses. Look.'
He saw the tracks. 'Perhaps they're up ahead.'
'Could be anywhere.'
Dubilier stared numbly at the hoofprints, feeling the place begin to wear him down: hard ground, city clothes, and a landscape he found quite illegible. He glanced at Lupio standing easily with his hands on his hips, the tensions of the city apparently drawn from him. He would survive. Dubilier hoped, guiltily, that he could continue to depend on him, noticing that he'd begun to already. 'Shall we keep going?'
'Mm. Let's walk until we drop. Then you won't mind where you sleep.'

'No horses?' asked Vyvyan with a doubtful frown. Hoodanu nodded emphatically, pulling at his lower lip. 'Where have they come from, then?'
Alex turned to Vyvyan and spoke as if Hoodanu weren't there. 'They're ferlem, obviously: out of the ground – pof! – like mushrooms.'
The mushroom man took the bait. He jigged up and down flapping his arms. 'You don't believe me! They are there! Sleeping like two-day foals – if the chezzerd hasn't got them first while you've been wasting air, tongue-teasing poor Hoo.' He sulked, pulling his hat over his face. 'Go and see,' he said in a muffled voice.
Vyvyan smiled. 'Aex?'
Aex didn't move.
Erthrim had been sitting on her heels, watching the men. She stood up and brushed her skirt. 'All right, I'll go. Will you show me, Hoodanu?'

The mushroom man grabbed her by the hand. He tossed his head, displaying Erthrim to everybody like a prize. 'Erthrim believes it. She doesn't let them both get eaten up while she's busy laughing at Hoo.' He strode out of the hut with her; then ran back in alarm to fetch his big basket.

A few hours before dawn Dubilier grew resigned to the inadequacies of his bed and fell properly asleep. There was a way out of the cavern, he was sure, but the old hunchback with the long white beard was being no help at all, and all the citizens standing around were making so much noise that he couldn't find it. The horses were making a noise too, and then Dubilier remembered that horses were important for some reason, so he opened his eyes to get a better look at them. There were only two: a little reddish one ridden by a man with a huge hat, and one other, which was a sort of bluish-grey and probably belonged to the woman who was bending over him.

'Ferlem-ar – my name is Erthrim and this is Hoodanu. Are you travelling? Can the Grach help you?'

Dubilier couldn't understand, but the rhythms of her voice told him she was greeting him, asking him something. He tried to stand up at once, but the hard road had sewn his limbs up with cramp.

'Look at him, Erthrim! He hurts. Is he afraid?'

'Aigui, I'm glad to see you,' said Dubilier, massaging his legs. 'I don't know your city and I can't understand your language... and I don't suppose you can understand me...'

He paused, feeling foolish, and couldn't think of anything else to say. He looked at Lupio, but he was still asleep. The woman was watching patiently.

'I am Dubilier,' he said slowly. 'This is my friend Lupio; we are Aiguda, from Thryn.' The angular man in the hat was staring at him.

'You cut your words like bad meat,' said Hoodanu. 'Don't you like them?' and he began to laugh. Dubilier had no idea what the joke was, so he smiled, which made Hoodanu laugh even more.

'Be quiet,' Erthrim told him. 'He's from another people; he doesn't understand. You shouldn't laugh at him.' She turned back to Dubilier who was feeling very uncomfortable on the ground and was starting to stand up again. 'I am Erthrim.' She pointed to herself, enunciating clearly. 'He is Hoodanu.' Then, miming great curiosity, 'Who are you?'

Her gestures made her meaning clear. Dubilier, extricating himself from the long arms of sleep, thought that through the dull vowels and nasal hum of their speech he could hear familiar Thrynian syllables: degenerate Thrynian, yes, but a recognisable son of the mother tongue. It was only to be expected that the Outwallers had forgotten how to speak correctly in the centuries that they had been deprived of influence from the city. He was relieved to find that they appeared to be human. 'Good morning,' he said. 'Dubilier. My name is Dubilier.'

'Lupio.' His friend was getting up now, with much the same difficulty. Dubilier smiled gratefully. Lupio went up to the strangers and reached out to fondle their horses.

'He likes us! See, see, Erthrim!'

'We're very glad to see you,' Lupio said. 'And very glad to see you have horses.'

'Hoh-sess! He said it. He can say "horses", Erthrim, did you hear?'

'Their language is like ours,' she said, 'but they speak so quickly.'

'Why? Are they in a hurry?'

'Will you come with us? Horses will help you.'

'Are you offering us a ride?' Lupio glanced delightedly at Dubilier. 'Thank you. We – he, Dubilier, and I, Lupio, thank you.'

'What's he saying? You like horses, stranger-man?'

'Climb down, Hoodanu. See if he'd like to sit on Weng's back.'

The little red pony was surprisingly sturdy: a breed of the marshes, compactly built, unlikely to fall victim to disease, bad ground, or malicious weather. 'Thank you,' Lupio said again.

'Is he saying ferlem-ar?' asked Hoodanu, holding onto his hat with one hand and steadying Erthrim's mare with the other.

'I expect he is,' she said, dismounting.

'Ferlem-ar too, guest! Ferlem-ar too! Oh, yes, you're of the Grach now, a great hunter riding out to battle the terrible chezzerd!' And Lupio and Dubilier, understanding nothing of his bright-eyed babbling, laughed anyway, riding inexpertly down the marsh road, led, perhaps, by friends.

Lupio tried to catch the attention of the man just leaving the hall after Ethsri. 'Aigu Aex!' he called, not thinking, and the man walked out without even pausing.

'Jeswed!' Lupio leapt up, dragging the sword from his belt. The Grach gave a gasp and fell silent: something sacred and old had been tipped over.

'Lupio.' Erthrim's hand was on his wrist. 'Throw down your sword. Throw it in the middle.'

'I've had all I can take from that – '

'Throw it!'

The weapon clattered into the ashes.

'Now kneel. Put your forehead on the ground.'

She spoke quietly; she was lovely; but she was commanding him like a servant...

'Kneel, you fool!'

He knelt, dipping his head perfunctorily to the dust. There was a general sigh of relief: the sacrament was ritually reinstated, decorum appeased. Animation came back to the frozen hall like a plucked string. Gracelessly Lupio scrambled to his feet, retrieved his blade and went out. There were no stars. He meant to stride into the mist, but he knew she'd find him; something she would do would make him stop and attend –

'What was that word you taught me? "Wild"? Because we live in the marshes without a "Wall". Are we wild, or is it you?'

'Aex insulted me.'

'So you insult the Grach.' The way she said it it wasn't even a terrible affront, just petty spite. She took away the glamour of sacrilege and made him a tiresome child. 'No weapon is drawn in Ethsri,' she said.

'I'm not Grach. I have different ways. You know that.'

'In Ethsri the ways of all are the ways of each. That is what Ethsri is.'

'Look, Erthrim, anyone who insults an Aigu must be punished. It's not just me, it's for the good of the city.'

'Stranger-man, I don't understand.' She left him.

He resisted the impulse to follow and shout and made his way back to the hut. Dubilier was already back from the meal and lighting the lamp. Lupio flung himself on the bed.

'What did you say to him?' They had discussed Aex often, too often.

'I called him. He walked straight past. Didn't you see?'

Dubilier made a guess: 'What did you actually say?'

Lupio paused. 'Well, all right, I called him Aigu Aex. I forgot. What's it matter?'

'Everything. He probably didn't even realise you were addressing him.'

'Gomath's eyes, stop peacemaking! He heard me all right. I was no further from him than I am from you now.'

'Even if he did – '

'He did.'

'Even if he did, it probably wasn't proper for him to answer, or he'd be accepting the rank you gave him. They don't have ranks, we've been through all that. What's wrong?'

Lupio didn't reply. His face was turned to the shadows. Dubilier looked at the position of his hands, the set of his neck. So much tension. Why? Sometimes the Grach pyroc-skin cloak suited him perfectly. Sometimes he slouched around in it like a wild beast with a grievance – an overgrown pyroc himself amongst these graceful people. Yet it couldn't be more than a month since he'd been surefooted and happy, looking for the horizon while Dubilier stared at hoofmarks in the mud. With the Grach Lupio was becoming more and more his old petulant self, with no alcohol to soften his rough edges. Why?

Lupio spoke, as if he'd heard his thoughts. 'They're so soft.'

'Soft? Surviving out here?'

'No, I didn't mean that. It's the tiptoe, self-effacing way they go about everything.' He rolled over. 'Look, you know me. I do what I want; I say what I feel like saying. But here I can't even speak without offending somebody. They're all perfectly in line, the whole time. Everything's controlled.'

'Well, that's how you survive. When we were on our own, you were controlling things.'

'It's not the same.' He relapsed into thought. 'They won't admit it,' he began again. 'Have you noticed that? They don't even have a city, just these – ' he hit the wall, ' – mud huts; tents and canopies. Animals wandering loose everywhere. Yet they keep perfect control – and they won't even talk about it. The social system – you've got Vyvyan, Erthrim's husband, he's the chief, a sort of Supreme Aigu, and then all the Aiguda: Aex and Achnar and Erthrim and Chejom and Mnirr and everybody. And then the workers, the servants, only they need more of them: breeders and ropemakers and bearers and skinners and tailors. It's like Thryn must have been once: move and you're out of place. But try to find out what your place is and you get a baffled smile. They tell you you're standing in it!' He laughed. Standing outside, Erthrim bowed her head. What she understood of his words and their tone upset her.

The marsh mists clung on stubbornly hours after sunrise, but the hunt went out, skirting the northern fens. Lupio rode with Achnar and Mnirr, a respectful pace behind them, listening carefully to their conversation and interposing a comment or a question from time to time. Dubilier watched him from the rear. He had chosen to ride with the boys and the bearers, knowing they would accept him and not press him to talk or work if he wished to stay out of the way and observe; nevertheless, in earnest of his good intentions he repeated his insistence that Broa let him carry some of the equipment.

Broa grinned through a full black beard that glistened with fog-dew. 'Well,' he said, 'it's good to share burdens,' and he offloaded one of the nets onto Dubilier's mount, compensating cheerfully for the Thrynian's clumsiness at taking it while trying not to lose control of the horse that still felt unfamiliar beneath him.

'I know I sha'n't be any use to the hunt unless I do carry something,' Dubilier said as he juggled the long roll into place.

Broa looked surprised. 'You are here, hunting,' he returned. 'How can you say you have no use?' He gave a quick wave and left the column to confer with one of the outriders before Dubilier could reply more than a hasty 'Ferlem-ar!'

It was an exchange Dubilier couldn't avoid reflecting on. True, he and Lupio had adopted the strange dress, strange customs, strange words (such as that blessing he had automatically spoken); they were riding Grach ponies, participating in the Grach hunt, and yet they were as far away as ever from knowing the marsh-dwellers, from living in their world, breathing its chilly air. Broa's parting words, for example: his language was no longer foreign, but his meaning was alien indeed. Though he had not stayed for a response, he had not, Dubilier felt sure, intended his question to be merely a piece of rhetorical reassurance. The man had been genuinely unable to understand how Dubilier could have meant what he said. Yet how could it escape anyone, especially a hunter, that he was a mere dead limb to the enterprise, a passive camp-follower in the train of action? It was as if he and the Grach started from incompatible ideas of the world, seeing the same things but with other eyes. Dubilier gazed between the riders ahead to the grey ghosts which were their leaders. He knew that Lupio felt himself quite as fogbound as he did. Could eyes habituated to the logic of street and square ever learn to interpret the cloud shapes of an intuitive perception?

A shout: someone had sighted prey. Lupio. Dubilier barely had time to register the irony before realising that his companions were spurring ahead, taking up the formation of the chase. The leaders raced away in a ragged triangle, decapitating the column, while the bearers immediately spaced themselves into a transverse line sweeping along behind them. Dubilier had to thrust forward faster than he had ever ridden before to keep anywhere near Broa and the others. Even as he caught up he saw that the phalanx was metamorphosing again: the outriders moved in from left and right while the wings of the bearers' line slanted to meet them, shaping a broad crescent around the rear of the killing wedge. Such skill. He remembered: all perfectly in line . . . control. Generated how? Discipline, he presumed. That's how you survive.

Lupio led, his unhappiness burnt up in momentum. Mnirr and Achnar flanked him a length or two behind. It was a pyroc, a great-grandfather of pyrocs, old and fat and already losing ground. His pelt was scuffed and scabbed, his flesh would be gristle and lard, but he was a pyroc, his destiny to be hunted and impaled – and Lupio was a hunter, a predator, a grinning phantom out of the fog. He felt the coldness in his bones. They were ringing him now, the hunters forging the iron circle, pricking the beast back to the centre wherever he tried to break it; and outside the hunters, the wall of bearers. Everyone was suddenly armed. Lupio looked about. Achnar had said that hunters rode light for speed and manoeuvrability; and there were the three bearers just behind him, one with bow and arrows, one with nets, and one with bidents and javelins. He had only to choose. The pyroc snuffled angrily round the circle. Everything crystallised, focusing all forces like white light for the blood-red detonation. It was calm and still. All lust transcended, there was only the pattern waiting to be completed. He heard a horse whinny somewhere far away. He reached for the net. Awkwardly, Dubilier put it into his outstretched arms.

There was no recognition in those eyes, no whisper of ferlem-ar or even thanks. Dubilier knew: this was a hunter, not a man called Lupio from Thryn; and there was another, one who had recently been Achnar of the Grach, coming round the ring to help him, but the two moved more like two halves of one. The net unfurled like smoke and drifted through the bleak air; and the pyroc was screaming, thrashing, on his back and kicking incapably as the hunter held out a hand to his spear-bearer.

There was a whistle on the wind; the pallid marshlight flared abruptly and abruptly died. Lupio looked back. The bearer was gazing over to the left, his mount shifting its feet, the spear sliding. Men were muttering.

'What?'

The shaft hit the ground. An old hunter was clamouring, his voice high and cracking. A horse squealed; Lupio felt his own horse stir, the hair of its mane twitching upright. A ragged wave tore the circle.

'Look!'

'I can't see wh-'

There was a horse, a big black horse, running past. Mist and marsh muffled any sound. A hundred yards away, swift and silent. It ran as from an enemy. All the horses swayed back in fear. A man fell. He lay prostrate in the bog as though he were praying.

'Mevn-dath.'

Then, something came – a shape; a thick stench, like rotten vegetation, like old blood. The earth quaked, and Lupio's mount writhed under him and ran.

'Lupio!'

He hung on across the dismal fens, arms wrenched, muscles aching, jolted and battered. The horse was heading south and east away from the scattered hunt, snarling and sweating. Lupio had time to consider letting go, being thrown into the turgid water and risking the hooves.

'Lupio!'

There was someone riding towards him, galloping along behind. Achnar on a frightened pony. Now he was abreast, ahead, shouting back at him.

'Don't understand!' yelled Lupio.

Shouting again – what was he saying? Lupio's mount veered left but Achnar was in pursuit, still shouting the same incomprehensible words.

And they were slowing, stopping. It came to a halt, legs splayed out, head down, foaming. Lupio slid to the ground, slipped in the mud, staggered about to get his balance.

'Achnar!'

He circled them, reining in.

'Achnar, how – ?'

'It's all right. You're safe.'

'How did you do it?'

'I told him to stop,' he said simply. He looked surprised to have been asked.

'But it was out of control!'

Achnar looked at Lupio as if estimating him. 'Your "control" . . . For the Grach, it's different.'

'You can – ' Lupio stared. 'You can just shout at it and it'll obey?'

'I can speak to him, and he will understand me, yes.' Achnar stroked the neck of the quietening creature, murmuring words of calm into its ear.

Lupio gazed behind him. The mist was thinning. A fine rain had begun. There was no sign of hunt or horse. The black stench had given place to the dull, earthy odour of the marsh. He had no idea how far they had come. 'What happened?'

'It was Mevn-dath. He is the First of the Horses.'

'The First of the Horses?'

'Mevn-dath is very old.'

Lupio understood. The black horse must have been the grand old leader of the marsh herds. He could imagine it, aged and powerful, surviving winter after winter to be seen with the new-grown mares trotting at its side. The Grach would respect that.

'Mevn-dath is very, very old. Older than the Grach. Older than any men. He is the First of the Horses.'

Lupio wanted to protest. Nothing could live that long. What he had seen had been a perfectly ordinary horse, except for its size – and its speed – and the way its hooves hadn't made the slightest sound . . .

Achnar was holding the steed for him to remount. 'We must return to the others,' he said, 'and join in Ethsri.'

They rode together without a word.

Erthrim was there already; Lupio saw concern and relief in her eyes. Ethsri proceeded. Lupio was singled out for honour as having had such good and bad fortune in the hunt. They blessed him, and food was passed to him first. Achnar and Mnirr undertook to tell the story of the hunt to the homekeepers, together with a boy who seemed to have a talent for dramatic narration. The word 'chezzerd' came up frequently and seemed to cause consternation. Questions and interruptions proliferated until the conversation became too dense for the Thrynians to follow. They withdrew. Lupio explained what Achnar had said about the giant horse.

'So what's "chezzerd"?'

'I don't know.'

The rain had stopped. They walked through puddles, breaking images of clear sky.

'It was bad that the pyroc got away.'

'Oh – yes.' Lupio had almost forgotten. It seemed trivial compared with everything else that had happened. 'What was that smell? Did you find out?'

'No, but I think that was what scared everybody, more than their phantom stallion. All the horses panicked. If it hadn't been for Mnirr, they'd have all made off after yours. They'd have had the Song of the Drowned in Ethsri tonight, with a verse for me.'

'What did Mnirr do?'

'It was unbelievable. He rode about calling something, over and over again, and then everybody joined in and all the ponies came back into line. By that time the apparition had gone and we all turned round and came home.'

Lupio was nodding. He told Dubilier how Achnar had saved him.

'Control. You were right,' Dubilier said. 'And not just social control either.'

'Unless it's all part of the same thing.'

Dubilier looked up, struck by a thought. Later he went to look for Achnar. Erthrim promptly arrived, as if she had been waiting for him to leave. Lupio let her in.

The talkers round the fire grew fewer. At last Erthrim stood up, kissed her husband, threw a square of peat onto the flames and walked out. Aex watched her go, picking morosely at a bone.

'Where's she going, Vyvyan?' he asked casually.

Vyvyan met his stare. 'Erthrim goes where she goes. Ask her.'

'Have you noticed she's been spending less time with us since the city-men came?'

Achnar shifted his position on the floor and spoke to Aex. 'My sister brought them here; she's been helping them understand our speech and customs. That's not a fault, is it?'

'No, Achnar, no. I was just wondering when she's going to finish the job.'

'What do you mean?'

'Take them away again,' said Aex.

There was a silence.

'Oh, come, man, you like having them here,' Mnirr said. 'You might as well admit it. Somebody to be mean to.' And he laughed loudly.

Aex would not be put off. 'They're not meant to be here.'

'Well, that's nonsense.' Vyvyan was between bewilderment and impatience. He had been waiting for this to break. 'How could they be here at all if they weren't "meant" to be here, as you put it?'

'They don't speak our language. They don't think as we do. Lupio argues with me because we don't think as they do. He drew his sword in Ethsri.'

'Oh, Aex,' began Achnar in exasperation. Aex overrode him.

'The mares don't like them. Now they break the hunt.'

'Break it?' Mnirr protested. 'Without Lupio there'd have been no hunt!'

'That makes it a worse omen,' said Aex.

'Aex is right there,' Chejom put in, taking the pipe from his mouth. 'Mevn-dath hasn't been seen since spring and he shouldn't appear until the death of Old Year. When he comes out of season there's some great event in the mist ahead.'

'It might be a good event.'

Chejom shook his head. 'Mevn-dath on the left, pursued by the chezzerd and breaking the hunt – that's a pretty foggy hope, Achnar.'

'They're not meant to be here.' Aex avoided Vyvyan's eyes, snapping his bone in two and hurling the pieces into the fire. 'What are they doing out of their "city"?'

'City-man . . . Is it difficult, being out of your city?'

'No. Not at present.'

'What are you doing?'

'Looking at your neck.'

'No, I mean, what are you doing that makes you be away from your city?'

'I don't know really. I just couldn't stay there.'

'That must be very – ' She searched for a word. 'Big.'

'Yes, I suppose it is. It would have been bigger if I'd stayed.'

'What do you mean?'

'There was this crazy woman. She thinks I'm a god.'

'What's that?'

'A god? Oh, dear. Let's say – someone who's more than a man. Someone who is all-important. Someone who lives forever – yes, Mevn-dath; Mevn-dath is a sort of god.'

'But you're not.'

'No.'

'Does it matter, what this woman thinks?'

'Yes. She's very important. She tells people what to believe.'

'I don't understand.'

'Like Chejom. He knows all about omens and signs and things, doesn't he?'

'Ah, yes. But he doesn't just say what he believes, he says what is.'

'That's what she'd claim too.'

'Ah.' She shifted. 'Is she a god?'

'No; but she thinks she is, because she's so important. I don't believe in gods anyway.'

'You know, I still don't understand it. Everybody's a god. Every man's more than other men. Achnar's a god at hunting; Vyvyan's a god at thinking and dealing with people; Aex is a god at sorting things out into order . . .'

'That's not quite the same. By what you're saying, Hoodanu is a god of mushrooms.'

'Of course he is.'

'Well, all right. But I'm not a god – I'm just me.'

'But you must be!'

He laughed, bemused.

'There must be something at which you're more than other men.'

'Not me. I can't settle to any one thing. I just keep moving about.'

'Then perhaps you're a god at moving about.'

'Rubbish. Look: I'm not moving at all.'

'Aha.' She drew herself across and started to tickle his face with her tongue. He put his hand inside her furs on her taut breast.

Achnar left the hall looking pensive and stern, but he smiled as Dubilier approached.

'May I speak to you, Achnar?'

The hunter spread his hands and smiled wider. 'You are speaking to me.'

'I mean, are you at leisure to speak to me?'

'Leisure?'

'Do you have anything to do just now?'

'Yes.' Achnar was almost laughing. 'Speak with you.'

The old confusion. 'I wanted to thank you for saving my friend.'

Achnar studied the ground. Dubilier hoped he hadn't said something embarrassing. Finally he replied, 'Several answers occur to me, Dubilier: that Lupio was not in much danger; that what I did was easy; that any of us would have done it. But those aren't the sort of answers you want, are they? I don't want to be unfriendly and reject your thanks, so – I thank you for them.'

'I wanted to say something else.'

'I expected you did.'

'I wanted to ask you how you did it.'

Achnar passed a hand through his hair. 'So did Lupio,' he said. 'It was the first thing when he dismounted: "How?"' He stopped and side-stepped to let a gang of children run past. 'You have that in common: you cannot just accept things, there has to be something behind them, a how or a why. Why do the children run? There is nothing chasing them.'

'Why did Mevn-dath run?'

'Yes. Something was chasing him.'

'What was it? Was it the thing that made that abominable smell?'

He nodded. 'It was the chezzerd.'

'What is a chezzerd?'

'He is a great beast – a terrible beast.'

'That smell – it was like something very old; something putrid.'

'It smells like death. The chezzerd smells like death because he is death. Death is very old.'

Dubilier realised how little the Grach distinguished legend and experience. 'Is he as old as Mevn-dath?'

'Older. Much older. If you had been a Grach child, you would have learned from your mother that the rest of his kind were turned into mountains when Ferla chose her clothes.'

He didn't understand the reference. 'So this one is the last.'

'Yes.'

'But how could – '

Achnar began to laugh again. 'You see?'

Dubilier had to smile. 'I'm sorry we have so many questions, but that's the way our minds work.'

'Oh, you would not believe a horse was standing up if you couldn't see the prop! What is it in a city, does no one trust anything?'

'No, most people do. But Lupio and I, we started asking questions and found that the answers everyone believed in weren't there. So we came away.'

'Still looking for the props.'

'Well, yes. We may not find them. Maybe they're not to be found.'

Achnar looked at him closely. 'That's a very Grachish answer.'

'Perhaps we're not as foggy as you think.'

'The fog doesn't go; we learn to live in it. We can't see things.'

'But we must try!'

'Then you'll leave us soon.'

It was a simple statement. 'Yes,' said Dubilier, wondering, not for the first time, what their motive was for dallying with the Grach instead of pressing on to Hisper Einou.

'But if you're not leaving at once, I don't doubt you'd like an answer to your first question.'

'Now I see why you don't need fences.' Dubilier stroked the silver-blue mare. She eyed him cautiously but didn't move away. Achnar had brought him to the watchman's shelter on the north-west perimeter of the settlement, where the horses congregated. He'd asked him to pick one of the herd and then called her over with three simple syllables. 'How do you learn to control them?'

Achnar was perplexed. 'You're repeating Lupio again. He talks about "control" and "obedience" – you see? I need to borrow your words. We don't have words for these strange things.' He spoke briefly to the mare. She tossed her head and trotted away again. 'I ask you to come to the hut; I ask her to come to the hut. What's the difference?'

'The language, at least. Where did you learn it?'

'Here.'

'I mean, how do the Grach know the language?' Achnar shook his head. 'Oh, that's another one for the Grachish children's stories, is it?'

'Even the mothers don't agree. My mother said that Mevn-dath taught it to Gum-dath.'

'Gum-dath?'

'The First Man.'

'What do the others say?'

'That Gum-dath taught it to Mevn-dath.'

'Hm.' Dubilier thought of something. 'Who's Ferla?'

'The First Mother.'

'I see. Is she still alive too?'

Achnar's eyes opened wide with astonishment. Then he burst out laughing.

Dubilier missed Lupio at the evening meal in Ethsri. Though he met Erthrim leaving as he got back to the hut, he didn't ask her anything, nor did he add the two things and make a conclusion of any kind. He was fed up with assaulting the insubstantial. But when Lupio announced it to him, and he found that he was spending more and more time on his own, he resumed his attempts to puzzle out the Grach – the search Lupio had instigated but abandoned on attaining satisfactions that transcended cultural differences. Dubilier spent a long evening in Chejom's tent, inquiring into their lore of herbs and charms and weather-wisdom, but left the hearth frustrated. If there were a single god from whom all the various superstitions diverged, he was long forgotten. Gomath was at least still remembered. 'God?' said Chejom. 'What's god?' It was infuriating the way that the Grach couldn't distinguish physical from metaphysical. Their immaculate naïveté was not in keeping with their uncanny capability for survival.

Sunrise swept the marshes, gilding inscriptions scrawled by snails on every roof and wall. 'Doobiloo!' called Hoodanu, galloping towards him on his absurd pony, 'Doobiloo! Come and fetch mushrooms.'

Dubilier was delighted. He stole into the hut, trying not to wake the sleeping couple, and pulled on a pair of waders. Meanwhile Hoodanu chose him a horse, a yellow-white youngster he had never seen before. 'He wanted to come.'

They rode out side by side, Hoodanu teaching his apprentice a long and complicated mushroom song. 'But yes, we must sing it, or they won't be there.' As he fumbled through the tune to alternate congratulation and reproof, Dubilier said to himself, Hoodanu is simple and strange. Of course he believes the song makes the mushrooms. But can I be sure Vyvyan and the others wouldn't agree with him?

'The song makes the mushrooms, does it, Hoodanu?' he asked when at last it seemed to be over.

'Ooh, no!'

'I thought you said – '

'Ferla puts them out for us. They're the ferlem she always makes first, every day. We sing to ask her for them.'

Out on the marsh road heading straight into an enormous orange sun, a flame mouth at the edge of the world.

'Let's run, Doobiloo!' The mushroom man clapped one hand to his hat and yelled, 'Ta-i-vi, Weng! Vi-o, vi!' and the spidery pony took off, running as fast as his crooked legs would go. The empty mushroom baskets slapped his flanks like half-blown bladders. Alarmed, Dubilier dug his heels in, trying to imitate Hoodanu's cry. Hoodanu turned round in the saddle, calling them and laughing. They bounced up the road behind him, the Thrynian unable to do anything but hang on round the pony's neck. He saw they were rapidly approaching a place where the green ooze had swallowed the road. In front of them was only a dark and shining mere. Weng was tripping across, hopping from tuft to tuft where the mud was firmest, Hoodanu singing as they went. Dubilier's mount ran straight on. Dubilier screwed his eyes up tight. There was an explosion of slime.

'Arrghh!'

Hoodanu stopped to laugh as they came lurching through covered in mud. 'Oh, you look like the first of the ferlem now, Doobiloo, in the juice of your birthing!' He helped him wipe himself and the pony's eyes and muzzle. 'Here, we leave the road now, but we do not go so fast if you like. Follow carefully.'

The mist was like curtains always opening just ahead and closing behind. It veiled the horizon, so that earth and sky blurred into one medium, and it blanketed the sounds of the marsh waking. 'Earth' is the grey wetness underfoot, thought Dubilier, 'sky' is the wet greyness overhead. And it's so silent. I can hear us all breathing – Hoodanu singing under his breath now. Not a landmark to be seen or heard. Which is why Grach philosophy isn't intellectual: there's nothing here to analyse. But it works. This man, the least adept of them all mentally, is finding his way as I might do down a familiar street in darkness, missing the pools and quagmires, making for what? A mushroom.

'How do you know this is the way?' he whispered.

'Listen.'

'I can't hear anything.'

'The mushrooms are singing.'

'They're singing?'

'They sing to let us know where she's put them out. Here. Here, here, here.' He slipped from Weng's back and shuffled forward, crouching. Dubilier dismounted, looking anxiously where he was stepping. 'Bring the basket.' Dubilier unstrapped one and went forward. The mushroom man was kneeling. 'There.'

Large, flat-capped mushrooms. Small, round mushrooms, greenish ones that seemed slightly phosphorescent. Branched clusters of mushrooms like soft candelabra. Fat, phallic mushrooms, grey and pink. Mushrooms in hundreds.

Dubilier gazed. 'That's unbelievable.'

'Why?'

'Which ones are good to eat?'

'All of them. Every one, good for somebody.' He kissed the soil affectionately. 'Ferla knows.'

Dubilier saw. Ferla the earth, she was the missing god, not missing at all. Everything in their lives was ferl, fruit of earth, which she put out; they themselves were ferlem, put out and in the end taken back again. How it had simplified them! There were no paradoxes when your god was under your feet, supporting you, everywhere forever, instead of lost, a thousand years ago, behind distant mountains.

He opened the pannier, imagining how Hoodanu must see the mushrooms: living beings, different from himself but going the same way, coming out from the same source and endlessly returning. His cousins. They made a pale congregation, luminous with the wet kiss of the mist as it dissolved. He reached for them. Hoodanu put out a hand to restrain him. 'First – '

'I know. Another song. Ferlem-ar, for the mushrooms.' Ferla's blessings back on herself, because everything returns to her in time.

'That's right! Good! One day you'll hear them singing too.'

'No, not me.' The white vapour was drawing off like slow smoke. 'I was – put out – in a city, and I'll end up there again. I won't need to hear mushrooms.'

'Why not?'

'There aren't any.'

'No mushrooms!' Round-eyed and open-mouthed,

Hoodanu tried to grasp this vision of horror. 'What a terrible place!'

'Perhaps it is.'

On their way home, swaying with baskets laden, Hoodanu stopped and pointed. 'Look.'

Dubilier peered through the fine drizzle which had replaced the early mists. A small shape, round and grey, lying at the edge of the road. 'What is it?'

'Baby pyroc.' Dubilier was surprised. Dead pyrocs couldn't be unusual. Hoodanu squatted, pushing his hat back. 'See.' Dubilier got down reluctantly. The rain was plastering his hair to his skull and sending irritating rivulets into his eyes.

'Is it important?'

The creature had been killed by something large and incredibly powerful. Half its side was gouged to the bone as if by one swipe. The blood was dry and black. Tiny bogworms wriggled back into the earth as Hoodanu turned it over.

'What did that?'

'Chezzerd.'

'Does it kill without eating?' *The chezzerd is death.*

'Poor pyroc is too small for him. I think he just got in the way.'

'Is it rare, to find things killed like this?'

'On the road – it's Grachish place. Chezzerd has his place. If we mix up, one of us will die.' He stood and stared abstractedly across the uncommunicative marshes. 'He didn't mix before. Something wrong.'

Vyvyan was at the watchman's hut with a small crowd. They too were looking at something on the ground. The horses kept away, fidgeting together. Hoodanu was about to call Vyvyan when he caught sight of the cause. He moaned. 'Chezzerd – what have we done to *you*?'

Vyvyan heard them approach and hailed them cheerlessly. 'See here,' he said.

'We were bringing this one to show,' Hoodanu said, lifting the dead pyroc. 'On the road. But . . .'

Dubilier joined the crowd and saw the stripped carcases of two horses lying in a heap as if they had been torn up and dropped from a great height. His head swam. He ran away and was sick.

'Evil. Evil. Angry. Evil,' said Hoodanu, over and over again, hugging himself.

'He never shifted ground before,' said Vyvyan. 'Never. Get Chejom.'

Somebody fetched the sign-teller. He seemed to draw unwelcome implications, and hesitated. Everyone watched him.

'I cannot see,' he said at last. 'There is something in the way – a shadow.' He looked into the crowd. 'Aex believes he – Aex now sees more clearly than I.'

He stopped, and Aex stepped forwards.

Afterwards, Lupio complained. 'You might have warned us.'

'I didn't know what they were doing. It all happened at once – so fast I couldn't think.' But he felt he had lived an age in desperate indecision while Aex was telling everyone exactly what was wrong and what needed to be done about it. 'What do you think will happen?'

'We'll have to go.'

'Now?'

'No,' said Lupio. He sat down. 'I must see Erthrim.'

'Is she coming with us?'

'That's up to her, I think.' In Lupio's voice Dubilier could hear Thrynian assumptions struggling with Grach.

'Will they kill us?'

'No. Aex can talk, but they're a peaceful lot, really. What was all that about the chezzerd, anyway?'

Dubilier told him about the three corpses. 'Apparently Aex sees it as a symbol of your violation of the tribe.'

Lupio snorted. 'Anyone would think I raped her.'

'Well, how do you think the city would react if one of this lot were surprised with an Aigui? In any case, I should think they have very particular ideas about sex.'

Lupio brooded, kicking his heels against the bed. 'I'll talk to her,' he said.

'I'm not sure they'll let you see her,' Dubilier told him. 'Achnar was pretty upset.'

'Achnar? I thought he was on our side.'

'Even so. He took it worse than Vyvan. He kept on about it. "My sister! My sister!" Terribly possessive. Unlike them, really.'

Erthrim took the afternoon watch, grateful for the seclusion of the lookout. For hours there was nothing to see but the birds about the mere. A pair of cories came down to feed. The kennet she had brought for company started to snuffle restlessly; she scratched his ears and quieted him with a word.

Daylight drained into the grey fens. It grew colder. The divers gave place. Tiny bats made untiring raids on the invisible millions of insects. The distance turned indigo, and then no colour at all. She wondered which of them would seek her out first: husband, brother, or lover. Lupio, she guessed. City-men were impetuous and demanding.

Night closed in. Erthrim put on her cloak, looking over the drowsy herd. A horse was coming out towards her, carrying someone with a lantern: not Lupio, she could tell by the way he rode. Probably the nightwatch. She waved. It was Vyvyan.

'Have you come to fetch me?'

The kennet was making a fuss. Vyvyan knelt to stroke him. 'No, not unless you want to come. I just came to keep you company, if you'd like that.' He didn't touch her. His voice was mild, without emotion. He hadn't come to bring her fear or anger or humiliation. 'It's cold tonight.'

Erthrim turned away slightly, not wanting him to see her face. Suddenly she felt tired, and realised she'd been tense, ready for a drama that hadn't happened. If it had been Lupio – She had imagined racing hooves like heartbeats, the darkness streaming past as she clung to his waist.

'I thought you were the nightwatch,' she said. Her voice was unsteady.

'I'll stay and wait for her,' Vyvyan said, 'if you want to go.'

His timidity broke her. Something bright and aching rose up and burst inside, and she clung to him. She cried and he didn't try to contain her. The dog nosed anxiously around them.

After a while the nightwatch arrived. They accepted her cakes and a pitcher, but told her she could go back to bed.

Dubilier was climbing stairs. Sometimes they were indoors, sometimes they seemed to be carved in a cliff face. It was very important that he reach the top. The cliff was crumbling as he went, and he wouldn't be safe until he reached the top. He was wearing Hoodanu's hat, and he had to keep grabbing to stop it flying off. Somebody was at his shoulder, trying to distract him. He was shaking him, shaking him right off the mountain. Dubilier blinked. The man shook him again. He sat up. Lupio was getting dressed, but it looked like the middle of the night.

'I'll light the lamp,' he yawned, groping for his spark-box.

The man moved to prevent him but Lupio said, 'We'll need it,' and lifted it down onto the floor.

'Get up quickly. Don't make any noise. Take your stuff and go.' The flame made a weird, flickering mask of his face, but Dubilier could see that it was Aex.

'Why?'

'If you stay we'll kill you. I don't want you killed; there's no point. The marsh is wide enough for us and you.' His voice was low and hard. 'You should have gone before. Go now. Horses are outside.'

He left. Lupio was stuffing their possessions into packs. Dubilier dragged on his waders. Lupio held out a bundle. 'Here. Look after these.' Aex had given them Grachish weapons: a bident, some javelins, a bow and a few arrows. There were two ponies waiting. He strapped the weapons to one. As he finished Lupio set his foot on the lamp and came out swinging a pack at him. Dubilier surprised himself by the ease with which he caught it and tied it in place. They set off, walking between the huts and making as little noise as they could. When they'd crossed the north-west perimeter they rode out of earshot, then turned right and began to circle the settlement.

'We should make for the road.'

'All right.'

'It's obvious, but it'll give us a better start. They have all the advantages in marsh.'

Dubilier was looking over to the right. 'What's that light?'

They slowed. 'It's not moving.' They came closer.

'It's the lookout hut. There's someone there.'

'Two of them. They've seen us.' He raised his voice. 'Ta-i-vi! Vi-o vi-o, ta-i-vi!' They rode recklessly, trusting the ponies, sacrificing secrecy to speed.

'Riders. Look.' She pointed.

'They're not Grach,' he said, reaching for the alarm-horn.

'Wait – no; it's them.'

'They won't last long. Your brother was stirring blood in Ethsri tonight. We'll be after them in the morning.'

Erthrim felt herself recede a little more. The city-men vanished in the darkness like ghosts impersonating what she'd imagined, the urgent ride.

Scrawny bushes on the bank offered scant cover. 'If only there were more trees!' Along the road someone – the unknown roadmakers, probably – had planted some. As they grew the soil yielded to them. Their roots plucked at the road metal like desperate fingers, and, unable to find support, they toppled immeasurably slowly into the bog. Dubilier, filling the water flasks, looked the length of the silver river. The enormous sun was climbing, trailing white filigree.

'The mist will hide us.'

'And them. And they're used to it. Are we ready?'

They left the road. Dubilier hoped the horses would show more of Weng's aptitude than the one he'd ridden the previous morning. They were doing well, presumably unaware they were serving the enemy.

Riding in silence, they heard the chant creep up out of nothing.

'What's that?'

'*Oo-oo-oo-ha! Na-ma-ha.*'

It was coming from behind them, but where and how far? The mist muffled it. '*Oo-oo-oo-ha! Na-ma-ha.*' High-pitched, meaningless, menacing.

'Human?'

'It's them. What are they doing?'

'*Oo-oo-oo-ha! Na-ma-ha. Oo-oo-oo-ha! Na-ma-ha.*'

They whirled left down a sudden incline. The sound was above them now, sweeping relentlessly across the rise. '*Oo-oo-oo-ha! Na-ma-ha. Oo-oo-oo-ha! Na-ma-ha.*' They made the ponies lie down and crouched behind them, knowing how exposed they really were.

'*Oo-oo-oo-ha! Na-ma-ha.*'

They stared upwards. The mist seemed to quake. The long line broke through, stepping with perfect regularity. The hunt had added beaters. The ones who were chanting, the ones who were marching with such apparent mindlessness, were the children of the Grach: a great lateral sweep of children arms' lengths apart. They intoned the dirge for their unseen prey. The nearest girl passed within twenty yards, glaring straight ahead without faltering.

Oo-oo-oo-ha! Na-ma-ha.'

Then they were past. The hunt followed, trotting quietly in loose formation, ready to leap ahead the moment their children signalled a view. They were looking in all directions, but none took notice of the mounds below, and the hunt passed on into the mist.

Lupio and Dubilier couldn't move. They lay shivering in the mire.

'Do you know where we are?'

'That's north – I think.'

'Maybe if we head north and then turn back south-east we'll miss them', said Dubilier, 'or do you think that wouldn't be safe?'

'I don't know. Perhaps when they've beaten the bounds they'll consider the ritual done and go home and sing about it in Ethsri tonight.'

Dubilier muttered something he didn't catch.

'What?'

'That was Ethsri.'

'What do you mean?'

'That's the answer. That's how they survive. They're part animal and they can act as a pack. Ethsri's not just a physical gathering, it's a mental one too. When the pack's threatened they can all unify their awareness and move together like – like *that*. That's why they don't have any notion of priority: they can see themselves as all different parts of one body.'

Lupio began to understand: those instances when comprehension seemed to jump from eye to eye around the hall and he'd felt suddenly cut off. And all that will-power. Everyone was tapped back to a source so full and strong they hardly ever needed to release it. When they did –

'Wherever we're going I think we should go.'

They worked, as far as they could tell, northwards, freezing at every odd sound mist or imagination filtered through. Later the mist lifted and they corrected course by the sun, which looked like a hole punched in the grey sky. They saw no more children. They camped early, setting the little tent among low scrub, and slept past daybreak until the ponies woke them, pawing the ground and whinnying querulously.

'What's wrong with them?'

Dubilier looked around. The morning mist was back in place; any dangers were not to be seen. 'Nothing that won't wait till after breakfast,' he said, 'I hope.' They rationed out the provisions they'd made: there wasn't much.

'We'll have to find food before the day's out.'

Lupio, already mounted, jiggled the shafts bound at his side. 'We can hunt.'

Dubilier saw a girl with clutching hands and staring eyes. He put her out of mind. 'Just the two of us?'

Lupio smiled. Dubilier remembered his other, cold, passionless smile, reaching for a net, and raised no more objections. He mounted too. They made for the road. Perhaps the Grach wouldn't patrol that part again.

Dubilier was uncomfortable. Since Erthrim Lupio had closed himself up, holding his bitterness with a firm hand as if determined not to relapse into his old rages of self-pity. At times Dubilier felt he was travelling alone. The mist which had seemed like curtains now turned into a wall; at any moment they occupied the ground immediately beneath them and the mist had the rest. They might be walking in a circle and not know it. Time and space flickered. Unease crept over him, but Lupio was so remote now that he didn't know how to speak to counteract it. It was like a poisonous smell. The mist was claustrophobic, yet at the same time they were horribly exposed, on a plain without defence. The hammering of his heart became the tramp of marching feet. Blood humming in his ears took on the rhythm of that sighing chant. He desperately wanted to stop and listen, but he was condemned to ride forever, slowly through limbo. The smell sickened him. He turned to his friend like a terminal drunkard, eyes wide with despair, mouth hung open, gasping to speak. Lupio was white. The silence thundered. Dubilier forced a sound, somebody's name, but it was only a croak. He saw Lupio respond, turning his head and lifting his hands like a puppet jerking, gazing up into an ancient face.

The chezzerd gazed down.

Now he could hear the words of the chant. *The rest were turned into mountains, the rest were turned into mountains.* Huge, it was a mountain, of purple-green scales, legs like the trees along the marsh road digging into the mud with the weight of centuries. This was cold, retching when the stench got into your stomach, the horse fighting under you, fumbling blindly for a sword because you couldn't look away from the eyes, or the teeth: the sword would be half the length of a tooth, say. Hoodanu and he had plunged into a great flaming sun: that would be the mouth, and that was thunder roaring. He wanted to tell Lupio, he knew why the marsh was grey, why there was nothing in it. Everything had been piled up to make that, there was nothing left, nothing else could exist beneath it. Dubilier didn't exist. Of course the chezzerd would crush them, they weren't real, it was the earth looking down, it was the eternal rock, the mountain, the mud, cloaked in mist. Why was he playing with his sword? He threw it away. What was Lupio doing with that bident? Didn't he realise they didn't matter?

But Lupio had forced his horse between the monster's legs and there was a wound suddenly brimming blood on its thigh. The roar wasn't thunder now, it was an earth tremor. Dubilier's mount was bucking and rearing. Dubilier clung to its neck for a few yards, but it flung him in the mud and galloped away.

Dubilier raised himself on hands and knees. The mountain was moving, swinging laboriously about. That great head – was it pointing at him now? Mustn't look. He averted his eyes. There was a tuft of marsh-grass just by his cheek: look – there's a tiny green insect climbing up the blade. How fascinating. He could see it so clearly all of a sudden. The tiny segments along its back collapsed rhythmically into one another and opened out again, and another step was taken. He smiled. He felt like lifting a finger to help it, but he might squash it by mistake. The ground was quivering.

There was another high squealing roar. Dubilier looked reluctantly back at the chezzerd. It was something like an enormous lizard balanced on its hind legs. There was a tiny horse bothering it, a little creature on a horse that kept darting about in the mist and hitting it, and that was what was making it roar. That must be Lupio. Well, it was his own fault. He was so arrogant, so headstrong. He'd annoyed the chezzerd and now it was concentrating entirely on him. What was he doing? Aex had given them those weapons to protect them on their journey. They weren't supposed to use them all so soon. But that was wrong – of course, they were going to die now, so they wouldn't be needing the weapons. That one had stuck in the knee, right under the first wound. He saw it vibrate as the beast took another step towards Lupio.

They were going to die, and it was all because of Erthrim. Women were like that. They didn't care. The chezzerd stooped and reached out a paw. There was a high scream, cut short, and another deep roar. That was it. Now Lupio was gone, and he was next. He might as well stand up then, and stop paddling in the mud. A black mound. What was that? Oh, Lupio's horse. But there was Lupio, still alive, and running towards him. He didn't have many weapons left. He was crouching down and the chezzerd was stamping towards them.

'Dubilier!'

'Yes?'

'Dubilier!'

'What are you doing?' Who said that?

'I – '

'You can't fight it. We're going to die. Achnar says and he should know – ' The voice broke off, giggling. Lupio was looking horrified. That's my voice, Dubilier thought. Me.

'Dubilier!' Lupio was shaking him. Was he asleep? No, there was the chezzerd, behind Lupio – didn't he know?

'Behind you!' Dubilier scrambled to his feet, pointing, laughing, crying. Lupio pulled him down again, looked up over his back, sobbing and cursing, and threw the last spear. It missed.

Lupio crouched back down, quietening, holding himself together. Dubilier saw his face change. He looked calm again; his eyes were peaceful and terrifying. Dubilier felt guilty. He wanted to appease him; if only he had another net . . . But no, this time the hunter was giving him something, a long heavy shaft with a sharp fork at the end.

'When I say, run at it with this. Yell. Try to distract it. Run around to the left. Stab it if you can get near enough, but don't throw unless you have to.'

Dubilier's mind was a cold clearing in the mists. He felt weak and tremulous, as if he'd been ill. He took the bident. 'Can't I – '

'Go now!' Lupio had gone, running low, arcing round and disappearing behind the bloody leg. It was a mad dream. Dubilier entered it himself now, staggering straight towards the monster, yelling, brandishing the useless lump of wood. It was heavy; easier to run without it. But no. Lupio had said.

'Yah! Catch me, lizard!'

The stink was overpowering. He stumbled in and clubbed at the other foot. Roar. The tail lashing from behind. Where was Lupio? The tail missed. Dubilier jabbed at it as it went by. The chezzerd started to bend to sort out the nuisance around its right leg. The mouth plunged out of the sky. Burning saliva. The earth and the sun and the stars, death falling on his head. So what? He stood there, aiming upwards with the stick.

Death falling; the mountain falling. A lurch and a deafening squeal, the chezzerd scrabbling for a footing in the sliding mud. A thousand tons of rock off balance. Lupio, framed in the old arch of the legs, waved: 'Get away! It's going down!'

It fell screaming. The earth shook so that they fell too. Mud rained. The chezzerd, leg trapped under it, clawed at the ground, couldn't rise. Lupio ran to Dubilier and snatched the fork, ran to the writhing head, in close. With all his force he raised the fork and hurled it. It sank home shuddering in the throat. The chezzerd convulsed, rolled over, claws thrashing wildly. Lupio jumped and put his sword in its eye, and again, piercing through to the tiny brain behind it; and out, stumbling back, landing awkwardly beside Dubilier.

It took a long time dying. It rolled and howled; blood rushed as though it would never stop, and the chezzerd wailed for each year of the hoard of ages ripped out and dribbling away in the dirt. Lupio had floored it, cutting at the damaged leg from behind so that it gave way, and he had lanced the poisoned brain with his sword. But Lupio was bleeding. He clutched his side; the ribs moved under his hand, where the tail's tip had caught him, barely flicked him. Lupio went blind, he was sick, he collapsed, he didn't move. The chezzerd was still moving. Dubilier put out a hand. Lupio didn't respond.

'Oh, Gomath, Gomath, Gomath, Gomath, Gomath . . .'

Ages passed in the chilly mist with the ancient one dying in its rage and Lupio lying senseless. Dubilier dreamed people in the mist, citizens and Grach; he dreamed women with veils, women in masks, looking on unmoving.

'Well, help me, can't you?' he cried.

He dreamed animals, caterpillars, pyrocs, bogworms swarming thoughtlessly from miles around to clamber and feed on the mountainous creature . . . fleas on pyrocs . . . horses galloping across the wastes . . .

'Help me, can't you? Help me!'

Weng came bouncing home, Hoodanu sliding from his back, dropping his hat. He ran to the hall. Achnar was there, squatting on his heels, his face painted. Aex stood at the fire. They had been quarrelling. The hunters waited for one of them to speak. Instead, Hoodanu burst in. 'The city-men!'

'You saw them?' Achnar snapped to his feet like a sprung trap. Hoodanu nodded energetically, gulping for breath.

'Where?'

He pointed.

Achnar signalled. 'Take – '

'No, no, Achnar, no: they killed him! They did!'

'What?' He shoved the hand from his sleeve.

Hoodanu clung on. 'They did! They killed chezzerd! He came to eat them, but they killed him!'

There was a cheer of laughter.

'No! We saw it, Weng and Hoo, we did, we did!'

'Aex . . .' Achnar was considering. 'What weapons did you give your city friends?'

Aex ignored the sneer; without turning round he said, 'A bow; a bident; three or four throwing-spears.'

'That's all?'

'Yes.'

'Hoodanu: in the mist things can seem – '

'No, no, no!' The mushroom man jumped up and down. 'The yellow horse ran away and he threw the man down and then the other ones, they rode round and round and he kept hitting chezzerd, and chezzerd hit the horse and then the first city-man got up and then they both ran at chezzerd and knocked him over – '

There was another roar of laughter. Vyvyan arrived with

Erthrim. Achnar gestured to the mushroom man. 'Sister, did you hear? Your lover is so cross he's gone and killed the chezzerd, with his bare hands!'

Erthrim looked at them all. 'I think he might have done,' she said.

'He did! They did!'

Erthrim went to Hoodanu and looked into his eyes. 'I believe you,' she said.

Achnar strode forward. 'It doesn't matter what happened. If the chezzerd didn't kill them, then they're wandering about without horses, am I right?'

'No. Wrong,' said Hoodanu quickly. 'Mevn-dath carried them away.'

'What?'

But Achnar was the only one laughing. Erthrim put her arm about Hoodanu. The hunters started to look doubtful. Some were already afraid.

Dubilier staggered, shouting at the dream-horses. He was trying to repeat the words Achnar had used to bring the mare to the hut. They tossed their sodden manes, snickered and vanished. He shouted at the black one that was grazing. A stallion. He lifted his head and trotted over. Dubilier stroked him with shivering hands. He looked wild, but Dubilier was too exhausted to be afraid. He muttered the words over and over again, coaxing the horse back to Lupio, huddled on the ground. He was a big horse; that was good. If only he'd stay. Dubilier bundled the body across his back and led him past the twitching chezzerd to the body of Lupio's pony. Murmuring soothing nonsense, he bent and stripped it of its luggage, transferring the bundles to the stallion who stood looking the other way, ignoring Dubilier. 'Good horse. Good horse.' They still had the bow and the quiver, that was good. This was good luck. Gomath, let it last.

He forgot the danger and the cold. His mind saw its time of safety and curled up to sleep, while his body went on with the work. Minutes passed; the great reptile heart ceased to beat, but the anonymous man loading up his horse didn't even look round. They could have been anyone, standing there in the mist: a man loading up his horse before setting off. For a moment they were eternal. Then the big black horse shook his head and the moment was done; Dubilier hesitated, afraid he might be about to bolt. They were back in the particular, the ordinary. He threw a saddle-blanket over Lupio, not knowing what else to do for him. There was no obvious injury; he'd stopped bleeding. It seemed natural to Dubilier that they should keep moving, taking his horse to replace the dead one and the runaway. He climbed up in front of the body. The horse began to walk away into the invisible world. Now and then Dubilier would give it an ineffectual prod towards what he hoped was the right direction – away from the Grach.

Behind them, someone else was flying home in the other direction, someone who'd seen the tableau, the transfiguration, the trick of the light. Yesterday one of those men, the one called Doobiloo, had knelt beside him with a muddy face and sung for the mushrooms, but he was someone else now. He'd killed the chezzerd, the thing that had never died, and he'd treated Mevn-dath like a packhorse. Perhaps he was Gum-dath. They couldn't hunt him, couldn't kill him; he'd gone beyond death into the world of the ancient ones, the swirling white world that had opened to admit him.

At intervals he was Mevn-dath the First Horse, sent by Gomath to rescue them and bound unerringly towards safety. At intervals the Grach were a gang of supersititous savages and it was a large black stallion which, unused to humans, had approached and allowed itself to be used out of sheer fearless animal curiosity. Then it became untrustworthy: at the slightest caprice it might toss them both into the bog and run away. The phantom women stopped to watch them go by. Far-off flickering lights revealed that there were more of them, hidden in the fog but somehow seeing everything. My mind is wandering, he thought, sitting upright with a jerk. Of course it is, I'm wandering. I'm lost. Where's Lupio? He shook him by the shoulder. Wake up. We're lost. Tell me what to do. But Lupio didn't stir. I should have asked Ibet. He wondered vaguely what time it was, sure that he'd been unconscious for some of the day. Food and water, he remembered. 'We can hunt.' 'Just the two of us?' And what would happen if he couldn't wake Lupio to eat and drink? He'd starve. Then he'd be there before him, transported to Taleg Ibnun because he'd been a hero, and he wouldn't need to eat. So Dubilier could help himself to what was left. He felt absentmindedly for the small oblong of pemmican and began to chew it. What did Mevn-dath eat and drink? The wind and the rain, probably.

Later he saw a pyroc and a group of larger, delicate-looking animals he couldn't identify. Starting out of a dream, he looked for the bow he'd taken from the dead pony, but the stallion had carried him past them before he found it. He left it where it was, venting his frustration by kicking Mevn-dath and screaming abuse at him. Mevn-dath ignored him and kept straight on. If it was straight, Dubilier thought suddenly, and not a circle. The thought plunged him into miserable reverie again, but when he spotted another of the unknown animals ahead, the bow was in his hand at once and he was reaching for the quiver. He'd never had to shoot from horseback before, and wished he had his crossbow with him instead. He glanced at the bow to make sure he was holding it correctly. It was unstrung. He howled and his quarry bolted.

Determined, Dubilier slapped the stallion's neck and spoke the word for halt, hoping his pronunciation would do. After the third repetition they stopped. Dubilier wanted to get down, but he was afraid the horse would run off. He struggled to bend the unyielding wood and slip the loop of the bowstring into its rest. It took time. Mevn-dath grazed fretfully, seeming to wish to go on. When the bow was ready, they did. Dubilier battled fatigue.

It was almost dark when he sighted another pyroc, worrying something in a bed of reeds. It wouldn't have been an easy shot for an expert archer, but it was no time to defer to probability. He managed to whisper his steed to a stop without alerting the creature and observed the scene with hallucinatory clarity. Each separate stalk stood up like a javelin. In their midst, the fat, vibrant body seemed to grow a deep and vital red. Is this how Lupio feels when the hunting frenzy's on? The pulses at his temples were beating quite audibly and he was shivering uncontrollably, but the hand that stole towards the quiver was deft and exact as a snake.

It was empty. The arrows had all fallen out. Dubilier lunged forward and the pyroc ran. Leaning from his seat, he thrashed at the reeds with the useless bow, somehow forcing Mevn-dath to carry him backwards and forwards over the ground while he hacked and cursed and cried. At last the horse took his head and made off into the gloom. Dubilier screamed and fell forward; he clung on whimpering, exhausted and enfeebled. Minute by minute he slipped from his precarious hold, uncaring or unable to do anything to raise himself. He hit the ground painfully, bounced and rolled. Consciousness deserted him as the hoof-beats faded.

He woke at first light, in rain. Hunger was like something physical pressing into him, and there was the shock of remembering he was alone. Numbly he crawled to the edge of a pool. He wanted to drink but the brown water terrified him. He saw his reflection, a giddy face disfigured by raindrops. Not me. It looked like the face of a man who's seen horrors. He rubbed his cheek.

He stood up weakly. 'Forward!' he shouted, and then danced about laughing. How could he possibly know which way was forward without the horse? How did he know that horses went the right way? The mountains. He'd have to see if he could see them. That huddled shape looked like a man lying on the ground. Dubilier staggered over, heart breaking wide open. Lupio lay, his face cut and bruised, an odd, disgusting twist in his body where he had fallen on his broken ribs. Dubilier dropped to his knees in the mire and clutched the cold hand; he screamed for nearly an hour. The big sun came up and the rain faded to a damp grey mizzle; then even that lifted. It was a fine day. Now they couldn't hide in the mist. Where were they? He glared around suspiciously. They were still there somewhere. 'Come out!' he shouted. Nothing moved but harriers, hunting steadfastly through blue sky. 'Come out! I'm not afraid.'

He stood up again, and saw the lake, and the village.

The ferrywoman climbed the steps and leaned out over the water to see what she was pointing at. There was a dark smudge moving erratically across the landscape. It looked like a man but misshapen, like a hunchback. It might be someone from the forest who'd strayed a long way from home. He seemed to be making for the water. The ferrywoman swung herself under the handrail and jumped back into her boat. It hardly rocked. At once she unshipped the short oars and pushed off. The other woman was watching the hunchback, who had fallen down but was getting up again. The ferrywoman paddled deftly in and out of the piles until she came to shallow water clear of the village. She stood up and poled herself briskly to the shore. She called and waved, but the man couldn't or wouldn't move any faster. He wasn't deformed, he was bent double, carrying someone on his back. She ran to help them. The man was weeping.

They lay Lupio in the bottom of the boat. Dubilier didn't know this woman; he thought she was Abredos and tried to fight her but couldn't summon up the strength. Now they were on the water, so soon they would be back in Thryn. He sat hunched up at Lupio's head, feeling the craft bounce and sway, thinking of Alita. Perhaps he'd have a bath and sleep for a few hours, and go to see her later. But this wasn't Thryn; Thryn had none of these wooden houses perched up above the river like water-birds.

'Where are you taking us?'

The ferrywoman rowed between the piles. The sun blinked in and out of them, laying angular blocks of light and dark on the lake. She asked him a question he couldn't answer, because he didn't understand it. They bobbed to a halt below one of the houses, at the foot of steep steps that went right down under the water. She tied her rope to them and gestured to Dubilier to go up first, but Dubilier was suspicious so he stayed and helped lift Lupio though it made him dizzy and he was scared of the gaps between the steps. Another woman put her hand on his arm.

'Ibet – ' No, who was she? Her clothes were strange. He felt the cloth, rubbing it between his fingers thoughtfully. Then he panicked and lurched towards the steps to escape, but Lupio's body was in the way, and the women laughed at him. They talked together in a rapid, skipping speech and then went inside, into a room full of beds. Ignoring Dubilier, they lay the body down and began to undress it. Blood had made a black mess of his chest and his side. One woman fetched cloths and a bowl and began to clean him. Dubilier's head was spinning. He leaned on the table.

'Don't touch him!' he shouted. 'Don't you know he's dead?'

The woman glanced at him and then spoke quietly to the

other, who answered and went away. Dubilier pulled at her wrists; he tried to make her understand but the dark thing behind his eyes was pulsing painfully, eclipsing the sunlight, and it made it difficult to speak. He began to cry again. She disengaged herself and went on with her work. Now the second woman came back with a beaker. She gave it to Dubilier; he didn't want it, but she wouldn't take it back, so he drank it. It was a thin liquid, scented and strange but not bad to taste. It was hard to stand the empty beaker on the table because his hand was so heavy. He tried to speak to the ferrywoman to draw her attention to the phenomenon, but she was far away now and something dull and silent was sloping down upon him. Someone caught him as he fell.

Dubilier was dreaming. He dreamed he was alone in the caves under the city, looking for Abredos the rivergateman. Abredos rose out of the water to meet him and they went crawling through long low tunnels dank with slime until they emerged into a vast cellar, as big as the wasteland, and the chezzerd was there to keep the rivergate. Dubilier was on horseback but he was frozen and couldn't move. The chezzerd roared, without making a sound. Dubilier watched it, fascinated, until he realised that obviously the chezzerd was Hisper Einou, the mountain he had to climb, even though it was so cold. Ibet was there, looking like the girl they'd seen on the Grach hunt, which made him afraid, but she showed him another part of the cellar which was a luxurious chamber, richly furnished and hung with clusters of jewelled fruit. If only he could reach the bed and lie down there he'd be warm again. He struggled and, slightly surprised, found he was already on the bed; but beneath all the silken drapery he could feel it was really just a block of stone, which made him very angry. He stood looking at the woman on the bed. She was wearing a blue gown and laughing at him, but reaching out for him too.

'Ali!'

He stepped forward, but there was no way he could cross the wild water. When he looked again it was Erthrim and masked handmaidens standing by with torches to see him make the jump. He longed for her. They stood together and she handed him a flower, saying, 'Isn't it time for the sacrifice?' and Lupio gave him the javelin; he was saying something too, but Dubilier forgot what because the pyroc was bustling out of sight in the reeds, so he threw the spear. The flower was scented and strange, but not bad to taste.

He woke up and saw Lupio in the next bed, washed and barbered and swathed in brown bandage to the neck: he looked almost as if he were asleep instead of dead. Then he went back to sleep and, when he next woke, Lupio was awake too.

'Lupio!'

'Good morning.'

'You were dead! Mevn-dath ... I found you! You were dead!'

'Mevn-dath?'

Lupio couldn't remember anything clearly except that he'd been in a fight. Dubilier was in a hurry to tell him everything, confused by fever and joy, but he left out the shrouded women because Erthrim had been one of them and he didn't want to upset him. He was rambling; he fell asleep again. Lupio began to understand that the ache in his side was where the chezzerd had hit him, and there was a woman, yes, he'd seen her sometimes by his bed, she'd dressed his wound. Sunlight came through a square window in the roof. Where were they? He tried to think but the question became less meaningful after a minute or two, and the pain in his head and side encroached. He felt sick. Later the nurse brought him soup in a bowl, but he was unable to take more than a few mouthfuls. Exhaustion took him and laid him back to sleep.

Lupio's dream was that his father was alive, leading him through fields. He was talking about a present he was going to make him, and gesturing expansively. Lupio understood that somehow the present would include everything he could see: rich and green, the long hills, dark earth and blue sky, and the city itself, which they were watching as if from a colossal height. Sparkling, proud, half creature, half machine, its labyrinthine arteries simmered ceaselessly. Councillor, courtesan, labourer, slave: each was a simple dot, one among thousands traversing the streets of Thryn, and it seemed to Lupio as his father pointed that this plexus of avenues and alleys, and the single silver thread of flowing water, was a gestalt, an ideogram complex but complete, decipherable in some great language.

Each travelling dot, visiting and revisiting the places of its concern, traced out its own territory on a grid and acquired identity from its activity. There were no two paths the same. So the meaning of it all, the great meaning, was the sum of all the lesser meanings, plus – Plus what? Lupio was a little boy wearing his young Aigu's cloak. He almost understood, but he needed to ask his father; he turned, but his father had gone. In dismay Lupio realised he'd forgotten where the present was. Up in the Iigril, down in the underhall, in a tavern, a ballroom, an armoury, a jail – he couldn't find it. Now he had to hide. There were pillars in the dusty museum, but when he hid behind any of them it vanished so that they could all see him. Kavi's voice echoed as she led them: 'He's the one! He's got it!' He was in the cold marsh wrestling with her, angry that she pretended to know where the present was, because she didn't, and then she was a young woman, and they went to see his father. All the men were sitting round a red fire in the middle of the hall. She was naked and beautiful under her furs; they made love until the roaring of the men alarmed them. He wanted to fight them, but she said, 'It's only the box,' and he realised she was referring to Thryn. He was amused to discover how easy it was: lift the lid off the city and the present's inside.

In that period there seemed to be more fine days than usual, so far as Lupio could tell day from day. Time passed in a smooth current, uninterrupted, undifferentiated. For most of it he slept, and never knew the hour when he woke. It didn't matter. The nurse brought him food, changed his dressings, shaved and washed him; she spoke to him as she might to a baby or a pet, aware that he couldn't understand the words, but in tones of encouragement, admonition, or comfort. He attempted some primitive conversations, bridging the linguistic gap with an object or a sign they could both appreciate; then he would tell her the Thrynian word and try to elicit hers. Even these efforts exhausted him, and it was clear she didn't feel it important they should communicate verbally. Except when she was attending him, he hardly saw her; he wasn't even sure it was always the same woman.

Dubilier hadn't been physically wounded. He was only resting and spent less time asleep than Lupio; consequently they were often awake together. As they talked Dubilier helped him establish what had happened to them between leaving the Grach (Lupio's last certain memory) and coming upon this new tribe. He recounted the battle, which the victor recalled only as a handful of sensations: a dim hulk that darkened his vision; a punch in the side; something like thunder; fetid gusts of decay. One by one he fitted these to Dubilier's narrative, and dwelt on it until he could be sure he was remembering, not just imagining, for it all seemed remote, in time and in probability. It had happened many years ago . . . to somebody else . . . (but there was an aching place in his side). Once he woke with a question, as if jerked out of his sleep by it.

'Dubilier?'

'Mm?'

'Do you think they've stopped hunting us?'

'I don't know. You said you thought it would probably be all right after we'd disappeared.'

'Did I?' He lay back, unsatisfied.

Dubilier said, 'Once they found the chezzerd we'd be all right.'

'Why?'

'Fear. Or respect, if you like.'

'I don't understand.'

'Well, the chezzerd was a terrifying thing. Remember how they reacted when it killed those horses? They were still afraid, too afraid to go and hunt it down – and then one man, one city-dweller, despatches it single-handed!'

'How would they know it was me?'

'Who else was out in the wilds with Grach weapons?' He chuckled. 'You're probably a hero now – the greatest hunter of all! It's a good job we left when we did, or you'd have found yourself set up as a god again.'

'No.' Not me – somebody else, many years ago . . . 'They don't think like that.' He'd had a conversation about gods once with Erthrim, but he couldn't remember the details. 'Only Thrynians think like that.' Every citizen eager to believe. Men twice his age trembling when he passed them on the street. The hem of his cloak sodden with the kisses of spastics. He shoved the thought back into the past; a new one took its place. 'It wasn't single-handed, either.'

'I was crouching in the mud at the time, gibbering.'

'You distracted it while I was attacking, you told me. I remember. I couldn't have done it single-handed.'

'It was still your victory. I wouldn't have done anything if it hadn't been for you. I would have lain there and whimpered till it ate me. You were the aggressive one, you always are.'

'That only makes what you did even more significant. You had to fight your own fear before you could even stand up. I'm a fighter naturally; it was automatic for me.'

'It's not the same,' Dubilier insisted, shifting in bed, 'it's not.' He knew Lupio was only being polite; he didn't have an active impulse in his whole being. All his life, in fact, he'd suffered because he couldn't assert himself. He'd been entirely passive with Alita and let her shrug him off with hardly a complaint; he'd run away from the city rather than confront her. Lupio had lived with the Grach, quarrelled with them, ridden with them, made love with one of them. He had only hovered about the settlement observing and analysing. Lupio was the hunter; he was no better than the hunter's servant, acting when told to. There was nothing heroic in that. Lupio was confused, he was feverish, he was talking nonsense. But it was taking Dubilier a long time to formulate an accurate reply, and Lupio was asleep before he found one.

The lake people, their rescuers, were fair-skinned with high foreheads, nimble movements, and tongues that raced and bubbled like a spring of water. Dubilier saw more of them now that he was better enough to rise daily and sit outside on the verandah. Boats beetled back and forth. Some were public ferries, like the one which had picked him up first; the rest were a regatta of individuality, in style as well as purpose – coracles, canoes, sailing dinghies, and strange lozenge-shaped rafts. Children squabbled and splashed, chasing in and out of the pier supports like graceful pink fish. On his third day up the nurse – one of the nurses – led him down the steps in the afternoon and a ferrywoman took them both to a much larger building. There were many women there, very few men. Nearly all of them greeted her as they arrived; several smiled in his direction, but otherwise he was ignored. She left him to go and talk with some of the women. He stood and surveyed the interior for far longer than he wanted to, feeling misplaced. Eventually, seeing her take a seat at a table where food was being prepared, he went over and joined her. She was chopping an unfamiliar dark green vegetable, a long hairy string bulging at intervals with large, lopsided bladders. He took a spare knife and began to help. She smiled, but said nothing. He tried to provoke conversation, first with her and then with an elderly woman across the table. They mimed brief replies when they understood and merely smiled sympathy when they didn't, and soon he shrank back, nervous and alert, into uncomfortable silence. He had noticed the women's cheerful reluctance to exchange speech with Lupio and him, rationalising it as a precaution against tiring invalids with the exertions of a new language. But the attitude of these women proved that wasn't it. They accepted his presence, indulged him when he sought attention, but generally went on as though he weren't there. A stranger at their table did not excite them, but nor did he seem to be embarrassing them. He helped as much as he could, and when the food was cooked they served him as one of themselves: they remained generous and considerate of his physical needs, but as a person, a character, a mind, he didn't interest them. Their reserve wasn't social or even sexual, apparently; among themselves, both male and female, there was chatter with hardly a pause. A gaggle of children ran in, wet and naked; while they were being coaxed and scolded, dried and dressed they too showed no interest in Dubilier. It wasn't as if they were shy – they disregarded him completely.

Dubilier found the woman who had brought him and demonstrated a wish to return. She gave him a small bowl which he filled with food for Lupio, then led him outside. He stood at the bottom of the steps, the bowl swathed in a cloth, and shivered. Evening mist wandered over the lake. The houses loomed dimly, purple, insubstantial. A ferry skimmed by; she waved. The woman let him aboard, recognising him with a smile, and rowed him swiftly back to the hospital. As he climbed out she touched him once on the arm by way of valediction, but would not speak. Lupio was lying in the twilight alone. Dubilier lit lamps and gave his friend the broth.

'Where have you been?'

'She took me to a large hut. I think she probably lives there.'

'What happened?'
'Nothing. I helped them make this, and they gave me some, but the rest of the time everyone ignored me.'
'No more friendly than our nurses?'
'Oh, amiable enough, I'm sure, just uncommunicative.'
Later Lupio slept. Dubilier was restless. He extinguished all the lights but one and took that out onto the verandah. Similar flames twinkled all around, like captive stars. There were birds sleeping in the eaves. Through the luminous mist a high flute was playing a long, repeated refrain. The village was so peaceful. Compared to it, the Grach's had been a place of permanent, unspecified danger. Looking back he could see that dallying there had been like lying down with well-fed wolves: inevitably, a time would come when the wolves would be hungry again. But this peace was not so temporary. This was high civilisation, improbable though it seemed that civilisation could arise here, in the wilderness, in the middle of a lake – and where did they get all the wood from? Equally improbable was this ambiguous attitude towards Lupio and himself, so careful and so careless. But improbable, indefinable or not, this atmosphere had enveloped them. They relaxed and breathed deeply; it was misty, but concealed no harm. The flute distilled it; the lake received it. He thought of the ministries being made to them. It was like being an infant again. The safety of the lake village was the safety of the nursery, the quality of home.
Home: Thryn . . . Had he ever known such safety there? Dubilier pulled off his clothes and went down to the water, entering it cautiously. He stood up on a step below the surface, shivering, and then descended until the water came up to his chest. He made swimming motions with his arms. He had forgotten, but it returned to him, and he launched out from the stair with hardly a splash. He swam with concentration until his body remembered; then he went with the same supple joy that animated the children, diving deep into roaring silence, breaking up and out into the chilly unfamiliar element of air, his face and hair streaming. Even in the underwater darkness he could steer slowly round the timbers of the houses, exploring the mazes that they made – trees, as it were, in some forgotten forest, still standing in an old formation of rigid squares and lines though the conspiracy of time and nature had swathed and

shrouded them in creeping weed, reclaiming them for chaos. When he broke surface again he saw the different world fixed on top of those obscure trunks – a world where things were the other way round, where the rule of artifice and architecture endured. There, in boxlike cabins, slept the people who had cut the trees and shaped them into these unnatural forms. Dubilier dived and surfaced, surfaced and dived. Two worlds, paradoxically joined, this above, that below. In the air, form enclosing nature; in the water, nature burying form.

While he swam everyone slept, except someone playing a flute. He swam towards the sound, twisting sharply not to crack his head on a drifting boat. Here it was, or somewhere very near. It beckoned in the air. He grasped the gunwale, balancing as he bobbed, then tipped himself over into the boat. It was a coracle, little more than a floating basket. He sat in the darkness and listened. The music was hypnotic; it certified the silence, undoing it. It called him to sleep. He found the paddle; then gradually, unsteadily, he sailed out from under the house, haphazardly to and fro until he gained control. He found out where he was and returned to the hospital for the second time that night.

The lamp had been taken. Dubilier gathered up his clothes and went inside. There was light in the next room. As he rubbed himself dry, the nurse came to the doorway with the lamp. Dubilier, naked, stood still. He saw her smile. The night and the mist, the quiet houses and the shifting lake were all caught up together in the shine of her eyes, incarnate in the geometry of her mouth, and her hands sheltering the flame. Through it all, repeating its way out of time into eternity, the distant music played, beckoning him to her.

She went by. He heard her at work, soft and clattering sounds, and her footsteps. Dubilier dried himself and climbed into bed. He had not touched, but he believed; and now he slept.

When Lupio was well enough to exercise they went swimming and boating in the daytime, rising late and going to bed early because there was nothing to do and no true company to bear them through this quiescence. One morning a nurse shook them awake. Lupio sat up. 'What's the matter?'

There was another patient, a heavily pregnant woman. She moaned from the bed nearest the door. The nurse gestured to her.

'Gomath,' muttered Dubilier, pulling on clothes, 'does she want us to help?' He was alarmed. Lupio shook his head, disclaiming understanding. The nurse left them to dress and knelt at the woman's side speaking to her in urgent rapid sentences, repeating herself as if asking for a reply. They stood by their beds, mesmerised by uncertainty. Neither of them had ever seen a birth before, or even knew what was done. It was very early. Weak light bleached the room and everyone in it so that they seemed to be in a pale zone out of time. No one moved, and that quiet, insistent voice went unanswered, disembodied. Impossible to think of birth in this bloodless, lifeless scene.

The nurse looked over her shoulder and saw that they were ready. She summoned them to lift the mother and carry her outside. Somehow they managed her down the steps to a waiting boat. Dubilier had a moment of panic because it looked too unstable; then the rest was simple effort, in a mood of urgency that came from being woken early and put to unexpected work.

The five – six – of them safely aboard, the ferry swept towards the middle of the village. The nurse was trying to calm her patient, and Dubilier realised that she was in labour already. Impulsively he took her hand, studying her face. She did not seem to see him, but only the pain and stress, and yet her eyes were not frightened. Something difficult confronted her; she gave it her complete attention so that it should not master her, even letting her body moan as it would while she kept her spirit silent. Isolated, stupefied by the rhythm of the oars, Dubilier cast about for something to distract him. The village looked shut off, sealed from the pallid sky above and the dreary lake below, closed to them in their desolate little boat. Her hand quivered under his. It was as if all the energy had been bled from the scenery to supply her psychic struggle. Lupio seemed to be caught up too. He sat in the bows, uncomfortably inactive. They had crossed the middle of the village and were passing under the buildings furthest from the hospital without changing course. Where were they going? Suddenly Lupio reached out, rocking the boat as he grabbed a length of driftwood. Dubilier stared as he shook the water from it and paddled determinedly with it for several minutes, but the boat did not move appreciably faster. He scowled and flung the broken slat irritably from him.

They emerged from the shadow of the last house into open water. The day had brightened. Sleeping waterfowl bobbed on the bow-wave; some of them woke and clattered abruptly into the air. Signs of life. The lake stretched ahead, narrowing to a point, and the banks rose steeply; there looked to be a waterfall there. The oarswoman pulled towards a part of the shore where they would be able to disembark fairly easily.

The nurse led them up the slope; the ferrywoman stayed behind. There was another lake, half the size of the one below the fall. Lupio and Dubilier found themselves walking clumsily, the heavy, plodding gait they had acquired inappropriate for this firm, uneven ground.

Lupio, carrying the front of the stretcher, saw it before Dubilier. 'Look!'

A bristling mass of green wrapped the far shore of the lake. Beyond, it seemed to stretch for miles.

'It's incredible!'

In the city they stood singly or tamely in file; along the marsh road there were sparse clumps, unhealthy and exposed; but here trees could grow forever, spreading profusely, unchecked even by the lumbering the village must have required. They were in among them almost before they knew it. The nurse marched them at a steady pace; their arms and feet were aching, but they didn't trip over roots or have to squeeze under branches. The trunks were widely spaced, but this was definitely a forest: a rich, musty, brown place, soft underfoot again, ages deep in withered needles. The cover was thin at first; and there were stumps left by forestry, many weathered and black, but some raw and relatively fresh. Ahead the forest seemed to swallow miles and years down its dusty colonnades. A city built to cover every inch of both lakes would not, Dubilier believed, have exhausted it. Meanwhile they, being human and small, subject to the hurts and strains that weak things collect by all their frenzied movement, were approaching exhaustion. The woman's contractions seemed to have subsided. She lay with her eyes closed, not at peace, but maintaining her reserves against the real battle.

The lake, bright and flickering between the trees, was past. They had come to the river that fed it, winding back into the forest and snaking across their path away to the right. They crossed a sturdy bridge of rough-cut logs, and on the other side the nurse directed them to a large tree several yards off, showing them that she wanted them to set the stretcher down. As they sank wearily to the ground she came up and looked at each of them in turn, but it was an inspection, a medical examination, not personal concern.

They all rested. The forest was very still. It was the time for morning birdsong, but what they heard was intermittent and far away. The river, close but gliding slow and deep, underlay the quiet and did not disturb it. Dubilier began to envy the sleeping woman, drowsy now that the tension had been removed. Why they had brought her, in labour, into the middle of a forest, far from the comparative comfort and hygiene of the village, he didn't know, but the place was too tranquil for him to feel anxious there. He looked down at her face again. She was young, with a strength in her features that reassured him; but at that moment her breathing quickened and she shook slightly. It was beginning again. He turned to the nurse.

She got to her feet and walked towards the bridge, signalling them to follow. They bent to pick up the stretcher but she waved them away from it.

'Where are we going? We can't leave her here.'

'I think we're going to.'

They walked briskly back the way they'd come. The woman and Lupio did not look round.

'Do you think we're going to look for something? Perhaps she wants us to help her fetch something . . . Surely one of us should have stayed with her.'

Lupio didn't reply.

'I should have stayed.'

'You don't know how to help her if she should need it.'

'I'm going back,' he said, but didn't.

They came to the edge of the lake. The nurse greeted the ferrywoman and sat down on the bank as if waiting for something. Perhaps they weren't deserting her totally. Minutes passed.

'It's horrible.'

'There's nothing we can do about it.'

Dubilier turned on him. 'I know what's happening. Something's wrong – she's going to have a miscarriage – a freak, or something. They're leav – we're leaving her to chance, on her own, in there. There are probably animals – ' There was fear in his voice. 'They leave them to die, so that they don't have to look after them. It's incredible, after the way they've taken care of us. It's savage.'

Despite himself, Lupio thought of it. Freaks – accidents by birth. The city was full of them. Many among his friends, in the old days when it didn't matter what shape you were so long as you could drink and smoke and pay your stake, or put up a fight when you couldn't. Many dwarves and cripples could match his own jaunty ferocity.

Kavi had changed all that. There was no difference in Lupio, but suddenly all of them wanted only one thing from him: 'Heal me, Aigu Cirnex, heal a poor cripple – ' They didn't seem to recognise him any more. They surrounded him, even while the depraved and the criminals ran away; set wrong from birth, the deformed had no such guilt. A woman with one leg twice the length of the other held up a baby with no legs at all. There was nothing he could do but hate them for believing. He said to Dubilier. 'I can see their point.'

Immediately he regretted it. He hadn't intended to side with the lake-people, only to reassure Dubilier that there were no grounds for supposing the birth would be anything but normal – the reverse, if anything: if they were abandoning the mother, why were they still sitting there? But it was done; by trying to repel that hideous memory he'd only convinced Dubilier that his apprehensions were justified. 'No, wait, man, I didn't mean – '

'I'm going back.' Abruptly, he ran off along the shore. One woman leapt up with a cry of alarm; the other was scrambling up the bank, but it was too late to stop him. Lupio hared after him, wanting for his own reasons to restrain him, whatever was going on, but he had reached the limit of his convalescent strength that morning. A vicious pain jabbed him in the side and pulled him up gasping among the first trees. The others were calling unintelligibly from the shore. Dubilier was gone.

He tried to keep running straight ahead, though it was impossible to tell which way they'd taken among the trees. He kept the lake on his left, but it seemed much farther this time, and there was still no sign of the bridge. Now there was an obstacle ahead, a felled tree lying across the path, all its branches lopped: they hadn't met that before, he must have missed the way. He looked around. The trees were closer here, with brown, wiry undergrowth tangling between them. He veered left to avoid the dead tree, but this shrubbery was tough and thick, impossible to run through without tripping. Detours made his path even more haphazard. Only the gleam of water kept him orientated.

Suddenly, drawing nearer, he saw to his horror that it was the river that was alongside now, not the lake. Without noticing he had cut the corner where they met; he must be running further and further from the bridge. Jeswed's nails! He went and looked downstream, but the river curved and was lost to sight behind bushes and brambles. He'd have to follow it back the way he'd just come.

The muted impassivity of the place angered him. Lofty, uninhabited, the forest acknowledged neither man nor his petty scales of measurement and significance. Its own infinity secure, it could afford to let him come and cut trees, haul them away or leave them lying, mutilated carcases; it held its own existence far beyond these trivial assaults. A tree dies, early or late, by axe, by lightning or by slow decay; a thousand trees die. The forest remains. One woman giving birth to one child: what was important about that? In a thousand unremarkable crevices a thousand seeds struggle for the light. Some grow, some perish. The forest remains.

Dubilier stumbled on. He had to find her, He had abandoned her and she was in danger. It wasn't guilt that compelled him, or fear, or love. It was the call of kind: one human seeks another. That was what was important. The lake-people didn't care, the forest didn't care, but he did. He wasn't like the forest; he was like her. He cursed and kicked his way out of the undergrowth and ran back down the river through the trees.

Almost at once he saw her, moving through the bracken on his side of the river. She had come to and found herself alone. Somehow she had crawled across the bridge and was staggering, like him, lost in the forest, looking for the way home. He glimpsed a white shape walking upright and then lost it in the tangles and the brown haze of the forest. He shouted and ran to where he had spotted her. No sign. He stood and looked about. There, passing between two trees. How had she got over there? There was something odd in the way she was moving. He shouted again and ran; he had to reach her. He didn't know how to speak to her, or how to help her; yet they could meet, as their hands had met on the boat, as all humans meet and make tentative connections. Whatever the birth was like, painful or joyful, he could be with her.

She was wandering among the trees, indistinct. He shouted; she vanished again. She was fleeing him, delirious, confused – or recognising him clearly as one of the ones who had deserted her. There was the bridge. He hesitated. Which way had she gone? He didn't want to waste time crossing if she was still this side of the river, but nor did he want to leave the bridge again now that he'd found it. He ran up it to the top of the span, and looked back. There was the big tree; and a woman's form on a stretcher. Her body was arched, her head back. He heard her cry faintly. It could not have been her loping through the forest; she lay where they had left her.

He clutched at the railings. Who had he been chasing? He'd been wrong in assuming the forest supported no tenants. There were wild people here – people still more savage than the Grach, who knew how to put off personality and go as a pack – exiles and outlaws, and the misborn of women like the one who lay over there. Outdwellers. The Thrynian word came back to him. Outwall; the Wall kept them out, though half the people it was protecting were freaks and recreants too. He had to protect her . . . but she, she was an Outdweller. He clung to the bridge as if it had some kind of security to offer. His wonderful impulse was gone, swept away on a tide of objections and counter-objections, all of them valid, none of them useful. Meanwhile a white figure stepped silently up to the stretcher and bent to look at her.

He had paused too long; now he was paralysed, transfixed by fear. Another approached from further off. He saw the deformity of its shape, recognised its peculiar gait. It might be monstrous. He couldn't even tell its sex. It knelt beside her.

What should he do? Lupio would have attacked at once, unarmed as he was. Nothing seemed to be happening. Some suspense and terror possessed him so completely that there was only one thing he could do. He couldn't run away; nor could he stand still any longer. His hand detached itself from the rail. His legs began to move. Agonised, exposed, he walked towards the captured woman.

As he came closer he realised that the whiteness of the interlopers was not clothing; they were naked, their flesh pale as leprosy. The nearer one had his back to him. No one had noticed him yet. The man's shoulders were abnormally narrow, his skull appeared to be pointed. Dubilier felt ill. Perhaps they would be docile and allow him to pacify them and lead them away without turning vicious. He should avoid startling them. Deliberately he made a slight noise. The man turned round. Dubilier was gazing into a face unlike any other he had ever seen.

The eyes were small and black, without any white or iris to them. They were set in rings of stiff white hairs, longer than the fur which covered the top of the head and the rest of the upper face. The nose was flat and had only one nostril, oval in shape; there were no external ears, and the mouth was small and protuberant, puckered into a permanent kiss. It was not a human face; not a deformed or subhuman face. It was a face which had nothing to do with humanity at all. These were quite different creatures. Dubilier stared. The man – male being – held out a hand in an inscrutable gesture. 'Keep away'? 'be quiet'? 'come and see'? or simply 'hallo'? Dubilier approached in silence, alarmed by what he was seeing, but trusting the lack of violence in their manner. Each being was shaking a hand over this woman, much as a human might shake his head in pity. Dubilier knelt. She still seemed either not to know or not to care who or what was around her. The child was very near. If the creatures became hostile there would be little he could do; meanwhile he should avoid doing anything that might provoke them. They were touching her, he wanted to cry out, to stop them, but they were pushing a log under her, raising and supporting her body: they were helping. They knew what to do.

Amazed and incredulous, Dubilier watched the birth. It was

slow and not easy, but the male received the baby while the female murmured to her, massaging her to encourage the contractions. He sat back, at a loss. What were they? How did they happen to be there? How did they know what to do?

It wasn't until the male took the baby, held her for the mother to bite through the cord, and ran to the river to wash her that Dubilier understood that this was what had been intended. They hadn't deserted the woman, but committed her to the care of beings skilled in delivery. With the habitual exaggerated respect of the lake-people, the nurse had withdrawn to allow them to work; it was he who had been intruding, and she who had been doing the best possible for her patient. If only she'd been able to explain! But then he wouldn't have seen the creatures, or the birth . . . It had been wonderful, even beautiful. Probably, he reflected as the baby felt the cold water and gulped her first air to complain about it, the villagers brought all pregnancies that promised complications out here and laid them under this tree, well into the forest and close to the water, for the wood-beings to tend.

His hand reached out and touched hers again. He felt lost once more now that it was over, in awe of the strange albinos. The female attended to the afterbirth and the male brought back the shrivelled and squalling baby. Then they repeated that peculiar shaking hand motion over her and the child, and over him, and went striding away at once. They had not been in the least perturbed by his presence, though he had been terrified of them. They must have taken him for the father. The woman was looking at him now almost as if she thought so too. She was spent, but the inner battle was done, and she came out to greet the world again, blessing everything with an exhausted smile. She opened her mouth to speak, but no sound came. Dubilier smiled and drew his hand away. He helped her sit up against the tree and gave her water. She bowed over the tempestuous infant, her tired eyes growing, if it were possible, still more radiant, and opened her shift to suckle her.

In a while Dubilier left them, walking back across the bridge and taking care not to lose himself again. He wanted to carry them back quickly, but knew it would be better to bring the others. When he appeared out of the forest the nurse greeted him with some apprehension.

'It's all right,' he said, not caring that she couldn't understand. 'Everything's all right. They delivered the baby. I'm sorry, I misunderstood, I didn't know what was happening, but it's all right. They're both fine.' She appreciated his tone and expression and smiled at him. 'It's a girl!' he said, and started to laugh, in relief.

Lupio was bewildered. Dubilier explained, as far as he could.

'Why are we still sitting here?' Lupio asked him. 'Why don't we go and fetch them?'

They sat till noon before the nurse decided it was time to do that. Dubilier hurried ahead. Lupio was looking for wood-people, but didn't see any. The forest was quiet as when they'd first entered it. 'If they're so well disposed, why are they so unapproachable?'

'I think that's the water-people's doing, not theirs.' He thought he was beginning to understand. On the journey back he supported the mother's head in his lap, holding her while she held the fretful baby. When they arrived she spoke to them, clearly expressing thanks, but then they were left to their own devices again. She and her child did not come back to the hospital.

They joined a band of young people diving for vegetables, coarse strings of round bladders which sprouted in tufts from the lake bottom. They went with another crew to the upper lake, fishing. They were always made welcome, but never quite included. Food was shared with them, but experience somehow wasn't. Nor was work. They had to take the initiative to participate at all, and that wasn't something Dubilier did readily. When on the third dive he finally hacked his way through the stalk of a bladder-string and gasping brought it triumphantly to the surface, he found the gang had already half filled a floating basket with five and six strings apiece. No one ever mocked his ineptitude openly, though he was suspicious of what they were saying amongst themselves; but his feeble efforts made him feel foolish, and he was not encouraged. Instead he settled back, half guiltily, into a typical Aigudan indolence. Life was sweet. He was well looked after. He loved everybody. The sun kept shining.

Lupio, though he was usually the one for initiatives, had

gone into a sulky decline. Confidence and vigour forsook him. He was not the resentful, prowling man Dubilier had seen in Thryn and again among the Grach, but he sat morosely in the stern of the yawl as if he were still making that unnerving dawnlight trip, crossing some cheerless lakeland of the mind. He languished, communicating nothing, even while Dubilier and the others cheered the spearwoman who jerked a huge silver bream kicking madly into the boat.

'This is marvellous,' Dubilier said, tilting his face up to the sun. 'I could stay here forever.'

Lupio grunted.

'What's wrong?'

Lupio gestured irritably. 'Everything.'

'I think you're better,' Dubilier said.

'Thanks. I've never felt worse.'

'Oh, nonsense. Relax. You might enjoy it.'

'I've had enough relaxation. I want to do something.'

Dubilier handed him a spear. Lupio grimaced. 'Show them,' said Dubilier. 'Catch one.'

'What's the point? It makes no difference whether I do or not.'

Abruptly Lupio dived over the side, spoiling the fishers' aims and almost fouling some lines. They cried out in surprise. Dubilier jumped in too and swam after him to shore.

'What did you do that for?'

Lupio shrugged. 'They don't care.'

'They soon will you carry on like that. Is that what you mean by making a difference?'

'Look: they're ignoring us.'

The fishers had settled down again placidly to wait out the fishes' disturbance.

'I don't like being ignored.'

'You've had all the attention you could possibly want,' Dubilier reminded him. 'When I brought you here you were nearly dead.'

'That's not what I mean,' said Lupio. 'You know that's not what I mean. They don't even talk to us.'

'We're foreigners,' said Dubilier. 'Remember everything you heard about foreigners when you were a boy? Now we're the foreigners.'

'No, in Thryn we wouldn't even let them in. They let us in. They *carried* us in. They put me back together.' He pointed to the fishing party. 'They feed us. Why don't they talk to us?'

'The Grach fed us.'

'The Grach nearly *ate* us.'

'Exactly.'

'What do you mean?'

'Well, this lot feed us but they don't want anything from us. They don't have a place for us. We're especially insignificant because we're men.'

Lupio nodded at that. 'The men don't do anything, do they? Nothing at all.'

'So they don't expect us to either, and don't recognise it if we do. They don't expect us to dive in front of them when they're fishing, but if we do, they won't be very surprised because they don't expect to understand us.'

Lupio looked at him. 'And you're talking about staying?'

'I rather like it.'

'You'll be lonely.'

'Are you definitely going on?'

'As soon as I can.'

Dubilier stood in the shallows. The air over the lake throbbed with sunshine. In a sky of blue jade there was not a speck of cloud, and the water was like glass. Beyond, the forest was still and cool. As always, there was a woman singing somewhere. The mountains looked impressive, but remote.

'I'm coming with you,' he said.

The village kept no horses. A dinghy was provided for them, new from the boat-makers' workshop. Dubilier was aware of the irony when he and Lupio spent more effort making themselves understood over their wish to leave than in any of their earlier attempts to communicate. The hull was of seasoned wood, caulked and varnished with vegetable gums and resins. There were oars and a pole with half a hook cut at one end, for poling and fending, as well as a small triangle of coarse sail which hooked to another pole that stood up for a mast. It was especially simple, primitive in design but exactly made, suitable for two city-dwellers whose only navigation had been done in the rivergateman's rowing boat. They spent an exhilarating day practising on the open water, laughing and splashing when, inevitably, they fell in. They were on their way. They loaded their few possessions, all gifts from the water-people. Of their former gifts, from the Grach, little remained: two pyroc-skin cloaks which had been admired, stroked, and carefully mended – the village had nothing like those; a pouch and water-carrier in flaking leather; a buckle of bone. From Thryn, he counted only a pair of breeches, a finger-ring, and a small chain. Could that really be the sum of their inheritance? Dubilier wondered about the intangibles. He looked at Lupio, who had started out thin and unshaven; now, stepping down to the dinghy, he would be called lean, had a short fringe of beard. Was the difference only one of words, two names put to the same thing; or was there something in the gap, something which had no name itself but whose presence or passing could be recorded in the shift from word to word? He tried to look at himself but came away unsatisfied. He had always been able to manage introspection, but this new objective scrutiny he couldn't. He looked at his hand. Was his body better muscled? more energetic? less soft-skinned?

'Dubilier! Why don't you bring that stuff down?'

They sailed the boat to the edge of the lake. Some of the women helped them carry it up into the forest. There was no leave-taking or any degree of ceremony, only four or five of the villagers who had come more to watch than to help. One of them was the woman with the new baby. Dubilier was surprised and pleased to see her. He waved, but she gave no sign. Feeling quite removed already, Lupio was paying no attention to the lake-people. He had nothing to communicate but gratitude, and that he could best express by the obvious joy he took in the boat, in getting them afloat and in motion. As they set off, the woman suddenly stepped forward, as if about to say something after all, but making up her mind too late. She lingered on the bank. Dubilier took a last look, and then turned away, oddly satisfied: some kind of valediction had been made, he felt sure. They rowed upstream easily for the current was weak.

The days passed them like the ripples on the water, merging and spreading into weeks. They travelled slowly and became quite proficient sailors on that placid river. While they were moored or moving under sail they fished with some success; they could catch fat and incautious waterbirds and pick wild fruit and berries from hedges along the banks. Everywhere, the greenery dulled as the year faded. It was a wild land. Haggard trees looked down on them. They crossed a great plain of brittle grass. Every leaf seemed shrunken, defensive, as if feeling exposed to some sky-borne threat. Unknown birds flocked or hung, solitary predators mapping their grounds. In other fields long-legged animals bounded gracefully away; creatures curled on the branches of thorn trees watched the pale hand of the sail ride along. Lupio played a wooden flute. The campfire spread gold across their corner of a deep blue landscape, between the tethered boat and the little tent. Overhead, stars blew in and out of the cloudless spaces. Once the music called a small beast with big triangular ears and good round eyes for darkness. It padded to the very edge of the firelight and sat. Lupio had no idea how long it had been there before he noticed it, unblinking, taking in the warmth and the glow and the flute as if they were all one shining thing. He said nothing. When he threw some more sticks on the blaze, the creature fled.

'What was that?'

Lupio described it. 'It was quite strange.'

'So were we, I suppose, seeing as it didn't find any reason to be afraid of us.' In this open, peaceful place where time was just the interval between waking up and going to sleep again, and space was a stretch of river the same, he felt somehow glad of that. But then they were quite alone, vagabonds through unmarked territory, and from mere unfamiliarity began to fear man themselves. A sound which might be a human footfall would wake them both at once; they'd sit up silently, reaching for weapons. By day they would stop talking and watch an upright shape ahead until it became a definite beast or bush or boulder. They didn't see anyone; they were quite alone.

The ruins emphasised their solitude, for they were signs that someone had been here and gone again. Without a word (their minds had drawn close during this time) they pulled for the shore and made fast.

First there were the white stones, on top of a hillock, describing an ample crescent with two tall black stones set between the tips like the posts of a door. Inside the ring were others, different sizes, standing or fallen in their places. At the centre was a conical one with a hollow knocked in the tip for a kind of cup or crater. Rain would have collected in it, but there had been no rain.

They trudged through the long grass and counted stones. Lupio heaved at a pillar to see if it would rock. 'I like this.'

'You do?'

'Yes. Why not?'

'You're not usually too keen on temples.'

'Is that what it was?'

'I think so. They put a lot of effort into building it, and it's not functional.'

Lupio laughed. 'A monument of futile endeavour? Right, it must be a temple.' Dubilier said nothing, aware he was being teased. 'Now they don't even cut the grass. Which do you think cleared off first, the god or the people?' But his enjoyment was undampened; he sat with his back against the black stone imagining festivals, the children perched on the white ones singing and clapping sticks together while men and women trooped through that sombre gateway with whistles and flowers.

Dubilier was cold. Preoccupied with thoughts of human sacrifice, he ran his finger around the rim of the dry cup, imagining it filled with blood. Men in furs with broken winter branches and stone knives.

He ran and climbed up a sloping stone. There was something else, hidden in the folds of the ground.

'What's that up ahead?'

The people had gone. They had had a city here, with gardens and colonnades, an architecture of space and light. The old road had run through here. They had been building a new temple, a majestic design. Something had stopped them; one couldn't tell what. Unfinished, the temple gaped inanely at the circling stars and clouds. Birds had nested in granaries; spiders veiled stained glass. The ruins were like dry husks that split. Tough grass chewed through the floors and splintered mosaic pavements; creepers dragged down walls. The grand stairways down to the water fractured and slid. The spring floods smashed their lanterned pavilions. Wild things hunted each other through stoa and schoolroom and mated in the cemetery. Lupio and Dubilier kicked their bones aside as they toured the ruins. They lit a fire in the colossal grate of the civic hall and sat on the dusty floor. Lupio was exuberant, ironical; his laughter echoed in the high roof, sparking sudden trickles of powdery dirt and rotten plaster. Dubilier was depressed, saying less and gazing more into corners as the evening shadows clotted. Then they slept. A nightbird visited the hall and sat creaking to herself in the rafters. Thin rodents scampered.

Dubilier woke. There was light, though the fire had long since shrunk to a mound of cold ash. It was the moon, pouring in through empty window-frames. He put his blanket over his shoulders and went outside.

The ruins shone silver, white and jet. The magic rays stripped off the daylight shapes and revealed the skeletal forms of a lunar world. Streets and houses became dry gulleys and grottos; a sagging wall and a pile of bricks turned back into a ragged outcrop and a scree slope beneath. Stalagmites and craters broke the plane of a ravaged plateau. He saw the ten thousand ghosts who thronged the canyons and lingered on the doorsteps of the caves. Their race was new to him: men and women with protuberant eyes, large hands, large hips. They welcomed him. Among them were a few of a different breed, long-necked, lobeless, emphatically erect, like the portraits of ancestors in the galleries of Thryn. They seemed to be gathering round him, pushing themselves to the front of the crowd. We are the road-makers, they said, but you are the greatest builder of all. Perfection on you, master, they hailed him, their parched voices like the wind in dead trees. Ibne, Aigu. Not me, he said. I'm –

He ran. They didn't follow. He came to the road. How could that be the same thing as the broken one they'd slept on, their first night in the marshes? That was a world away; this was a broad road on the moon. From here it drove straight ahead for miles, then plunged and twisted through the jumbled foothill country, lost to sight. Perhaps it reached the mountains. The moonlight turned brick to rock; rock it sublimated, rendering it pure crystal. Hisper Einou loomed above them all, a flawless diamond. Somewhere on those glassy slopes. He was like a pilgrim in an old romance, sent by his lady to fetch an impossible treasure from the lap of a jealous god. What would it be? He thought of a fountain of flame, or an eternal blossom tended by gentle gardeners in grey cowls. Silly, you're dreaming, he told himself, content to continue. It would be enough. In a moment the old shadow would fall from him; the wall would be breached; the secret chamber entered. He thought of an old hand offering him new fruit, the grey sleeve falling back.

He turned and retrod the crazy pavement to the hall. The ghosts clustered. Master builder, they cried. He smiled. You've been dead too long, he told them, you've got the wrong man. No, they insisted. He passed between them and went back in to sleep.

When he woke again Lupio was already up, studying a frieze. Paint flaked from the faces of great men and women grouped round a table for a stylised, frozen feast.

'They didn't leave much,' he said.

'The stones,' yawned Dubilier.

'Stones,' said Lupio, 'bones.'

They rowed away. Lupio stood up in the bows to guide them through a rocky stretch; he laughed and sang nonsense, jeering at every rock that failed to split them. Later, in idler water, he threw stones. 'Thryn is dead; Thryn is dead; Thryn is dead,' he chanted as they spun and splashed. 'We're alive,' he said, tossing away the rest of the handful. 'No, we're not; we're dead too. We won't ever go home. We'll die up there, on the spears of the savage snow-people.' He jerked his head to the mountains. 'Aristocrats of Thryn, done on a spit for a snowman's dinner.'

'We'd be pretty tasteless,' Dubilier said. 'He'd leave half of us round the edge of the plate.'

Lupio laughed. 'That's better than banging our brains out against a Wall.' He sat down and took an oar. 'Thryn's dead already, but the difference is – the difference is that we're going to get a bit further before we drop.'

They reached the broken country. The river ran broad and shallow along a canyon floor. For three days they fought and stumbled against it, cut and bruised themselves humping the boat over boulders, through rapids, out of petty whirlpools. The hillsides rose and darkened; the sky receded.

'We're going to have to leave it,' Lupio announced.

'It'll be better ahead.'

'You think so?'

At last they manhandled the dinghy out of the stream and jammed it among high rocks, for no good reason, but they couldn't bear to abandon it where it was certain to be smashed after the next heavy rain. Then they divided all they could carry and, rather than clamber back over the loose rock downstream, penetrated further into the canyon, following the river until they found an easier place, or until they should be forced to climb the precipice. They walked for days and ran out of food. The scenery became even barer. Then the river widened. It was clear they would have to go up. The walls were sheer and grudging of footholds, but they managed to scramble up to a fault that formed a continuous ledge at about a hundred feet. There, perilously but in desperation, they cornered a stray goat and killed it. It fed them for several days. In its stomach was barely a trace of green food. They toiled. Far below, the river boomed.

'We'll need to keep four bags back for the players,' said Andwaldo.

Knesh said, 'Ah.' He had forgotten that. It was a good job Andwaldo remembered – but that was what Andwaldo did so well, the measuring, the stock-keeping, the – what did he call them? accounts, and things. Numbers. There had been no numbers before Andwaldo, and probably would be none after him. Knesh himself could manage two, of course, and five (if he had time to consult his fingers), but he muddled three and four as often as he got them right, and six and seven and all those were really too much for him. Before Andwaldo they'd used to sow this field and that field and that field, and reap them, and then use the grain how they wanted, until it was all gone, in which case they got hungry, or there was a lot lying around going mildew, in which case they distilled it and got drunk. Now Andwaldo worked it all out with numbers, and there hadn't been a glut or a dearth for – well, for a long time.

Knesh had been just a boy when Andwaldo arrived. They strolled up and down the fields while Knesh took great pains over Andwaldo's language lessons. It fascinated him that a grown-up needed to be taught to *talk*. Andwaldo was pointing at the stubble. Had it been a good harvest? Yes, said Knesh, the grain was fat and brown. So had the harvest been better than last year's? Knesh thought about it. Well, the grain was fat and brown last year too. It was generally fat and brown. That was what grain looked like. But had there been more of it last year, or not? Knesh laughed. How could he tell that? Last year's had all been eaten up. Andwaldo tried again. How many sacks had they gathered this year? Knesh couldn't say. Many. What did that mean, *how* many? Oh, look. He pointed to the ground just ahead. The butterflies are dancing. Look, Andwaldo: but-ter-flies. So while everybody taught Andwaldo words, he taught them numbers. Some of them understood better than others and walked about counting things joyfully for a week or so; then the novelty faded, and numbers were forgotten again. So Andwaldo had appointed himself numberer, to do all the counting, measuring, and sharing: that was how people did things where Andwaldo came from.

In those early days, Andwaldo had talked of leaving. He was on his way somewhere, he said; he had come to Evpa Hsu by chance. At dawn and dusk you'd see him staring out towards Bilovan: there was someone waiting for him there. If it wasn't an enemy, Knesh's mother used to say, it was surely a sweetheart. But he didn't go, and he didn't go, and it was astonishing there were so many things that needed numbering; and now Andwaldo was an old man. He hardly ever looked dreamily at the hills any more. He'd never go. He was indispensable. He said so, and so did Knesh. Four bags were put aside.

Andwaldo left Knesh to supervise things. When he saw that, the boy left off swinging on his beam, jumped down and followed him. 'Andwaldo!'

The white head bowed towards him with the mixture of kindliness and reservation adults make to protect themselves from excesses of childish enthusiasm.

'Andwaldo, did they have kites where you came from?'

'Kites, Qepez?' Like catching fish in the clouds.

'Javeth and me have made a kite, come and I'll show you.'

Tugged, Andwaldo walked on in his own direction. 'Qepez, I'm busy now.' When the sky bobbed with a fleet of stars and flowers, scowling demons and yellow birds, knocking and tumbling together . . . 'I'll look at it later.'

'Did they, Andwaldo?'

'Did they what? Did *who* what?' He paused, looking exasperated and amused.

'Have *kites*, Andwaldo! I bet they didn't. I bet they didn't have any harp as good as ours.'

'"Half",' said Andwaldo.

'*Harf* as good then, they didn't, did they?'

'How do I know? I haven't seen yours yet, have I?' The sky sucked them up. We had to pull to stop them flying off.

'So *come*!' Qepez was hanging on his arm again.

'Later.' He flicked the boy's ear.

'Ow!'

'I'll come and see it this evening, if you haven't forgotten all about it by then.'

'Andwaldo!' recriminated Qepez, rubbing his ear. 'You're the one who's always forgetting things.' The old man crossed the yard. Qepez called after him. 'Will you tell us about the kites they had where you came from when you come and look at the kite me and Javeth made?'

'We'll see.'

'You promised! Yesterday, Andwaldo, yesterday you promised me a story!'

'A story, a story! You think I've nothing to do but tell you stories? The players will be here soon; they'll tell you a story.'

'The players? Today?'

'Soon.' He walked on, gazing over the pitiful fields, but seeing a shining city and kites on the long green hills rising into the running clouds.

The kite Qepez and Javeth had made was a red wing. They tried it out on Snail Hill, and when it had dived and battered itself a few times, and Qepez had cried, and they'd blamed each other, it suddenly climbed into the brisk air, swaying and fluttering its fringe, and soon went as high as even their ambitious string would let it, and tried to go higher; but they pinned it down with a stone and chased each other round, squealing and jerking the line to feel the awesome authority of the kite pulling back.

Below, Oulhie put her hand on Andwaldo's arm, distracting

him from his slate to watch the red thing cavorting in the sky. Later she called him from the next room.

'More kites?'

No. There were two men coming over the dead land from the south, where the river and the road were. His eyes narrowed, half in scrutiny, half in suspicion. Few people visited Evpa Hsu, none from that direction. I'm a superstitious old woman, he told himself; but it was as if the kite-tossing wind had suddenly pierced the walls of the barn and was blowing cold and relentless through his stomach.

'Which way?'

Lupio shrugged, rubbing his feet. Their boots were giving out, cracking and peeling. The land-shy lake-dwellers set little store by going soundly shod.

'There's something over there.'

'Where?'

'There. D'you see?'

The buildings were as drab as the rest of the scenery. It was a large farm, or a small hamlet.

'They're actually cultivating!' Lupio kicked the ground. Dust flew up.

'How?'

A tracery of green struggled along sketchy furrows, stretched thin to cover the fields. Small animals nosed the dirt unrestingly, governed by little figures as thin as the sticks they waved.

'It's incredible. They must starve themselves to feed the pigs.'

Lupio had already started off, scuffling down the slope. He followed. Soon they were in the fields, and taking tortuous care not to step on the gangling, unhealthy-looking vegetation. In this shallow basin there was indeed a layer of manageable soil, though everything looked thoroughly leached. The children surrounded them, their shrill shouts turning to smothered giggles and shyness when they realised that the strangers couldn't understand what they said. Lupio and Dubilier stumbled downhill, children everywhere underfoot.

'Hey! Be careful!' Grubby fingers plucked at their baggage. 'There's nothing for you in there.' He shook his head. 'Get out! Get away!' But still they jostled. The Thrynians broke into a run, careering down the narrow strip between fields. The children followed, whooping, and chased them into the village. Parents appeared, and elder brothers and sisters, wading in with shouts to disperse the pack, but gathering the children rather than dismissing them because these men were strangers, not looked for in Evpa Hsu. Dusty and travel-worn, Lupio and Dubilier stood panting and grinning as they fought last skirmishes with the more persistent of the welcoming committee, their belongings scattered at their feet. Dubilier smiled at the cautious faces, lifting empty hands in a gesture of goodwill. We are like you, his hands declared; we have nothing, we are at your mercy, at the mercy of hard earth and fickle winds. Your children are safe with us; you and your property are safe from us. We are as you are. Some smiled back. The children started to chatter again. Lupio looked around them, searching, he suddenly realised, for another young face, better fed than any of these, that he had last seen in a very different courtyard, far away. Suddenly the travelling was a weight upon him and he wanted to go home. But not to Thryn.

An elderly woman approached them. To look at she was no different from the crowd, but she spoke to them in a public manner and seemed to ask them in. She stooped to help Dubilier pick up their gear and Lupio hurried to follow, grateful for her initiative. They entered a kind of bakehouse, the source of the tendril of smoke that had helped them locate the village from up in the rocks. Someone gave them a dipper of water from an urn; Lupio showed pleasure and drank deep. It was tepid but refreshing, drawn from a clear spring. Their hostess brought bread from a batch cooling on a high sill. She broke it in half and gave them one each. It was brown and dense, and slightly bitter. They attacked it with the single-mindedness of the starved. Lupio noticed that the woman was eating too as she called out in tones of approval to the bakers: in the simplest manner possible, his friend had broken his own portion and given her some back for herself. Subtly he demonstrated that they wished to share, not to be served. Lupio felt a pulse of confidence. This was all right. It might be good to stay for a while.

He leaned forward, put his fingers to his chest. 'Lupio,' he said. 'Lupio.' He indicated Dubilier and spoke his name slowly, separating the syllables. In the background the cooks were putting down their work to watch this unusual event. Gracefully and unselfconsciously repeating Lupio's eager gesture, the woman touched her own breast and said, 'Oulhie.'

Lupio and Dubilier glanced at one another: a small triumph. Already they had come nearer these people than all their efforts had brought them to the lake-dwellers. The wilderness, its arid rock and lifeless canyons, was ahead of them as well as behind, but there was food and water here, shelter from the cold and the prospect of good company. 'Oulhie,' they said, struggling with the unfamiliar sounds.

She opened her arms, turning from side to side to embrace, notionally, an indefinitely large area. 'Evpa Hsu,' she told them, 'Evpa Hsu.'

'Evpa Hsu,' they imitated, and Oulhie corrected their pronunciation.

'The village or the people?'

'Maybe both.' Oulhie was regarding them intently. Lupio walked two pairs of fingers along the table top, pointing to show they represented Dubilier and himself. He repeated their names. He repeated the walking action, and tapped the surface at the point where his fingers stopped. 'Evpa Hsu,' he said, reinforcing it with a gesture like Oulhie's to take in the whole village. Then he drew one finger back along the line of the walk and tapped the point where it had begun. 'Thryn,' he said, 'Thryn,' gesturing to the two of them again.

The woman looked surprised. She got up at once, motioning them to follow. They took the remainder of their bread with them, and waved their thanks to the bakers. Oulhie led them across the yard and into a barn. The air smelt of chickens and smoked with grain dust. A narrow flight led to an upper storey; brown feather bundles bustled frantically off the steps in front of them and went to roost among the sacks as they reached the landing. 'Andwaldo!' she called.

He came out. 'What is it?' The eagerness in her voice told him what: she'd brought the foreigners. Somehow they'd impressed her and she wanted him to meet them at once. He felt reluctant without knowing why, self-conscious and on the defensive.

She swept him back into the room before her. 'Andwaldo, they say they come from Thryn!'

Andwaldo was startled. He inspected them warily. Beneath the gradually accumulated camouflage of foreign haircuts, foreign beards, stains and strains of travel, there was something aristocratic in their emaciated faces. Long necks; taller than the Evpa Hsuan . . . He was uneasy, like an old man revisiting his nursery and finding how little everything has grown, how familiar and yet quite altered it all looks. 'Are you sure?'

Lupio guessed what she'd told him. She'd mentioned Thryn, and 'Andwaldo' was a recognisable name, much less foreign to him than 'Oulhie'. 'We're from Thryn,' he said. Nobody spoke. Oulhie was standing back, looking as pleased as if she'd invented the pair of them herself. Andwaldo, a weathered old man with disconcertingly steady eyes, was gazing at each of them in turn. The silence was becoming absurd. 'I'm Lupio,' he added, merely to break it. 'This is Dubilier. From Thryn.'

The old man's voice was deep and warm, with a hint of some obscure emotion – regret? weariness? nostalgia? 'Aigu Lupio,' he said, 'Aigu Dubilier: welcome to Evpa Hsu.'

'Four of us,' said Andwaldo. 'Uthien, me, and Sarol and Ylma. Just married, d'ye see. And they were determined – well, leastways, Sarol was, Ylma didn't seem to have much say in it – he was determined Thryn was no place to start married life. Look at the children, he'd say. Look at the women. You must have noticed the women. You remember their eyes?' Dubilier shifted in the chair, uncrossed and recrossed his legs. 'All dull, aren't they? No gleam to 'em. There's no hope for 'em, you see. No prospects. Not any more. Well, this is, what, thirty-five years back now, it must be worse today, isn't it?'

Lupio nodded as if bowing slowly. 'I expect so,' he said carefully.

'It had to be better outside. I should think you know what I mean. Whatever there was, Outwall, it couldn't be worse than what was inside. Not with a young wife and all your dreams for the future. You're not married?' They shook their heads. Andwaldo smiled affectionately at Oulhie. 'Well, we found our spot, and we waited till after midnight, and then over we went. I should think you did the same. And didn't that feel good? Like setting foot on a new world. Pioneers. Head down against the wind, trudging through the marshes, you can walk for days and not hardly tell you've moved, it's that empty. Great. Great feeling.'

'Until you fall in.'

'Eh?'

'You must have fallen in, in the marsh? Where we were, it was – '

'Oh! We fell in. We fell in all right. At first we did. But you soon learn, what's good ground and what's not. You find the paths. There are paths, it's not so bad. We'd have dry enough ground to put the tents up at night, and Uth and me, we used to talk, tell each other how good it was, and not listen to the shouting and screaming in the other tent.

'Then we had some luck. Well, it seemed good luck – we came upon this farm, d'ye see – oh, scant half the size o' this place it was, but they took us in; didn't say much, didn't ask much, let us sleep in the outhouse – and we worked for 'em. Up to our knees in the wetfields, with the schinni.'

'Schinni?'

'Don't you know? Odd stuff; won't grow unless you drown it. Wouldn't touch it now; not that there's much chance of it taking up here. But that's how we went on from day to day, always planning to move on and find our own place, but somehow – Well, we were glad enough not to have to keep struggling, truth to tell, glad of some food and a roof to eat it under, you know? And then it was harvest. They brought in help, labourers, half a dozen of them; regular, they were, lived somewhere not too far off, or travelled round all year from job to job, I never did find out. Loose lads, they were. Loose-talking, loose-moving. They'd be there, trussing and bailing as fast as we could bring it to 'em, doing it one-handed, almost. You could see it in their eyes when she walked into the yard and back again to the fields, like they were flowing round her. "Oh, let's leave, Sarol," she kept saying, "I don't like it," and him making and muttering his threats, what he'd do if they touched her – and him no bigger than a schinni-stalk.'

He took another mouthful. They didn't speak, waiting for him to continue.

'They had her. All of them. First thing we knew was Sarol screaming and carrying on; middle o' the night, he'd brought her back in and she was lying there moaning, blood on her, and

Uth and I there trying to calm her down and trying to stop him from rushing out. Well, we had him sitting down, gasping and blowing he was, and we turned round to see to her, and we were half-asleep anyway, and what with one thing and another, time we looked back he was gone.

'Sorry, love, it's not a thing to talk about at table I know, but I won't go into details. We found him, Sarol, in the morning, and buried him. The farmer wouldn't do a thing to them. "You can use that spade," says he, "and mind you bring it back by noon." I ask you! Half-hinted it was our own fault – though we never did find out what she came to be doing off on her own that night. He made out they'd carried her off while we were all asleep, but that hardly seems . . . well, picture it: kidnap a new-wed woman and not wake the husband? But I'll speak no ill of the dead.

'She took it very well, though, when we told her what they'd done to him – told her the half of it, leastways. "This wouldn't have happened if we hadn't hung around here instead of doing what we set out to do," she says, and we were off in a couple of hours. She led us, as good as, making for the mountains – '

Dubilier and Lupio exchanged glances.

' – never sleeping two nights in the same place, if she could help it. "We owe it to him," – that was it. Whatever we said, that was always the last word. "We owe it to him."

'Then we had to split up. We fell in with some travellers, queer types, foreigners, come from beyond the mountains and making their way home. They had room for two, no more. Uth and I decided Ylma had to go, so we drew for the other place and he won it. I didn't like that much, travelling on my own. You wouldn't like it. You get – well, you get to feel loose that way too, no hours to follow, no master to obey, no one to call you here and there. You think you own it all. Then, oh, there's a storm, and you've twisted your ankle and there's not even a tree for shelter, and you know you don't own any of it, nobody does, 'cause it's as free as you are, if you know what I mean. The lack of company, that's what does it. I'd said we'd meet, at Bilovan; go to the best place, I said, and wait. I'll find you there somehow. But, well, by the time I got here I'd had enough; I wasn't going anywhere. I kept saying, Oh, I'll go, I'll go soon; but why throw away a place like this when you're miles from nowhere? What was in the mountains for me, you tell me that?'

'Why were you making for the mountains anyway?' Dubilier asked him.

'Now that's a funny thing. I'm sure that came later, you see. I'm positive, when we started out, we didn't have any idea where we were going. Just away, somewhere better. You know what I mean. But then they did for Sarol and Ylma was talking about the mountains, we'll head for the mountains. Maybe it was just that that was what we could see, sticking up the other side of the marshes: like swimming to the opposite bank, you know?'

As they turned, involuntarily, to the window, he went on.

'It's a funny thing. Here am I, talking, talking, talking – never letting you get a word in! Having you here brings it all back. What's Thryn or Thrynian been to me these last thirty-five years? But here I am, pouring it all out like a barrel with a hole in the bottom. And yet it's a queer thing: try and try, I can't recall the name of the big mountain, that one there. Bilovan, we call it, but that's not what it was back in Thryn.'

Dubilier was about to tell him when, to his surprise, Lupio cut in. 'I don't suppose it cares what we call it,' he said, slipping easily into Andwaldo's manner. 'It's been sitting there since before there were names, or men to use them, and it'll be sitting there still when we've gone and taken our tongues with us.'

Andwaldo approved of this, striking the young man cheerfully on the shoulder and offering him more yoghourt.

Bertollo drowsed at the reins. A meaningless bit of a song circled in his head, buzzing like an importunate fly.

Farewell to my mother by the cold hearthstone
And never return till the walls be down.

Walls be down, walls be down. He shook his head. The aged yellow mare plodded on, half asleep too. Walls be down, walls be down. Farewell to my mo-

'Ez!'

'What, my love, my flower, my precious, my topaz treasure hung on a chain at my heart?' The ridiculous voice came from inside the wagon. 'A golden chain,' it added as an afterthought.

'I'm falling asleep!'

'I'll awaken you with a kiss.' Ezra Dmdnny Dmdnny appeared in a grubby singlet and spangled trousers, embraced the young man from behind and kissed him on the cheek. Bertollo didn't respond. 'I'll entertain you.' Ezra went in and came out again pulling on a baggy coat. He had difficulty finding the second sleeve. Then he stood swaying on the box beside Bertollo, bowing to an audience as clamorous as it was invisible. 'Yes, yes! Patient, generous ladies and gentlemen, your eager, wretched, loyal Ezra Dmdnny Dmdnny will make a marvel for your eyes' astonishment. A marvel to startle you from your sleeping. I'll find an egg in the air!' He snapped his fingers, muttering.

Bertollo gazed around the barren landscape. 'It would be a better marvel to find the chicken. We'll get no supper from this.'

'We'll eat the egg,' said Ezra, proffering it. Bertollo gave him his look of long suffering. 'You don't like my wonderful egg, plucked with great effort from the thinnest of airs, purchased by years of strenuous physical labour from the great Invisible Mother Chicken Spirit – '

'It's made of clay.'

'What, love of my loins?'

'We can't eat clay.'

Pouting, 'You don't like my great marvel?'

'I think you'll find,' said Bertollo tenderly, 'I have a similar great marvel up the sleeve of my own coat.' He turned his face up to be kissed.

'Bitch.'

Ravens followed the rainbow caravan, in hope of scraps. The waggoners' clothes were motley: strong leathers and workingman's sackcloth mixed with the beads and happy rags of the mystery. Paint lingered on cheek and forehead, a feather or a shred of tinsel in someone's hair. The lowland herders had welcomed the players and let them play from sunset almost to dawn. Now they rubbed their eyes, searched for their clogs, and went to the feeding and the milking. The departing vagabonds, like ghosts, had no such provisions to make.

Bertollo stretched. 'What's a hearthstone?' he asked.

Ezra at his side woke the horse with a jerk at her reins. She snorted and trotted faster as he crooned to her, dmdnny dmdnny.

'There'll be food at Evpa Hsu.'

'Knesh! Knesh!'

Looking harassed, the farmer came back. 'What is it?'

'Are we to shift these four?'

'Ah . . . four?'

'These. The sacks.'

'Ah. No, those are for the players.'

'The what?'

'The players.'

Lupio looked at Dubilier, but the word was new to him too. 'Right,' he said to Knesh, who hurried out again. 'It's odd, isn't it – they really do have no conception of numbers.'

'And no curiosity about them either. Everything above ground level gets only a baffled stare and then prolonged neglect.'

'It's not really surprising – '

'Oh, no, I know that. They really don't have time or energy to spare for anything but work.'

Lupio was dusting off his hands and stepping back. 'Well!' he said, 'apparently we do: this lot's finished.' They walked out into the yard, pausing to gaze at the mountains that dominated everything, and at the one that dominated the others. Clouds flocked over it, herded by the vigorous wind. Some boys were flying a kite from the hilltop.

'I want to ask you something,' said Dubilier, 'but I'm not sure it's wise.'

Lupio gave him a delighted smile. 'How will you choose?'

'What do you mean?'

'Which you're going to satisfy, your hunger for knowledge or your hunger for wisdom.'

'Why are you being so reticent with Andwaldo? Are you afraid of him?'

'Afraid? No, of course not. I'm very fond of the old boy. How do you mean, reticent?'

'Whenever he mentions Thryn, you gloss it over or change the subject. The other night, when he wanted to know why we left, you really didn't tell him. You left out all the important details.'

A shadow crossed Lupio's face. He shook his head. 'He doesn't want to know all that.'

'But he does! That's just it. He'd like to be reminded of the old place – he's still very attached to it, in his way.'

'So are you, by the sound of it.'

A whisper of the old city arrogance stirred in Dubilier. It was easier to be patriotic in exile, well away from the rancid streets that contradicted all the doctrine.

'I don't know – since talking to Andwaldo I've started to think about going home. Eventually.'

Lupio was reminded of his feelings when they first arrived at Evpa Hsu. 'I think about home too. But not about Thryn.'

Lupio was the one who had stood up in the dinghy, throwing stones in the river. Stones; bones, he had said. Dubilier asked him, 'Would you rather stay here?'

'I don't know.'

'When I wanted to stay at the lakes you wouldn't let me.'

'Not true. I merely drew your attention to the fact that the place was driving me mad and would likely drive you mad too. You'd have ended up like Andwaldo – always moping about your sacred mountain.'

Dubilier glanced up sharply. 'My mountain? That was your idea. The first time we met, remember? You said: We'll go to the mountains.' But he heard himself, trying to deny responsibility: it was a poor defence.

Lupio waved this aside. 'That was in Thryn. In Thryn, Hisper Einou is the only other place in the world they've ever heard of. Like Andwaldo and his pals. It's somewhere to aim for when you start out. Then you look around and realise you're not obliged to walk in a straight line for the rest of your life.'

Dubilier began to be afraid, as he had when they'd talked by the upper lake, as he did whenever the prospect of separation from Lupio arose. On the road, there had been unanimity: they were going to the mountain, when they could see it, and when it was lost in the mist. They had fantasised about what would happen when they got to the mountain, to give themselves incentive or compensate for wherever they were at that moment. But now that the mountain was all too visible, crowning their view every day, a conflict had emerged. They were not even seeing the same mountain. To Dubilier Hisper Einou seemed to rise up over them like an imperious third party determined to interrupt their conversation. He felt challenged to say something definitive, quickly, and couldn't.

'Don't you want to go and look for Taleg Tivoriun, and the real Cirnex?'

'Not in the slightest,' said Lupio. 'There's nothing there.'

Now Dubilier knew he had lost his grip on the argument. 'But to prove it. To Kavi.'

'Who's Kavi?' asked Lupio blankly.

'Well, to your own satisfaction, then.'

Satisfaction was what Dubilier had wanted in Thryn; it was why he'd left Thryn, to seek it on Hisper Einou. Now the mountain threatened him with satisfaction. Perhaps the mountain was really nothing but a mountain. Perhaps satisfaction would be the most unsatisfying thing of all.

Lupio was turning round idly on one foot, scratching a circle around himself in the dust. 'I'm satisfied,' he said.

On Snail Hill Lupio helped Javeth and Qepez strengthen the lashings that bound together the sticks of their red kite. It was firmer, more aerodynamic, but they still had difficulty getting it aloft and soon tired of running up and down with it. They flopped on the grass and began a debate that mounted to squabbling. 'Ask Lupio then if you don't believe me,' Qepez finished, 'he knows *everything* about kites.'

'I don't,' he called over to them, 'but I do know there's an art even to tying a piece of twine round a piece of wood.'

'Well you should,' insisted Qepez, undefeated. 'You come from where Andwaldo came from, don't you?'

'Yes.'

'Well then, Andwaldo told me that everybody flies kites there, everybody. He said there's a day when people fly them out of their windows and the children all run along the hill, much, much bigger than this one. And they have battles with the kites until only one kite's left and that one's the winner, the best kite of all.'

'Andwaldo said that? Kites in Thryn?'

Qepez nodded emphatically.

'Perhaps he was making it up.'

'No! Everything Andwaldo says is true, all of it, isn't it, Javeth?'

'How do you know?' The great city loomed up in Lupio's mind, more vivid than he could have wished. The fallen moon of ignominous roofs huddled like swine at the trough; the sprawling lawns and courtyards of the Aiguda; and, above it all, the inflexible hauteur of the Iigril and the temple declaring absolutely, against all evidence, that everything was best, that the shrivelled seeds and warped blossoms would fruit into perfection very soon now. That humourless sky, spattered and hopping with kites, the frivolity of string and coloured paper? Andwaldo might be able to remember some lapsed festival, he was more than twice Lupio's age; but could there possibly have been one?

Dubilier was coming up the hill.

'Dubilier remembers it too,' said Qepez. 'He told us yesterday. Dubilier! Isn't there a kite-day, in Thryn? Lupio says there isn't. There is, isn't there?'

'A kite-day in Thryn? Like Andwado was telling you? Yes, of course there is.'

Lupio was bewildered, but Qepez and Javeth were pleased with their champion and claimed his attention for themselves.

Javeth asked, 'Are there players too, in Thryn?'

Dubilier caught Lupio's eye. 'That word again, "players". What is players, can you tell us?'

'The players are people,' Javeth protested, 'they're not a something.'

'Are they? What do they do?'

'They do stories, and dance and sing.'

'And they make magic, and they fly, and then they have a fight,' Qepez chimed in, hacking and thrusting with an invisible sword, 'da, da, daa! and one of them gets killed and falls down, and then they make some more magic and make him better again.'

'They sound like wonderful people,' Dubilier said.

'Oh, they are, they are!' Qepez affirmed, bounding back from his fight to the death with eyes wide and shining.

'Where are they? Can we see them?'

'They're not *here* yet,' said Javeth. 'They go from village to village in a big wagon – '

'Lots of wagons!'

' – and they build a stage in a field and play on it.'

'That field, that one there!'

'No it wasn't, it was that one.'

'It was! It was that one there, Hnaga told me!'

'Can't you remember?'

'No, we were too young to stay up late.'

'So you've never actually seen these players you praise so highly?'

'Soon we will!' said Qepez, the reminder serving only to increase his enthusiasm.

'So they don't come very often?'

'Every – every – ' Qepez stared in supreme concentration at a distant tree. Javeth, the more practical one, spread his fingers and began slowly numbering them off.

'Five years!' announced Qepez triumphantly, his tree having presumably signalled his answer to him.

'Not it's not, it's – '

'It is! Five, it is, I know!'

'No it's not, it's seven, 'cause – '

'Five!'

'Seven!'

Javeth forsook the dizzy heights of arithmetic and pulled a face at Qepez, who chased him off down the hillside; then a gust took the forgotten kite and began bowling it rapidly through the grass, so they raced to rescue that instead.

'What's this about kites?' asked Lupio. 'How can you remember something I've never even heard of?'

'I don't.'

'Why did you tell them you did, then?'

'I don't know. It sounded like a beautiful story, entirely preferable to the truth, so I thought, why spoil it for them?'

'I like that! Who was it yesterday who was rebuking me for failing to keep Andwaldo up to date on the condition of his beloved birthplace, in all its great grisliness?'

'No, I don't know; it's not the same.' Dubilier was uncomfortable; standing over his friend as he reclined on the slope, he seemed to be about to deliver a lecture, whereas he was really only exploring an intuitive impulse of his own, probably an irrational one at that. He sat down and pulled a blade or two of grass, making himself relax before he answered. Lately he'd become so defensive. He said, 'I'm not sure disillusioning people is a good thing, not when it's unnecessary.'

'I don't understand this. You're the one who's on a quest for the truth. Are you going to go round Evpa Hsu telling them all what a beautiful place Thryn is just because they happen to be simple enough to believe it already, and then go home to Andwaldo's and say, Actually, old man, you're quite right, it's the most terrible pigsty really? I mean, where do you draw the line?'

'I just try to look at it from their point of view,' said Dubilier. Perhaps that was it. 'Andwaldo feels guilty about running away. He makes *me* feel guilty about running away. So I want to talk to him about Thryn as it is, instead of helping him hide from it. I think we should assure him that he had every reason to run away. But the others – it's their present that's so wretched, stuck up here on bare rock trying to scratch a living. They need to think that there is somewhere else that's better – to look up to Andwaldo with admiration because he can count, and he comes from this marvellous city where *everybody* can count. Who knows, they might be right. Perhaps in some mysterious cosmic reckoning that actually does outweigh the squalor and the crime.'

Lupio was laughing, more in surprise than derision. 'You've changed your mind since yesterday, then. Yesterday you had to go on to Bilovan. Evpa Hsu simply wasn't good enough. *You* wouldn't be content to stay here with your comfortable illusion that Taleg Tivoriun is somewhere up there, bright and shining, full of old men with long white beards who can recite the Seventeen Secrets of the Universe backwards while picking their toes.'

Dubilier grinned. He couldn't cope with anger, but ridicule was all right. This whole thing seemed ridiculous to him, sometimes. But it wasn't as comfortable as it might have been. 'I'm not comfortable,' he answered. 'that's the trouble.'

'You should have brought a cushion.'

'No, I mean the illusion: Taleg Tivoriun and the seventeen old men, all that. I can't be comfortable in it the way the Evpa Hsuans can be comfortable believing in Thryn. I'd like to be, but I've been given cause to doubt it; so now instead of belief

I've got to have knowledge, choose the fact instead of the illusion, whether the fact makes me comfortable or not. I suppose that's the trap of being human.'

Lupio was thinking. 'Like me and the Grach,' he said.

'Or like you and Kavi's Cirnex.' He felt very still. Such moments were the nearest he could come to Lupio's comfort here in Evpa Hsu. Or had he made Lupio uncomfortable now too? He studied his face but couldn't tell. That was a trap, too. Even now he was pursuing knowledge, looking for the fact behind the illusion – and who could say what constituted fact? *Perhaps in some mysterious cosmic reckoning* . . .

They sat unspeaking in the chill wind, watching two boys who were happily squabbling over a battered kite as if it were all they needed, all they could ever need.

The players arrived one night. Their rainbow snake creaked in from the north-west, down the narrow track into a field, where it coiled itself into a rough circle and waited for an hour or two. Gaspau the Buck slept. Ezra Dmdnny Dmdnny and Bertollo slept. But before dawn someone was up brewing tea over a bonfire, passing round torches and handing a mug to each sleepy riser. Their speech was scattered and low. Some began to exercise on the hard ground, jerking dumb-bells and doing press-ups. Then Gaspau came out to the fire, fastening his overalls with one hand, accepting a beaker with the other, and sent people off to the spring to fill the butt and some waterskins. Everyone congregated and the jobs were portioned out. A few of the vans were moved back and then the horses were unharnessed. Bertollo vaulted back into their wagon and began searching for something.

'Get up,' he said.

There was no response. Bertollo lit the lamp and continued rummaging. Ezra groaned, screwing his eyes up, and burrowed under the bedding.

'Get up!' Bertollo pulled the blankets from his face and tilted the lamp so that it would annoy him.

'Go away. Take that horrible light away.' Ezra wriggled, burying his head again.

'It's time to get up.'

'Let me sleep. Poor wretched Ezra, kept awake all night by an insatiable boy and then dragged from his lovely warm bed before even the cock's up . . .' He fumbled blindly for the covers which Bertollo had pulled away. The young man turned to disembowel another trunk.

'It's you that's insatiable,' he said. 'Where's the pick?'

'Mmnnmmnn . . . '

'Where's the *pick*? We need it. The ground's so damn hard – '

'Mmnnmm!'

'Ez!'

'Dono. Goway. Mmnn. Let him dream, Ezra Dmdnny the great . . . m'jish'nn . . . Got to have dreammszzz . . . '

Bertollo found the pick, sighed audibly at the bulge in the blankets and reached up to snuff out the light.

'Thank you, my butterfly,' said the bulge lightly, not moving.

The stage was going up. Shortly before daybreak, when the first villager pushed back the shutters, it was all but complete, dark and incongruous in the old familiar field, commanding a region between the worlds, an outpost of the dominion of dreams.

It spread its power over everyone that day. The children's play spiralled towards it and tentatively onto it, but never into the secret zone behind. Between the wagons they glimpsed the phantom figures strolling, resting and preparing for the coming spectacle in eerie quietness. Once in a while it was broken by a sudden thunderflash, the blare of a trumpet, or a shout of mysterious laughter. Then the adults paused to look across at the gaudy temple and its encampment, and bent to work faster in the thought of the holiday to come. The players waited, limbering up, retouching costumes, checking lines and props. It would begin at sunset.

'Light the lamp,' said Andwaldo to Oulhie. He frowned at his slate, on which the sums seemed longer than ever.

'Aren't you coming?' Dubilier asked him.

'Got this to finish.' He tapped the slate with the end of his stylus. 'More important than plays.'

'You'll miss it,' Dubilier warned him, thinking he intended to join them later. 'Only once in seven years, remember.'

'Well, it's nice for the children. It's for the children really, not old scarecrows like me.'

In fact, Dubilier reflected as they hurried towards the music, Andwaldo was very little like a scarecrow at all. His burly frame cramped at the table, that leonine head bowed over a slate, showed power he withheld, like a shuttered flame. The fist that clutched a pencil had once torn him a path through the badlands. Onstage a dancer was juggling fireballs, summoning the crowd with a nonsense song.

'How long is it you've been in Evpa Hsu, dear?' asked Oulhie.

'Thirty-five years.'

'And how many times have the players come in that time?'

'This is the sixth, love.'

'And how many of those times have you missed seeing them?'

'Don't remember.' The answer was too curt, came too quickly.

'I think I do. I think you've avoided every one since the first, just after you arrived.'

Andwaldo looked up at her. He made his voice kind. 'Don't disturb me, love. I must finish this. You must go, quickly, before it begins. I expect Dubilier and Lupio will need your help to understand the play.'

The players' patch was round, like a little world, a pocket of strangeness comfortably contained by the fields where everything went on as normal. Inside the ring the players rested, making no disturbance, as though time were inverted on their borders and it was night there while it was day here. Now that day was finishing the magic inner world shook itself and woke. Darkness took the mountains, the hills, and the rest of the fields. The juggler's fire stood in for the sun, growing brighter while the western afterglow faded. The people gathered, and the little world grew. It was the only world now, so they gave it their faith, and its unnatural properties became merely natural. The king showered gold on his subjects, and it was gold, not just sand; while the horses on which he and his captain rode out of the castle were thoroughbreds, though their backs were like stripped branches. The travellers found their way by invisible stars, or by painted stars held up by children clambering on the scaffolding. Later a demon made his own stars from a tube which he lit, little buds of fire that spurted out and hung in the air for a long time. The audience accepted them all.

Lupio was disappointed. In the city there were masques, on occasion, and skits: sophisticated amusements whose wit he applauded. Nobody expected you to believe in them. This was a different matter. Some of the stagecraft was just crude. It confused him. If you saw how it was done, or if there wasn't even a pretence, how could you believe in the stars? He wondered if that was what Andwaldo had felt too. Naturally the old man would be too kind to let them see that he didn't enjoy their festival, so he stayed away. But there was Dubilier: he was having a good time, booing the long-tailed green King Demon and his army of clowns when they attacked the castle. Lupio shrugged and returned his attention to the stage, to the things that would happen suddenly and catch him unawares. Men disappeared, women flew, a tree grew onstage in seconds: impossibilities, yet no sign of the strings and mirrors that dangled haphazardly, ruining the rest for him. If they could do this magic, why did they bother with the tricks, the illusions anyone could see through?

Oulhie touched his arm. 'Can you follow it? Isn't it wonderful?' She was as happy as the rest of them, happy to forget everything they knew, to abandon it all in the grey world outside and come streaming into the magic circle at the first bidding of the juggler. The torchlight danced, and they didn't wonder what sleight had happened in the unseen moment between one flicker and the next. Their faces were vacant, like masks. It wasn't a difference between two kinds of illusion, Lupio realised, but between them and him. The human capacity for self-deception appalled him. He wished it could be done away with, grown out of altogether. These stories were childish. They had to do with a king and his faithful captain, who set out from their palace to look for a magic treasure, and all the ridiculous creatures they had to vanquish on the way. It was the sort of thing the grown-ups told Qepez and Javeth, or that Lupio's father had told him, if it came to that. Strange to find something so intimate recurring in such an outlandish setting, so far from home.

Lupio began ignoring the crude pantomime embellishments and concentrating on reconstructing the original story behind them. It really did seem remarkably familiar. If only it weren't all in a foreign language. He felt that one name would bring it all back to him in a flash. But then the play began to ramble. A meandering sequence of adventures befell the heroes. A peril arose, clamoured, challenged, was met and dispatched, and they rode on, to the next. The tension slackened, and Lupio lost interest again as the players moved their play into its indefinable middle. They freewheeled, they improvised. They wandered down into the crowd, starting sideshows, disseminating all their power into random games, acrobatics, conjuring displays. The crush lessened as people moved to other parts of the field, following the various distractions, and Lupio stood up. Dubilier was trying to attract his attention, pointing to where one of the heroes was fighting the King Demon, cheered on by a ring of watchers. Lupio caught something they were shouting and then he knew what the story was.

'It's the only logical explanation.'

'We'll ask him.'

Andwaldo had not come to the festival. Everyone else had stayed until the end. Reassembled, the play reached its final, climactic battle of fireworks and flowers, and then the whole gathering, players and farmers, men, women and children, had melted into a great dance about the bonfire. The music was mad, dissonant, spontaneous; it was inspired, it was all wild flame, circling forever no matter who took the tune, how skilful or ignorant his fingers. Gaspau the Buck was in the middle, leaping the blaze, his horns on his head, his tattered dress flying. He leapt; he seemed to dance in the air, in the fire: no one could tell if he were really aflame, a burning devil or the great hurtling god of the deer.

Now the bale-fire was in embers. In the dim outer world something began to suggest the shapes of mountains in the eastern sky. The sun was to be resurrected, the balance of light and time restored. The players hurried to dismantle their impertinent creation. Evpa Hsu was already well into the middle of a brief sleep, but the celebrations which had exhausted the farmers had left Lupio and Dubilier preternaturally awake. The end of the play precipitated them to a new beginning.

'Do you think that's the reason he stayed away?'

'What do you mean?'

'Guilt again. The play reminds him of the culture he abandoned.'

Lupio stretched. 'Ingenious as ever.'

'Mm. I suppose I should be tired, but I'm just not.'

'You are really, but your head hasn't caught up with it yet.'

There was a pause.

'Do you still feel like staying?'

'No.'

'I didn't think you would. Will you admit – do you think there might be something in it now?'

'Of course I don't! But everyone else seems to. It's determined to haunt me. No getting away from it, even out here. No, you're right: it would be mad to come all this way and not go and see for myself. Nobody else is going to lay the ghost for me.' He laughed then. 'What a stupid way to live.'

'Whereas I . . . ' It was too complicated. Dubilier thought for a few minutes. 'It comes down to the same thing, I suppose,' he went on. 'It's a good enough phantom to chase.'

'What do you mean?' Lupio said again, but his friend didn't reply. They both fell asleep as the sun got to the top of the mountains. The players drove away a few hours later, taking all their secrets with them.

Andwaldo was up before anyone, raking around in the yard. He checked in the barn that the players had taken their provisions: four sacks he'd set aside, no more, no fewer. Later he went into the field where the play had taken place. When Dubilier came out of the house he was poking at a small fire. It seemed a mockery, a satirical replica of the sacred blaze.

'Good morning, Andwaldo.'

'Morning?' The old man squinted at the sky. 'Only just, you know, only just. What's the matter with them all? Sleep the day away!'

'Well, you weren't up all night!' Dubilier was about to go on and ask why he hadn't come, but he saw how Andwaldo had turned away, already defensive at this slightest implication of criticism. He wouldn't give much of an answer, Dubilier was sure, no matter how casual the enquiry. Why was he so sensitive, in his placid exile, to this one reminder? Dubilier reserved the question. 'What are you burning?' he asked instead.

'Bits and pieces. Rubbish.' He jerked a thumb at the well-cleared field. Dubilier saw a length of silvery ribbon in the flames, and shreds of painted paper. The updraught caught a burning feather and sent it spiralling between them. The smallest of remains, a handful of litter that even the scrupulous players hadn't found; but it mattered to Andwaldo, so he had to light a special fire and destroy it before he did anything else that day. Dubilier was startled out of his resolution. He spoke quietly.

'Why do you hate them so?'

Andwaldo prepared a jocular denial but he caught the young man's eye. Damn his impertinence.

'They get in the way, in the way of the work. Look at it.' He gestured at the farm. 'Everything still to do. Everyone still in bed. Takes us weeks to get back to normal.'

'You begrudge them one day in seven years?'

'We can't afford it. You'll know when you've been here as long as I have. Before I came it was all – anyhow. Slapdash. No sense of proportion, no routine. People starving because nobody had bothered to see the harvest home properly. I changed that. Made them see what's what. Got them working. Sorted things out, d'ye see.'

'And the players are the last things that won't be sorted? You can't organise them, so you won't recognise them?'

'Recognise?' Andwaldo shuffled. 'I'm an old man, you can't expect me to change now . . .'

'Andwaldo, can I tell you something?' They stood over the twitching ashes as the last of the smoke rushed away. 'You've seen one of the plays?'

'The first one, just after I got here. I've no time for that sort of – '

'*Did* you recognise it?'

'Never seen it before.'

'Well, no, no, of course not; but the story. It's the story of Gomath, isn't it?' The old man was bewildered. 'You remember. The castle, that's Thryn; the king is Gomath and his friend's the Cirnex. The King of the Demons is Jeswed: they call him something that sounds like that. He kills the Cirnex, but the Outwall magicians revive him. Then they go to the mountain, that's – ' he pointed, ' – Hisper Einou, the one you call Bilovan, and the castle on top must be Taleg Tivoriun.'

'I don't – '

'Taleg Tivoriun, the Citadel of the Departure? And then it all gets muddled in the middle, when they put on their circus, and when we get back to the story again, it's the return: the Cirnex leads Gomath down the mountain and they come back to perfect Thryn and establish Taleg Ibnun.'

'All such a long time ago,' Andwaldo was muttering. 'Don't remember the details . . . never paid much attention to the – '

'We thought perhaps you did remember,' Dubilier said, being brutal. 'Better than you'd have liked. We thought that might be why you never go to the plays, because they really are about Gomath, and that reminds you of everything you left behind. " . . . *none should pass in or out. They perceived in themselves the seeds and blossoms of perfection in all things that men should be and do, and they said, Let us also come to fruit in this perfection free from the taint and corruption of the Outwall.*" Isn't that it?'

Andwaldo was looking towards the mountains. The old expression had come back to his face, the stare of baffled anger. Dubilier saw he had distressed him more than he'd intended. 'I'm sorry, all that's not important. But you must see, that if the play really is about Gomath, then that's some kind of confirmation, for us, Lupio and me, I mean. I didn't mean to – well, what I mean is, anything you can tell us about it might help.'

Andwaldo's eyes had dropped again, as if wearied by peering back through so much time. 'You won't be staying on here after all, will you?'

'I never meant to.'

'No more did I.'

Dubilier hurried to repair the damage. 'You get the best of it, anyway. What you have here is far more valuable than whatever might or might not be up there. You ask Lupio what he thinks! Taleg Tivoriun may not even exist. Gomath – '

'I don't know anything about Gomath.'

Andwaldo looked miserable. Again Dubilier saw the image of a defeated old lion. It was a shame. The old man couldn't even stir himself to talk about it. Insisting had done no good at all.

'I am sorry. We really have caused you quite a lot of disturbance, haven't we?'

For some reason that seemed to surprise him. 'Disturbance?' he replied. 'No, no. You fit right in. You've done all right.'

Dubilier smiled, relieved. 'Even though we talk about Thryn all the time?'

A spasm of annoyance shook the old man's features. 'All that's not important – Thryn and all that. I don't mind Thryn.' He lapsed again.

Dubilier didn't understand. 'Then why does the mountain haunt you?' he asked gently.

Andwaldo's voice was choked, as if he was saying something forbidden to him. 'Ylma,' he said.

Dubilier didn't know what to say.

Andwaldo poked the fire. 'It's all very well for them,' he said. 'Come here strutting about with their toys and their hobby-horses and their fine words. It's a mockery, that's what it is. It's not like that. It's not fighting dragons,' he said, with scorn. 'Demons. What do they know about demons?'

Dubilier made a gesture to hold out a hand to him, but drew it back again and walked away. The old man stayed vividly with him, wretchedly tending his embers, the mountains above him clear in the cold noon. Dubilier had quickened his own resolve, at the cost of Andwaldo's peace.

He was in a confusion of urgency and remorse when Lupio hailed him. 'Come and gather your things. Oulhie's going to drive us. If we leave now we should catch them.'

'The players?'

'They're heading south-east. She thinks they might be going all the way there.'

'Will they take us with them?'

'Well, we know now there must be Thrynians among them – or someone who knows something, at any rate – but come on, we're not going to sit here speculating about them!'

They came upon the caravan in the early afternoon. The horses were grazing in a small valley, the wagons drawn into a rough circle once more. No activity was visible. Lupio and Dubilier climbed down and thanked their driver.

'There's no need. You had poor fare from us.'

'You gave us everything we need. We have nothing to give you in return.'

'You have given my husband pleasure. He loves to remember Thryn. You have given him memories.'
'Too many memories,' said Dubilier; but Oulhie didn't seem to understand, so he let it go. She wished them luck and turned the buggy around. When she was out of sight they shouldered their gear and hurried down to the circus. There was nobody to be seen.
'Which one?'
'Let's see if we can find the man who played the king.'
The first van was empty. Masks and costumes hung on the walls. Lupio reached one down. 'This was one of them. The loyal captain?' He held the mask to his face.
'Mm.'
Lupio followed him to the next. Two men were in the bunk. One of them, his white face still streaked with whiter make-up, sat up and said, 'Bertollo, save me! The barbarians are attacking!' There was no response from the other.
'You were the juggler,' said Lupio.
'Take what you want, it'll do you no good! The sanctity of true art will turn to spindrift in the hands of ignorant plunderers, temple-pillagers, reavers, rapers . . . '
'We haven't come to rob you, we've come to ask your help.'
'That's it: the struggling visionary compelled to serve a brutal and brainless master. What do you know about the spiritual world?'
'How did you do that one with the three balls on fire?'
'You wouldn't even understand.'
'We're players too, you know.'
He folded his arms disdainfully. 'Show.'
Lupio put on a mask and mimed, posed, leapt up, whirled about and posed again.
'Rubbish. What's your play?'
'It's about two men trying to get to a mountain.'
'Oh, *that* old thing. I know it, I've performed it, oh, all these years, my talent, what a *waste*!'
'That's why we thought you could help us. You know all about it, don't you?'
'Why should I tell you?'
'We're from Thryn. You know where that is, don't you? We know what your play derives from. We're looking for Taleg

Tivoriun, up in the mountains. That's all there, in your play: Gomath and Jeswed and everything. You must know. You can help us get there.'

Ezra looked from one to the other. 'Oh well,' he said ungraciously, 'if that's all. I thought you'd come to rape and ravish.' He sounded offended.

Dubilier stepped forward. 'Then you do know what we're talking about.'

'Not a word of it, my travel-tarnished heroes. Total gibberish. But then – ' he smiled archly, ' – we're used to that in our line; aren't we, Bertollo?' Without looking he jabbed his companion with an unkind finger. Bertollo woke and grunted angrily. 'Bertollo, flame of my passion, sit up and make yourself look respectable. We've got visitors. I thought they were brigands and iconoclasts, but they've only come to ask the way.'

Bertollo lifted his head an inch, stared at them without deference, and lay down again. 'Whadda they wan?'

'They want to get to the mountains.'

'Thass where we're going. Whassa probl'm? Wan' go back to sleep,' and he did.

'Well, gentlemen, there you are: the adjudication of our company's most astute young intellect. Now Ezra Dmdnny Dmdnny, sorcerer and artificer supreme, condemned by cruel gods to starve and scrape through life as a vagabond clown, must likewise turn aside and rest awhile from his tedious exertions. You'll have to ask Gaspau, you know,' he added suddenly.

'Gaspau?'

Ezra Dmdnny Dmdnny crooked his index fingers and held them to his forehead.

'The fire-dancer?'

He nodded. 'The Buck. The Chief.'

'Where do we find him?'

'Ooh, you mustn't wake him, dear, nc. Puts him in a huff. Like us. Goodnight.' He lay down abruptly, faking a ridiculous snore.

They went outside. 'I can't believe they know nothing about Thryn. The story – '

'Coincidence,' said Lupio. 'In any case, they're going our way.'

'Coincidence? It's so close to the scriptures.'
'So was I.'

'Yes, we're going to Pepache-ti-Bilovan,' said Gaspau the Buck. They were speaking a tentative Evpa Hsuan, which was the only language they shared with him, though other members of his troupe spoke languages as close to Thrynian as Grachish had proved to be. They were as various in race and tongue as in their antic and dramatic skills, but the Thrynians had found no one who knew of their city or of any traditional or religious significance in the play. It was late evening, time for the wagons to move off. According to the season, the players maintained this largely nocturnal routine: rest by day, travelling or performing by night.

'Will you take us there?'

'Yes. You will have to work.'

'Whatever we can.'

'Why do you want to go?'

Gaspau's wife Neione took the reins and led off. The rest of them followed on in no fixed order, bumping along the scanty tracks. A night-bird began to cry. The moon slipped through a crack in the clouds; then it was gone. Creatures of the stone ground bristled and clicked: bats skittering from the caves, scorpions and small shiny lizards from under rocks. Lanterns were lit in the wagons, glowing through hessian and canvas, sparkling through chinks in woodwork. Dubilier, telling the whole story slowly and carefully, paused while Gaspau went forward to light the driving lamps. A skinny animal with saucer eyes and foxy ears had been running along since the train left the valley. Now a girl called it from the back of her wagon and it leapt in at once. Gaspau unrolled a cracked scroll of vellum, the last relic of an ancient abstract of the play; but the play itself was older than that, he said, and players had been performing it before that writing was invented. They studied it together. Some of the parts Gaspau interpreted excited Dubilier especially. Invisible great hills slid by; then they were climbing one, and Neione had to drag to check the horses from cantering down the other side. An hour passed. The jolting of the wagon had begun to seem less uncomfortable. Down the line someone was singing in a drunken voice. Gaspau frowned but did not interrupt what Dubilier was saying. Lupio got up and relieved Neione so that they could finish their discussion. After a while she came back out.

'My husband would like to talk to you.'

He gave up the reins again with a sympathetic smile and ducked inside. Gaspau was taking a pan from the stove. He poured out a drink for each of them, black, hot and thick. It was bitter, but spiced, and invigorating.

'I don't understand,' he said. 'I don't know how we can be playing about a missing god; I don't know how a god can be missing. I don't know how these things could be and we don't know them. I don't know what you'll find on Bilovan. But we'll take you there.'

'Thank you,' said Lupio. 'Very much.'

'You are lucky you met us. Perhaps that is done by these gods, hm?'

'Perhaps it is,' said Dubilier. He began to talk about Gomath, and the legends. Lupio sat back. The after-effect of the play had had a strong effect on Dubilier's faith: he was practically preaching to them. It disturbed Lupio. He had to restrain himself from making sarcastic comments. What Dubilier was explaining accounted for his own motives, perhaps, but they were not Lupio's. Lupio did not want to be associated with them.

Dubilier looked across at him. 'Why don't you go and take over from Neione?' he asked in Thrynian. Dubilier knew.

Out in the open, the reins in his hands, Lupio felt more at ease. He could hear the murmur of his friend's voice, but he ignored it. He took a swig from his mug and settled down, hunched forward on the seat, staring intently into the dancing flood of the lanterns and beyond, into the darkness of the unknown country. The sound of Dubilier's explanations was lost under the beating hooves and rattling wheels. Lupio began to whistle. He was travelling.

When Dubilier had talked himself to silence, Neione leaned over and took his hand. 'You're tired,' she said. 'It is not a surprise! You should stay with us. You could join the troupe, help with the scenery, act in the play. Then you could go to a mountain and back every week!'

'No,' he said gently, disengaging his hand. 'I couldn't. You drive your wagons from here to there, day to day, night to night. Your dreams are small enough for you to put them in your pocket and carry them along. Hope for you means to do a good performance; success and reward are a good meal and a good sleep. I respect that, but it's not for me. I wish it could be. I can't drive on like you; I'm driven. My dream is a big one. It's far ahead, calling me; and at the same time it's behind me, pushing me forward!' He mimed a comic display and they smiled politely. 'I can't be satisfied with small dreams,' he said. 'Once you've looked up from the road and seen that big dream, like sun shining on the mountains early in the morning, you just can't rest, tonight or any night, whether you believe it or not.' He paused. They did not speak. 'We met a man who tried to stop,' Dubilier went on. 'A lot of the time he manages to keep his eyes on the ground. Day by day, he's very successful. But he'll never be at peace. He can't let go and dance and sing like you. Every time he looks up, there are tears in his eyes.

'But how can Gaspau the Buck understand that? I'm sorry, I'm talking too much. Your great blessing is not to have to think about it all. Your joy is that you can perform the play, which no one who understands it can ever do.'

Gaspau and Neione talked for a few moments in another tongue. Then Gaspau said, 'Dubilier, we have a word: it is *enethricca*. It means, doing without knowing, following what you can't see. Usually it is a bad one. Now I think it is a good one. We don't know what it is, this dream, but we can help you to it. We are due in Hoag Ciane the night after tomorrow night. They've waited seven years, they can wait a few days more. We go straight to Pepache, and don't stop. Two days, three, you'll be on Bilovan.'

With no performance to prepare until then, there was little work for the Thrynians to participate in. The caravan crawled onwards, to the annoyance of some of the troupe who resented the break in tradition.

'Well, I don't know about you, boys and girls, but I can remember a time when we were travelling players, spinning magic, mirth and mystery across bleak and stupid lands, bringing heaven down to earth once a week. What an age! Wizards and tambourine men are in disgrace, we're nothing more than a glorified transport service, and not too much of the glory either. Humping passengers! Ragged tramps without – '

'Shut up, Ezra,' said Lupio.

'Without so much as a civil word in their knapsacks for the great Ezra Dmdnny Dmdnny, world-weary mage and sage, dust of the way on his proud brow, scorned and spat upon – '

'Ezra, what I do have in my knapsack, among other things, is a usefully shaped piece of metal we tramps and vagabonds rely on to dispatch annoyances we meet on the road. Would you like to feel it or will you get up front and take your turn at the reins?'

Ezra liked this blond, gaunt young man. 'Come out and keep me company,' he said. 'Tell me how a civilised boy like you comes to be wandering among savages, and Ezra the thunderous will be as quiet as a fish.'

The river was just below once more. They pulled off the road to rest a while. Dubilier, leading a pair of horses back from the water, looked up and saw how the road plunged straight ahead, lancing between the hills as if its builders had merely shouldered them aside in their impatience. Idling now, he was conscious of the enormity of that ancient, forgotten power. Here, where there were no marsh-waters to attack it, their creation endured, a monument to arrogant will. Dubilier could feel some of that now, pick up the spirit that had thrust those ancients across the wilderness. Tomorrow they would reach the road's end, Pepache-ti-Bilovan, the little quarry town at the foot of Hisper Einou. Above, somewhere among the mountains, would be the source of this river.

Lupio and Dubilier trudged up the steep little streets and thought about Thryn. This wasn't like Thryn, whose architecture was bizarre and neurotic, an illegitimate breed of fantastic luxury on fantastic poverty: these houses were low and plain, all grey or whitewashed stone. But it was a town, the only other one they'd found, and the citizens, especially the older ones, watched them go by with curiosity and a polite and respectful air, which reminded them both of being Aiguda, and how much they'd forgotten of urban things.

One of the company, a woman who'd been born there, was helping them around. They bought new boots and a few pieces of clothing, and then started to seek lodgings. The woman made enquiries, hoping to find somewhere for them before it was time for her to go back to the rest, who were camped on a hill just outside the town. As she spoke with one old woman they heard surprise in her voice.

'What was that?'

'She says you should ask hospitality from your own kind.'

'What does that mean? Have they decided they don't like us so hugely after all?'

'Oh, no. She means the people from your city living here now. She told me where.'

It was a modest but noticeably more affluent district, set apart among woods a little uphill, and the house, though unremarkable by Thrynian standards, seemed imposing in its setting. A man in his late fifties greeted them at the door.

'I'm glad to see you,' he said. 'We were hoping you'd find your way out here sooner or later.' He had been generous in adopting the local accent but his Thrynian was still fluent.

'You knew we were here?'

'*You* knew *we* were here.' The smile broadened.

'A lucky accident.'

'Ah, there we had the advantage. We were informed this morning, not long after you arrived.'

'You keep a lively interest in the affairs of the town, then.'

'Oh, no; but when the players arrive for the first time in seven years, and some days early at that, people start to talk: such trivial change is news in Pepache. Early, are they? That's not like them, is it? And what's that you say? Strangers? Travellers? Aha! Where have they come from? From Thryn! Goodness me! Better and better!'

'Are you going to ask our guests in or is it the fashion now to entertain on the doorstep?' It was a woman's voice upstairs. With much suave apology the man led the way. Lupio followed, taking to him immediately. The impersonation of local gossip had been unexpected, exact, and very funny. But Dubilier felt ill at ease. The man was a true Thrynian aristocrat, an ancestral portrait perfectly preserved. Dubilier had forgotten the fine sound and the subtle touch, the precise fingering of the sensitive instrument of social grace. Its tone recalled discomforts and compulsions he'd left behind him as he came; but as he turned the corner of the stair he smiled. It was just another artifice, another pleasant lie.

Lupio was saying, 'We'd noticed the interest the townspeople were taking in us.'

'Traditional, my friend; we're part of their history. They love us.'

Lupio didn't understand. He glanced back at Dubilier who said, piecing thoughts together, 'The road – ?'

'How else could they have transported it?'

'The stone!'

'That's right. You didn't know?' He rapped on the wall above the banister. 'Hundreds of years ago our forefathers lugged this stuff off in tons, to make the Wall. They had to lay the road specially for it. Thrynian wealth built the industrious little community Pepache is today.' They entered a reception room. The woman stood up.

'I thought you were never coming,' she chided him. 'Introduce me.'

'I'm sorry,' he said to them. 'A chap gets rusty living so far from civilisation – you are – ?'

'Lupio.'

'Dubilier.'

'Aigu Lupio; Aigu Dubilier.' He saluted them. 'My name is – '

But Dubilier had interrupted smoothly, reciprocating the bow. 'Aigu Uthien; Aigui Ylma.' He was amused to enter the game by scoring this point.

The woman turned to the man, eyebrows raised in perfectly controlled surprise. 'They know all about us.'

'I assume – the townspeople – ' He looked to Dubilier for verification.

'Actually, no. We met Andwaldo.'

That startled them. 'But he's dead!' The clasped one another's hands, as if unconsciously afraid they were about to be separated. 'You've seen him?'

'He lives in a little farming community called Evpa Hsu. We've just come from there. In fact there wouldn't be a community at all if it weren't for him, so it seems the Thrynian spirit of colonisation survives.'

'But how marvellous!'

They stayed and were entertained. The play was not until the following night, so civilities continued through the evening. Dubilier's sense of detachment increased; it seemed strange, after struggling so long towards an ill-focused dream that beckoned from the remotest horizon of awareness, to sit and sip old wine in a town where the dream was a mere natural feature, underfoot as well as overhead, its substance prosaically chipped away to provide a livelihood. They mentioned it, the goal of his quest, with perfect urbanity; allusions to gods and citadels would provoke a smile of sophisticated indulgence. Lupio and Dubilier became, in the eyes of Ylma and Uthien, two respectable but eccentric archaeologists. There was a sort of path leading a long way up, it seemed. Nobody much went above the first slopes; no, they themselves had to confess they'd never even ventured that far. This was quite high enough, said Uthien, and named a figure. Well, the view, yes, that must be quite something; but then we're not so badly off here, are we, Uthien? Here, take a look from this window.

'It's difficult to remember,' Lupio commented as they were going to bed, 'that these are actually the people who went through all the things Andwaldo used to talk about.' A thought occurred to him. 'Were they Aiguda, in fact?'

'I don't think so. But they certainly are now.'

'I wonder if *they'll* see the play tomorrow.

'I hope we'll be away by then.'

'Don't you like them?'

'Yes. I admire them; I admire their poise. You're right, they never once mentioned it, any of it: being refugees, hard labour, rape, murder. They seem to have written it out of their past altogether.'

'Well, they couldn't know how much Andwaldo told us.'

'And we couldn't mention it.'

'Not done.'

'Quite.'

They laughed. A strange, boyish excitement was creeping over them.

Lupio yawned, relishing the warmth of thick bedclothes. 'It's nice to be élite again.'

They both laughed again. Dubilier understood perfectly. Lupio believed in nothing, took everything for what it had to give him, quickly growing tired, so that he sometimes seemed to embrace what he hated. But Dubilier found a true nobility in Uthien and Ylma's arrogant pretence. Thryn decayed, the players mocked and parodied, but still they held up their image – here, in the very lap of disillusionment. Lupio reckoned he had no illusions; privately Dubilier wondered. In the high chamber of the Iigril, a long time ago, in an atmosphere hysterical with the rhetoric of undischarged emotion, they had chosen the disillusionment and condemned themselves to the truth: knowledge, not belief. Somewhere overhead it was waiting, the answer, on bare rock, and soon they would confront it. Then there would be no more choosing.

As if carried by their own momentum, the ancient Thrynians had ploughed their road through Pepache and a couple of miles beyond. Awesome tools had disposed of solid rock. The last of the grass was far behind; only moss grew here, and that had not completely covered the striations marked up the walls of this cutting. Each layer sandwiched a thousand, two thousand years? Their ancestors had sliced twelve million years into the past to make a way for themselves and their wagons. Above were the oldest workings, a pit now filled with water. As they approached the sun turned it to a mirror, white and blinding. Further round the road finally gave out and a track took over, not direct and imposing like the road, but compliant with the tumbling contours. It took them up over a ridge, clear of the marks and relics of quarrymen, past the last heaped earthworks; then they could see.

The world was below them. It occurred, belatedly, to Dubilier that in fact they had been climbing the mountain ever since the day they had had to abandon the boat, for they had reached quite an altitude already. He at last managed to shake his lowlands assumption that mountains would be exactly as he imagined them: separate cones sticking up independently from a common base, like a shelf of hats. On the contrary, from up here the distinction of one mountain from another seemed largely academic; to climb one was actually a question of making always for higher ground until it was impossible to go further. The rising sun enhanced this new impression by gliding and burnishing every available face of rock and twisting the high clouds all around into spectacular aureoles until splendour concealed all the particularities of the scene. The path curved and the ground dropped away on their right. Below them the river churned sunlight. Lupio ran ahead and posed on the edge, head back, arms akimbo, saluting the view. He was climbing erratically, sprinting, stopping, darting off the track and back again – wasting energy, Dubilier realised, but enjoying everything with a gladness he hardly felt himself.

('Dubilier! Dubilier! Are you awake?'

'Not quite.'

'Then you shouldn't have answered. Let's go.'

Creeping out of the house before Ylma and Uthien rose, more like truant boyservants than pilgrims of destiny.)

Dubilier followed slowly. He had slept badly and resented the dullness it had left in him. He felt unprepared and, compared with Lupio, unresponsive. He reached the spot and stood at his side. 'Where do you get all this energy?'

'From the sun!'

Dubilier squinted against the glare and then turned round. Pepache and the field where the players were starting to build their stage were out of sight. He thought that there it might not be dawn yet, under the almighty shadow. 'You'll be exhausted by evening.'

'So will he.'

In Thryn it was the legend that the source of the river was up on Hisper Einou, but now Lupio, ahead as usual, saw it was also true. He shouted through cupped hands.

'Come and look at this.'

They stood on a ledge and looked up at the fall. Dubilier realised it was what they'd been hearing for hours, a continuous boom that now drowned out the thrashing of the river miles below. It was immense, a sheer column hanging free in space, enveloped in the mists of its own spray. High above the sun glinted on a silver thread that thickened as it careered down the rock face, rebounding from shelf after shelf, gathering strength for the last leap. Below lay a boiling white confusion lanced with fractured rainbows, the haze in which the cataract perpetually destroyed itself. It hurtled from the crag to smash on the rocks below; and out of that destruction it was reborn as the river, a wild laughing thing here which would grow calm and pensive when it crossed a deserted prairie, and then dark and dumb in a forest where it would settle as a pair of lakes. Later it would creep stinking and muttering beneath an ancient city, soured by drains, the tributaries of ten thousand households. Shattered and reborn, at every turning; each league sloughing an old skin, becoming a new serpent, and yet it was also all of them at once. All the snakes were one snake, all the rivers one river, and it began up there.

If Lupio were shouting, Dubilier couldn't hear him. The hiss of it was deafening. It hung, writhing, out in space, so startling and immediate, as if he could reach over and touch it. And the drop looked so deep. He closed his eyes against the temptation of its vertigo. The great hiss surrounded him, filled him, seeking out his heart and silencing it. It became absolute and entire. He let it overwhelm him. What did it mean? That the next step forward was oblivion. He swayed. He felt himself fall. It seemed he was falling for ages, turning and returning like the water.

Lupio shouted his name though there was nobody to hear it.

Dubilier woke. He was lying awkwardly on hard ground. When he opened his eyes he still couldn't see anything. Perhaps he was blind. He couldn't hear anything either; but he could move. He wriggled backwards a little, feeling to either side with his hands. Nothing but rock. There was a musty, nostalgic smell in his nostrils, like stale woodsmoke.

He called out. 'Lupio!' He heard that. The echoes batted it around and made nonsense of it. He waited, lying in the dust. Nothing.

Then he remembered the fit on the cliff. He was dead.

Lupio was gazing at the waterfall in pure admiration. The noise was exhilarating. This was something to see: it would go on forever, though, simply falling, careless of whether anybody were there to see. It really was magnificent. No wonder the ancients had put their gods here.

'Superb!' he yelled, enjoying pitting his voice against something so entirely overwhelming. 'Dubilier! Isn't it superb?' But his friend was behaving very oddly, swaying about on the edge like a drunkard. Lupio started towards him as he collapsed. 'Dubilier!'

He dragged him away from the edge, knelt and supported him with an arm round his shoulders. His head lolled; he seemed completely insensible. Lupio put an ear to his chest but he couldn't hear the heartbeat for the noise of the water. He thought he seemed to be still breathing. After agonised minutes of unskilful fumbling he found a pulse. Dubilier was alive. He had to go and get help. He tried to sit the body against the rock wall, but it slid into a heap. He'd definitely have to move him to safety, or he'd probably roll over the edge by the time he got back. He took off Dubilier's pack and his own and put them to one side; then he hoisted Dubilier onto his back and carried him on up the path. A few yards ahead he reached a spot where it twisted away from the falls and followed a gap in the rock. The high walls kept out most of the noise: that was a relief. Lupio set the body down and searched until he found a hole that seemed to open into a cave. He left Dubilier just inside while he ran back for the packs; then he scrambled to a ledge where a sparse clump of thorn was clinging and broke off an armful of dead wood. In the darkness he scooped it into a pile and set spark to it. It flared high and bright. The cave looked larger than he'd expected. He hoped it wasn't the lair of anything savage. While the light lasted he tried to rouse his friend, calling him and rubbing his face. There was no response, but he was breathing soundly. That meant there was nothing for it but to leave him while he went for help. He fled heedlessly down the path, and reached the highest of the quarries just as work was packing up. His acquaintance with their language was minimal, but his distress was far more eloquent, and some of them seemed to remember noticing him go up that morning. Eventually one who appeared to be a kind of foreman, stolidly refusing to accompany Lupio himself, took him to a long low hut where several mules were stabled and untethered one for him, then stood and watched suspiciously as he mounted and rode back up the slope.

The creature knew the path and climbed quickly, but it was dark before they reached the cave, and if it hadn't been a clear and starry night, Lupio would have had difficulty locating it. The ashes were quite cold, but there were some branches that hadn't caught, so he gathered a torch of them and lit it. Dubilier had moved from where he'd put him, but he was unconscious again. There was nothing Lupio could do for him. He had to be taken down to Pepache, immediately. Ylma and Uthien would help; he could recover and go hunting gods another day. The Cirnex had waited a few centuries for someone to visit him, so another fortnight shouldn't put him out unduly. Lupio shivered, reshaping his fear and fatigue into anger and directing them at the mountain's improbable guardian. He tried to picture him, sitting up there, and when that failed, tried to imagine what it was they were actually supposed to be going to find. It resisted him. He didn't know what Dubilier was expecting, but he'd be lucky if there were even a couple of bones, or a shrine of some kind: a rudimentary cairn, or a small scorched hearthstone. Probably there would be nothing, a bare peak where even the eagles never came. But even that he couldn't picture. He stepped outside and walked a few yards down the path. It seemed impossibly dangerous in the dark. He went back and managed to lift Dubilier and prop him across the back of the mule, where he swayed alarmingly. The mule seemed to sense the dubiety of the venture and grew restless. After working since first light the extra trek up to the cave was all it was going to put up with. Then Lupio's exhaustion rushed him like a sea. He tugged at the bridle and moaned for a while before giving in. Dubilier still showed no sign of coming to as he dragged him into a corner and arranged his cloak around him. The mule pawed and scuffled in a vain search for food and then went to sleep.

Lupio was hurrying all over the city. It was late evening and he had to leave in the morning on a very important journey. He was feeling hot and irritated because there was someone he couldn't find, someone he had to see first and persuade to go with him. To begin with it was Dubilier, but when he realised he could expect to find him at the temple it became Kavi that he was looking for. When he got to the top of the hill the temple wasn't there, but it didn't seem to matter; it was a beautiful day, and there was Kavi sitting on the grass. Hifran was there too. He was trying to say something to her, or to both of them, but Lupio had to get his message in first. It was overwhelmingly important, and, he thought, very funny as well. I've come to tell you, he heard himself say, as Hifran stood by opening and shutting his mouth without making a sound, I've come to tell you, I've come to tell you, I've come to tell you, I've come to tell you. He danced slowly around the Previs, who wasn't moving.

When he woke he had cramp in his neck from sleeping on the stone floor. Everything was very still. It took him several minutes to realise that both Dubilier and the mule had gone.

Dubilier didn't notice the mule straight away. Returned suddenly to full awareness, he felt thoroughly rested. He got slowly to his feet and then the creature snorted, stirring in its sleep. Dubilier went over to discover what it was. He reflected distantly on his own sudden fearlessness, stroking a large unidentified animal in the dark. Either it was a dream, or else one or each of them really was a ghost. Death seemed to be nothing like his apprehensions or those of his religious educators. The mule woke and nuzzled his hand. Dubilier was hungry. He thought the mule might be too. In his pack was some of the hard travellers' biscuit. He broke off a piece for each of them. They seemed to be in a cave of some kind. It was night. All this accounted for those strange sensory deprivations he'd experienced earlier. He took a look outside, wondering where the waterfall was and whether he'd really fallen into it. Perhaps the reincarnation heresy was true and he'd been remade when he hit the bottom and put back on the mountainside with a second chance. He heard a noise behind him. The mule had pursued him to the end of its tether. Dubilier freed it. Perhaps the mule was Lupio, reincarnated at the same time: my faithful captain, he thought. At any rate, the beast seemed to want to go down, but reluctantly followed the man with the food. Later, when Dubilier hesitated, unsure of the trail in the dark, it pushed on ahead of him. Dubilier was glad of a companion who knew the way. It became steeper and the mule was leaving him behind; at the next opportunity he spoke softly to it and climbed onto its back. They rode on. The stars clouded over. He couldn't see a thing. Was that rain? Large drops began to fall, more rapidly. Dubilier tried to tent his cloak into a cover for both their heads. It was not very effective. The rushing of the river was inaudible in the downpour of rain. There was a flicker of lightning, but no thunder. In the moment of blinding green glare the mule faltered and trembled. Dubilier, who'd been talking to it for half an hour, began to murmur more soothing nonsense into its ear, urging it onward and upward. 'We'll find shelter.'

The next flashes revealed nothing, but after that Dubilier saw that they had emerged from the tumble of crags and boulders and were walking up a bare ledge again. There was sky on all sides, above and below. The lightning seemed to leap up at them, startling the mule and searing their eyes. As Dubilier lurched forward and threw his arms around its neck, he glimpsed a dark shape like a recess in the rock just above them. 'There it is!' he shouted, though he had no idea what. They managed to negotiate it in the blackness, passing through a curtain of streaming water. It was another cave. Thunder boomed. Lightning cracked a great void, showing huddled, floating forms, giant rocks or clouds. Dead or not, they were both very wet. Dubilier wished he had something to dry his companion with. He slid, almost fell from its back. 'Not far now, I expect,' he said, patting it vigorously. 'We'll rest and go on tomorrow. Or you can stay here if you'd rather.'

Flash. The ledge outside looked quite regular. There seemed to be a parapet of some sort around it. Dubilier hugged himself, his knees drawn up to his chin, his cloak wrapped tightly around him. Crash. The thunder was getting nearer. Each peal bounced tirelessly from mountain top to mountain top, vaulting the far valleys, as if it would never fade away. This floor was uncommonly smooth. Dubilier ran his hands over it. Could it be man-made, a shelter for stranded climbers? Flash. He turned round just in time to see that the rock had indeed been worked: a livid after-image showed him the shape of a doorway. He felt his way across to it and nearly broke his neck: the arch was the top of a flight of steps. Still feeling somehow remote from everything, untouched by the danger and the darkness, he stole down them. They turned a corner. He heard the thunder, and the mule snuffling as though to call him back. Not yet. He could see the next steps, as pale golden bars cut horizontally into the gloom. There was a light down there. It was shifting about, rising and falling. Firelight. Dubilier had read of fire-mountains, in legends of other lands. Their throats belched flame, rising from oceans of fire hot enough to melt rock. He should be afraid now and climb out again. He got to the bottom of the stairs and felt the heat embrace him. It was an iron brazier of coals, glowing in the middle of a small stone hall.

He hesitated.

'Come and dry yourself at the fire,' she suggested, stepping into its light.

Dubilier gazed at her. Her mantle was the colours of pigeons' feathers. Her face was still shadowed.

'Who's there?'

'A friend.' She sounded amused.

He walked over to the brazier, holding out his hands in a mechanical salutation to its warmth, all the time looking at her.

'Do I know you?'

'Do you?'

Challenged, he went up to her and pushed the cowl back from her face.

'No.'

Her hair was chestnut brown, plaited and coiled, secured by a leather keeper and a plain bone pin. Like a child, he touched her.

'You're really there.' He was visibly relieved.

'What did you expect?'

'I thought I might be dreaming.'

'You might. How do you know you aren't?'

'You certainly look as if you might be out of one of my dreams.'

'There you are, then,' she said, with a certain satisfaction. 'You *are* dreaming. You're also making me wet. Why don't you take your cloak off and put it by the fire?'

Fumbling, Dubilier complied. 'You speak my language.'

'Or, to put it another way,' she said, pretending to be pedantic, '*you* speak *mine*. Do you want some wine?'

'Please.'

She fetched two beakers and gave him one. 'I've been waiting for you,' she said.

'I haven't the faintest idea what's happening,' Dubilier told her.

'No,' she said. Her eyes were brown and full of glee. 'That's nothing new. Drink up. We're going to have a look at the beacon.'

A beacon? They'd never seen a beacon on their travels. Nobody in the valley had mentioned a beacon.

She took a brand from the fire and went past him to the foot of the stairs. Its light bloomed and curled around her. Dubilier put down his cup and hurried after. By the time he reached the top she was already stepping out into the rain. Her torch hissed, but it didn't go out. The mule was nowhere in sight. He followed her on up the path. He had left his cloak inside and was drenched at once. The rain was heavy, the rock slick underfoot.

'Where are we going?' he yelled.

'This is it.'

The path curved to the left, climbing steeply, bringing them out on the roof of the rock shelter. There was a second brazier, with wood and coal already laid, and nothing else. Dubilier looked around. This must be the top of the mountain, he realised. All around them was empty darkness and the ceaseless falling rain.

'It's time to light the fire,' she said.

'But it's raining! It'll be no good!' The rain ran down his face and into his mouth.

Her torch was still flaming. 'It's all right,' she insisted. 'Come here. Come and stand where I'm standing.'

It was like walking up a river. There was, in fact, a little rivulet springing up out of the dead rock just by the foot of the fire. It ran between them and away down the mountainside. That must be the source of the river, Dubilier thought. That's impossible too. The thought gave him confidence. It was a dream. He was dying, and this was his dream while he died. The river had been with him and Lupio since they set out, always somewhere nearby; and now here was the river's beginning, as if he had unwound everything, undone the past, unmade his life and come back to the point where it all began.

Of course they couldn't light the fire. It was all over. He stepped lightly across the water and took her hand.

'Here.' She had split her brand into two tapers. She handed him one. 'Take it.'

Together they touched them to the sodden fuel. Nothing happened.

'It won't work,' Dubilier said. He turned to her to explain and looked into her eyes.

The whole dream, everything he had wound and unwound, was in her eyes. She was smiling. She saw all he had unmade and undone, and it didn't matter. She knew who he was.

'Once again.'

They touched the wet wood and the fire burst out of it, leaping up into the sky.

They clutched each other and shrank from the blast of heat, laughing as they stumbled backwards. Dubilier's heart was racing, and the fire was throbbing too as it flamed against the rain. There was also a deeper pulse somewhere, like a drum reverberating in the valley. She turned in his arm and pointed down into the abyss.

'Look,' she said. She put back her hood and unpinned her hair.

They stood and gazed into the darkness, feeling the heat of the blaze at their backs. Something was beginning. On other peaks there were fires springing up in reply, like candles flickering in the rain. There was fire on the hills, on distant mounds and tumuli; and further off, on the ice crags, and beyond them on hills where it was still spring. Flame by flame it crept around the sky. They could see the clouds and the rain lit up in crimson and silver and gold. People were laughing, because the beacons were alight and the rain could not put them out. Dubilier was straining to hear. It sounded like music. Something picked up the drumbeat. The fire was spreading too, passed from hand to hand. People clustered to take it along. Torch lit torch all the way down the mountain-sides to the thousands swarming in the valleys. Multitudes came and went, climbing and descending in shadowed files to carry the impossible light. They were singing. Dubilier knew there must be many different languages with many different songs in each, and many different voices singing each song; but he couldn't hear any of the words, and they all blurred into one song, a chant to the rhythm of the heartbeat and the drum. He and she were holding each other close, bound together by the fire and the rain on their skin. Dubilier felt there was fire inside him too. They watched as the light went away in an endless procession into the world, chains of fire turning in the night. There were scrabbling noises on the path below.

'Right,' she said, disengaging herself. She kissed him. 'Back you go.'

The rain was slackening, becoming fine, like mist, and it mingled with the smoke from the fire. As she turned from him he saw her robe wasn't grey at all, but the colours of flame, as if he could see the fire through her body.

'Wait.' He clutched at her and missed.

'What's the matter?'

'I don't even know who you are.' The footsteps drew nearer, and Dubilier knew he must find out at once, before they were intruded upon. 'You seem to know me. Who are you?'

'You came all this way to see me, and you don't know who I am?' She didn't seem surprised. She was doing something at the fire.

'Dubilier!'

'You'll need this.' She held out a taper, like the ones they had used to light the beacon. As he reached for it he tried to grab her arm, but she wasn't there, and he overbalanced and fell down. She was laughing at him, but not unkindly. 'Not me,' she said. 'You'll learn. One day.' And then she was gone.

'Dubilier – '

He was lying on the wet rock. Someone was leaning over him: Lupio, with his hands cupped around his spark-box to shelter it from the wet. So he'd received some of the light too. Dubilier sat up painfully. It was bitterly cold. The beacon had disappeared and it was dark all around, but he thought by now it really ought to be dawn, so he said, 'Good morning.'

Lupio looked distraught. 'What are you doing? How did you get up here? I've been searching for hours.' He helped the shivering man to stand and led him back down to the shelter, where the mule was tethered.

Dubilier gestured weakly. 'Taleg Tivoriun.'

'For goodness' sake. It's just a cave. There's nothing here.' Lupio lowered him to the ground in the corner, holding the flame high to look around. Somebody might have chiselled this out of the rock once, a long time ago, but it was just an empty cave now. He wouldn't have lasted long up here, whoever he was. Some hermit, probably.

Dubilier was trying to speak to him. 'Lupio, we – '

'It's all right. You can rest now. We'll soon have you down.'

He sat beside Dubilier and tucked blankets round them both. 'I caught your friend wandering down alone,' he told him, nodding to the mule. 'I didn't know where you were. I thought you'd gone over the edge! You'll be all right now. It'll be light in a little while.'

'She gave me light.'

'Shh . . . '

'I dropped it.' He laughed weakly. 'But it's all right – the light's inside.'

'Have you been dreaming again?' This creepy place was enough to give anybody hallucinations.

'The Cirnex – '

'Forget it!' Lupio's voice sounded harsh in the stillness. 'There's nothing up here. You can see for yourself. There's nobody here. But it's all right. It doesn't matter.'

'No, no – I must tell you.' Dubilier was agitated. Lupio let him speak. 'The Cirnex: she's a woman.' Lupio looked uncomprehending and Dubilier laughed again. 'It's not you after all.'

It was taking Dubilier a long time to recover from his collapse on the ledge by the waterfall. Whatever delirium it was that had driven him up the bare mountain in the middle of that ferocious storm, its delusions still possessed him. Lupio had tried to keep him quiet on the way back to Pepache, but instead of resting he'd gone down prattling and singing, laughing at incomprehensible jokes, giddy with fatigue. When they returned the mule to the quarry he had embarrassed Lupio by spending more time thanking the animal than its master; and at Ylma and Uthien's he'd been worse. He went on and on about the Cirnex and divine light, as if his mind had refused to accept that his pilgrimage had been a complete waste of time and was frenziedly spinning fantasies to distract itself from the truth. All their hosts wanted was to hear about the climb, the scenery, and the view from the top, and then to commiserate about the dreadful weather: the worst storm any of them could remember. Rivers were in full spate; bridges had been washed away. The whole thing had been more than enough for Lupio, but Dubilier had scarcely noticed. Gomath only knew what *he'd* seen. Lupio couldn't control him, and it was obvious that his continual excursions into spiritual fantasy made Uthien and Ylma uncomfortable. It was sheer bad manners. Lupio had drawn Dubilier aside. 'Can't you see you're annoying them?'

'No, no, they're annoying themselves, you see. They don't want to know what we saw. They just want to hear what they expected us to see.'

Lupio didn't answer. He knew what he'd seen, at daybreak on Hisper Einou. There beneath them, blurred by drizzle and low cloud, was the whole world – not just the bad lands of the north and west, but the world beyond, over the mountains, where there were fields and woods, and other rivers; and villages, towns, cities, spread about like stars in the sky. There were more there than he'd ever have believed, glistening as their roofs and gutters caught the morning rain. Each of them was alone, so they reached out to each other; he could see that the roads were also awash, flowing like arteries. He had felt their pull. Automatically he pulled in return, tugging at the rein, and half turned in his saddle as if he expected still to be able to see them, spread out for him like a living map: the whole world. The mountains were only the beginning; all the journeys lay beyond.

But Dubilier needed him. Something which had been implicit in their relationship from the beginning had now crystallised out fully. Dubilier needed help because he was wrapped up in the weavings of his own mind. His sufferings had unbalanced him. Perhaps he would recover in time. Probably when they got back to Thryn being on familiar ground would help him. It was like having a little child in tow – vulnerable, easily moved, but full of wonder, and responding with an odd, untouchable logic of his own.

(Late evening. They were sitting after supper in the low room over the barn. Oulhie had hardly touched her food. She sat gazing out of the window. Purple skyline and indigo sky faded into each other. No one had spoken for several minutes. She dropped her head on her arms and started to sob again.

'You shouldn't cry for him,' Dubilier said, 'he's not very far away.'

Lupio stiffened with discomfort. That was a tactless thing to say, hardly likely to do anything but make her more resentful. He wanted to interrupt and override what Dubilier had said, but he'd been feeling uncomfortable with words all day. None of them seemed any use. He gave Dubilier a sharp look instead, but Oulhie was replying already.

'He should have been; far away. He should have gone, like he wanted, to Pepache and the mountain, but I wouldn't let him. I should have let him, let him go when he wanted.'

Involuntarily, as he always seemed to do when he was sitting in this room, Lupio glanced out at the mountain, hating it. Four lives it had spoilt, swinging its arrogant shadow over them – and how many more? He hated the superstitions it had fostered, and the stature with which it upheld them. He would have liked to pluck it out of the dark skyline, rub it out into the night so that it wouldn't be there in the way when the sun rose next morning.

'No,' said Dubilier. 'His body wanted to be here, on the farm, near you. Only his spirit wanted to fly to the mountains.' He looked out of the window too: he seemed to see an entirely different view. 'For the first time now he has both.')

All around Lupio saw only trees and rocks. He put all those other roads out of his mind, because he had to concentrate on this one, the road home. Dubilier was like a child and had to be looked after. Lupio kept an eye on him as he rode through the trees a little way ahead. Well, in two respects he wasn't like a child at all. He never seemed to need to be led, and he asked no questions.

Dubilier's mount stopped and bent to drink from a flood pool. He climbed down and knelt to drink at her side. The mounts were wiry creatures, something like long-legged oxen. From Evpa Hsu Knesh had directed them round another way to avoid having to climb back down into the ravine. It took them via another little farming community, rather more prosperous, where they bred these creatures and others suitable for the steep and crabbed terrain, like goats and llama. The thuum made excellent beasts of burden, and would find their own way home when released, so long as the travellers kept to the banks of this river, their habitual watering-place.

Already they had reached more fertile land. The ground was stony, but it held a good alluvial layer that encouraged trees and lichens, and grass of a spectacular green along the river valley. Everything was still rich and sodden from the storm. Lupio urged his mount down to join Dubilier, who was getting to his feet and greeting him – no, greeting them both – as though they'd been apart for a day at least. As he got back into the saddle he remarked, 'It'll be easier if we turn off soon and skirt round the hill.'

Doubtfully Lupio looked ahead. It seemed probable that before long the river would entrench itself in a steeper gully where they'd have to leave the thuum behind, but they knew that as long as they followed this tributary they couldn't miss rejoining the mainstream somewhere.

'Shouldn't we keep going?'

'It'll be easier and quicker.'

Lupio didn't ask how he knew. Soon there was flatter ground on the left bank. It certainly seemed to offer a pass between the hills.

'This is it.'

As soon as they were unloaded, Lupio's mount turned and trotted off, but Dubilier's seemed to want to stay with them. The last they could see of her between the trees, she was standing on the bank turning unhappily this way and that, as if trying to choose between the humans and the other thuum, who was lowing imperatively at her, sensing something amiss.

Lupio and Dubilier stumbled about on the scree, following the contour to their left while the slopes to the right grew steadily steeper. Lupio was saving his breath for the exertions of the trek, or he'd have begun to complain to Dubilier and challenge his choice of route more forcibly. But before dusk they heard running water. As they headed towards it the hills fell away to either side and they found themselves slithering down a long incline to the bank of a river. It flowed faster and more voluminously than the tributary, but its bed was no less rocky. Lupio gazed upstream to see if he could recognise the place, expecting that they were somewhere at the northern end of the canyon. Precariously he balanced on a high rock. In the distance he spotted something jutting up from behind boulders on the shore. He went towards it. Dubilier heard him shout and he came back running.

'Dubilier! It's the boat!'

Dubilier nodded, unsurprised.

'The floods must have picked it up and swept it here. It's a wonder it's not smashed.' Both the poles and the oars were still there. The dinghy was dry, intact and pointing roughly downstream, as if waiting patiently to be relaunched.

But first they had to get it off the rocks and lug it along the tumbling watercourse, as they had done coming. They had it in clear water within two days; the current and the gradient were with them this way. But there was something else. Waking from a hectic dream the second night, Lupio felt how frightened and suspicious he was becoming, and how little he liked all this responsibility. While he strained and cursed, hampered by loose pebbles and immovable boulders alike, Dubilier worked with a placid goodwill, remaining calm and composed through all the heaving and shoving. It disconcerted Lupio. Plainly they no longer saw even the rocks in the same light, as though they were living on different planes. If Dubilier wasn't going to come down from his wretched mountain, what could he do about it? But if this were madness, it had a very even temper.

The wind dropped as they approached the ruined city, and it started to rain. The cliffs gleamed. The shattered stairways dripped long, slow cascades. The sail hung limp, as if the dinghy wanted to stop there.

'Let's go and have another look round.'

'Wouldn't you rather keep going?'

'No.'

They made fast to a block of stone, part of a toppled balustrade that jutted out of the water. Dubilier leapt nimbly ashore and ran up the slippery, tilting steps. Lupio called after him. 'Let's take some food. We can light another fire up there.'

Grinning as if at some private joke, Dubilier came splashing down again for the food and kitchen equipment. He bounded ahead of Lupio all the way up even though, with his hands full, he had no hope of saving himself if he tripped. Forty feet of wet, broken stone into deep water. Lupio was about to shout out to him to be careful, but he bit his lip and watched his own step. Ever since finding him on top of the mountain he'd been giving Dubilier advice and been ignored or laughed at for his trouble. What Dubilier wanted to do, he did, careless of common sense and his own safety. It was annoying that he so rarely seemed to encounter the setbacks and dangers that Lupio was warning him against. When he did, he negated them by being undismayed. He didn't seem to recognise adversity. Lupio resented that. If the journey had taught him anything, it had only confirmed his previous beliefs. The world was random, senseless, obdurate in its refusal to conform to any ideal. You had to watch out for yourself. He felt protective towards Dubilier. He thought, If it hadn't been for me – but then Dubilier would pluck another fish from the water, or find an unguarded nest of eggs, and it would be apparent that the world was good to Dubilier, however it seemed to him.

Dubilier was far ahead. Lupio reached the safety of the promenade and looked around for him while he got his breath back. The ruins seemed to express what he was feeling: the futility of ambition, the meaninglessness of ideals. He couldn't find Dubilier. He roamed around the cluttered streets. They delighted him in a savage, almost morbid way; he'd been taken with that last time, but not so completely. Failure was chart ed in the fractures of the skyline. The rampant weeds and creepers were the blind fingers of a nature that was brainless and incontrovertible. Last time, without believing in it, he'd at least had the slim purpose of the quest to carry him on. Now that that was all over, evaporated, as he had always expected, into disillusionment and inconclusiveness, he had nothing to do but fall back to earth, like a dart thrown at the sun. They scarcely needed to row any longer; the river was fuller and the current carried them easily down to the city again.

Lupio had lost his old wild fire. There were no more heroes. Life, even life dressed up as heroic endeavour, fails to reproduce the shapeliness of the old tales. Ventures don't end, they trail off or are aborted. The triumphant return is really only a failure to continue. The colourful pretences of the players came back to him. He remembered his own excitement; they had persuaded him to leave Evpa Hsu when he might have stayed, perhaps taken on Andwaldo's job. Or if Dubilier hadn't collapsed, he might have gone on beyond the mountains, essayed some of those further journeys. The roads haunted him. On and on, always going beyond, and never looking for an end. But instead here he was going back, crossing old ground again, renegotiating that same river. Why should he stay with Dubilier? Some part of his heart still clung to principles and ideals, whatever his intellect understood. He was sick of it.

He climbed a dangerous tower, little more than a swaying pile of masonry, and went out onto a crumbling balcony to look for Dubilier again. Up here he was above most of the ruins, every building gaping open to him. They were all empty. Nothing lived in them. From this height he couldn't see the rats and birds and lizards that had been scampering around them before. The rain was falling, indoors and out, as if to make a final demonstration of their inadequacy.

Dubilier had seen a woman dancing in the shadows over a wall. The wall was only half finished, and half of that was sliding into ruin. This was a new temple that they'd been building. He put the baggage down and ran lightly across the treacherous floor, then climbed the tiers to the place, ducking beneath leaning beams and shafts of stone. When he reached it, she was gone, and it was only a filthy rag caught in a crack, fluttering and dangling as the wind came and went. No, he decided, not 'only'. Nothing was 'only'. We limit in order to comprehend and manipulate; but the definitions are arbitrary as fear or desire, a full stomach or a light head, the flickerings of air and fire and water, or the flapping of an old tarpaulin in shadow. So it had been a woman too. He held it out, as if he were holding the woman, to dance with her; but it was a rag now and the woman had gone, whisked away through time. Down those twilit corridors he might have pursued her forever, over the hills and down the streams that flowed from them, always catching at her just to lose her among the trees. She had come and gone, so that her identity was the one certain thing: an abiding uncertainty. She had no face, only a mask, or something he had glimpsed as she turned her head and ran. He might see it here or again everywhere or nowhere, its lines caught for an instant, its subtle geometries echoed in another, a case of mistaken identity. Perhaps all masks approximated it, and every young girl was a bud that would blossom into it once, even if there were no one to see. Perhaps it was something about the eyes, or the shape of the mouth. Was she smiling? Had that been a laugh or a cry she gave as she fled, turning her head from him? He thought it was probably the wind whistling in a deserted gallery, or moaning among the rocks. Not being subject to the frailties of actuality, she was perfectly beautiful as her cowl fell back. To detect her everywhere made life worth living, so that the nightmare of running became the dance itself. He stepped out of the ruined temple and saw Lupio standing on a balcony to watch the weather. He was right, they'd have to find shelter for their cooking fire.

As they drifted on past the old moon-monument, Lupio saw how thick the grass and moss had grown, and with a start, like waking from an unexpected doze, he realised it was spring. Escaped from the long clutch of winter, fertility swaggered and crept over the wild plain in a thousand different shapes and directions. Woods and wild orchards flourished, and grey tracts of thorn trees sprouted little knobs of yellow-green which here and there unfurled into incongruous flowers of white and pink. A herd of deer were running, and they saw them against the horizon intermittently for days. There were butterflies and dragonflies soon, and moths that visited the fire. The boat had to be coaxed along a stretch where reeds were dense, growing in large island clumps. It kept raining. Where there was no shelter to be had they covered the boat at night and lay listening to the rain falling ceaselessly into the river; in the morning the canopy glistened with the silver tracery of snails.

It was easier sharing the dinghy now. Dubilier seemed to be recovering. It was possible to hold a lucid conversation if he could be kept off the cosmic symbols and metaphysical paradoxes, though he still maintained, without ever speaking of it specifically, that something extraordinary had happened to him on top of Hisper Einou. Well, the inner apocalypse of a breakdown would be a dramatic and ghastly experience – one vision which Lupio, when he thought of it at all, was glad not to have shared. He kept both their minds strictly to ropes and poles, dry firewood, meat and vegetables, and the natural commonplaces of the landscape.

Now they were travelling between colonnades of trees whose mournful dripping was belied by the green brilliance of their new leaves. Beyond, the woodland thickened and grew dark. The river flowed deep and slow. Soon they would be able to return the boat to its builders. Small furry creatures made for the banks in a flurry; something snapped among the rushes; a fish rose for a swimming beetle; but birds were rare and a solemn quiet prevailed.

They sailed across the upper lake and hailed a solitary boat. The crew replied in considerable confusion; it was a while before anyone remembered who they were and how they came to have a craft of local design. They made two journeys to carry the boats down to the lower lake, and then one of the women punted the travellers to a small house on the north-east side of the village, set slightly apart. There were a few people there already, cleaning up and arranging furniture; they smiled welcomingly before leaving, and then a woman came in with a meal of fish and fried grain. She stayed to eat with them, and Lupio was surprised how emphatically she and Dubilier greeted each other. Not remembering her at all, he kept studying her covertly, but without success until she had taken the empty dishes away and returned with a wickerwork carrying-cradle and a soundly sleeping child. Knowing she couldn't understand and feeling rather foolish, nevertheless he whispered to Dubilier, 'Isn't she the one we – '

'Yes. I think she's come to help us this time.'

The woman took Dubilier's hand and led him to touch her baby, speaking one or two words carefully and repeating them. Then Lupio came to the cotside. The child dreamed on, unaware that above her head was now being conducted the first in a long-delayed course of language lessons.

Her name was Aldellena, her mother's Piripheis. Her father was unknown: the lake-people did not practise monogamy since the women outnumbered the men by nearly four to one. Men occupied a special place in their society, well looked after and generally not expected to do much that was arduous or dangerous. Though they might work in nurseries, they were rarely present at births, and it was clear that Piripheis considered Dubilier had done her a great honour by going back to her in the forest, especially when the Thrynian explained how he'd thought she was in danger. It was for that reason that she'd volunteered to remove the barrier of aloof politeness that had kept them at bay last time. It was just a question of a simple, informal undertaking given to the Fulthfol, a group of four women and one man that seemed to uphold the nearest thing the lake-dwellers had to social government and jurisprudence. Their responsibilities were casual and mainly consultative; they were notified that Lupio and Dubilier were returning the boat to its builders and came to see, just as they had stood around and watched them take it away upstream.

Piripheis was slender but strong. Her dark hair, cut short when they had seen her before, now hung in a shaggy fringe that flopped repeatedly over her eyes. Though she affected not to care about it, the impatient shake with which she would continually toss it back became a characteristic and oddly attractive gesture for her new friends. There was a permanent curve in the fingers of her right hand where the bones had misset after a building accident years before. She would come in whenever she had time from her daily work, kick her clogs into the corner and settle down cross-legged to play with Aldellena and talk to the men. Sometimes it was a race between the child and the visitors, to see who could understand first. Piripheis was friendly to both men, but with a special warmth for Dubilier, and he, by temperament an eternal student, responded by learning faster and more eagerly. He would sit with her sometimes late into the night, talking in a low murmur for Aldellena's sake. Lupio preferred communication through shared activity and went boat-repairing, hut-building, fishing and food-gathering. The villagers remained rather in awe of him, a male so impulsive and free-ranging, incautious of his own comfort and safety. He felt few regrets that once again they were idling unnecessarily instead of pushing on, for the place was more suited to him now – and certainly far more attractive than any prospect of Thryn. But especially he was relieved of his sole responsibility, and the rest was doing Dubilier good. His conversation with the water-woman was lively and enthusiastic no matter how it stumbled. They would both frequently break off in laughter at their own frustrations. There was an urgency to express and an urgency to receive, as towards the crisis of a ball game; both of them would have to dive deep to search in the dark tangles of ignorance and confusion, often having to go back and work again at something they'd cleared already, and then understanding would surface into the daylight and the exchange would begin again, swiftly, hand to hand. Lupio couldn't see which of them had the advantage, but he was observing Dubilier; he was definitely coming back to earth, if not by the most direct of routes.

It was a mild evening. The sky had made itself up in topaz and rose and was bending to touch up the water and the buildings from a generous palette of reds. Lupio had been over to the nearest kitchen to help clear up and was canoeing back. There was little traffic at this hour and he took a short cut between the legs of the houses, paddling and coasting, ducking as he had learnt to do. He moored at a corner post and left it to swing with the current, free for anyone who needed it, though hardly anyone ever took a craft from that hut. For one thing it was inconveniently situated, out on the edge of the village, while there was no shortage of boats nearer the centre; but more important was the assumption that the freedom of guests should not be hindered. Nevertheless, it was obviously taken for granted that in their present condition of probationary intimacy (as Dubilier had classified it) the visitors would share the normal communal work. This was not a paradox any more, for they were beginning to appreciate the local conception of freedom: apparently there was no distinction between labour and leisure.

Another paradox Lupio found still puzzling, and that was how the even, easy-going life here was sustained only by a rigorous moral unanimity. This matter of the boats was a fair example. There was nothing to prevent an individual from appropriating some particularly fine craft, the product of half a year in the boatshops, and maintaining it as private property, neither letting others use it nor operating it as a public ferry. Not everything was held in common; people had possessions . . . yet they had no locks . . . yet there was no theft. There was a gravity of social integration, of communal orientation, which kept everyone materially at the same level: it was reminiscent of the pack instinct of the Grach, but it was neither savage nor mystical.

The house was in darkness and Lupio thought Dubilier must have gone off somewhere with Piripheis. He lit the lantern and put it up on its hook; then he caught sight of them at the other end of the room. Dubilier was still sitting on the low bench with

Piripheis on the floor beside him, leaning her head on his knee; Dubilier turned and smiled to see him. She must have fallen asleep, Lupio thought, and Dubilier, with his usual exaggerated respect for her, hadn't moved to get up or light the lamp for fear of waking her. But she was speaking, saying something quietly to Dubilier, and still she didn't turn or get up. It was odd.

'Hello,' Lupio said. 'Isn't the lesson finished yet?'

She laughed and murmured again. Dubilier looked round, knowing he would need a translation. '"Just begun",' he repeated. He stroked her hair.

There was a pause. Lupio couldn't think of anything to say. Disturbed, elated, he lifted the lamp down again and stood it on the table so that the ends of the room swooped into shadow again. He sat down and picked up a pair of boots he was working on, reinforcing them against the rough country to come. They had decided to leave soon and go on overland, for below the lakes the river strayed north and went through miles of double bends. His bodkin slipped and twisted, and one piece of leather wriggled round back to front and had to be cut free before he could correct it. He stabbed his thumb. Then the lake-woman got up and went outside. Dubilier undressed and got into bed. Lupio abandoned the boot. Piripheis returned with dripping hair and sat and dried it before turning the lamp out. She slept there that night, in her own bed, and the men rose before her next day.

They went to the kitchens for breakfast, put water on to boil, prepared three pitchers of schinni tea, exchanged yawns with the cooks and firstcomers, and took mugs and plates to the table. Lupio sat down across from Dubilier, who scrutinised him.

'You look worried.'

'I am. I'm happy for you, you know that, but you must realise the danger.'

'You're thinking of Erthrim, aren't you?'

'Yes.'

'But Piripheis and I are in love.'

How easily he'd said that. 'So were . . .' But Lupio hadn't loved Erthrim, nor she him. Greed and boredom on his part, casual inquiry – play – on hers. 'That's not the point. What do you think will happen if you try to take her away?' A thought occurred to him. 'Unless you're thinking of settling here.' A hope.

'No. I must go back.' He smiled. 'You've already fixed my boots for me.'

'Don't.'

'Lupio, don't worry. It's lovely of you to care like this, but it'll be all right. Nobody owns Piri. She can go where she pleases.'

'They're a community. No one ever leaves, they're all too committed to each other.'

Dubilier shook his head slightly, as if unconsciously imitating her mannerism. 'Piri and I are committed. I think.'

He switched to the native tongue and asked his neighbour for a piece of bread. She smiled as they still did to congratulate the foreigners on their use of the language, and passed him a chunk from her own plate. He turned back to Lupio.

'What's theirs is ours.'

Lupio made a dismissive movement. 'It's easy to give someone a piece of bread . . .'

'Then why are there people starving in Thryn? No, there's a secret. They know that here. You can only give someone something when you both realise that it doesn't belong to you any more than it belongs to him. Then it *is* easy, if he needs it.'

'So you need a piece of bread.'

'I need Piripheis.'

Dubilier's neighbour looked round again, recognising the name, but she appreciated the young men's intensity and didn't interrupt.

'Well, what *about* Thryn? An Aigu attempting to come back from voluntary exile and bringing an Outwaller with him. It's not exactly going to win you popularity.'

'They don't matter. There's only one citizen I owe anything to.'

'Oh yes, your mysterious lady from the shadowy past. How's she going to react? Why won't you ever talk about her?'

'Do you want me to? I used to think it was all very complicated, all mazes and masks on lots of levels. But it was probably very simple.' He traced a shape in the juice on his plate. 'Like the wallflowers you see all over the city, all shrivelled. It was like that, a tender thing beginning to grow in a cramped place, poisonous air – so it grew up askew and stunted. Leaning over to one side. We kept getting caught in things like dependence and power. Who controls whom. Off balance – so it never had a chance to grow into anything better.

'I owe Ali a terrific amount. I don't expect to be able to give her any of it. That story's over.'

'Will she be all right?' Lupio asked. 'There's rough going ahead.'

'I can manage her,' said Piripheis, jogging up and down.

'Mwa,' said Aldellena, patting her mother's shoulder. She leaned this way and that, testing her freedom. The padded bands of the papoose held her safely spreadeagled on her mother's back. She began to tug at Piripheis's hair and stuck a finger into the ear she found beneath it.

'Ow,' said Piripheis, grimacing. Aldellena crowed, bouncing as if in anticipation of the ride. 'I think you can come down again, my friend, while I finish packing. Can you hold her?' She slipped out of the straps while Lupio caught the child from behind, pretending to drop her. She squealed, and he did it again. Piripheis regarded them both with stern good humour as the cries became louder and more excited. 'You treat her too well,' she told him. 'She won't be interested in her mother any more, who just ferries her from here to there. I think it's you who should wear this.' Waving the harness she approached him. Lupio thought she really meant to hang it on his back, but instead she merely put an arm around him. He tensed. 'What's the matter?' She hugged him. 'You like her but you don't like me, hey?'

It was a shock of two histories clashing. Monogamy was the tradition of the possessive society of Thryn. Lupio's scorn for discriminations of class and sex had gained him the reputation of a libertine even before he attained majority. But he still saw sex as a matter of adventure and conquests, and he respected property, as long as he respected its proprietor more. He didn't have the light touch of casual affection; though he wanted to squeeze her back, he couldn't, and knowing that made him even more awkward. It was not the first time she had embraced him; he knew she was amused that a vagabond man could be so squeamish.

Just then Aldellena twisted round in his grasp and threw her arms around his neck, pressing her face into his. Lupio and Piripheis burst into laughter, and so the baby laughed too; she caught his eye and they both relaxed, beginning to enjoy each other more.

Wandering about in the wilderness was a familiar, almost welcome experience. He hadn't intended to go far, just to find horses and bring them back; but the herds had eluded him, and the temptation of the trackless waste was too strong to ignore. Last time he'd done this, delirious after the battle with the chezzerd, he'd been in a frenzy of anxiety and filled the misty air with his legions of phantom women. Now he could take the wasteland on its own terms, merely drifting until he sighted a herd grazing. There were two that didn't shy away, a mare and colt that responded, after dozens of attempts, to his few phrases of First Language, to soothing nonsense in every tongue he knew, and most to the bag of dried fruit he'd brought. He bridled them and mounted the colt, leading the mare along beside and hoping they wouldn't decide to get rid of him. He tried to direct his mount what he thought was the right way, but eventually gave him his head. It was exhilarating but hard work to be on horseback again, and they were finding their unfamiliar burden uncomfortable. Dubilier, preoccupied with keeping both of them calm, suddenly realised that the dark streak ahead was a river. Either they were much too far north, or this was a different river and he was entirely lost. The light was failing and the horses were making a strange deep crooning sound and dipping their heads as if to drink. Sometimes just trusting things to work out wasn't enough. Through the mist Dubilier saw an unidentifiable black shape pacing restlessly on the far bank. It looked huge.

The others had expected to leave that day and it disconcerted them more than they'd admit to have to unpack in the afternoon things they'd confidently packed early that morning. They joined a team building a landing-stage on the western shore so as to see Dubilier as soon as he returned. They kept busy and each of them, conscious of the other, was careful not to turn too frequently only to scan an empty skyline. In the evening they conversed as far as Lupio's vocabulary would permit. He assured her alternately that it would be a difficult and chancy thing to catch horses in the marshes, and that Dubilier couldn't possibly have come to harm. They were too glad of the mutual consolation to consider that his assertions might contradict each other. Aldellena slept, having quite forgotten that there had ever been a special flavour to the day. Near her cradle the conversation encroached more and more upon Lupio's ignorance until he was learning and she instructing, just like the lessons she had given Dubilier. They were even sitting in the same customary places, Lupio on the bench and Piripheis a few feet away on the floor. He was aware that he was trying to replace Dubilier for her, as though that would annul the concern caused by his absence. He couldn't. He lapsed into silence, staring at her bowed head until he felt uncomfortable and leant back in despair to gaze out of the skylight. There were two tiny stars, a veil of torn clouds dragged endlessly across. He could hear music, wooden flutes and a drum and simple strings, as there often was in the vacant hours before midnight. The room with its lack of possibilities constricted him. Waiting and worrying in silence, just to leave, seemed so negative when there was so much here, richness and beauty and vigour, no matter how modest and plain it all appeared.

'Let's go out.'

'You want to look?'

'No; let's go the other way, up to the forest.'

'But when he comes – '

'If he comes now, we'll see him when we get back. If he doesn't we'll just sit here fretting all night.'

That was as foreign to her nature as it was to his. Yet she struggled. 'No. Suppose he's hurt.'

'There'll be someone to take care of him.' He thought of how Dubilier had described their arrival at the lake village. 'Ettenepit will have him tucked up in a sick bed before we know he's here.'

She shook her head.

Lupio was tired of logic. If she wouldn't come, he wasn't

going to stay and mope with her. It wasn't like her to be so depressed. Perhaps he'd get his flute and go and join the music.

She looked up at him. 'Go along without me. Feel free.'

It was a phrase they used all the time here, as a sort of greeting, a conversational tag. 'Feel free,' he repeated.

She would come only on condition that they went the long way, around the village instead of through it, to make sure, and before they even reached the site of the new jetty they saw the four of them on the bank, the man, the colt that was scarcely two hands shorter than his mother, and the great black stallion.

'Are you all right? We thought something had gone wrong.'

'No, everything's all right, but we'll have to feed them now or they won't stay.'

Piripheis was in awe of them. She had never been so close to any large animal. She patted the giant carefully but he did not deign to notice her, chewing gravely at the unfamiliar stuff they were strewing for him. In the darkness he was like the thunderhead of an imminent storm: in a trice he might snap his rope and turn into a blur of crashing hooves, swift and impersonal as lightning. The others were pale, and almost ethereal beside this elemental.

'He is – ' She had no adjective they'd understand. 'How did you get him?'

'The others led me to him. He looked us over and condescended to come.' He embraced her for the first time, holding her lightly. 'Lupio and I have travelled with him before, but Lupio won't remember that.' The First Horse lifted his head as if displaying himself to them; then he stepped to the brink and drank.

Aldellena was terrified. She wept and fought, would not be brought anywhere near the horses, and then wouldn't let Dubilier tie her to her mother's back. The horses grew nervous. He gave Piripheis the agonised child. 'Take her over there and calm her down; she's upsetting them.'

That made Piripheis angry. The unease of the previous day had been inauspicious; she was feeling sad at leaving home for the first time, perhaps forever, and apprehensive about the journey. 'Land-shy', the water-people called it. Instead of comforting her, Dubilier seemed to be accusing her. 'Do you think it's my fault she cries?'

'No, but I know Aldellena won't let anyone else pacify her.'

Distressed, she held the baby roughly to her shoulder and carried her out of earshot. 'Shh, my love, it's all right,' she murmured, but with eyes as mournful as her daughter's.

The plan was for Dubilier to take most of the baggage on Mevn-dath, since the stallion knew him best, and for Lupio to have the rest on the mare, leaving Piripheis and Aldellena the colt; but riding proved to be more difficult than Piripheis had anticipated, certainly not an art to be mastered in a morning. Dubilier was glad that the horses were so amenable, but hoped they wouldn't have to meet any emergencies. He tried to adopt the Grachish manner of sympathetic address, but Mevn-dath wasn't listening, and resolved the arrangement in his own way, manifesting disapproval of any attempt to treat him as a pack-animal. He refused anything on his back except Dubilier and Piripheis, with Aldellena squalling in her sling. Lupio offered to carry her, but it seemed better she should stay with her mother to start with. He rode the colt and guided the mare, laden with all their belongings. Several people helped with the last of the preparations, having gathered eagerly if cautiously on the bank. Dubilier tried to thank them and say goodbye, but even the Fulthfol had no sense of ceremony and, except for a few handclasps and brief valedictions, ignored him: they were far more interested in the horses.

They went into the wilderness. It was a pale, muted day when nothing seemed to possess much energy or solidity, and nothing made any noise, as if the world were holding its breath. Their little caravan made no disturbance, reduced by the blank grandeur of the landscape to three insignificant shapes in a great limbo. The spell overcame even Aldellena. She grizzled for nearly an hour and then, finding herself ignored and unharmed, took to looking about her with an odd solemnity. Later, tired out by her protests and hypnotised by the monotony of her view and the rhythm of the horse, she fell asleep. Unshod hooves made a soft, kissing sound. Marsh creatures flickered among long grass. Harriers hovered, making their eternal observation, but it was several days before they witnessed one dive and strike. It was a shock to realise that that dull grey stillness was a surface illusion over millions of ceaseless tiny movements, growth and death exchanged as dramatically as the plunge of the hunting bird or imperceptibly as the creep of green scum.

Lupio could negotiate the natural order. Piripheis would lead the mare while he rode ahead with a spear and a net. There was a spindly creature with a long neck which was rare but easy to catch once sighted. Piripheis called it ewku, and its meat was light but tasty. Then there were pyrocs. Once he found two together, a rarity, and managed to transfix both while they were nuzzling the glistening remains of their own prey. Piripheis knew the snare her people used to trap waterfowl. She would ride up and set half a dozen before they made camp for the night. When they reached them next day there was often a bird and occasionally two. There were even eels to be fished from the larger meres, though very few. Aldellena adapted quite well from a largely vegetarian diet to the new abundance of meat, though she needed it thoroughly chewed for her first. Otherwise she was not very happy in this strange environment and often maintained a withdrawn silence and inactivity which proved alarmingly unshakable. She liked it when Lupio carried her, however, and would babble enthusiastically when he whistled or sang.

They saw the old marsh road ahead and improved their speed by following it for a day, circumspectly. Primarily at Piri's insistence they stopped to inspect the site of the battle with the chezzerd, but the mud had shifted and little remained. A row of yellowing bones protruded from the marsh, and there were remnants of the tail and one leg; but for the general barrenness, they would scarcely have found so much. Unusually sentimental, Piripheis rescued one of the smaller vertebrae. 'I didn't think anything so big lived,' she explained. 'I am glad to think it was still not too big.'

They continued circling north and west, retracing the course of their escape in the hope of avoiding the Grach. Proceeding with care, accompanied by a mother and child unused to travel, they had taken almost twice as long to do the same journey that they'd done before in fear and desperation, eventually in madness, galloping night and day. For the sake of Aldellena, even Lupio was now eager to get out of the wilderness as soon as possible, but it was obvious that they wouldn't be able to complete the detour and pick up the road again before nightfall. They agreed to make camp early, east of the settlement, and move off before dawn so as to get clear before many of the Grach were abroad. They slept without keeping watch, trusting to wake in time. The mist enfolded them like the ambiguous welcome of an old enemy.

'Weng!'

He was usually patient, even acquiescent. But this morning he lay in the corner and pretended he hadn't been called. It was wet, like every morning, but he could smell a permanence in this rain which indicated that it would go on all day. He felt no desire to rise.

'Weng! Get up! Get up! You think you can stay here, you can choose whether you come or don't? You think I can carry these by myself?' Hoodanu stood behind him and shook the great baskets, but Weng wasn't stirring. 'Well, then! There are others, then, who don't turn their stupid backsides on the one who feeds them, brushes them . . . sleeps beside them when they have the fever, shivering all night like a frightened mouse, you were, and barely twice the size, a little foal . . .'

The man knelt beside him and scratched his ears. Then he jumped up.

'Pooh! Hoo doesn't need you. No, no, he doesn't, then. He'll go on his own and fetch them.' He stamped out demonstratively. 'Where's my hat?'

Weng got to his feet and walked slowly after him, shaking his head to ease a wry neck. He blinked as the first drops hit his nose. No good would come of setting out today.

They had to go further from the road than usual and jog through the wet for nearly an hour. Weng might perhaps have resented it, but he knew it wasn't malice on Hoodanu's part. The little man had no such spite in his nature. They had to go where the mushrooms had gone. Weng was listening for the song.

'Shh.'

Hoodanu slipped from his back and moved forward, crouching and extending an arm as if to part the mist like a tent curtain.

Weng followed. There they were, far over there, like a spread of silvery bubbles. And what was that shape? It looked like huts; but Weng thought they were far from the settlement now. There was a man coming out, however. There was talking. Weng could smell Hoo's unease. This was not normal. A current plucked the mist and Weng could see the tents more clearly, and the creatures by them. He couldn't tell if he'd seen any of the people before – people all looked the same, except Hoodanu and four or five special ones he knew – but he recognised the horse, the big one. He trembled. His coat prickled with apprehension, between fear and joy. Something great was imminent, about to rear up any moment with a cry, as if all spring were to happen at once and burst in his face.

Hoo thrust his sleeve into his mouth, stifling a squeak, and jumped back on Weng. They ran away. Him. He'd seen him once before, yes, just like this, in the mist with the Horse. He'd been loading up then, as if they were preparing for a journey, and now, worse still, he had him tethered, and he stood grazing as quiet as any brood mare, Mevn-dath. Tether Mevn-dath. And Mevn-dath didn't mind. Horrible, it was.

But the First Horse knew that that Man was powerful. He killed the chezzerd. He did, yes, though they all laughed and didn't believe. Well, so he wouldn't tell this time. No. He wouldn't let them laugh at him again. There. And because he was frightened too he wouldn't tell them. He began to sing, in a high-pitched voice and very quickly, his thanks-song to Ferla, although the panniers were flapping empty behind. Even if they all ignored him, Hoo remembered the old stories. He remembered who killed chezzerds, and was with the First Horse at the Beginning: the First Man. Gum-dath, and Mevn-dath – he'd come back, but they'd all driven him out and tried to hunt him. But poor Hoo, he was faithful. He'd shown Gum-dath about the mushroom-song, and now Ferla put them out especially for him, round his tent while he was sleeping. Poor Hoo had seen, but he wouldn't tell anyone, not even Erthrim and Vyvyan. He gave Weng a squeeze to ask him if he could run faster.

The pony snorted. His baskets were light. Hoodanu had gathered no mushrooms. It was no good today, he'd known it.

Lupio put his knife down. 'This reminds me of the little man with the hat. Hoodanu.'

Dubilier nodded. Piripheis looked at each of them, expecting elucidation. She was most puzzled by this food which seemed half flesh, half vegetable, and interested to hear more. But Dubilier, scraping Aldellena's plate while she bobbed up and down mouthing impatiently, said nothing because he'd been thinking of Hoodanu already. The mushroom-man had probably been up and harvesting hours before. It was good he hadn't got to this patch: there were plenty and to spare for them. While they had gathered them Dubilier had knelt and spoken to the earth-mother, Ferla, apologising that he'd forgotten the formula Hoodanu had taught him by saying ferlem-ar as best he could.

It was this sort of nonsense that still gave Lupio worry about his friend's mentality. Once upon a time he had grown used to being dazzled by Dubilier's intellectual competence; it had made his own sophistication appear mere affectation, city foppery. But Dubilier was going soft, still mesmerised by his own mysticism, kneeling in the rain to pray like a superstitious peasant. He'd lost his touch – but that was better than losing his mind, which was what Lupio had been afraid of back in Pepache-ti-Bilovan. Exhausted by the dangers and deprivations of living rough, Dubilier's sensitive mind had come close to the edge, and the disappointment of that hideous night on the mountain had unhinged its fine balance altogether. But the human brain was a wonderful organ, resistant to the hardest knocks; it went under only to initiate the mysterious mechanisms of autonomic recovery, just as he himself had gone into a coma after fighting the chezzerd.

At any rate, he'd say nothing to Piripheis. She, evidently, saw nothing to suggest that her mate was in anything but his right mind, having no prior standard of comparison. There was no point in alarming her, especially since their devotion to each other was the main force in bringing Dubilier round. Lupio was glad for him. He'd always been in need of a good woman.

The sky was enormous, exaggerated by the flat and nondescript terrain. The view was always three-quarters sky, once the early mists had shrunk back into the sodden, crumbling earth. The rain was colourless, and even the sunshine seemed anaemic. Pale, indefinite tints came and went through the day. The birds made their endless, random circuits, unnerving her, mirroring the formlessness of her own apprehensions. She was full of questions she couldn't finish. She kept them to herself; they had no meaning but vague anxiety, like the whimpering of Aldellena waking at night. They would cling together, and Piripheis would take comfort from soothing her with the pretence of reassurance. Then she would sleep herself, to dream of something comfortable and ordinary – diving, cooking, cutting wood, the silver delicacy of water – and wake not knowing where she was. For all its greatness the sky had no answers, and the meagre land yielded no clues.

But today they came in sight of it: a dark blue lump on the horizon. The end of all the emptiness, where the answers would be found. It looked ominous . . .

Of course it looks ominous, she considered, exasperatedly putting her frail, querulous child-self back to bed for the hundredth time. Of course it's ominous, things are going to happen there – isn't that what 'ominous' means? She shifted her seat, holding on to Dubilier. Aldi clings to my back; I cling to Dubilier's back; he clings to Mevn-dath's back. Everybody depends on everybody. What will they be like? How stupid, to build a wall round yourselves and forget what it looks like outside. But imagine, a city – that's much bigger than a village. What had he said? Thirty women for every one back home and more than a hundred times as many men? As many men as women. And to be able to walk from house to house. She was a bit in awe of them. He had told her how they had ravaged a mountain to build themselves this road. Unable to conceive them in imagination, she repeated all the things to herself. It sounded a grim place. But she was going. Why was she indulging herself in all this feebleness? She was acute, and strong, and used to survival; unlike city women, she did not require a continual supply of luxuries. She had a scornful disdain for the image of Alita. If they didn't like her –

That was odd, and she mistrusted it, that dividing of people into 'me' and 'them', instead of taking everyone as 'us'. Now 'us' had a new meaning: Dubilier and me. That was real already; something she'd not experienced before, and she thought that not many of her people ever discovered it. Sometimes there were groups of two or three that seemed unusually stable, and a preference for one particular partner could endure long after sex had stopped being important, but these were never exclusive, more like familiarity and habit than devotion. They didn't have this sense that two became one, a unit in reckoning with itself and with everybody else. Perhaps that was necessary in a society that was arranged by division instead of union. She thought of what they'd said about 'class'. Such people were servant class because they did this sort of – what was it called? – 'work'. But which sort? She couldn't remember. She knew the distinction between 'wanting' to do it and 'having' to do it was all-important, but that confused her completely.

She grinned and tossed the hair out of her eyes, taking care not to bump Aldellena as she did so. Well, she might be ignorant and afraid sometimes, but one thing was certain: the Thrynians were a very strange people who did many very silly things very solemnly. That night Dubilier tried to give her a serious talk to prepare her for their arrival in the morning, but she made fun of him to shut him up, and then they passed the time more pleasantly. She had made up her mind to ride straight in – well, crawl straight in, under their silly Wall – and take what came.

They left the river, which had started to smell quite noxious. The ground was very wet, and rose towards the city. Piripheis became impatient. Everything was still foggy. Lupio and Dubilier were talking. They decided not to try the way they'd come out by, nor any of the other Gates, because they'd be impossible to open from outside. They went around slowly, hoping to find some access point. The city was silent, an interminable succession of angular silhouettes going by. Lupio rode closer to look. He shouted and came back into view.

'Right here – there's a gap straight over here.' They climbed the slope. 'It's new,' Lupio said, slight apprehension in his voice. 'This is the distillery. It looks as if it's been half pulled down.'

A breach in the Wall. The grass was strewn with broken masonry. The horses picked their way forward and the riders looked up and down. Anile and decrepit, the city hugged the mist to it like a cloak, but they could see its nakedness underneath. The Wall was down.

3

And I saw that there were temples at both places.

Miguel Serrano

The temple was cold and as dark as night. The torches were all too high for him to reach without a lot of effort, so he always brought the lantern. As he moved the mounds of shadows fluttered up and vanished like bats. He bit his lip and rehearsed the things he still had to do. Determinedly he swept the dancing stage and sprinkled it from the inch or two of sacred water that remained, then went to make his obeisances to the pool itself. Lit from below, the face of the god wasn't smiling in benediction but chuckling at a private joke. He ducked his head, his heart beating fast, and didn't look up again. There were different flowers and leaves in the pool, the wrong sort, and they were sodden and brown among the slime which sealed the surface and ran a forlorn tide-mark up the sides of the basin. It needed cleaning; he'd have to clean it. He rolled his sleeves up and began. Suddenly, before he'd finished, he yelled in fright and jerked his hand out. The building echoed. He moved the light and peered in with disgust and fascination. There was a frog in the god's pool: a brown shiny thing with a blunt head and four twitching legs. It darted into the muck, kicking up a cloud of debris. He looked about but couldn't see where it was now. His own reflection bobbed, his wet hands sparkling. In the depths beneath was the statue's face again, upside down, its jewelled eyes and bright mouth seeming to flicker while the water settled, as if it were babbling madly. He scrambled to his feet, bowed perfunctorily, and ran, up the hill, along by the Iigril grove, and onto the road. As he ran he saw smoke curling up from somewhere on his right. Another house gone. He passed several villas, but didn't see anybody. His arm ached from carrying the lantern. He went past the house as usual, and then doubled back under cover of the ruined vineyard and came through the unkept kitchen garden. Mad or not, they'd never set this alight; there was nothing here. The grimy scullery had been ransacked more than once, and what could not be carried – the stone flour bins and burst vegetable sacks – had been left for the rats. Some of them didn't even bother to run away when he came in, watching him fearlessly as if sizing up a potential meal rather than a potential threat. He ignored them, found the crowbar and began wrestling with the trapdoor. It fell back loudly. Before he went down the steep steps he relit the lantern which had blown out in his running.

She was much as he'd left her, sleeping silently.

'Previs?'

He cradled her ancient head. The lids fluttered open, but the eyes were a long time focusing. He gave her water.

'Previs, I'm back.'

A long pause.

'Hifran?'

'Yes, Previs.'

'Have you been to the temple?'

'Yes, Previs.'

'Is it – worthy?'

'Yes, Previs.' He felt guilty for running away. Should he tell her about the nasty thing in the pool? No, it would worry her. What would she do? Only tell him to catch it. It was his duty. He looked at her. Her eyes were wandering again. 'I did my best. Previs, when is he coming?'

No answer.

'Can I do anything for you?'

She fell back, her head lolling on his arm, and he laid her down. Was she trying to signal to him? If only he knew what to do.

The Wall was down, the great Gates splintered and gaping. Smoke from bonfires and smouldering houses mingled with the mist, making it sullen and slow to lift. Within, the city loured dark and dying. Presiding over the ruins whole buildings lingered as if reluctantly immune to the general dissolution.

They stared. Piri, who had never seen Thryn before, could not understand; but Dubilier felt a flash of outrage, a wave of self-reproach, and then calm again. The last time he had been in the city he had had the sense of history requiring him not to leave it, an accusation of desertion in the flap of a dingy tapestry high on the council chamber wall. But there had been that other hanging, the loose tarpaulin in the deserted city of the moon, making the same claim for attention to a race that had scattered and died . . . That same last day, meeting Lupio, he had felt the inception of a new design, the pattern of a game destined to be played out, regardless by whom. Their desertion had not caused the rout; rather, they had been preserved, cut free of history and set down to get on with the future. The smoke got in Aldellena's eyes and she began to complain. That smoke was the logical conclusion to the Thryn he'd known. Nothing can prevent the end of a story. Then he heard a laugh: Lupio.

'The distillery! Whoever accomplished this had an entirely misguided sense of priority.'

It was a ghost speaking, a ghost who wore rings and flashing silk, careful that they were of the best workmanship and the richest colours, but careless that they were all tarnished and tattered. Dubilier waited. There was nothing he could do. Lupio did not see in the same perspective as he did; he saw only the immediate, in one pulse of the heart. His city-life had been a grisly mime of love and hatred, guilt and pride, holding up excellence with one hand and defacing it with the other. He had dropped the pose on leaving the city: another mask they'd left behind. But Thryn was the city of the empty eyes, and masks had their own life here. Lupio's came to him through the broken wall, welcoming him back like a ghost. But then, while Dubilier watched, Lupio gave a sigh and the mask fell from him again. He had seen too much Outwall to be possessed any more by cynicism and sentimentality. No ready-made response would do. Tired and dirty, Lupio sat on his horse looking up into a ruined city.

'What has happened?' Piripheis asked.

'Perhaps I started a fashion,' said Lupio. They looked at him. 'I set fire to my house before I came away,' he explained. Piri plainly didn't understand. She rocked Aldellena, who was grizzling. Lupio considered them. 'What about the Iigril?' he suggested. 'Or do you think they'll have had that too?'

'We'll go to what used to be my house,' Dubilier decided.

'Can we find food there?' asked Piri.

'I don't know,' said Dubilier, helping her down.

They unburdened the mare. Dubilier spoke detailed and courteous thanks to her and her colt, but to Mevn-dath he said only two or three words of Grachish, and touched his shoulder. The black giant gazed down at the man, and then up at the city. He looked so utterly aloof and alone then that the Grach's awe of him seemed wholly justifiable. It was not easy, at that moment, to be sure what sort of creature Mevn-dath was. Then he tossed his head, lifted his tail, and galloped off without another glance, the other horses following.

The travellers picked up their belongings and went into the burning city.

The distillery was destroyed, the streets all around it deserted. Under the stench of burning was another smell, rank and rotting. Nothing moved. They skirted a slew of refuse and made for the food dispensaries, where Lupio was already hammering on boarded doors. The only reply was a hollow echo.

'I'll find someone to ask.' Dubilier turned down a narrow street, avoiding the patches of scum between the broken cobbles. He glimpsed a figure in a doorway and called out. It ducked inside. He followed. It was a woman, her hand already on the handle of the back door. 'Just a minute, please!'

Perhaps because he sounded more courteous than commanding, she waited. Her bearing was youthful, but wretchedness and want had aged her; he couldn't guess how much. 'We need food,' he said, avoiding explanations now that he had her attention. 'The dispensaries have been closed, haven't they?'

She said nothing.

'How do you manage for food?'

She laughed loudly in pure derision, and wiped her sleeve across her nose and mouth, still laughing, regarding him as the unsympathetic might regard the insane.

He persisted. 'What do you do for food?'

'Anything.'

He looked at her. She was filthy, scarred, disfigured by violence and disease. She resembled her city, except that she was still defiant as it broke her down. Her spirit was a wire holding taut the battered pieces of her body.

'We've been away,' he said. 'Outwall.' Still no response. 'I don't know what happened here.' He stopped. She wasn't about to enlighten him. 'Hasn't there been a special arrangement made to provide food?'

'Yes.'

'What is it?'

'This.' There was a knife in her hand.

Dubilier contemplated it. I'm not meant to die now, he thought. I don't believe things are that bad. It would make nonsense of everything if I were to die now, here, like this. I'm unarmed. Perhaps she'll wound me. He saw brown smears on the blade and felt sorry for those whose stories had ended in that arbitrary way. He stood looking at the blade she held lightly in her hand.

'I admit,' said Lupio, 'that I couldn't reach you before you put that knife into him, but I think I probably could before you pulled it out again. Do you want to try?'

She glanced at the newcomer who stood framed in the doorway across the workshop. He held a sword. She continued to open the door behind her and, leaning through it, gave a loud whistle. As she did so Dubilier stepped forward and took the knife out of her hand. He hadn't thought he would do that at all, and they looked at one another with some surprise. An old man with long moustaches came in behind her. He was only five feet tall. The younger man with him was taller. They were both armed. The old man registered the shock in her face, her knife in Dubilier's hand; he and his companion saw how easily the strangers stood, how casually they bore their weapons. The old man muttered impatiently, guiding the woman back outside. He glanced back and shook his head.

'Just a moment,' Dubilier called again, but they had gone. He held the knife out hilt foremost to the younger man as he was following. 'Please give it back to her.'

'Jeswed's eyes!' said Lupio.

Dubilier went out into the street. 'Thank you,' he said.

'What did you want to do that for? He could have killed you!'

'I wanted to give her the knife back. It's probably all she has.'

'So that she can go and stick someone else?'

'What she does with it isn't for me to say, is it?' It was a genuine question. Lupio didn't answer it. 'And she'd be killed herself without it. Should I choose that? It's a bad time, Lupio. There are no good alternatives.'

Piripheis looked from one to the other, not knowing what had happened. On her back Aldellena began to sing, an incongruous sound in the shattered street. Dubilier smiled and twisted a lock of her flossy hair round his finger. She laughed and tried to pull her head away, hitting his cheek to tell him to let go. They crossed the bridge and Piripheis stood still while he showed Aldellena the river, all choked with rubbish and ruined furniture, and explained to her that it was the same river that Lupio and he had carried her mother across just a while before she was born. Lupio stood at a distance, looking restlessly all round, his sword still drawn. There was a peculiar stain of slime high up on everything still standing, on either bank. Wasn't that a body in the water? He wanted to move. His own fighting talent, honed along these same streets in less desperate days, would see him through, but Dubilier didn't even seem to recognise the danger. He had stood there looking at the woman's knife as if she'd offered to sell it him as an antique. He wasn't safe. Meanwhile his lover and her baby hardly knew what a street was, let alone what might happen to them in one like this. Disaster didn't strengthen, it divided. In the chaos after catastrophe only the lawless survived; the scavengers, those who put self before standards. But what was the exact nature of the catastrophe?

Among the ruins he saw someone move, and another over there. 'Come on,' he said.

They got safely through the city, travelling quickly with Lupio as ostentatiously armed guard. They met no one on the road beyond except fugitives, some laden with loot, some who had nothing at all. No one would speak to them without first begging food or money. Dubilier tried to answer them, but most shambled on ahead without listening to more than the first words of his apology. They didn't need tales of woe; they had plenty of those already.

Piripheis looked at the villas they passed with some amazement. She had just about grasped the idea that they had been private property, not communal houses, though they were three and four times as large as the largest huts she knew. She could certainly not understand why so many of them had been ransacked or abandoned, instead of occupied.

But when they came to Dubilier's, it was clear to Lupio that here there were new occupiers. Broken windows had been patched, and there was a cart in the driveway. The ground to either side had been partly dug up, and it looked as though a few trees had been felled.

'*You* lived here?' Piripheis asked Dubilier, taking his hand as they walked up the path.

A boy came round the side. 'Get away from here,' he said. He held a peeled branch with a blade lashed at the end.

Lupio cursed quietly and stepped forward, his hand on the hilt of his sword, but Dubilier restrained him with a glance. The boy looked uneasily from face to face. 'What do you want? Go away.'

'We need food, and a place to stay. We've been out of the city a long time. It would be kind of you to help us.'

Different places and different languages had altered Dubilier's accent. Lupio wouldn't have noticed, but it was no longer the diction of the Aiguda. The boy frowned, inspecting them anew. 'From outside?' he said. 'Who are you?' and then, once again not waiting for a reply, shouted, 'Da!' There was a pause. Lupio moved towards the boy, but he motioned him back with the spear. The front door was flung open and a man appeared, scowling. 'Outwallers, Da,' said the boy.

'Stinking marshers,' said his father, coming up the path. He had a heavy chopper in his hand. 'Madness, pulling the Wall down. Go on, get out of it! They'll be everywhere, I told 'em they would. Go on!'

Dubilier took another step. 'My name's Dubilier,' he said. 'This man is Lupio. We've been away, Outwall, for a time, but before that we lived here. This was my villa.'

The man dropped the tool to his side, standing his ground and surveying them as hard as his son had. 'Citizens?' he said. 'You don't look it.'

'We have been away, travelling,' Dubilier repeated, patiently.

'How long?'

'A year. Two, maybe. I can't tell.'

The man looked astonished. 'You mean – before the Wall went down? You went Outwall?'

'Yes.'

He made a wordless exclamation of utter bewilderment. Nothing followed it, so Dubilier said again, 'Before that, this was my home.'

That roused the man; he shook the chopper. 'Well, it's mine now! You can't just stroll off when you like and come back when you like and expect to carry on as if nothing had happened, you know.'

Dubilier shook his head, smiling, and went up to him. 'I'm sorry,' he said, 'I didn't mean you to think I wanted to reclaim the house. But we all need shelter and food. We can't pay you for it, but we can work. We've nowhere else to go.'

The man still couldn't work it out. '*You*,' he said, pointing, 'used to live *here*?' jerking his thumb over his shoulder at the house.

'That's right.'

'*You're* Aiguda?'

'We were.' He grinned as the man looked over their grimy clothes, the patched cloaks, the dusty boots, the cumbersome baggage.

'What did you say your names were?'

Still Dubilier refrained from adding the conventional title. 'Dubilier, and Lupio. This is Piripheis and her daughter Aldellena.'

Lupio winced. The man was sure to recognise those as foreign names and turn them all out, whatever claims he and Dubilier might have. But he had let them go by and was staring at Lupio instead. 'I remember you,' he said. 'You're the one who told everybody you were the Cirnex, come back from the dead.'

'No,' said Lupio, going forward in turn. 'The Previs said that, not me. That's why I left.'

'Old Kavi?' The man smiled, unexpectedly, as if at some droll recollection. 'She's dead. They did for her. I don't hold with all that guff,' he announced suddenly, with a suspicious stare.

'Nor,' said Lupio firmly, 'do I.'

'Can we come in?' asked Dubilier, picking up his pack.

'Aye.' He nodded slowly. 'It's not your house,' he reminded him, 'it's mine now. You remember that. You come along in.'

'Oh, thank you,' said Piripheis, her exhaustion and relief breaking into a smile as she too came up to him. He stood looking stern, but swaying a little on his heels, taken aback by friendliness and goodwill but determined not to be taken in as well. Poor man, she thought, he's been little used to them. How could people live together in such hostility and mistrust? But Dubilier was one of them, and Lupio too, so she wouldn't despair of it all yet, vile as everything seemed.

Unable to think up any more warnings to issue, their host had turned his attention to his son. 'What are you hanging about here gawping after? You get back there and finish that planting.'

The bushes rustled. She froze. They were coming for her. Even here, even with all the care and precautions they took – Ah, no, it was only a coot that had wandered up from the water's edge. It hadn't seen her. If she sat very still . . . The coot paused and then came nearer, its head darting right and left as if it were looking for something. Which it probably was. Was it a male or a female? It was so close; surely if she put out her hand very slowly and gently, thinking peaceful things all the while, he wouldn't mind if she just – The coot was gone with an ungainly scuffle of wings, and all the other birds too. Now she'd have to wait. It was so depressing. Why didn't they trust her? They were all so timid; they'd never do what she wanted them to, though she didn't mean them any harm, she only wanted to hold one, to cradle him in her hand and feel his tiny heart pulsing through the warm, soft down of his breast. She wanted to stroke the top of his head with one finger and watch his nervous little eyes flick from side to side, perhaps a wood-pigeon, to hear that tremulous, brooding sound they made. The sparrows were the first to reassemble, and thrushes and blackbirds, and there was that dark green one, what was it called?

'The green one there, Ibet, what's that one called?' asked Alita.

'That's a nuccyx, Aigui.' Ibet put her bag on the ground and sat down beside her. And they all flew away again.

'They're so timid . . .'

'They're only doing what we're doing, Aigui, which is being

careful. It's not like it was, with everybody in their place and keeping to it. Everyone's your enemy who hasn't proved himself your friend.'

There was a pause. 'How are things in the city today, Ibet?' So as not to seem too eager to see what was in the bag. She wasn't a beggar; she still had that much self-control.

'I didn't go down. I don't think it's worth the risk any more, not until we have to. There's nothing there we need; nothing I can't get from friends, people up here. We're better off with them, we know where we are with them.'

'But Ibet, the house! We must make sure – '

'You listen to me, Alita: that house is going to go sooner or later. It's only luck that it's not been done over already. They're much more interested in the villas, but there's others, you know. The unlucky ones – starving, nowhere to go, no one to look after them. It only needs one of them to break into that place and they'll be all over it before you can turn round.' She sat back. It was obvious this had been on her mind for a while and she was glad to have got it said. 'You've got to face up to it. You might as well say goodbye to the house now.'

'Ibet, I sha'n't. Whatever's happening down there, that's my house and nobody else is to touch it. Unless I say. You must go down there and see to it.'

'"Must"? "Must"? Aigui, I risk my life for you daily. Hourly. If Mengac or that slimy Himithet find out I'm keeping you hidden away out here, they'll have me as well as you, you know. I'm not going down to that city again. I've got a responsibility towards you – what'll you do if anything happens to me?'

'Then I shall go myself.' She stood up, brushing the dirt and debris from her skirt with frantic hands.

Ibet seized her wrist, pulling her down onto the fallen tree again with a humourless laugh. 'You're not going anywhere. Do you think I'd let you go off and get yourself killed? Give us both away? You're staying right here.'

'Ibet, take you hand away! I am still mistress here, Ibet! I am still mistress here!'

The birds flew round about the island, in and out of the ruined aviary where Ibet was keeping her hidden. They flew over the lake and around the estate, as the grass grew ever taller and the weeds flourished unchecked. The birds pecked at the neglected apricots still rotting beneath the unpruned trees. They built their nests among the chimneys and crenellations of the house itself, and they skittered in the rafters, pattering on the ceilings of the empty rooms. Their droppings stained the beams and floors. Everything worth having had been removed. Only Ibet lived there now. There were those with whom she had certain arrangements. She got by. The house was safe enough now. She reckoned Mengac's marauders had had all they could want from it, and the homeless were too demoralised to come up out of the city; but it made sense for the Aigui to stay out of the way, on the overgrown island. There was no telling. And it did make life easier.

'What do you have in your bag, Ibet?'

'What do you think? I've brought your food. Don't I always?'

'Yes, Ibet, thank you, Ibet; you are good to me, I'm sorry I . . . Is there some bread? For the birds, I mean. Can I feed them?'

'Yes, Aigui, you can feed the birds. Just let me sort this lot out.'

'Give it me, Ibet. Oh, there, look, look, there's the green one again, she's come back, I knew she would! Now, where's her mate, I wonder? What did you say their name was again?'

'Hold *still*, Diwy . . . Oh, do please hold still; you can go back to him in a minute.' Piripheis was losing control.

The nanny-goat strained at her tether. 'Blëë,' she said. She began to graze but each time Dip-Dip bleated she lifted her head and tried to go to him. Well, she was tied fast, and Piri would milk her somehow. She spoke soothingly to her.

'Yes, I know Dip-Dip wants to drink too, but he's a big boy and we need your milk now, don't we? Dip-Dip can eat grass – yes, grass, that's right, you can too. We can't eat grass – there's a good goat, that's it, you stay just like that – so we need you to turn it into milk for us. We – '

'Eëëë,' shrilled Dip-Dip from the other corner of the paddock.

'Meëë,' replied his mother, coming near to kicking the bucket over.

'Oh, *Diwy*! Hold *still*!' Piripheis impatiently swept the hair out of her eyes and parked it behind her ear. Privately she decided she preferred fish, who didn't need tethering or milking and didn't have silly voices. They were much more sensible creatures than the goats – or else brainless altogether. But then they couldn't turn grass into milk, or into goat, and she was enjoying this new diet. And Aldellena liked them too. She looked over Diwy's back at the baby who was rolling happily around near Dip-Dip – not too near, she hoped. 'Aldi!' she called and waved to her. Aldi saw her and waved back, both hands, laughing idiotically.

'Eëëë,' said Dip-Dip.

'Meëë,' replied Diwy.

There, said Piri to herself, now I'm being as stupid as the goat.

Dubilier came over to help her finish. He was good with animals; they seemed to respond to him. He squatted in front of the nanny so that she could still see her kid while looking at him, and talked to her. The yellow milk spurted into the bucket. Piri left some for Dip-Dip and Dubilier went to untie him, and to play for a minute with Aldellena. She lifted the bucket with both hands and carried it to the house, stopping to let Frujos come out.

'Less today,' said Piripheis.

The farmer grunted.

'Will she dry up soon, do you think?'

'What?'

'Will she, Diwy – "dry up", can you say that? We say "dry up" for a river, when there is drought . . .'

Frujos looked into the bucket and over at Diwy and the insatiable Dip-Dip. He avoided meeting Piri's eyes. 'Can't tell. Shouldn't do. You mind,' he said, striding away looking back at her, 'you tell me if she's going to, all right?'

Piri nodded obediently. She smiled to herself. She knew Frujos couldn't bring himself to trust her, but she'd been so careful to be polite and friendly to him right from the start, before he'd had time to gather his suspicions and ask where she came from, that now he could find nothing to complain of. It entertained her, going out of her way to be nice to him when he'd have preferred to ignore her: it embarrassed him, and then he would retreat to his customary defence of pompous righteousness. For a while he had assumed she and Dubilier were married, and when he'd discovered they weren't, he'd made noises that that baby was one more mouth than he wanted to feed; but he loved her, though he did his best to conceal that, and the men said they'd leave too if she and her mother had to go. Frujos had no wish to go back to the way things had been before, when he and his family had been running the estate unassisted; and no more had been said. Oddly assorted though they were, they were together, and this was their home.

Dubilier had gone back to his continuing task of digging up slabs of stone and brick. He had had a paved terrace with ornamental walkways; now that area was to be put to use like all the rest. It was not really his sort of work, and he did it slowly, but he never did or said anything, even to Piripheis, to indicate that he was bitter or regretful. Well, perhaps he had a moment or two of nostalgia, but he was as enthusiastic as Frujos about getting the property into shape for the present and for the future.

Taking him out and showing him the work he'd done, Frujos had been curt and defensive that first afternoon. 'That's the way it's going to be,' he concluded, raising his voice. 'I know it's a bit different from the way it was in your time, but things have changed, and you can't afford to sit around idle all day; nobody can. Especially not Aiguda. You've got to be sharp. Look after yourself and your own. There's men walking about, Mengac and his revolutionaries, the ones I told you of that're living in the Iigril – if they could get everybody on their side, there'd be no more Aiguda. If you'd been here the months after the flood, they'd have had you and all, most likely. Strung up on the trees. I thought that was what had happened when I come along and found this place deserted, but there'd been no burglars, so it was all a bit of a mystery.' He looked sideways at Dubilier then, and at Piripheis. Clearly there was much that was still mysterious. But he left it and returned to his theme. 'I know it must be a shock for you, seeing all your ancestral flowerbeds dug up and full of cabbages, but – '

Dubilier interrupted him then, as if unable to keep silent any longer. 'Farmer Frujos,' he said, turning to him with smiling eyes, 'I think you've done miracles. It's all alive and growing – I can see the love and care shining back at me! I hadn't realised how dead it was, this earth, weighed down with shaven lawns and formal gardens. But you've brought it all back to life. It doesn't matter about the past, it's the present and the future that matter. My ancestors have got what they need: they're under the earth. Why should they dictate what goes on on top of it too?'

It had been a supremely embarrassing moment. Frujos's expression was changing rapidly as he tried to decide whether he was being congratulated or mocked. Lupio was looking agonised, fingering his sword and clearly wishing Dubilier would shut up before they all got thrown out. But Piripheis had been amused and impressed that Dubilier could think and speak that way about somebody else's upheaval of what had been his home.

For something – no, *everything* in his voice and his manner displayed that he really did think it. If she had said it, it would have been to jostle Frujos, the extravagant praise being thrown in for his benefit because she didn't care either way. But Dubilier was inspired, and when he was inspired he forgot all the paraphernalia of convention and expediency and just spoke. He was almost naïve in his idealism, so that he could be high-minded without being aloof, and she loved him for it. But the most astonishing thing was the way the world always fell in with him. The people you were expecting to turn round and laugh at him or walk away insulted broke into smiles and agreed with him instead, looking surprised at themselves as if that had been what they were expecting too. Things arranged themselves for him, like the mushrooms that morning in the marshes, or the fish he coaxed from the pools. Even Diwy the goat responded to him. She had never met anyone so – so in tune. She felt sometimes that whatever her own emotions for him, they were no different from those that the rest of creation might feel for him, given the chance. She thought she hardly recognised him as an individual man, but instead as a factor of harmony which would resolve anything to rightness – as a magical amulet, a talisman which would always point the right way. And then she thought that that was what love was: the illusion that the beloved offered the hope of completeness, not just to you but to the whole world. She put down the bucket and ran to him, hugged him. 'My talisman,' she said.

'What?'

Frujos, talking to his son, looked hurriedly away to pretend he hadn't seen. But his wife leaned out of the kitchen window. 'Priphyis!'

'Yes, Win?'

'I don't think I'll be wanting you to help with the churning today.'

'Why not, Win?' she asked, hurrying to pick up the bucket.

'Well, you've took so long getting the damned stuff out of the goat, girl, and now you're taking so long getting it into the kitchen, that I reckon it'll be cheese before I clap eyes on it!'

'Gomath, it's cold in here. Why don't you shut those windows?'

The doors thudded to behind him, sending echoes booming up and down the tower. The draught played with the rags that hung from the walls, flapping them to and fro. He walked around the long table, disarranging the papers that lay on it, glancing at each before sweeping it aside with a heavy hand. The breeze snatched one, drifted it quickly down the table and dropped it on the floor.

'Shut the windows!'

The man on the balcony didn't move. Himithet sighed and went out to him, leaving the paper where it had fallen. 'What's happening? There's nothing in that lot that's less than a week old, and most of it's inaccurate.' He followed his companion's gaze down to the devastation below. 'Mm, yes, fascinating, isn't it. Inspiring. The hustle and the bustle of the great city. The happy singing of its proud, healthy citizens as they go about their daily work.'

He went back to the table.

'Listen to this one. " . . . where I heard tales of an army of marshmen, led by a spirit who laughs at our weapons, and whom swords and knives cannot harm – " Ha! " . . . accompanied by a witch who – " Gomath's teeth, come in and shut that window!'

The man on the balcony was dark and powerfully built. As he turned, his face had the look of one whose life is labour, to whom words are a waste of breath, but something in his brow warned that it would be a severe underestimation to deduce that no great or serious thoughts occupied him. All this in contrast to Himithet, who was slight and irritable, his restless movements betraying a brain that was too quick, too urgent – that might boil over at any and every moment into violence. Himithet was all tension, while the other was all solidity. Himithet's appearance also suggested a life of toil in service, but the life of a clerk, a storeman, or a domestic supervisor. He showed no gratitude or even pleasure now that his demand was being complied with, but merely sat sideways on his chair, swinging his feet and scowling around the ruined council chamber.

'What we need is a blaze. That'd warm things up. A blaze, eh, Mengac? We could have another fire, eh? There's plenty more villas – one or two big houses left in the city, too.' He paused. 'What were you doing out there, planning your new city?'

'Yes.'

'Can't build without clearing the ground first, Mengac. Lots of rickety, rotten old places to come down yet. Lots of Aiguda that need winkling out. You ever seen big spiders, Mengac? Fat old spiders that spin themselves into corners? You should have. Plenty of them in here.' He stood up swiftly, angrily, spurning his chair, and started to roam around again. 'It's still cold. Why don't we burn this place? Burn the Iigril. The Iigril, going up in flames. That'd shake them. What a symbol! Another public execution, only this time cutting the head off the city itself. Why don't we burn down the Iigril?'

He put a hand on Mengac's arm, staring into his face.

Mengac threw him off. 'That's all you know, isn't it?' he said bluntly. 'Burnings and executions.' He gestured at the smoke hanging above the stricken streets. 'Have done with it.'

Himithet grinned. 'I intend to.'

Mengac was not smiling. 'Have done with it,' he repeated. 'What we need now is thought – planning – co-operation. New order,' he said, with the tone of someone who has said a thing a thousand times to an unresponsive world and intends to say it a thousand times more. 'You're so handy with lynch-mobs, get me a working party.'

He turned back to the sombre view as if he knew the demand wouldn't be answered. He ran one huge hand through his hair. 'This lot are no use at all. All helter-skelter, higgledy-piggledy. Burn this, burn that. Finish off the Wall. Enslave the Aiguda. Abandon the city. Some of them are even talking about Gomath!'

Himithet snickered. 'You're as bad,' Mengac told him. 'I'd give twenty of you for one decent mason, straight I would.'

'You want to get the citizens together, Mengac? Light a fire. That's what gets them together. Light a fire. That's what fetches them. They all come, creep out of their holes to come and look at the pretty flames . . .'

It was a cold morning, and Lupio was looking for work to do to keep warm. He sat on the kitchen step and pulled his boots on. Frujos came past him, his arms full of tools.

'Leave me the long spade,' Lupio said. 'I'll make a start on the new patch.'

'Doesn't have to be done yet, you know,' said Frujos, almost apologetically. 'Week or two'll do.'

Lupio smiled. 'I need the exercise.' He was amused by the odd relationship he'd struck up with the farmer and his wife. At first they'd been more cautious of him than of Piripheis even. Frujos was determined to show that he was a realistic, earth-bound working man with no room in his head for flighty nonsense about gods and mountains and such, while Win, though anxious to be faithful to her husband and 'right-thinking' by his standards of common sense and practicality, nevertheless maintained a kind of awe of Lupio and asked questions (when Frujos was elsewhere) about Kavi and the prophecy and the incident in the library. That his answers were as prosaic as her husband's might have been, though less impatient, obviously dissatisfied her. She wished there might be marvels somewhere in the world, even if they weren't in her kitchen or her husband's vegetable beds, and Lupio was insistent that there was nothing at all miraculous about himself, his friends, or their rather unimpressive adventures. She took more consolation from Dubilier, whose metaphysical approach could conjure wonders and mysteries out of the most common-place material.

By now the couple had come to accept Lupio's ordinariness, and to appreciate him as a ready and dependable fellow worker, but still they kept their distance, their appreciation showing itself as respect rather than friendliness. He hadn't turned out to be what Frujos secretly feared or Win secretly hoped, but he did come from a different, unknown world, bringing with him a wealth of experiences far wider and more various than their own. He wasn't what they'd expected, but they couldn't tell quite what he was. Priphyis (they couldn't get their tongues round that funny language of hers) was a nice girl, and a pity she was a foreigner – but she would keep speaking foreign to that poor baby. They made a firm point of talking to the child in proper Thrynian whenever they were near her; else how was she ever going to grow up, with her head full of that nonsense? And Dubilier was a strange one, not quite right in his wits, but harmless and entirely good-natured – and such a talker! He looked at things all different, somehow, and things he told you seemed wonderful, all shining and good. And he and Lupio Aiguda, but not a bit proud; and there were Mengac's folks going about saying the Aiguda had no goodness in them at all and promising to kill them all. It didn't seem right somehow.

Andos came out to help Lupio in the new patch. He followed him with a trowel, eradicating any weed that had resisted the spade and removing the stones. He too was rather shy of Lupio while liking him considerably, but he was his father's son and so his shyness came out as a gruff self-sufficiency: he was grown-up, he knew what was what. But he was a boy, and had a boy's impetuous, insatiable spirit, so that he was like his mother too, and his questions often betrayed him. Crouching down in the new furrows, he looked up at the man he was helping. Last night Lupio had played his flute, which was a rare event and special enough on its own, but then he had topped it by being prevailed upon to recount one of his adventures, not in the waste lands, but here in Thryn, when he was a boy.

'I'm glad you're not the Cirnex,' he said suddenly.

'What makes you say that?'

'Well, it's daft, isn't it? Sitting up on that old mountain waiting for a god when you could be down here . . . There aren't any gods anyway, are there? That was just Kavi and her nonsense.' Andos habitually made all his questions rhetorical by going straight on before there was time for answers. 'She was mad, that one. I'm glad she's dead.'

Lupio laughed. 'What have you got against Kavi? I bet you never even saw her.'

'My Da says she was the one that kept things the way they were, in the bad days, before the flood and everything.'

'That was her job.' He stopped and leant on his spade. 'She had to wait for the Cirnex; it was just bad luck me being there. A case of mistaken identity.'

'You ought to *hate* her.'

'Nooo . . .' Lupio felt a sudden access of benevolence here in this safe little corner of the world, digging a hole and putting seeds in it. 'She couldn't help it. And the city might be a nicer place with a god, and everyone always knowing what they ought to do. We'd all be happy; there'd be no misery, no poverty, no fighting . . .' He looked at Andos, who was completely bewildered, and realised he was just being romantic. 'Well, no, people could never really be like that; but once upon a time citizens used to believe in Gomath and talk about perfection, Taleg Ibnun, you know? We know nothing'll ever be perfect, but it must be nice to believe it could be.'

But as he spoke he'd already lost heart in it. He was just delivering Dubilier's lines, about ideals and illusions being good for you, and pretty as it was sometimes, it didn't match up. He'd been to the top of the mountain and there was nothing up there, just the view: more lands and more journeys, all the places beyond.

'Do you really think so?'

'No. Don't take any notice of me, Andos; I can't do the philosophy, I'm just waffling. Stick with what you know and forget about gods and perfection and things. They just confuse everything. It's much better to stay down here with the plants and the seeds – and the weeds too.'

Andos, however, was not paying attention. He looked as though something important had just occurred to him in Lupio's rambling. 'I suppose,' he said, 'even then . . . you're only planting seeds because you believe they're going to work, aren't you? You never really know, do you? Everybody's got to believe in something, or nothing would ever get done.'

'You ought to *hate* her.'

Dubilier was sitting up in bed, leaning against the wall. What she said amused him. 'Why, love?'

'She treated you abo – abombally.'

'Abominably.'

'Yes. To shut your door on somebody, somebody you used to

love, like that – it's not human. Why didn't she just say, I'm tired of this, please go away?'

'I think perhaps that's what she did say – in her own way.'

Piripheis was not mollified. 'In her way, in his way.' She hit him lightly on the leg. 'Why don't you all just do and say what you mean instead of all this pretending and hiding and giving secret messages all the time?' She could get annoyed with Dubilier's insistence on unfolding layers of meaning out of everything.

Dubilier was thinking about masks. Alita and he had hidden among the trees of her orchard, beckoning each other, running away. Masks by torchlight. How could he possibly be sure what she had really been saying to him? And what about Ibet?

He stroked Piri's shoulder with the back of one finger. 'I must go and see her.'

'Yes, of course.'

'There's something . . . an unfinished story there.'

'You said it was finished. You said, before you left the city it was already finished.' She turned her head and kissed his finger, nuzzled it with her cheek. 'You can't make it anything now.'

Dubilier knew the idea of his seeing Alita didn't worry her. She cast no shadows of jealousy because there was no tint of possessiveness in the light of her love. She was just puzzled, as by a new word she didn't understand.

'Of course I can,' he said. 'In fact, the past is probably all made up in the present.'

She rolled over, playful now, holding his fingers in the way that Aldellena might have done. 'Oh, yes, and what about the future?'

'That's made up in the present. It must be, because it doesn't exist. I am sitting here now making up a good future in which it's a fine thing for me to go and see Ali tomorrow.'

'And say it doesn't – what do you say? – "come true"?'

'*I* don't say "come true" because I don't think anything ever does come true. Everything always is true.'

'No, but what if it's horrible, and she screams at you and cries and says she'll kill you and you have to run away again?'

'Then I'll sit here tomorrow and, well, no, in fact, I won't sit here tomorrow because I've got the rest of that stone to break, but I'll stand outside breaking stone tomorrow and make up a good past in which that was a fine thing to have happened when I went to see Ali yesterday.'

'You are impossible.'

'Nothing is impossible,' he declared, 'given sufficient illusions and fools enough to dream them.'

'Am I an illusion?' She pressed herself against him, seductively.

'Oh, yes. The best I've ever done.'

'Goat.' It was her favourite insult at the moment. 'If I am an illusion, you won't want me to come with you.'

'No. I'm not trying to hide you, Piri, or hide her, or even hide myself. I think that whatever happens tomorrow, Ali and I will have work to do. Tidying up. I think we'll be able to do that better if we reduce the random factors.' He explained what a random factor was. 'Having you there, there'll be three illusions going on instead of only two. On the other hand – '

In the event, it didn't matter, because random factors swept the board and Alita wasn't at the villa after all. Nobody was, and it looked as if nobody had been for quite a time. After walking through stripped and lifeless rooms he was glad to come into the kitchen and find birds living in the rafters and lizards in the larder. He spoke to them all and then wandered out into the grounds, through the orchard whose uncut grass and ungathered fruit seemed like a silting up of time, an accumulation in one place of vegetable equivalents for all that he had been through, all that had happened here while he was away. He stood on the shore of the lake looking across at the island aviary her grandfather had built. There was so much still that might be used. He wished that the farm might attract more people so that they could take this estate and cultivate it too. It was time for reconstruction.

Ali was presumably dead, unless she had found some way of procuring food and safety in her town house. Now that he had started the process of finding her, he should finish it; whatever Piri felt, he did still care. He did hope that this woman, who had been enigmatic and inaccessible all her life, had not pulled her final trick, perfected her ultimate disguise, and vanished without trace. He did want to know what had happened to her. The birds flew across to the island and back, and didn't care. For them there was no past, no future. It was the curse and the glory of humanity to have these illusions, and to grow attached to them.

'You went off alone?' said Frujos at supper that night. 'Well, if you've really got to go down to the city too, take someone with you, for goodness' sake. Take Lupio to look out for you. There's people as'll recognise you, don't think they won't. And there's plenty more as'll slit your throat just to brighten a dull five minutes.'

Piripheis opened her mouth to say something but closed it again. She didn't want to revoke in fear what she'd said in tranquillity. Let him go. Dubilier was not a twig in the water, to be pushed this way and that as the wind willed.

Now that the beggars owned the city, new outcasts claimed the Hall of Glory – rather, were driven into it, the only place where they could huddle. They came in twos and threes, drawn by a chance word, an accidental meeting, the nod and the glance of a stranger passing in an alley by lantern light. There they found one another, but no safety: there was no safety in the city to be had under sun or moon, indoors or out. So they went down, lower than even the beggars had, down the slippery stair where the weed had surged up and now clustered dead and stinking, down into the underhall and the stone caverns below the city. They worked, and perpetual darkness grudgingly gave way to their fires until the smoke thickened in the airless colonnades, and the river fog rose to meet it. There was a lot of work for them to do since the river had stretched itself and settled back to sleep: the floors were strewn with filth and putrefaction, rags and sticks from the homes its arms had swept away. Stark, bloated bodies grinned through the sunken wrecks of their own furniture; a disembodied arm clutched a jug full of mud. In the ruins of the Wall where the rivergate had been they found the corpse of a deformed old man. He lay on his back, his stiffened hands like talons clawing at the brickwork, for the flood had come upon him in his den as he lay dreaming. They shovelled and swept. What was dry they burned; what still oozed they scraped reluctantly back into the river. There was little to breathe but poisons and the fingers of disease had marked everything they touched, so that many died, and even when the restoration was complete many more, for it was hard to live there. Even so, they grew in numbers, but remained out of sight because they had no strength. They were waiting for that, but not the strength to live above ground: the brute strength of the packs or the cunning strength of the lone survivors. Or perhaps that would be it after all; perhaps he would prove a great warlord.

They gathered round the fire and prayed, and talked, and sang, and were silent. They pieced together scraps of news and rumour and conjecture: the Previs was dead, but who had killed her? and where was the body? Two women sat in daylong trances, conferring with her spirit through the smoke of magic herbs: yes, there was a successor; no, she was none of them, she was to come. So Kavi was more important after her sudden, mysterious death than ever she had been in the great length of her life, but there was no irony in that: it is the way of presiding spirits. They listened for her word. They knew the hidden ways and could travel them faster than the fractured and perilous streets above. With faith, this skill could bring them food, and when it did not, they fasted. They wept, they shouted, they quarrelled, they were reconciled, but always they sang, Lead us, Gomath, lead us, lead us. These days, their songs echoed more than ever.

The conventions of society die late, often after the society itself. Dubilier reached to ring again, but Lupio touched his arm and said, 'Mad as it may sound, I think we'll attract less attention by breaking in than we will by standing on the doorstep ringing the bell.' They slipped round the side of the house and Dubilier stood on Lupio's shoulders to force a suitable window.

They didn't stay long. The memories were thicker here, for the house had escaped ransack and only perishables had been evacuated. The furniture was gradually turning into soft white ghosts; the house was shuttered and stale, and nothing disturbed the slow fall of the drifting dust.

'There can't be many places left intact as this,' said Lupio. He lifted the corner of a tapestry to admire the workmanship. 'I wonder why no one's stripped it.'

'The destruction hasn't been methodical.'

'No, but I'd have thought a place like this, standing above the flood-waters . . . and we found it easy enough to get in.'

'It's probably just another random factor,' said Dubilier. He was aware how they were accumulating. It was difficult to see the shape of events. The journey home had been simple and lucid; since then, the unforeseen had dominated, and though he now had a good acquaintance with the forces at work in Thryn, predictions and even intentions eluded his grasp. At the moment of his flippant formulation to Piripheis of his theories of time, they had ceased to apply. The past he had in mind, his life up until leaving the city, now seemed incoherent and vague. He could see himself, and the events with which he had surrounded himself, with clarity, but without understanding, as if remembering some vivid dream. And the new past which he had just adopted, the story of Thryn from then until his return, at least left traces. The entire city had been changed; nothing did not reveal it. But here, throughout the gracious, sepulchral rooms so redolent of associations, he found no clues: nothing to tell where the two women had gone. Everything was in place. They had left the house intending to come back at some time. Or was it only the efficiency of Ibet's housekeeping, that – unlike him – she had tidied everything up before leaving?

So the future was equally opaque. There was nothing on the horizon. He and Lupio and Piripheis might stay working on the farm until they grew old and died. But in this uncertainty, the feeling of void after the completion of enterprise, he trusted that something new was arising. They were freewheeling, moving into new time, beginning again in a different direction. Time is an illusion by which we differentiate pattern out of chaos. Dubilier believed that his failure to recognise, and thus to create, the pattern of the future was due to the fact that time had been renewed; the patterns would be new patterns. Events were working, but as if underground, unseen, even by him. The people were disrupted, their city demolished, as if to clear the ground for new development; the Wall was down in preparation for the new demarcation of space which must accompany the new time. Standing at the door of Alita's bedroom, reviewing as in a museum the locales of his past life, the functions of his vanished identity, he hoped that he would duplicate the openness that he saw in Lupio, that readiness for new roles. What would they be?

'It was a fine house,' said Lupio, rejoining him after touring it. 'I hope it survives.'

'You burned your own house down?'

Lupio seemed to pick up his thoughts. 'Breaking with the past,' he said. 'This woman obviously intended to come back one day.'

'Maybe.'

'What do you want to do? Did you search the villa thoroughly?'

'No, but it seemed even more desolate than this. I don't know. I can't relate to the past very well today. Let's go back to the farm. I want to see Piri and think about the present.'

Himithet came in with Bruki. For once Mengac addressed him before he could start speaking. 'Cheredep here has been telling me a story I think you'd enjoy. Cheredep, this is Himithet and his wife Bruki. All of us here work for the New Order. You can say safely what you've just told me.'

Cheredep was a dark, sober-looking man whom Himithet couldn't recall seeing before, but he said, 'Himithet; Bruki. I've seen you both several times. We've sacked a number of houses together, and I worked with you at the Wall one week. I came here because I thought you all – we all should know that Lupio's back.'

'Lupio? No. He'd never come back to Thryn, not now there's no Previs to protect him. Can't have been.'

'He's not the only witness,' Mengac put in.

'Oh, it's definitely him, Himithet. I know him. I used to be his cook. He was coming out of a house, a big place, one of the old Aigudan mansions.'

'We should have knocked them all down long ago.'

Cheredep went on, disregarding him. 'It looks like he's taken a drop in self-importance since he's been away.'

'How do you mean?'

'He'd none of the finery he used to wear, except for a great sword. He was dressed in ordinary labourer's clothes – '

'Disguise.'

' – and there was another man with him I didn't know. Could have been a foreigner, I suppose, someone he picked up on his travels. And if he's taken to housebreaking and living down in the city – well, he was always a wild one, but he liked his comforts and he was ready to fight for them.'

Bruki had been listening carefully. She asked, 'Who is Lupio?'

'You remember the religious revival, the year before last? Kavi telling us Perfection was at hand? Do you remember what was at the middle of all that?'

'No. Some prophecy, wasn't it – somebody . . . Oh, right – '

'Hm? The Cirnex, remember him? Come back to tell us how wicked we were?'

'That was Lupio?'

'Right. Right. She pretended he'd appeared in a flash of lightning – where was it?'

'Downstairs,' said Mengac.

'Eh?'

'In the library.'

'Yes.'

'And that's how she got killed; he ran away – '

'He's no fool. He could see it wasn't going to stick. She had to tell everyone that unfortunately the second coming had been postponed, owing to a slight – ha! – indisposition.'

'And then there was that riot, and the temple – '

'They stove her head in for her. He must fancy himself, strolling back home like that!'

'He always did,' said Cheredep.

'Well, I don't know,' objected Bruki. 'He was very popular, wasn't he?'

'And very unpopular when he disappeared.'

'But people will still listen to him.'

'They're not that stupid.'

'People are stupid,' said Mengac bitterly. 'I see what Bruki sees. Even the hard ones living out in the ruins; there'll be some who'll be glad to see him again.'

'More than that,' said Bruki, 'there's all the fanatics down underground, the religious ones.'

'The Hall of Beggars? There's no one there now. You're a bit out of date, love – eh, Mengac? You, whatever your name is? We did out the Hall; cleaned it right out.'

'They went underground,' Bruki said calmly. 'To the underhall. There's a whole colony of them down there. You didn't know?' She turned to Mengac. 'They'll be a pushover for an opportunist like Lupio: all shut up in the dark, fantasising like mad . . . They'll be so keyed up they'll believe anything. Has he been back long?'

'Hard to say,' said Cheredep.

'When's the earliest report?'

Mengac shuffled papers wearily. 'A week ago the first positive, but there's so much nonsense here – '

'Still, he might not have found the fanatics.'

'Who knows?'

'We've got to get to him before he does.'

Himithet started to smile again. 'Oh yes,' he murmured, 'oh yes. I'll get some assistance. You, come with me and show us where you saw the mighty Cirnex.'

Cheredep followed him out. Mengac sat deep in thought for a few minutes, and then said, 'You're right, Bruki. Your husband, he's not interested in what I think; he only thinks about enemies, the Aiguda – '

'Lupio was an Aigu? Yes, of course, he was. Oh yes, that'll be why Himithet's so keen all of a sudden. A special holy Aigu to hunt down.'

Mengac rubbed his head.

'I don't know how you see this, Mengac,' Bruki went on. 'I don't know what your plans are for that lot down in the underhall, but it's not just them; not just the loonies. We can't afford another revival. All right, so Kavi's gone, but that might make Lupio more dangerous.'

They heard the door of the Iigril boom shut.

Bruki asked, 'Are you going to give him his head?'

'Your husband? It's what he does best.'

Bruki sat and thought about it, kicking her heels on the table leg. 'I suppose,' she said. She looked grim, accepting an unpleasant task under obligation. 'We've got to kill Lupio, and before the fanatics can make him a martyr.'

Last night it had rained hard. Today a blinding sun was climbing a steady blue sky, and everything gleamed, rinsed and draining. He would go to the temple today, and after that perhaps to one of the safe farms, where he could get an afternoon's work. Perhaps to the one where they'd given him this pony. But first there was the Previs to feed. Hifran had often wondered whether it was sinful to steal food for her, but there seemed little alternative, so he consoled himself with the thought that in a proper city it would be the duty of the citizens to look after their Previs, so that he was merely making sure they did, by a roundabout route. Also, he spread the burden as thin as he could, trying not to raid one place too many times – and this had the added advantage of making his visits less susceptible of detection.

He'd been to this one a few times before. It was mostly vegetables and grain, but they had a family of goats, and some chickens, and he'd once or twice been able to steal from the kitchen. It seemed a prosperous little place; one of the old Aiguda houses, like Aigu Lupio's had been. He heard agitated voices. Had he been seen? He burrowed into the hedge and crouched there, scratched and wet all over.

Piripheis was brushing her hair. She turned from the mirror to look out of the window. The sun beckoned. A fresh day. Last night's rain smoked off the drying roofs.

Who was that?

'Dubilier.' Her touch pulled him out of shallow sleep. 'There are men outside.'

They hadn't often been bothered, never seriously. There were enough of them in the villa to deter most vandals; there were still many places less well defended. The urgency in Piripheis's tone brought Dubilier out of bed and to the side of the window. There were four of them; he recognised none. At that moment one cupped his hands to his mouth and called out.

'Farmer!'

'I'll wake the others,' said Piri, pulling on a gown and hurrying from the room.

Dubilier opened the window, staying cautiously to one side. 'What do you want?'

'We don't want any trouble. You're harbouring an enemy. Hand him over and we'll leave.'

'An enemy?'

'An Aigu.'

Dubilier smiled. How stubborn they were! How long would

it be before they realised they were living in a new age? 'There are no Aiguda any more,' he told them.

'Is this your place?'

'No.'

Frujos came hurrying in, his hair disarrayed, his eyes wild. 'Let me talk to them.' He stood in the open window.

'Frujos, you be careful,' urged Win, coming in after him.

'What do you want?'

'Just the Aigu, friend. Send him out and we'll go away, hm?'

Frujos looked at Dubilier.

'Be a good citizen and send him out, eh? For Mengac and the revolution.' There was something insulting about the voice.

'Is that Mengac?' asked Dubilier.

Win shook her head. 'No, that's Himithet. Watch him, he's dangerous. Son of a snake and a rat.'

Dubilier stepped into view. 'Himithet,' he called. 'I used to be of the Aiguda. Now I'm a farm-worker. What is it you want with me?'

'Come out and we'll tell you,' grinned Himithet, shading his eyes from the sun that flashed off the glass. Cheredep was squinting too; he shook Himithet by the shoulder.

'That's not him.'

'Not him? Not the one?' Himithet tried to size up the figure. 'You sure?' Cheredep grunted dismissively. 'He's Aiguda, anyhow.'

'We're after Lupio,' Cheredep reminded him. The two thugs they'd recruited waited impatiently for the talk to end and the damage to begin.

'Your name Lupio?' Himithet shouted.

'No.'

'Is he there?'

'No.'

'He's lying,' Cheredep muttered, signalling brusquely to the other two. They stepped forward readily. 'He's the other one, the one who was with Lupio in the city.'

Himithet looked at him. 'Are you sure?'

'Sure enough.'

They looked back up. There was nobody at the window.

'Aigu,' shouted Himithet.

There came a sound of doors opening and closing, and hurrying footsteps.

'They're making a break for it.'

'The back way. Run!'

But before any of them had got more than a few yards, the front door opened. They stopped.

'How can I help you?' Dubilier asked.

'Lupio,' said Cheredep, pushing in front of Himithet. 'Where is he?'

'He's not here.'

'We'll see for ourselves, if you don't mind.'

'Come in.' He held the door for them. 'I'll show you around.'

'It's a trap – '

From inside came the voice of Frujos: 'Don't you go letting them murderous, good-for-nothing vermin into my home – '

Himithet smiled, showing all his teeth, and bowed slightly. 'You're very kind.' He went in and stood looking around the hallway with obvious pleasure. He hung his coat on a peg. 'You really keep it nice, hm? Tasteful. Cosy.' He spoke to Cheredep who was still hesitating on the step. 'Aren't you coming? Shall we take the Aigu up on his kind invitation?' Cheredep came in, the others following. 'Oh,' said Himithet, 'perhaps you wouldn't mind if our friends took a look at the grounds while you're showing us round? I'm sure there's a lot to see.'

'Not in quantity,' Dubilier said, 'but we use the space as fully as we can.' He shut the front door. 'Where would you like to see first?'

Frujos stood glaring on the stairs. They went round the house looking in every room. Himithet checked every cupboard, every hiding place. Cheredep came downstairs. 'He's not up there,' he said. There was the sound of a baby crying.

'Now the grounds, Aigu, eh? Let's see what our friends have found.'

The chicken coop had been torn open. Birds and feathers were everywhere. One of the men was holding Frujos, a knife at his throat. The other was standing in the middle of an onion bed, an egg in his hand. He crushed it as they approached. His fist bled viscous white and gold. 'There's no one.'

'All right. All right. Bring the farmer. We'll go down to the wall.'

In Dubilier's time a low stone wall had marked the extent of his land. He and Lupio had helped Frujos reinforce it with rubble from the demolished terrace. Here the goats were penned. Himithet stood stroking Dip-Dip for a moment as they all assembled. 'Now,' he said. 'Lupio was here, wasn't he?'

'Yes,' said Dubilier.

'But he's not here now. He went away.'

'That's right.'

'Where? Where did he go?'

'I don't know.'

Himithet smiled again. 'Well now,' he said. 'This is what we're going to do.' His men grinned at each other. 'We're going to start here, and work our way – systematically work our way – back up to the house – all the way up there – and then through the house, until you remember. I'm sure that between us we can manage to do something to jog your memory.' Suddenly the hand fondling Dip-Dip showed metal. The kid tried to back away but found himself held.

'You'll have to destroy everything,' said Dubilier amiably. 'We don't know where Lupio is.' Diwy began to bleat fretfully. Himithet caught the eye of his unoccupied lieutenant and indicated the nanny with a jerk of his head. The man stepped into the pen and cornered her firmly. Himithet looked round. Her mate Dioc was tethered at a distance, behind a hurdle. The knife bit. Blood splashed the butcher's sleeve. Dip-Dip screamed horribly.

Dubilier watched sadly. Was this the end of the story? Perhaps Lupio was to be the saviour of Thryn; it seemed that something must have helped him, his escape had been so quick and so successful. Perhaps his life was protected. But they were all to die as martyrs for him, even the animals. Dip-Dip was dying, struggling. Couldn't he help? They would kill him too, before he could move. But –

'Dioc,' he called. 'Dioc.'

Himithet looked up. 'Thought of something?'

There was a snap, and the sound of wood splintering. Himithet looked back and yelled. The man guarding Diwy lunged sideways; she leapt past and ran to her kid. Dioc was there, hooves and horns and teeth. Himithet stabbed and missed, yelled again and went down. Diwy turned, her nostrils flaring, as her captor tried to avoid her. Dip-Dip had fallen. His wasn't the only blood. Dioc jumped the fence, his eyes fearsome and yellow. 'Call it off!' shouted the man holding Frujos. Dubilier had a stone and was bringing it down on the side of the man's head; Cheredep yelled, thrusting. Dubilier stumbled back from the sword, dropping the stone. Himithet got to his feet, shaking and cursing. His right arm dangled. Dioc ran at him again. The man in the paddock aimed a vicious blow at Diwy, barely missing her. And then the men were regrouping.

Dubilier was calling something in a strange language. Chickens: there seemed to be more of them now, flapping out of the bushes shrieking. Beaks and claws. Cheredep was striking at them, trying to keep them from his eyes. They were a storm of wings, scratching, biting. Dioc, abrupt and terrible, blood across his face. Frujos too, with the chopper Win had run to snatch from the woodpile. Dubilier rose, the cut stinging. Andos was running from the house with his home-made spear, and Piri following with Lupio's sword. How strange it all looked.

This was the first battle: the defenders of the new against the destroying forces of the old – parents fighting for their children, farmers for their seedlings, birds for their eggs. He went to see what he could do for Dip-Dip, but he was dead, and so were some of the chickens. So it is, he thought; martyrs. But not us, not yet. Mustn't be. Only the first battle. It was turning into a rout. One man was on the ground unmoving, and Himithet was trying to flee. He had been beaten off more easily because he hadn't understood the nature of the battle. He had come looking for Aiguda, a decadent race, expecting to drive them nearer extinction; he had thought to push over what was already rotten and decrepit. On a hundred estates, this was what he had done; here for the first time he had encountered not old enemies but new ones, and they had routed him.

But the line between defence and attack was a delicate one. The forces of life could turn murderers too, in the blink of an observing eye. Dubilier ran to them, calling each one's name again, but to pacify and quieten.

'Previs Kavi! He's back! The Cirnex – '

'What, boy? What?'

The Previs was recovering. She could sit up now and read unaided, sometimes, in the volumes Hifran had brought her from a perilous raid on the Iigril library. He was really a very skilful little thief. She was glad that it was he who had been looking after her rather than one of those faithless temple girls. It had been Hifran who had insisted that she was not dead after she'd been struck down in the rioting, and had made them bring her here. They'd left immediately, and never returned. They'd played their small part for Gomath, and good riddance.

'Aigu Lupio, Previs – '

'You've been to the temple? What did you see?'

'No, Previs, I saw him. He's back, and another man I've never seen before.'

'Tell me. Sit on the bed. Catch your breath and tell me.'

He told her about riding to the little farm and hiding in the bushes. 'I heard them coming, running, and I thought they'd seen me, but I looked out and I saw them at the back door. It was Aigu Lupio, Previs.'

'Are you sure, Hifran? You were frightened; you saw somebody that – '

'No, Previs, I know him. I know him better than anyone. I used to sleep – ' He blushed and bowed his head.

'Go on, boy. Pull yourself together. Tell me what he did.'

'He and the other man said something to each other; they were in a great hurry, and the other man disappeared back indoors. Then the Aigu, the Cirnex, came running down towards me. I didn't know what to do. I wanted to stand up and call out, but I was scared. He came to the hedge and scrambled over it, and then he ran past me through the trees.'

'He didn't see you?'

'No, Previs, but he took my pony, that was how he got away.'

'Why was he running? Did you find that out, eh?'

'Well, after he'd gone through the trees I got out of the hedge and I shouted, but by the time I got to the road he was a long way down it. I didn't know what was going on, and I didn't know what to do; but I was hungry . . . and I knew you would be too, Previs – '

'Stop dithering.'

'And so I went back to the hedge, but when I got there some

men were there and they were beating the hedges and shouting, and they had weapons; and then one of them started kicking the hen-house, and I ran away again.'

'How many men?'

'I saw two, but there might have been some more.'

'Did you know them?'

'No, Previs.'

She sat for a long while saying nothing. Hifran began to be afraid he might have excited her too much and tired her. At last she said, her voice gathering strength as she went on, 'If you're right, Hifran, and it was the Cirnex, the ones who tried to kill me must be trying to kill him. This is a terrible time, boy. The enemies of perfection are strong. The Wall is down. Deshingena-aw-Jeswed are creeping in. We must have faith. We must find the Cirnex and rally the citizens for the time when Gomath comes.'

'He's coming, Previs. He isn't far off, is he?'

'No, Hifran,' she said; and she thought, Another man, a stranger ... who helped the Cirnex escape while he himself stayed to brave the attackers ...

That evening Hifran was sitting by her while she slept when he heard a noise. He stole upstairs and looked in the yard. It was the pony, riderless. 'I wish you could speak!' murmured the boy. The creature nuzzled him.

When the farmers woke next morning their patient had gone. He had been sullen and resentful at first, when he'd come to and found himself in bed with his head and chest bandaged, deserted by his companions and watched over by an Outwall woman. Then he'd grown embarrassed, refusing food and attention, and at last turned to the wall in a stubborn pretence of sleep.

'Like a child,' said Piripheis.

'Leave him,' Dubilier told her. 'He'll feel better about it in the morning.'

But he'd left without waking anyone. Win had some words to say about folks' ingratitude; Frujos assured them *he'd* not expected anything different, though he was surprised, he admitted, to find they hadn't been burgled or murdered into the bargain; but Dubilier just remarked that he hoped the man wouldn't come to harm in the city.

'They'll be back,' said Lupio.

'We'll find somewhere else to hide,' said Piripheis.

'We should leave the city altogether,' he said. 'Go back to your village and leave Thryn to die. There's no future here.'

'On the contrary,' said Dubilier, 'there's only the future, and it's only just begun.' He didn't try to explain. If he stayed, they both would. But perhaps it was time to leave the farm. To stay would be tempting destruction, for all the others if not for them.

Andos said, 'You ought to stay and fight.'

His father looked awkward and put his knife and fork down heavily. 'I hope you'll not be leaving us to look after this great place on our own.'

Though she had gone many streets out of her way to pass it, Ibet barely glanced at the house before hurrying by. Somehow, she felt, if she didn't notice it nobody else would. So far it seemed to have escaped vandals and looters. If things stayed quiet, she told herself, she might move back in one day. Alita would never know. As long as she was kept properly afraid, she'd stay cooped up in the aviary. Not that she could get off the island without help, anyway. Already the ravages of damp and exposure were weakening her pampered constitution.

The place Ibet was hurrying to had formerly been a simple tavern, a hearth glowing like a beacon for all the shiftless and shapeless of the city. Now the only light in the river quarter came from bonfires where survivors crawled to warm their bones. The tavern had become a dark, tight little fortress, and only the known and the knowing could get in. Behind the shutters smoke and drink changed hands as before, but now on a market with other commodities, food and clothing, jewellery, skins and spices, and every service you could put a price on. Whenever Ibet's friends and relatives and debtors let her down, she came here. Alita's money was good coin.

Ibet argued with one of the proprietors until she went to see about what Ibet was asking for. Then Ibet took a seat among the crowd, accepting pipe and bowl as they were passed on, withdrawn and anonymous in her grey cowl. Her brain idled. She let the fumes rise into it. The acrid night flowed through her, thick with tales. There was a big man with a broken arm who had some rubbish to tell about magicians and their familiars attacking him. The clientele, gullible as ever, were enjoying it. She heard them speculating about the return of the Cirnex – would they never get tired of that? – and a man who could either talk to animals or turn into one, she wasn't sure. The tale had an unusual teller though. He seemed to make no boast of his claims; indeed, he was frightening himself as much as his audience. He was in awe of this fabulous stranger, a man who'd been out across the wastelands and back again . . . A thought darted into her mind and out again at once, but it left her listening with more than half an ear.

'It looks as though we've lost before we've started,' said Bruki. 'They're making legends already. I was in a tavern last night, listening to one of them, one of Himithet's men. He doesn't know me, or he'd probably have shut up for my benefit.' She sighed. 'It's beginning again.'

'Lupio?' Mengac frowned.

'Lupio and a horde of demons, apparently. This other man, the one my husband talked to, he's a nuisance. I think we could persuade them against Lupio, remind them what happened with him last time, but we've got nothing on his mysterious friend. Nobody seems to know him at all, so they're having a banquet over him.'

'What do you mean?'

'He's the one they've been waiting for, the one Lupio went off to fetch – from Hisper Einou, would you believe? He's their Gomath, come back to perfect them.' She laughed. 'It's so ironic it's beautiful! They're so ready – if only *we* could get at them the way Lupio can, we could have the New Order shaping up before nightfall! They're milling around like sheep, bleating for someone to lead them, but they're facing the wrong way. Back into the past, always the past. What's the matter with this city, Mengac? Don't they recognise the future when they see it? Does it have to jump up and hit them over the head first?'

'It begins with violence, the future. They need that shock.'

'My husband and his merry men.'

'That's right.'

'I wish he'd get it over with,' said Bruki.

'What is it, Andos?' Dubilier looked up from his weeding.

'Ma says there's another of 'em at the door.'

People had been coming for days, most just to gape and pry, some to praise the little commune for standing up to the brigands and to offer their support to his cause. He was bemused to find himself so readily identified as a leader and sent them away.

'What do you do?' he would ask them.

They were farmers, toolsmiths, wheelwrights, nurses, clothiers.

'Go away and do that, then. That's the best way you can serve the "cause", as you call it.'

Of those he had seen and spoken to, a few had understood. He was sure that many more had been dismissed with more acerbity and less encouragement by Win or her husband – though the effect was the same: it made them go back to their own work. For Win to send Andos to fetch him, his latest caller must have been very importunate indeed.

The woman on the threshold lowered her cowl at his approach.

'Ibet!'

'So it is you.' She paused, taking in his ragged hair, patched smock, dirty hands, heavy boots. 'Things have changed, Dubilier, haven't they?' She gestured at his villa, now a farm.

He recognised her old self-assurance, developed and strengthened now that she was no longer restrained by the obligations of service. 'They have. I tried to find you. I went to the villa and the town house, but they were deserted. I've got much to thank you for.'

She lcoked arch. 'It's a servant's pleasure to serve, I'm sure.'

Dubilier was surprised. She plainly thought he'd used the phrase sarcastically. 'I mean it,' he said, stepping forward to her. 'You told me where to look when I didn't even really know what I was looking for.'

She searched his face again. 'You went? You went to the mountains?'

'Yes.'

'And came back again?'

'Yes.'

Now she was surprised, almost laughing in amazement, but

recovering herself immediately. How controlled she was. He had envied her before, but now he merely observed, impressed.

'What did you find? No, don't tell me, I don't want to know.'

'You don't?'

'No.'

'You must be the only person in the city who doesn't. Won't you come in?' he said. 'Have something to refresh you.'

'No. I just wanted to see you, to make sure.'

Now it was her sense of purpose he admired. Satisfied with having seen him, she was already back at her own plans and calculations.

'What do you do now?'

'Survive.' She stood very straight, almost defiantly. The line of her shoulders suggested someone who has put down a laborious burden and has no intention of picking it up again.

'How?'

'There are ways. Fortunately we don't all have to break our backs and our fingernails grubbing in the dirt.' He had noticed the paint on her nails and bracelets inside the capacious sleeves of her old robe. She seemed half scornful, half pitying.

'No,' he agreed. 'You your way, I mine.'

'You enjoy it, don't you?'

'Yes.'

She had spoken to taunt him. Now she shrugged, clearly dismissing him as beneath contempt; but she couldn't resist another prod.

'You didn't come across your dearly beloved, then, when you went visiting?'

'Alita – where is she?'

Suddenly her mask was back. The old Ibet stood before him, canny and close. 'Well . . . A mistress doesn't always tell her servant where she's going, does she?'

He heard the menace in her voice. 'Is she dead?' he asked.

'Dead and buried, most likely,' said Ibet, turning to go. 'Dead and buried, like all the Aiguda should be. Don't fret yourself, Dubilier: you just go back to your work.'

Instead, he went to talk with Piripheis.

'I'd like to kill her,' she said.

'Hush, Piri, of course you wouldn't! If it hadn't been for her, how would I ever have met you?'

She conceded the point unwillingly. 'All the same, I would. Treating you like that!' Her eyes burned.

'And possessiveness too! You are coming on!' Then she had to laugh, and dissipate her anger; and he observed her as he fondled her, feeling her relax. At the right moment, he said, 'The thing is, I think Alita is still alive.'

She stiffened, but he held her. 'I thought the woman said – '

'Her words didn't match her eyes. What do you think: why did she come to see me?'

'To see if it really was you; she said that.'

'Mm-hm, but why was she interested in me?'

'She wanted to gloat over you. The Aigu working on the farm, like a servant.'

'Right; but that's exactly what she didn't do. Once she saw what I am, what she thinks of as defeated, she discounted me altogether. Her interest moved on elsewhere. And yet when she arrived she was so urgent – she even cowed Win into letting her see me! I think it was what I represent that was important to her. Was I a threat to her?'

'How?'

'I don't know, Piri, but the only way I can see is if she's keeping Ali prisoner somewhere – in the cellar at the house, probably – and living off her somehow. She wanted to see if I were still passionate with love for Ali, and particularly if I were still the great Aigu with power and men to command. As I'm not, she's decided I'm no threat: I'm not about to rescue her prisoner.'

'That sounds like a story,' Piri said doubtfully.

'Well, whatever the explanation, I'm convinced she's hiding Ali from me; and the only reason to hide something is because you possess it and you don't want anyone else to.'

'Possess . . . Perhaps it's love, Dubilier. Perhaps she loves Alita and is scared you'll steal her away again.'

Dubilier paused to recall Ibet's manner, her tone, her expression.

'I don't think so. There's a hollowness in Ibet, a heartlessness. She needs to control everything because she has no faith in anything being good to her of its own accord. Or is that love? It can wear strange faces in this city . . .'

'Don't go, Dubilier. Don't go looking for her. Whatever they have together, let them keep it. We don't need Ali.'

'She might need us.'

'If you go back down to the city, you'll be killed, I know it.' She let her arms fall from him. 'You're right,' she said, 'I am growing possessive. I must let you go. If you want to find Alita, go.'

'Piri, darling.' He held her. 'Don't you start building mazes for me too. Soon I shall have to go because if I don't I'll be encouraging you to be possessive. And then I'll have to stay because if I go I'll be encouraging you to be a martyr.'

The door banged open and Aldellena stumped in. 'Ook,' she demanded. She had brought a speckled feather for them to see. There was dried blood on it.

Piripheis scooped her up. 'Aldellena,' she said in astonishment, 'I left you under the tree; how did you get upstairs?'

'Walk,' said Aldellena, unconcerned. 'Ook,' and she brandished her treasure again.

'You walked all the way upstairs?' Dubilier asked her.

'She's tried to before,' Piripheis told him, 'but she's never managed.' She was proud for her daughter, but taking great care not to overburden Aldellena with that.

'It's a lovely feather,' said Dubilier. 'Piri, I'm going to go down to the city and look for Alita.'

She gave him a smile. Aldellena had lifted them both out of the labyrinth. 'Come back.'

He kissed them and went to speak to Frujos, who was also alarmed.

'Don't worry; I'll borrow Lupio's sword.'

'Lupio's gone off too; he'll have it with him.'

'Has he? Where's he gone?'

'Said he saw somebody creeping about the hedges and took off after him. Oh, you're a pair of rot-brained chickens, you are, going out there with all the world hunting for you. What'll we do if you don't come back, hm?'

'Now don't you start. There's a long knife with the bailing gear, isn't there? I'll take that.'

There was a strange nostalgia in him. Memories waited every yard along the road, though it had changed much since he'd last taken this way to the city to visit Alita. Again he felt the sensation of destiny, of past time being gathered together and wound up so that new time could begin to be unwound. He would find her there, in that tomb of a house that was also embalmed in memories and yet entirely altered. He would see her so differently, clearly, as he had Ibet; he could help her now, and no matter how many times he might see her again afterwards, it was now that their last goodbyes would be said. His feelings for her had been plagued by phantoms because they were phantom: formal but lifeless, a transparency without a heart, wavering in the orchard at twilight. Now he had come into clear day, and that hopeless apparition could be laid to rest between them. Piripheis had no need to fear it.

He passed a man he didn't know, but who evidently recognised him. He greeted him uncertainly, hesitating as Dubilier walked on, and then hailed him.

'What's the matter?'

'You're the one lives on that farm with the man who used to call himself the Cirnex?'

'That's right.' The man was highly agitated. Was he dangerous? Dubilier didn't think so. Perhaps he was just another miracle-poker, ready with a thousand questions. 'What is it?'

'They got him. They've taken him. I saw them.'

'Lupio? Is Lupio in trouble?'

'The revolutionaries. I saw them. He was fighting them off, half a dozen to one.'

'What happened to him?'

'If he's not dead, they'll have him in the Iigril, and he's as good as dead there; you'll never get him out again.'

Alita struggled out of the water spluttering and hugged herself, looking warily about. She coughed and shivered. It was nearly noon. She'd wasted hours bullying herself out of the fear that Ibet would return, which was infuriating seeing that she'd waited how long? a week at least, surely, for the one day when Ibet could not come back in time. Alita had almost despaired of her ever going down to the city again, but this morning she'd announced she had to. Could it be a trick? Could she be waiting somewhere to catch her and punish her again and drag her back to the island? No, she told herself, though she was still shivering with more than cold, Ibet had no reason to suspect this escape, for Ibet didn't know what she knew. Ibet hadn't been there that morning when she'd crawled through the bushes and peered out and seen him standing there. Where she was standing now. It was a long way across the lake but she'd recognised him at once. He was back. She'd called out once but he hadn't heard, and she'd been frightened to do it again in case Ibet were there and she heard instead. But now Ibet was down in the city and wouldn't catch her before she got to Dubilier's villa. There she'd be safe. Whatever he thought of her now, he wouldn't let Ibet take her back and punish her. First she needed clothes; her dress had been too heavy to swim in and she'd torn it off. There'd be something in the house.

There wasn't. She was shocked and angry to find everything gone: all the lovely clothes from the wardrobes, and her jewels, and her books. Then she grew frightened again, dried herself on an old blanket, wrapped it around her shoulders, and hurried out. The sun was shining and there were birds above, singing as if things had never gone wrong, as if it had always been summer and Thryn had never been destroyed. She wondered if they were the same birds that lived in the aviary with her. Well, they were free and so was she, and neither of them had to go back to that if they didn't want to. She was going to see Dubilier, who would protect her.

There was someone coming, just around the bend. Ibet. No, unless she'd brought men and horses with her. Alita crouched down by the hedge and covered her face.

There were fifteen of them, mostly men, some on horseback. They travelled easily, as if anticipating no hindrance. Their leader was a small, noisy man who was walking backwards addressing them all, with much gesticulation.

'Chickens,' he was saying, 'chickens and goats. That's all. Not demons, not ghosts, not witchery-woo. Who's afraid of chickens here? Eh? Anyone afraid of chickens? Anyone afraid of goats, then? Anyone? No one! That's good, that's very good. Then we won't be having any trouble, will we? No trouble, eh? What we'll do – what we'll do is this. When we get to the farm –'

'Himithet.'

'What?'

The man pointed to the figure huddled against the hedge. 'Well, well. What's this, then? Come here, my dear.'

Alita didn't move.

'Bring her to me, one of you – she appears to be a little deaf.'

There were sniggers of expectation. She was lifted to her feet and dragged back to the road, her hands held behind her. She cowered.

'We're not going to hurt you, my dear. Look at me, hm?' He thrust a fist under her unwilling chin and forced it up. She saw him then, him and his crew, and something revived in her. They were servants, servants and beggars and thieves and even idiots. What did they mean by holding her? She tossed the wet hair from her face and held her head proudly, staring down at the grinning captain.

'Let go of me.'

There were gasps and shouts of laughter when they heard her voice. There was no mistaking the aristocratic tone. Himithet was delighted. 'Who are you, my sweet?'

'I am the Aigui Alita; I'm *not* your sweet.'

'An Aigui! Did we all hear that? A genuine Aigui! And we thought they were all *extinct*, didn't we?' There were shouts and cheers from the men, raucous suggestions. He raised a hand for silence, relishing the moment. It was perfect. Something to whet their appetites. The farm would be a pushover once they'd warmed up on her. 'I *am* sorry, Aigui, I didn't realise we were talking to an Aigui, Aigui, or I'd have been more respectful. I must confess, Aigui, we took you for some tramp or other, wrapped in that blanket.' He seized the folds and jerked them apart. There were whistles and cries of appreciation. He smiled, staring at her body just long enough to make her realise how helpless she was, to blunt the edge of her defiance on the cold stone of fear. She would do anything soon, to save herself. 'It's lucky that you fell into our company, Aigui,' he went on, letting the blanket drop closed again. 'Someone of your standing shouldn't be travelling alone, Aigui; she needs looking after, Aigui; she doesn't know what sort of scoundrels and villains there are lurking along this road. Don't worry, Aigui, we'll look after you. We seem to be travelling the same way; why don't you just jump up behind my first lieutenant and ride with us, hm?' He signalled to one of the mounted men and they began to hoist her onto his horse.

She struggled. 'No – ' The blanket rode up her thighs, caught between her and her captor as she kicked. Himithet drew his sword and gave her bottom a sharp smack with the flat of the blade.

'Don't be *alarmed*, Aigui . . .'

Her hands and feet were tied and she was slung face down across the saddle-bow, half-covered by the blanket. The horse was apparently familiar with this kind of treatment and took no notice of her. She stopped squirming when they rode on, afraid of jerking herself from the horse's back; she was even glad to be hanging head downwards so that she didn't have to look at the men on foot who clustered around and pestered her. She was almost unconscious from her exertions.

They were badgering Himithet. 'Let's do her now. What are we waiting for?' But let them wait. I can command them as long as they know there's a juicy reward at the end of it. Let them get worked up, they'll appreciate her more. After all, Aiguda practically *are* extinct. Mengac, we're winning.

He hardly noticed the rider approaching from the other direction. Suddenly one of the gang gave a startled yell: 'It's him!' Himithet came to. The man was riding off the road to circumvent them.

'Who?'

'Lupio! It's Lupio!'

'What? Well, get after him then!' He hesitated as the horses were spurred into a gallop; why hadn't he come on horseback? There was one left. Cheredep's. 'Give me your horse.'

'What?'

'Get down, man!'

'But the girl – '

Himithet strode up to them. Alita felt herself gripped by the legs and hauled down. It wouldn't be so bad. There weren't many of them now that those ones had ridden away. They were in a hurry; they'd be quick. They weren't far from Dubilier's. He would rescue her.

Himithet held her to him with his left arm. Her head lolled. She saw something gleam in his right hand, coming up fast under her chin. He dropped her as she slumped and pushed past Cheredep to leap onto the horse, wiping his blade on its mane as he dug his knees into its flanks. There were shouts of protest, but he'd left them behind.

It was the same pony, Lupio was sure, standing among the trees just off the road where he'd grabbed it before. This time there had been someone on its back, someone who had made off the second he called out. He had dropped the rake and hared back into the house for his cloak and sword, shouting to Frujos, 'There's someone snooping about again! I'll get him this time.'

'You'll get yourself killed!' Frujos shouted upstairs after him. 'Like as not it's only another damned sightseer.'

Lupio ran out without replying, seized a horse from the neighbouring estate, waved to the astounded farmer, and rode back, but it was too late. There was no sign of the spy. He rode up to the top of the hill and looked down, hunting for any scurrying figure. Nothing. He argued with himself. Of course it was a sightseer, one a bit shyer than the rest, come to see where the battle had actually taken place. But his intuition persisted. There was the coincidence of it being the same pony, the one he'd found there saddled and waiting an hour before the trouble even started. The rider, whoever it was, had been hanging around then, before there was any reason for the farm to interest anyone at all. Privately Lupio reckoned that it was one of the gang hoping to attack by surprise – in which case he should be back at the farm now, preparing. He wandered about dissatisfied for a few minutes more before turning his mount back along the road.

There were people ahead. The rest of the gang; he was right, then. The farm was between them. Could he get there first? Hardly. In any case there were too many for them, even supposing Dubilier could pull his trick with the animals again. Lupio veered off to the left. Raise help and go back to the rescue. Where were the sightseers now that they needed them?

The leader had spotted him, sent riders after him. Perhaps he could draw them away from the farm. He urged his unfamiliar steed faster. What was it the Grach shouted? 'Ta-i-vi! Vi-o, vi-o, vi-o!'

Hifran almost fell down the steps. 'Previs, Previs, he's chasing me, what can I do?'

'Compose yourself! Do you come into the presence of the

Previs-aw-Gomath in such disarray? I'm ill, and so you take advantage of it!'

She seemed so much better, so much more alive; and yet to Hifran's expert sight there was a flush in her face which told him it was the fever that animated her now, burning in the haughtiness of lip and eye. Its fire had rekindled her ancient spirit, brittle and desiccated as an old stick. He hated alarming her, but the frightened boy in him shouted down the gentle nurse. He went to her bedside, standing as erect as he could, and forced a measure of calm into his voice. 'The Aigu Lupio, Previs, the Cirnex.'

'*Chasing* you?'

'I went to the farm again. He saw me and came after me on a horse but I escaped.'

'Did he see you come here?'

'No, Previs.'

'There's no mistake this time?' Hifran had 'seen' the Cirnex so many times since the first, and raised so many false alarms, that she had had to send him back to the farm to watch for the man and confirm his belief. 'Don't forget all our faithful in the city are waiting only for your word.'

'It was him. I'm sure.'

'And did you see anything of – the other one, the man he brought back from Taleg Tivoriun?'

'No, Previs.'

'Well, then.' She sat a moment in meditation. So it would come. It had been vouchsafed to her to be the one, her of all the line of Previsten. She took a grip on herself, furiously commanding the drums of the fever to stop beating in her head, directing her hands to stop shaking as she lifted one to the anxious boy. 'Take me to the temple.'

'Previs – '

'I must give the word. We must be ready for him when he comes. We have been unready for centuries; let us at least get it right now.' She chuckled, feeling light-headed as she made to rise, but her legs ignored her. 'Take me there, boy.'

'No, Previs.'

She grew irate. 'You'd disobey?'

'Previs, you're weak. It would kill you to take you to the temple.'

'Not – true!'

'I've sat and nursed you for months, Previs. It's not long since you could hardly speak, much less sit up.'

'I am better!'

'Much better, Previs; but not well. I'll ride to the temple and give the word if it's time; I'll do anything for you, but I sha'n't let you kill yourself.' He shook his head. 'Not now.'

'I must receive my Aigu . . .'

'If it is the Aigu, and he has come all the way from Taleg Tivoriun, then he won't mind coming a little further to see his Previs,' said Hifran. 'I'll bring him myself.'

He took his leave of her and she heard the hoofbeats fade quickly. It worried her. The dancer of the lord and her legs didn't obey her. She was unworthy.

Himithet cursed silently, leaning against a tree. A few yards away Cheredep leaned on another, wiping his face and neck, his chest heaving. The other four moved quietly through the spinney, looking all around. The man was cunning as all demons, no doubt of it – presumably how he'd got the citizens to believe in him at the outset. He'd evaded them with ease for an hour on an old farmhorse – including the time they'd wasted following hoofprints when he'd hopped off and let the horse go on without him. They'd been lucky to spot him again, running across open ground, but then he'd plunged into this thicket and they'd made so much commotion blundering in after that Himithet had had to order everyone onto foot. But Lupio had cornered himself now. They'd catch him among the trees; or if they didn't they'd flush him out, and then it was all over, for the thicket was just below the temple, and the temple was just below the Iigril, and it wouldn't take a moment to rouse everyone there.

'*There he is.*' Unbelievably close, standing on the path that led down to the city, waving and shouting to some peasant making his way up.

'Quietly, you pigs,' Himithet hissed. Two of them were ahead, grabbing Lupio as he tried to break away; and now the other two. The peasant was running for his life. Himithet smiled, gratified. He'd been annoyed with himself ever since making that mistake over the girl; they'd hate him now, though they'd doubtless had what fun they wanted with her body before it got too cold. But he'd been in too much of a hurry to concern himself with the politics of leadership. It was getting Lupio that mattered – and now they'd got him, though it was a struggle.

'Caught your breath?' he said to Cheredep with a smile quite devoid of sympathy. 'Shall we go and supervise them before they tear him to pieces, hm?' He sauntered down out of the trees, his first lieutenant limping behind.

Lupio was kicking, fighting to free his arms. He drew his blade and hacked wildly about him: there was no fine swordsmanship in trying to hold off four. He connected and heard a yell: one man spinning, clutching his side. He saw blood on his own arm and felt it running down his face, shook his head, blinking it out of his eyes. A face loomed as one of them made a lunge, bare-handed. Lupio felt a pang of calm, curiously recognising an old companion, one of a hundred rogues he had known in a hundred lost places . . . a hundred years ago. They disarmed him and held him fast, bullying him now he was safe. There was someone strolling down towards him: Himithet, probably, and the bigger man behind would be Mengac. Or – no – he recognised him too. Jeswed's spit. Cheredep. He heard weak laughter, his own, a terrifying sound. His eyes were closing. The blood tasted rich and sickly on his lips. Abruptly they dropped him and he sprawled on the grass. They were running about again, crying out. There were more of them than he'd thought, and fighting amongst themselves now, probably for the honour of killing him. He lifted his head. A whole host coming up the path. He was seized and pulled upright again, making the token jerks of the unwilling captive.

'Is he all right?'

'You're safe. Don't struggle. We've got you.'

Who? He turned. Himithet running away, Cheredep face down in the dirt, the others falling to these newcomers, men and women in filthy robes, squinting as if the early afternoon sun hurt their eyes. 'Let me go. Let me go.'

'No, no, Aigu, it's all right now. Praise Gomath we got here in time.'

They carried him uphill into a place of echoes. He opened his eyes, seeing nothing but shadow and the lurching colours of pain. Hard stone under him.

'Let me see him.'

'It's him, isn't it?'

'Guard the doors.'

'We knew him. *We* could – '

'Get out of the light.'

'The Aigu protects him. The Aigu brought us at the . . .'

'Bring some water.'

'Yes.' Fingers on his face. 'It's him.' Who was that? He made the effort to open his eyes again. A boy, kneeling over him. It hadn't happened. He grinned to realise it. None of it had happened. It was a drugged dream, and he'd got into a fight as usual, and the boys had brought him home and Hifran had got out of bed to look after him. Dream . . . Hifran . . . Now he could dream some more; let himself slip into the dark waters and dream some more.

Piripheis waited until they'd stopped shouting at each other and Frujos and Andos had gone off to get help. Win came past her in the hallway and Piri stopped her. 'Where are you going?'

'I'm going out to see who I can find. Your man's right: if all they busybodies want to help him, then here's their chance. Though, just atween you and me, Priphis, I reckon they won't be so keen to show their noses when they hear what – '

'Win, don't go. They can manage. Will you stay and look after Aldellena?'

'And where will you be?'

'I'm going with Dubilier.'

Win shook her head emphatically. 'That's no place for –'

'I must. Something's wrong. I know.'

'Well, I should just about think something *is* wrong. Didn't you hear what he said? Lupio ambushed and took off to the Iigril?'

'No, there's something else, Win. Please. You know how Aldi loves you.' She smiled and held the older woman's hands in her own for a moment. Then she went to Dubilier. 'What is it?'

He paused, scanning her face. She understood. Through the panic and the preparations for battle, she'd seen there was something he hadn't said. This determination was new and frightening. It was not that there was no rage or fear in him, though Frujos had blustered enough for all of them. He had harmonised his emotions, readying himself, submitting to the inevitable. He was like a sword: there are rage and fear in a sword, but you see only the silent gleam and the sharpness of its edge.

'Is it Alita? Did you find her?'

'Yes.'

'She's alive?'

'No.' He told her about the pale ruined body under the hedge. 'If only I'd gone out that way this morning, perhaps I'd have been in time to save her.'

'Dubilier, don't. You know that's a trap – a maze.'

'I know, love.'

'You need your strength for now. You can't fight yourself and Mengac. It would destroy you.'

'Piri, this might destroy me anyway. I've been preserved till now, saved for this battle. This might be the end of my story. If I don't come back – '

'No, my love, I'm coming with you.'

'Piri – '

'Dubilier, respect me enough not to try to make me stay behind.'

Himithet burst in.

'I know,' said Mengac.

'Who in the marsh are they?'

'Gomath's faithful few,' said Bruki. 'Remember, darling? The ones you cleared out of the Hall of Beggars?'

'There's scores of them!'

'Exactly.' There was little warmth in her smile. 'Now they're in the temple: prophet and people and all.' She put her hands together in the motions of the children's game.

Himithet recovered at once. 'Oh, well, that's it, then, isn't it? That's easy now. They've cornered themselves, haven't they? Done it all for us.' Mengac looked up at him, his eyes oddly mournful. 'Well, come on, Mengac! We've got them now. We can just walk in and clean up, hm? Well, come on! We did it before, when we killed the witch.'

'More fires,' said Mengac.

'More fires? I should think so! Naturally more fires!'

'Tell me when it's done. Tell me when there'll be no more fires.'

'What do you mean?'

'Who will you be chasing when you've burnt these? Me?'

'What's got into you? This is it! Get this lot and – pop! – no more god!'

Mengac nodded. 'Tell me when you've finished.'

'Mengac, now listen. You want support? You want the citizens on your side? It's you against him! He's got them – you want them – you go and take them! Simple as that! You've got to come and do it, Mengac. Then they'll see. You'll be the strongest. They'll come to *you*. They'll be frightened. You killed the Cirnex. Then they'll follow you.'

'I don't want following. I don't want fear. I don't want any more destruction.'

Bruki shook her head. 'I think he's right this time. Only Lupio really stands in our way. My husband puts it in his customary crude fashion – '

'Thank you, my dear.'

' – but we have to communicate with them. They need to believe in you, and they won't believe unless you show them.'

He stood up, precluding further persuasion. 'Well,' he said.

'Can you wake, Aigu?'

'Uughh ...' He raised himself on his hands. They had spread their cloaks under him. The smell was unpleasant. He felt refreshed, light-headed. This was the temple. Hifran was at his side with a steaming cup. 'How long have I been asleep?'

'An hour and more. Can you drink this?'

The tone was deferential, subservient, but not that of a frightened boyservant.

'What is it?'

A scent of herbs. 'A stimulant.'

He took it and sipped. 'You've changed.' He was thinner. Boys grow rapidly at around thirteen, fourteen, but this was a face that had experienced many years in that time. 'Are you a doctor now?' he asked, indicating the cup. 'Or a temple boy? What are you doing here?'

Hifran bowed his head, neither yes nor no. 'Serving the Aigu,' he said quietly.

'Hmm.' He felt along his arm. Dressings. 'Am I wounded?'

'Scarcely. The Aigu protected his servant.'

'Now look – ' But he hadn't the will to start arguing. If they still believed that nonsense, there was nothing he could do to dissuade them at the moment, certainly. 'Was that Cheredep? With Himithet?'

'Yes, Aigu. They're evil men.'

'Mengac's lot.'

'Yes.'

'Everything changes, doesn't it, Hifran?'

'On its way,' the boy agreed cautiously. And what was that supposed to mean? What had they done to him?

'What happens now?'

'We'll stay here, working together, as long as they'll let us.'

Belatedly it occurred to him. 'You think they'll attack again? Yes, of course they will.' He looked around, surveying the place and its people from a defensive point of view. To judge by the way they'd rescued him they were a spirited bunch, but could they organise if there were a siege or an assault? 'Who are this lot?'

'Your followers.'

'Mine?'

Hifran made a deprecatory gesture. 'The servant's servants serve the master.'

Lupio looked at him shrewdly. 'Who taught you all this?'

'The Previs.'

'She's supposed to be dead.'

'The Aigu protects his – '

'No. You've been looking after her, haven't you?' He drained the potion.

'It's the same.' And that was something Dubilier might have said. 'She won't die until Gomath returns – I believe that.' Lupio was nodding moodily, mechanically. 'Aigu Cirnex,' Hifran went on, a little diffidently, 'that other man – the one you brought back with you – '

But at that moment there was uproar and a great commotion at the doors.

Unworthy. That was like the name of some repulsive disease. So it was. A disease is a tendency to imperfection. She was an imperfect bride who could not rise to greet her bridegroom when he came; who couldn't dance for him, work with him, or stand at his side against his enemies. How long since she had danced? She had been a cripple for years, even before the uprising in the temple. She was useless to him.

Then why was she still alive? All the citizens thought her dead, except Hifran and the two or three who helped him with food and gifts, and some of the faithful. They must be waiting at the temple by now. It was sometimes not wise to contradict people who thought they knew. Many of the faithful spurned her name: she had brought bad luck, flood and persecution and disaster. Many more preferred to believe in her as a spirit presiding and refused to think she might be alive somewhere. A spirit is easier to deal with than a sick old woman. A spirit is simple and pure. And worthy.

Why was she still alive? Would Gomath punish her by making her endure until his homecoming and then have her die at the last minute? There were precedents in the scriptural history. She turned up a reference but let it fall aside unread. She would be Gomath's symbol to his citizens of all the imperfection he had come to repair. He would cast her from him and take a new bride, young and vigorous and fertile. She had waited so long. But she had never given up waiting. Others came and went like hungry sheep. No one had been faithful as she had. He could not dismiss her unsatisfied.

Then why was she still alive? The god must have some plan, something that he could do even with her, broken and dying as she was. He would have to come soon.

Then she heard something: footsteps of people and horses, and a sound of rumbling wheels beneath heavy loads. She heard few noises, for the road was high above; but this was clearer, like a dream. Why had she always assumed he would come alone? I was a child once, she thought suddenly. A little girl. She had not thought of that in years. Where was the part of her that had been then, that had sung and cried and wondered and sulked – and danced? There had been a noise like that when she had left her home. For days she had stayed confined with only the Previs and the eldest and youngest temple girls visiting her.

They would question her about her dreams and her thoughts and read all the signs about her person. On the last day she had asked and been told that her parents were giving a party to celebrate her acceptance; and then her father had come with a carriage all decorated, and all the guests to wish her well, and taken her half asleep to the temple. Now she was waiting again, half asleep; but no one would carry her now.

Urgency filled her with a force more vibrant than any fever. The rolling noise was passing by: Gomath on his builder's dray, piled high with stone, as in the old pictures. She had to go to him.

Getting up was not so difficult with this force impelling her. It almost carried her upstairs, though her lungs were aching by the top. She rested in the kitchen. A broken chair yielded a walking stick and she hobbled outside, getting used to the feeling of walking again. There was no sign of anyone on the road. For a minute she was tempted to return and rest – but what a waste. No, she was to go on. Either he had come and she would follow him, or he was still to come, and would find her in her proper place welcoming him to his temple.

It was chaotic. Neither side had very large numbers, nor superiority in tactics, arms, or position. It was infuriating. Lupio hadn't understood that it was actually for him that they were fighting, which meant that he wasn't allowed to join the guard at the main doors. He had expected, somehow, the attackers to have the advantage of better leadership and the resources of the Iigril, but their leaders were only Himithet and Mengac – Himithet, apparently, had a desire for destruction that virtually overruled any regard for which side was being destroyed, while Mengac, the legendary ogre of the revolution whom nobody ever saw, stayed well back and let Himithet and his ruffians get on with it. As for the armouries of the Iigril, they had been rusted or ransacked into harmlessness long ago, so the army outside had nothing that the refugees inside, used to being hunted and in danger, could not match. It became clear to Lupio, before Hifran insisted on his removal to the vaults below, that the revolutionaries had pursued their devastating career with impunity through small but sufficient advantages: simple terror, and their habit of moving in large mobs. Now it seemed any chance could decide the outcome, for a mob is not an attack force, and the power to frighten is useless when there's a solid stone wall between you and your victim. Lupio was angry that he was prevented from adding his own weight to such a precarious balance, but he knew if he did go out and get killed, Mengac and Himithet would eventually overrun the temple and kill everyone. Hiding in the cellars, hardly hearing the din overhead, he didn't witness Dubilier's arrival.

A boy with half his side caved in had dragged himself to Mengac's feet. A chill wind was blowing clouds into a bank below the sun. There was hatred in the dying eyes as he craned his neck at the shadow standing above him. He lifted his hand and made a clawing gesture, an old sign to ward off evil spirits. 'Deshingen-aw-Jeswed,' he whispered, 'deshingen-aw-Jeswed.' Mengac didn't move. Then Himithet came and prodded the boy with his toe.

'Thank you. You've delivered the message. You can go now.'

It rolled a little way down the hill. Himithet looked at it, wiping his nose and forehead on his sleeve. 'We'll have 'em soon. One by one. It's hard work.' He slapped Mengac on the shoulder. 'But we'll have 'em soon.'

Bruki ran and leapt, catching the sill with her fingertips and using her momentum to run up the wall and balance there. The shuttering dangled. A man with an antique mace knelt above her, growling. She tipped herself up onto the sill and struck him before he could fend her off, but the collision threw her backwards. She swayed, using the couple of seconds to turn her fall into a leap, and swore as she hit the ground clumsily. Those seconds had been enough to show her the party coming over the hill.

Spread out in a long line, they came to the battle like a sweep of the scythes they carried. Dubilier had remembered the Grach. He stood up on the cart as Piripheis jumped down from behind. He tried to speak to her, but she ignored him, running to where a knot of Mengac's men had already set upon the new arrivals. Dubilier scanned the mêlée. Whoever the rabble in the robes were, defending the temple, they must have Lupio in there.

Hence the desertion of the Iigril and the forces massed against them here. The action was sporadic, ugly and uneven. Two crowds jostled over the threshold while others made futile attacks around the building, tussling with anyone who came out. Unless Lupio was already dead.

Himithet saw the whirling chain just in time to duck. He opened the man's chest with his sword and turned back to glaring angrily up the hill. A few spots of rain fell. The sun dazzled him, seeming to lend a rainbow aura to these visitants.

Bruki was panting at his side. 'It's the other one!'

'What?'

'The one with the animals! Lupio's pal the god.'

'How did he know? Who are that lot?'

She shrugged. 'Disciples.'

'More?' His wife saw a ripple of uncertainty cross his brow; and then he was his smiling feral self again. 'Convenient. The gods come to their own temple to be sacrificed.' But, as if in mockery of his speech, the temple doors began to squeeze closed against their avenging deity. To left and right the men of Himithet's gang were turning to meet the newcomers. After all, there weren't so very many of them.

'Aigu – '

He threw off the beseeching hand and got up, striding to the foot of the stairs. 'What's going on?' The prolonged scrape of heavy wood on stone ceased. There were angry yells, cut short by the boom of the bar falling into place. He ran upstairs. 'Why are we falling back? What's happened?'

'Aigu, reinforcements – '

'More of you?' Lupio looked uncomprehendingly at the survivors.

'We don't know who . . . '

'Help me up.' He scrambled to the high window-ledge and stared between the broken slats. Hill-folk. Mengac would slaughter them. Where had they come from? The light dimmed as an edge of cloud cut across the sun. Hifran was climbing up beside him.

'Come down, now, Aigu, I think you ought to rest.'

Lupio ignored him. A woman ran past. Piripheis? It couldn't

have been. She'd be mad to come down here. He leaned out into the open and looked about, Hifran at his shoulder. There was a familiar figure standing up in a cart, up on the ridge. He stooped to get down and the sun swam into view again, flashing on the blade he carried: silver fire. 'Gomath!' The fool! He'd be killed – and he'd brought Piripheis too. Lupio jumped down. 'Come on. We're going out.'

There was no resistance. He looked at them all, bewildered. There was awe on their faces, an electric expectation. 'What is it now?'

Behind him, standing on the ledge, Hifran spoke. 'He has come. He has come!'

'Bringer of Perfection . . . '

'Lead us, lead us, lead us . . . '

They hummed and muttered, looking up to the boy at the window, waiting.

'Go.'

Piripheis fell heavily. A boy ran up holding a stone above his head, but then there was an arrow sticking awkwardly out of his shoulder. He tumbled across her making strange cooing noises and lay still. The stone rolled free. His blood spilled across her breast and neck. Her knee was twisted; she couldn't rise.

Himithet ran backwards and forwards, but they were hemmed in. The fanatics burst out of the temple, Lupio at their head, chanting some horrible dirge. Working together at last, they bowled over the rebels who crowded the doors and came on unscathed. Now they were yelling the name of their god. Himithet collared a youth who stood trembling, his dagger in his hand. Himithet slapped his face. 'Wake up! They're only a lot of rot-brained peasants and beggars. We can tear – '

Something tripped him and something struck his head and shoulders and back. The pain was surprisingly small. Where he touched the ground he was numb. There was a bright red fireball, a very tiny one. He swam towards it, and then realised that it seemed so small because it was a long, long way away, falling through the void – a red spark like a falling star, plummeting through the blackness. He felt he might follow it forever, and never lose sight of it.

The atmosphere played strange tricks. It was too early for mist, but something was making everything indistinct, muffling the cries and clashes, slowing the movements. Someone came at him from the side, but Dubilier was able to dodge. Where was Piri? 'Piripheis!' There was a bright patch, there, of normal daylight: perhaps she would be there. He went to see. There was a man standing in it, looking at him as he approached: a big man, solid as a statue and dark as one in his pool of light.

'Where is she?'

'You're the one they're saying is the god.' His voice was ponderous.

'Where's my Piripheis?'

'She's dead. We'll kill your Cirnex; kill you. Then perhaps we can stop killing.'

Dead. Piripheis dead.

'Let me see.'

Dubilier didn't resist as the man took his right hand and examined his knife. 'Dead?'

'You've only a little knife, Gomath. You must be very confident. I – have a big sword.' He drew it.

Distantly, Dubilier admired it. 'She's not dead.'

'You know I have to kill you. You know that, don't you? I'm going to tell you before I do: look how clean my sword is. I've killed no one else today. Do you believe that?' Dubilier didn't answer. Mengac shook his head. 'No one will ever believe it. There'll be a statue of me holding your head, and they'll put a number on it – how many I killed in this battle.'

Someone else: another spot of light, zigzagging towards him. 'She's not dead; I won't have her dead.'

'Oh, yes – your Previs is dead.' There was another gust of rain.

It was Lupio, racing towards them shouting, with a huge spear.

Dubilier ignored them. 'SHE'S ALIVE!' Here came a third light, hovering up the hillside. It was an old woman pointing a stick. The breeze fluttered the remains of her cloak and hair as if toying with the idea of blowing her away. She pointed. She saw Lupio running to help someone. Him.

'Aigu Gomath! My lord and husband!'

'SHE'S ALIVE!'

But the big man wasn't listening. He was grunting and struggling, trying to remove Lupio's spear from his chest. His face looked as though he wanted to explain something. Then he sagged and went over on his back. The old woman was stumbling down, shouting about Gomath in her weird, cracking voice. The light changed again to a paleness, and everyone stopped fighting. There were wailings and murmurings. The old woman upset them somehow. Dubilier paused. He thought he'd seen her before. But he went off through the trampled grass, tears in his eyes, looking for Piripheis. 'She's not dead,' he told everyone, 'she's not.' They backed away. Some of Mengac's men knelt down and made signs of deprecation. He ignored them, turning over bodies. He found her, pinned under the corpse of a mongol youth shot from behind. Her face was white, her breast a mess of blood. He shivered, and nearly looked away; but he picked her up and carried her back to where he had been standing. If he was right, that old woman was the Previs – what was her name? She probably knew what to do; whether he could save Piri, or what words to say over her. People got out of his way.

Lupio hurried towards him. 'It's Previs Kavi.'

'That's right.' That was the name.

Lupio was staring at him, surprised to find he wasn't surprised. Then he noticed what his friend was carrying. 'Oh, no. Gomath, no.'

'She's not dead, is she?' His tone was peremptory.

Hifran. He'd know what to do. He was at Kavi's side; Kavi had collapsed.

'Bring her over here.'

Lupio helped Dubilier lay her down at a little distance from the dying Previs, then turned to Hifran, who was saying, 'You shouldn't have come.'

'My Aigu; my husband . . . '

Hifran looked up at Lupio, miserably. 'She's dying, Aigu Cirnex.'

'Then leave her,' Lupio told him. 'Come here.'

The boy lingered wretchedly, gazing at the crumpled face. 'I must take care of her.'

'Gomath's sake, Hifran!' It was only an oath, but it drew Hifran's attention. Lupio showed him Piri's body. 'Let the old woman die! What can we do for this one? This one's young. Don't you understand?'

Dubilier moved out of Hifran's way, found himself almost falling over the sprawling old woman. She raised herself on one elbow, glaring at him with a manic intensity of joy. 'Welcome, Aigu,' she gasped. 'Aigu Gomath, I am unworthy . . . '

Dubilier knelt, distracted.

'It's all right,' he said. He cradled her head. The crowd sighed and quivered.

Kavi weighed nothing. 'Is she – the new one?' she was asking him.

'She's my love. She's not dead.'

'I understand,' murmured Kavi. 'I was unworthy . . . '

'No one,' Dubilier said hurriedly, 'no one's unworthy.' He saw something white on the ground, caught up in Kavi's hair. He plucked it and showed it to her: 'Look, you see this flower – ' Then a spasm shook her and he forgot what he was going to say. He smiled instead, and she gripped his arm with great force while she died.

He lay her back on the ground. Hifran stood up, looking at the two bodies in turn. 'I don't know what to do.'

'She's not *dead*,' Dubilier said again. He picked Piripheis up again. 'My love.'

There was a long embarrassed silence. People were starting to move away. Hifran tried again. 'Aigu Gomath, she's – ' And then she opened her eyes and made a sound.

Somebody shrieked.

Andos had come to fetch him, almost stumbling in his haste. 'Lupio! Lupio! They're bringing the bones!'

So he had had to go and supervise. The boy had marched in front of him all the way. People stopped work on the building sites to watch him go by, and he smiled and waved to them, still feeling rather silly. But Andos ignored them, proud to be the one to be escorting the Cirnex.

He could sense the tension in the little square. The masons

and engravers stood in an awkward little semi-circle, while the foreigners moved about energetically, leading in the horses, manoeuvring the great sleds and carts. The bones were filthy.

'Gomath's sake!' cried Lupio, pushing through the spectators, 'isn't anyone going to help them?' He rolled up his sleeves and strode across, caught a rope-end and started to tug a knot free. One of the foremen greeted him and began to describe how they'd dug what was left of the skeleton out of the mire. That was all it needed. At last the Thrynians fell in to help with the unloading. There was much laughter and gesturing on both sides – it was the language problem as much as ancestral xenophobia, Lupio knew that. The one word of Grachish that every Thrynian seemed to understand was the one Lupio wished had never been mentioned; but to the citizens it was obvious that when these strangers talked about Lupio and Dubilier killing the 'chezzerd', they were really trying to say 'Jeswed'. What they meant was that the Cirnex and Gomath ('Dubilier' was the name he'd taken to disguise himself on his travels) had slain the old devil of the waste lands, as had been prophesied. And so the scheme to unearth the bones and build them into a triumphal statue, here in the square by the Hall of Glory.

They got the skeleton down and scrubbed it while Thrynian doctors and Grachish hunters ran from bit to bit with notebooks and old anatomical texts, puzzling out which went where. Their design incorporated a pedestal with an enthusiastic description of the fight. Lupio ignored it. He knew it would only make him insist that the reality had been less grandiose and more unpleasant. Unfortunately, as usual the citizens preferred their own fictitious versions. Dubilier, however, had managed to have alterations made to the statue they'd erected to him. In the original drawing he'd been standing with one foot on the body of Mengac. It would be impossible to expunge all the disapproval that now obscured the citizens' memories of the revolutionaries, but Dubilier had done well by rejecting that sketch, publicly adopting ideas and terminology from Mengac's scraps of plans for the New Order, and taking Himithet's widow into the Fulthfol.

That was another foreign word that Thrynian tongues were reluctant to negotiate. Most people simply called the advisory group the Aiguda, which caused much confusion. 'Piripheis' too had been generally shortened to 'Previs' – at least there was a logic to that, as well as wilful ignorance. In any case, she and her husband welcomed it since she had become far more popular than Kavi had ever been in the role (Aldellena's presence helped enormously), and any sign that she was accepted boded well for other integrations.

It suddenly occurred to Lupio as he grappled with a huge femur that he might be risking opprobrium. Perhaps it didn't look good for a man to assist at the erection of a monument in his own honour. Lately he'd had too many thoughts of this kind. The niceties of politics came to him with difficulty, and always with doubt. Already he wished for the old days when obscurity, or notoriety, had kept him free of this dull incubus responsibility.

No, he thought, if the people don't like it, I don't care. And they know it. Dubilier, he's the man for the policies, the calculations. I'm Lupio. I'm the one that lugs bones about and shares a bottle with the gang. They know that. He looked around at them. They watched him drink, taking in that action as if it were an entertainment. Yes, he was Lupio, but in a new way. His life had changed completely. He was himself. What he did, he did for them, whether he wished it or not. These days he could feel the moments leaving his hands and watch them flicker and turn into legends as they floated through the crowd. With a flourish, he took a third pull before passing the bottle on, rapt with an irrepressible, exhibitionist glee: Lupio still, but Cirnex too, since they'd have it so . . . And for the first time, his fate amused him.

Mid-afternoon, he stopped work and strolled up to the Iigril. They were all there. Win threw up her hands in mock dismay. 'Now I suppose I'm to do more food!' Dubilier was carrying a basket.

'What's this, a picnic?'

'There'll be plenty, woman, stop fussing,' said Frujos.

'I see – going off for a picnic without telling me.'

'We knew you were happy where you were.' Dubilier told him. Lupio smiled. From anyone else, the remark would have been facetious; but Dubilier – architect, leader, and god he might be, but he preserved intact that dubious gift he had brought from Hisper Einou, his simple, devastating candour.

'Well, I'll be happy here now. What can I carry?'

'Me,' said Aldellena, stretching up to him.

So he did, and after the meal they played together. Lupio held her tightly and rolled down the hill with her, over and over. Shrieking and laughing they ran back to do it again.

They walked through the trees and looked at the new city. It hung in its scaffolding yet, roofless and half done. Soon they would be bringing in reeds and straw for thatch; and eventually, with barges and some temporary repairs to the marsh road, perhaps wagons of slate and building stone from the quarries of Pepache-ti-Bilovan. There was so much to plan, so much to hope.

Dubilier turned about and heard distant crashes and rumblings. All the old Aigudan villas that couldn't be used were being demolished – as much for the symbolism and to channel the citizens' new-found energies as for the sites and materials. He wished Himithet had survived to take charge of all that. Ali's old mansion would be going. He closed his eyes to summon its image and bid it goodbye. He remembered the day he had gone to look for her, and saw the lake again, and the overgrown island in the middle of it. Her grandfather had built an aviary there, though all the birds had left it now, frightened by the din of the house-wrecking.

There was a woman there.

She was standing on the shore, half hidden among the tenantless bushes, dressed in a grey gown. A cowl hid her face, so he could not see the expression with which she looked towards the ruins. He moved closer, approaching her silently as though gliding across the surface of the lake – but Piri was calling him, because he had turned back at the top of the hill, lost in his daydream. She took his hand. He felt the warmth, the vitality of her touch.

'Have you forgotten something, my love?'

The woman in grey was receding now, snatched away by an implacable wind of time. She was so far off he would never see her face. He turned and looked at Piripheis.

'Yes,' he said.

'What?'

'I've forgotten.'

'Silly!' She hugged him.

Aldellena and run ahead and rolled down the slope again. Now she was coming trudging back up to see what had happened to them. She looked determined and happy. She shouted, 'Come *on*!'